The GIRL *from* PARIS

JOAN AIKEN

sourcebooks
casablanca

Published by Sourcebooks Casablanca, an imprint of Sourcebooks,
Inc.
P.O. Box 4410, Naperville, Illinois 60567-4410
(630) 961-3900
Fax: (630) 961-2168
www.sourcebooks.com

Originally published as *The Young Lady from Paris* in 1982 in the
United Kingdom by Victor Gollancz Ltd. This edition issued
based on the hardcover edition published in 1982 in the United
States by Doubleday & Company, Inc.

Printed and bound in Canada.
MBP 10 9 8 7 6 5 4 3 2 1

One

WHEN, AFTER TWENTY YEARS, MATTHEW BILBO CAME out of prison, his first impulse was to climb to the top of the nearest hill.

It lacked several hours to dawn when the great gate clanged behind him and he walked, a free man with a heavy heart, into the middle of the city of Winchester. The shadowed streets were still empty and silent, dankly glistening from a light rain that had fallen overnight; he could see no signpost or people to advise him of his homeward way. Yet a long-disused shepherd's faculty soon asserted itself, and he began, slowly but with certainty, to make his way toward the east, up the long hill that led in the direction of Petersfield, Midhurst, and Petworth. His legs felt strangely weak. His eyes ached from withheld tears. Getting to be an old man, he supposed, fifty or thereabouts. Life in jail had been so uneventful that his memory seemed to have slipped a cog or two, and spun round vaguely these days, presenting some facts clearly enough, but drifting mistily past others. His original sentence for poaching had been fifteen years; but then, a couple of times, he had tried to escape, first when word had come that Martha was going to marry somebody else, then when his parents had been evicted from the cottage. He had been recaptured and that, of course, had added to his term, and he had been transferred to Winchester. But resignation had set in, after Martha's marriage and his parents' death; he had learned calm with time, suffering the slow years to come and go at their own pace. Solitude had always been his friend, for silence is much the same whether experienced in a cell or on a rainy hillside with one's flock of Southdowns huddled against the turf. The long hours of his own company afflicted him less than they did most prisoners. It was true, he had missed the cry of the sheep and the song of larks; now, making his way rather slowly and stiffly along the Petersfield road, he discovered how much he had missed the air of the hills; it tasted pure and cold as spring water.

After five or six miles his prison stiffness began to wear off, and he moved better; besides, he had reached the top of the ridge and come to a level stony track; ahead, the domed summits of the Hampshire Downs were outlined against the paling eastern sky. Like a row of mushrooms, thought Bilbo with pleasure, and, the image reminding him of food, he presently sat on a fallen log by a spinney and munched a bit of the penny loaf, yesterday's ration, which he had been too bemused by thoughts of coming freedom to eat when it had been given to him. Stale though it was, the fresh air made it tasty; even so, he could eat no more than the crust. At rest, he began to think immediately about his forsaken protégé, and trouble came down on him like a cloud.

He rose and walked on.

The prison authorities had supplied him with a suit of clothes, for his own, taken from him on admission, baked, fumigated, and stored, had long since mildewed away. They would have been too big, anyway, he reflected; he had shrunk somewhat in jail. He now had a coat, waistcoat, breeches, and stockings of dark, cheap woolen. By the permitted occupation of weaving horsecloths he had managed to earn eighteen shillings, of which ten had gone to pay for the clothes; the remaining eight now jingled in the pouch he had made himself. But I'll need to get me some better gear than this, he thought, for I can't tend sheep in these taffety things; a couple of weeks'd see them worn through and torn to shreds. I'll be wanting a hard hat, and a gabardine smock, and some leather leggings, and a pair of iron-tipped boots. Time to worry about that when I'm home to Petworth.

The sun, having extended a long band of light—prune, lemon, and chestnut-colored—along the dimpled horizon, now appeared in a blaze of rainy glory.

Ah, thought Bilbo, that's summat, that be! And he inhaled a deep breath of satisfaction. But for the first time in many years an intimation of what he had lost now came to trouble him, and the breath he drew ended in a strange, painful groan; buried memories began to stir, of rainy mornings on Barlavington Down, with the sheep's wistful chorus echoing far and near, and his young sister Sarah, a dot in the distance, bringing his breakfast tied in a red-spotted handkerchief.

No use to make a fantigue over what's gone, though, he thought, and strode on firmly, for he had more than thirty miles yet to accomplish. Despite the resurrection of old griefs and the presence of a new one, his heart was hopeful; he was, after all, going home to Petworth in sweet, auspicious April; the larks were skreeling their hearts out in the sky overhead, and down in the valley the timber trees were covered in pink buds.

~

He did not reach Petworth until evening; out of condition after the long wasted years, he was obliged to rest every five miles or so, and though he was eager to see his native place again, there seemed no reason to overtax himself and get there all tired out and vlothered. He followed bridle paths rather than turnpike roads, so as to avoid encountering people, for he felt nervous of human contact; so dusk had fallen over the small market town by the time he was tapping at the door of a cottage near the toll gate.

A child opened the door, blue-eyed, straw-headed, finger in mouth.

"Your ma about, liddle 'un?" he asked. "Say her brother's here—your uncle Matt."

"Ain't got no uncle Matt," said the child, removing finger from mouth.

This was a blow; but a fat, suspicious-looking woman now arrived, who cleared up the puzzle.

"Missus Bowyer? She moved round the corner into Darner's Bridge arter her husband was took bad. You'll find 'em there, third house along."

The street called Darner's Bridge was, luckily, only a few steps farther; but Matt's reception there was hardly more welcoming. He would, he thought, hardly have recognized his sister; although ten years younger than himself, she had aged much more; all her teeth had gone, her once flaxen hair was gray and scanty, her eyes faded, and her face, lacking teeth, had become haggard, pinched, and shrewish in expression.

"Sairy? It's Matt."

Her gasp was not one of delight; rather, his arrival seemed the last straw.

"*Matt?* What the pize are *you* doing here?"

"I just come out," he said simply. "Didn't you get word? I sent you a message by Toby Hedges, six months past."

"Oh, ah. Reckon he did say summat, but it slipped my mind. You can't stop here, Matt," she went on hastily. "There's ten of us in the two rooms as 'tis. We've not room for another nipper, let alone a grown man."

Matt began to feel discouraged. His feet burned after walking all day along rough tracks in the cheap prison shoes; his toes throbbed like glowing embers.

"Maybe I could just come in and have a set-down?" he suggested mildly.

"Oh well—I daresay." Reluctantly Sarah Bowyer stood aside to let him in. The small stuffy room, opening directly off the street, was below ground level, and smelt dankly of burning waste on the tiny fire, potatoes boiling in their skins, old grubby clothes, and unwashed human bodies. There seemed to be five or six smallish children in the shadowy, shabby place; Matt edged himself gingerly onto the corner of a torn horsehair couch.

"Ned about?" he asked.

She shook her head.

"He's working at the clog factory now; he got too crippled up with rheumatics to blow the bellows for Sam Budd." Ned had been a blacksmith's assistant. "Sam and Cathy's at the clog factory too now," she went on.

"That's good," said Matt tentatively.

"Good? For six shillings a week? Times are terrible hard, Matt. And we've ten to feed; and only three bringing anything in." She looked with exasperation at the skinny, towheaded children huddled about the room, as if calculating how long it would be before any of them rendered some return for all the potatoes they had consumed.

"Well, I won't be a charge on ye," said her brother pacifically. "All I was wanting was a bed for the night, time I'll go to Mus' Strudwick and ask for my old job back."

"Strudwick? *He* won't have ye," said his sister contemptuously. "He've long since found himself another shepherd. Time don't stand still while ye're in jail, brother."

Slowly, reluctantly, she inched him a half-cupful of tea from the brown pot that stood on the hob, filled the cup with hot water, and added a drop or two of milk from a metal can.

"Thankee, Sairy." He drank the tea with pleasure; in jail it had been a luxury served only at Christmas. And he reflected soberly that what she said was perfectly reasonable; somehow in all these years it had not occurred to him that his job would not be waiting for him when his term was done.

"What did you expect?" Sarah demanded bitterly. "D'you think they'd be awaiting with red carpets when you come out? To my dying day I'll never know why you done such a tarnal foolish thing as take that hare. Couldn't you *see* the trouble as'd come from it?"

"I didn't take no hare, gal. I never took no hare in all my borns. I—I—I wouldn't." Matt had a stammer at times, when he was trying to express something that was of importance to him; he had to help his words along by hammering the air with his hand. He did so now. "There's summat—ellynge—about a hare." Haunted, he meant—unchancy. "Remember how Mum allus used to say as how they belonged to Old Scratch? I don't reckon to that. But I'd never touch one—nor sell it—nor eat it—not for dunnamuch! And so I told owd Mus' Paget the Justice—over and over—but he 'oodn't believe me."

"*Paget!*" Sarah turned and spat into the fire. Her brother was somewhat shocked at such a gesture. Mum 'ud not have liked that, he mused. She told us to behave like gentlefolk.

"If a blessed angel came to tell Paget the Day of Judgment had come, he'd not believe it," Sarah said.

"He still on the Bench here?"

"Oh, ay. Still sending chaps to jail, or transporting 'em. But if you didn't poach the hare, brother," persisted Sarah, "then who did?"

"Ah, who knows? Maybe young Barney Lee. He was allus half a gypsy. And he'd chuck it in my cabin when he knowed they was after him. He'd be sore at me, because Martha'd never look at him, once her and me was promised."

She looked at someone else soon enough once you

were in jail, thought Sarah, but she kept this thought to herself and said, "Well, if it were Barney, no one'll ever know, for he died twelve years since of the typhus, time Mum and Dad and the others was took."

"God rest his soul, poor chap; he were allus a scrawny, ill-set creature."

"God rest his soul? Aren't you rued about it at *all*?" burst out Sarah. "Twenty years you been in the lock-up, your gal lost, your job gone, all on account o' that lying rapscallion and that stone-hearted Justice, yet you sit there smiling like a sawney. If it was me—I'd be up-atop-o'-the-house angry! I'd want to do summat."

"Do what?" Matt looked at her, honestly puzzled. It was a long time since he had engaged in a conversation of this kind; ideas came to him slowly.

"To Paget! To make him remember me! He busted up your whole life; and there he sits in his fine house. Now he's wed to Lady Silk-Satin Adelaide, widow of the Earl of Muck."

"What's *she* ever done to you?" Matt asked, struck by Sarah's vindictive tone.

"Sits on the Parish Relief Board. Won't give out so much as a candle, 'less you go in the Union."

"What come to Paget's first wife?"

"Died, poor soul. Ah, a right nice lady, she were."

"Well then," suggested Matt, "he've had his troubles too."

"Huh! He didn't care! Wed again afore the grass had sprouted on her grave."

Matt sighed. The world was so full of trouble, it seemed to him there was no use dwelling on it. Better, if possible, to turn one's mind to more comfortable matters.

"Larks were a-singing, loud as a tempest, all the way I come along," he said. "And the merry trees was out on the hill; I'm glad I didn't miss that."

"Larks!" Sarah sniffed. Then her ears picked up a

limping step outside the house. "Here's Ned. He'll wonder to see ye, surely." She did not sound as if she expected her husband to welcome the arrival of his brother-in-law; and indeed, Ned Bowyer, when he hobbled in, stopped short, stared hard at the visitor, and then lowered himself onto a stool with a kind of gloomy grunt, suggesting resignation rather than pleasure.

"Matt's only here for a sit-down and a cup of tea," Sarah said conciliatingly. "I told him we couldn't put him up."

Ned, as was his way, immediately contradicted her. He was a thin, twisted man, totally bald, with large transparent outstanding ears and a facial expression made irritable by the constant rheumatic pain he suffered; he was, however, obstinate rather than bad-tempered, and liked, when possible, to put his wife in the wrong. "Turn away your own flesh and blood?" he demanded. "What kind o' set-out is that? Matt can bide out in owd Tom Boxall's shed, I reckon. Sam fed Boxall's chicken, time he were laid up, he owe us a good turn."

Matt said the shed would suit him very well; and some bits of sacking were found, to make him a bed. He refused to share Ned and the elder children's supper of turnip-and-potato stew, saying he had eaten already, and that he would go to bed directly.

"Dunnamany years 'tis since I walked thirty mile," he explained with his diffident smile.

Sarah shook her head over him when he had gone out of the room.

"Matt don't change. He were allus a bit natural," she said, meaning simple. "Fancy! He reckoned he could just pick up his old job again; it never crossed his mind as folk wouldn't want a jailbird as a shepherd."

"Dunno why they wouldn't," said her husband instantly. "Matt were a 'countable good shepherd, I heard. Mus' Noakes, over to Duncton, were wanting a chap for the sheep since owd Ted Goodger died. I'll tell Matt, come morning time. It'd be a fine place for a man without a wife or family; there's a cabin, top o' Duncton Down, goes wi' the job."

Sarah sniffed again. Fine for some, her expression suggested; they only have to come out of jail and suitable jobs are handed them on a plate. But still she had, in the old days, been sincerely fond of her brother. Some of this feeling still lingered; and it was a relief to learn that he was not likely to be a drain on the family's slender resources.

Despite fatigue, it was some time before Matt Bilbo fell asleep. The little wooden shed was draughty, and colder than his prison cell; and there were the added distractions of large bright stars, visible through gaps in the planking; the hooting of owls in the garden of a large house called Newlands not far off; and all the unfamiliar nostalgic smells of things in the shed, turpentine, peat, linseed, and straw.

Matt was deeply troubled, too, about a friend left behind in jail. Poor Simmie, how'll he ever wrostle through in that place without me to watch out for him when he gets in a pucker, and stop him trying to fight the Beaks? Still, fretting won't help him. Trying to put such thoughts aside, Matt thought over the conversation with his sister. Some of her words about Paget came back: "There he sits, in his fine house! If it were me, I'd want to do summat to make him remember me!"

❧

Matt slept late next morning, tired by his wakeful hours, and the unwonted exertions of the previous day. Sarah let him lie till she had given the children their scanty breakfast; then she roused him with a cup of warm milk and a crust of bread.

"I can pay ye for the vittles, Sairy," he said, confused and made humble by this kindness.

"Bless the man! Can't you take nothing for granted?" Sarah was in a better mood today. She told Matt about the possible job at Duncton. "Ned says, best go after it directly."

"Ah, I will. And thank him kindly, Sairy. I'll let ye know how I fare. 'Tis nought of a walk to Duncton. If I work there, I could come and see ye, of a Sunday."

"Bustle along, then; don't stop here a-talking," she said good-humoredly.

Matt took the road south out of the town, toward the South Downs, which could be seen as a blue undulating ridge five miles away.

It was a cool, windy season; the ploughed land was beginning to dry out on either side of the road. Hawthorn buds pearled the hedges. Yesterday he had avoided the turnpike roads, but today he must cross the River Rother, which obliged him to follow the main road so as to make use of its bridge. He still, however, felt nervous of all the riders, cart drivers, cattle drovers, and foot passengers who frequented this busy road. Eh dear, what a lot of folk there be, he thought, and took to a footpath beyond the hedge, once the river was past.

Soon another surprise awaited him. No wonder there had been so much traffic. For while he was in prison the railway had come to Petworth—or at least as near as Lord Leconfield, the landowner who lived in Petworth House, would permit. A mile out of town, beyond the river, a neat weatherboarded station presided over two gleaming iron rails which ran east and west; and a wooden two-coach train was loudly chugging eastwards, dragging its plume of smoke behind it.

"Dang me," said Matt, scratching his head. "You'd think that'd fritten the hosses and cattle all to blazes—the noise it makes! But I reckon 'tis a 'countable fine way o' getting about the country."

The cattle, apparently inured to the noise, continued

to graze placidly in the water meadows; the horses trotted biddably along the road, ignoring it. A carriage and pair could now be heard approaching as Matt climbed the heathy ridge beyond the station. He caught the sound of hooves rapping smartly along the graveled roadway, the creak of harness, the crack of a whip. Still wishful to avoid human encounter, Matt swerved away from the roadside onto a sandy track that meandered off at an angle through gorse and heather. Beyond a holly bush he almost tripped over a large brown hare, which was sitting upright, sniffing the air and sunning itself. Alarmed, the hare bounded off toward the road, taking huge, erratic-seeming leaps, so as to gain a view on all sides. Equally startled, Matt came to a halt, screened by the tree from sight of the road. He heard a violent crash, a shout, a woman's scream, and the terrified whinnying of horses. Other shouts followed, and the clatter of running feet.

Matt, standing still, began to tremble.

Oh, geemany, he thought. That there hare has been and gone and run in front of a carriage and made the hosses shy, and there's been an upset.

But *I'm* not going to go and get muxed up in it. One hare's done me enough harm in my life. This one can carry its bad luck somewhere else; this time, Matt Bilbo's a-going to stay clear.

He was able to make this decision with a good conscience, for, from the number of different voices and the sound of running feet in the road, it could be judged that a good few helpers were already engaged in succoring the victims of the accident. There was no need for Matt to add his assistance; indeed, very likely he would only be in the way. And maybe nobody's badly hurt, he thought hopefully.

He strode on at a steady pace toward Duncton Village.

Two

"YOU WOULD CONSIDER PARTING WITH *MISS PAGET*?"

Lady Morningquest was a tall, impressive personage, with a commanding air, an aristocratically curved nose, and a high, incisive voice; her tone indicated disapproval, such as might be displayed by the donor of a handsome and valuable gift, on discovering that the recipient intended to pass it on to a charity bazaar.

Her companion, however, wholly undisturbed by the note of censure, replied equably, "Well, you see, *ma chère amie*, this is how it is: certainly I am devoted to *la petite* Elène Paget, I regard her as I might my own daughter (if I had one)—and *that*, my friend, is the very reason why I would not wish to stand in the way of her advancement. In the city of Paris, how much wider a vista would open before her. Without doubt, as your protégée, dear madame, she would have the opportunity to hear the words of savants, of philosophers—there is the Comédie, the Opera—whereas, here in Brussels—pfah! What a narrow, provincial scene!"

Nevertheless, Madame Bosschère glanced with some complacency about the room in which the two ladies were standing. It was the salle, or largest classroom, of her school for young ladies, a handsome spacious chamber with double glass doors opening on one side into a hallway tiled with black and white marble, on the other into a garden half screened by a large grape arbor. Everything in sight glittered with cleanliness and prosperity.

Lady Morningquest also turned to survey the room benignly through her lorgnon, before repeating in a tone of perplexity, "You are really offering me Ellen Paget? But, *ma chère*, I thought she was your right hand in the school, your *première maîtresse*? I fear she might be wasted in the post I am seeking to fill; though, of course, I should be happy to have my dear little goddaughter in Paris! But I had hoped merely for some worthy person—steady, sober, not prone to agitations or high flights—perhaps a young teacher who found large classes too formidable; or an older one, approaching retirement, wishful to secure a less exacting position in a quiet household—"

Here Lady Morningquest paused, possibly arrested by the recollection that no stretch of truth could designate the Hôtel Caudebec a quiet household.

But Madame Bosschère had not noticed her hesitation.

"My dear friend, Mademoiselle Paget is as steady, as sober, as could possibly be desired, I assure you: imbued with sense and integrity, she has the head on her shoulders of a person three times her age! *Elle est pleine de caractère*—formidable, indeed—honest as the day, wise as an advocate, upright as a judge!"

Madame spoke in rapid French, which had the effect of making these qualities seem, somehow, less reliable. But she added with vehement sincerity, "I say all this to you in full confidence, I who know her thoroughly, and have done since she was a *petite fille*. She is ruled by conscience—your English Calvinist conscience! She would not knowingly commit the slightest fault, she would bitterly repent the most trifling error."

In that case, and if she has all these virtues, I wonder why you wish to be rid of her? reflected Lady Morningquest, intently regarding her *chère amie*, who bore the scrutiny with aplomb. Usually, at this time of day, late morning, Madame Bosschère would not yet have assumed her full toilette; she would be comfortable, though perfectly businesslike, in wrapper, muslin nightcap, shawl, and felt slippers, bustling about the administrative duties of her school. But in honor of her august friend and patron she had today dressed early and appeared convenable, if not downright elegant, in dark-brown silk, admirably fitted to her plump figure, and a Brussels lace fichu. Madame was not tall, but she possessed immense dignity; she neither flushed nor paled under the thoughtful gaze of the ambassador's wife. Indeed a skeptical observer might have wondered how her face could remain so unmarked by the traces of care and authority; was this due to an untroubled conscience, or a lack of scruple and sensibility?

"Let me see," said Lady Morningquest, "how long has the child been with you?"

"She is hardly a child any longer, *chère amie*! She came to us when she was fifteen; her elder sister Eugénie was still with us at that time; *non*—I mistake—it was Catherine, the middle one. Eugénie had already left to wed her baronet. Two years *la petite* studied here as a pupil; one, by her own request, as pupil-teacher; and now three as full teacher. During which time, as you say, she has become my right hand."

"Has she never been home during that time?"

"Oh, *mais oui, bien sûr, plusieurs fois*. The father, who is a very correct English gentleman, as you know, madame, requested permission for her to attend her sisters' weddings, and the christening of a niece; and his own wedding…but each time she returned, and I believe was happy to do so. I understand that *la petite* is *not* loved by the father's second wife."

"Six years in all." Lady Morningquest counted thoughtfully on her thin, beringed fingers. "So she is now twenty-one."

"And how deeply indebted I am to you, dear friend, for introducing me to the Paget family; for giving me the chance to acquire such a treasure! Indeed all three Paget girls were amiable, well-disposed, serious young ladies—"

"You would hardly call Kitty Paget serious?"

Madame gave an indescribable grimace, half moue, half shrug.

"Serious when it came to her own interests! A light heart, but a hard head. I understand she married an exceedingly wealthy bourgeois—how do you call him?—an ironmaster."

Madame pronounced it *irrenmastaire*. There was considerable irony in her tone; bourgeoise herself to her blunt fingertips, she nevertheless had the same dispassionate regard for her friend's aristocratic connections that she would have for a piece of fine Meissen or Dresden; it was plain that she deplored the social aspect of Catherine Paget's marriage while admitting its utility.

"You think Ellen would be less hardheaded? Less regardful of her own interests?"

"*Douce comme une ange!*"

The benevolent Directrice seemed to be assigning some rather contradictory characteristics to her young assistant, reflected Lady Morningquest. But she merely remarked, "Ellen will need more than gentleness, I fear, if she is to hold her own at the Hôtel Caudebec. She had need, rather, to be a female Metternich."

"And she can be that too," responded Madame Bosschère without a blink. "But are matters, then, come to such a pass in your niece's establishment?"

"They could hardly be worse! That young man is behaving like a monster to my poor Louise. He neglects her atrociously—gambles all day and most of the night; his companions are drawn from the worst sections of society. And the wretched Louise, instead of trying to grapple with the situation, merely reclines in her boudoir and reads philosophy! As for the child—I am in despair. A village brat would get more care. I tell you, madame, the ménage is a disaster—I have a migraine for two days after each visit."

The widow looked suitably horrified by these revelations. "*Tiens!* It will be difficult, I concede. But I do believe you have found the right person for the task, my friend. I am certain that such a situation would not daunt *la petite* Elène. See, here she comes now."

The two ladies were standing on the estrade, or teacher's dais. Leaning on its balustrade, they surveyed the bustle of activity now commencing in the long classroom, as the young-lady pupils prepared the establishment for an evening's festivity. Today, May 5th, was the feast of St. Annodoc, the school's patron saint, and was traditionally celebrated by a collation in the school garden, a dramatic performance, and a dance, to which parents and selected friends were invited. Hence the arrival of Lady Morningquest from Paris. Her daughter Charlotte was to play Ophelia in a heavily edited version of *Hamlet*, and though Lady Morningquest, a realist, expected small pleasure from the performance, she had traveled to Brussels since she had her own reasons for consulting Madame Bosschère.

Now she turned with interest to follow the direction of the headmistress's glance.

Although drawn from the cream of Brussels society, the young-lady pupils at the Pensionnat, many of whom continued their education till the age of twenty or beyond, were, in general, tall, big-boned, and brawny. Exuberant today, and unrestrained, since it was a holiday, they laughed and screamed like herring gulls, energetically lugging the furniture so as to clear the floor. Some brought in vases of flowers, others directed the aged gardener where to place blossoming orange trees in pots, and palms in tubs—all this without the least embarrassment, despite the fact that most were *en deshabille*, clad in calico print wrappers, their long flaxen hair in curlpapers, their large feet in list slippers. Every now and then a shout would come from the *salle à manger*, where the hairdresser was established with his curling tongs: "Mademoiselle Eeklop au coiffeur!" The few English or French girls in the group were instantly recognizable because of their smaller stature, darker coloring, and greater modesty of demeanor.

A young lady differing from the rest in that she was already dressed, in a dark-gray gown whose Quakerish plainness of cut was mitigated by a decided elegance of line, appeared to be in charge of the proceedings, and was giving orders to pupils, gardener, and servants, in a low, clear, decisive voice which was immediately and unhesitatingly obeyed by everybody, despite the fact that she was several inches shorter than most of her charges.

"Yes—that will do very well, Emilie—the pots in rows across below the estrade, and the ferns in those baskets along the side; *non*, Marie, together, not separately. We shall need a great many more. Clara, run and tell the little girls in the *première classe* to come, as many as can be spared, and they can act as porters running to and fro. That will keep them out of mischief, too."

At this point, looking up, Miss Paget perceived the headmistress and her guest. She smiled quickly at them, revealing an unsuspected dimple in her thin cheek, and curtseyed, saying in a friendly way, "Excuse me, madame, that I did not observe you before! There is so much to do that one need have eyes in the back of one's head. Lady Morningquest, how do you do! Charlotte has been counting the hours to your arrival. She is going over her lines in the Green Room—shall I send her to you?"

"No, no—leave her to con her part," said the fond parent. "I had rather be sure she knows it by rote and will not disgrace the family. There will be plenty of time to talk to her after—and you, too, my dear, I hope, when you can be spared! I have messages from your father and your sister Eugenia, for I have been in Sussex recently. But I will not distract you now."

With another quick, smiling curtsey, Miss Paget availed herself of this dismissal to dart across the room, exclaiming, "Maude, Toinette, take care with that bench, or you will mark the plaster. Set it down *away* from the wall—so—then you can drape the baize over it."

"What a pure Parisian accent she has," remarked Lady Morningquest approvingly. "Her speech has not been contaminated by your hoydens of Flemings."

"She takes pains to converse every day with our dear old Mademoiselle Roussel, who has the diction of a truly cultivated person."

"She need do no more than listen to yourself and your cousin, my friend. Both your accents are exquisite. How is the Professor?"

"He is well, I thank you, madame," responded the Directrice; but a slight cloud became evident on her brow, and this was not missed by the alert eye of her guest.

"I had no idea," idly remarked Lady Morningquest, watching the activities of Miss Paget through her leveled lorgnon, "that Ellen Paget would turn out such a pretty girl. Her sisters were handsome creatures enough, but she was an ugly, skinny little shrimp of a thing when I saw her last, all hair and eyes and hollow cheeks. She is a credit to you now, my friend."

"Pretty? I would not go so far as to call her that," replied the headmistress rather sharply. "One does not require prettiness in a teacher; in fact, it is a disadvantage, leading to unhealthy devotions among the pupils, and unsuitable regard from visiting teachers."

Aha, my friend, thought Lady Morningquest; so that's where the wind sits? She remarked mildly, "Still, it is an engaging little face."

More fitted to the stage than the classroom, she reflected, surveying the expressive countenance of Miss Paget. If she had any theatrical gifts—and had not been a gentleman's daughter—she could have made her way on the boards as a soubrette. Her face was piquante and pointed, with wide-set dark eyes and a neat, straight little nose. Dark, strongly marked brows kept her from insipidity, and so did a charmingly shaped mouth, always curved in what seemed the beginning of a smile even when she was serious. Dark hair, confined in a knot on the nape of her neck, was so fine and soft that tendrils escaped at the back and also curved down over her brow, giving her an air of childlike appeal. Viewed beside her massive pupils, she seemed more of a child than they— until her firm, confident voice made itself heard.

"Softly, Léonore—ease it through the door. See— there comes Monsieur Patrice—you do not wish to knock him down!"

"*Quoi donc—mon cousin*—what is he doing here at this hour?"

The cloud deepened on Madame's brow, as the pupils parted respectfully to allow a slight active man of her age, or a little younger, to make his way to the dais.

"Ah—Miladi Morningquest—*bonjour*—" He made a hasty, nervous bow in the direction of the distinguished visitor, but Lady Morningquest could see that he wished her at the devil. He continued rapidly to his cousin, "Marthe, here is catastrophe! I told you how it would be if the wretched girl was permitted to go home for her *jour de fête*—"

"What?" exclaimed Madame Bosschère, grasping his meaning with positively telepathic speed. "Not Ottilie de la Tour? You do not mean to tell me that some misfortune has befallen her—?"

"What did you expect? Not five minutes ago a servant delivered *this*!" Furiously, almost grinding his teeth, he flourished a crumpled piece of paper embossed with a coronet. "Broke her miserable nose riding one of her father's horses in the park—without permission, I need hardly say! I wish it had been her neck! Now her idiot mother writes that she is under a doctor's care and cannot return to school. *Du reste*, what use to me would be a Hamlet with nose bound up in court plaster? I should be the laughingstock of my colleagues at the Seminary. Oh, these cretinous giggling lumps of girls, with their fetes, and parties, and their minds on nothing but pleasure— how can one do anything with them? I would tie all their necks together and drown them in the Seine! Why in the name of reason did you allow her to go home before the performance?"

"My dear cousin—her father is the Count of—"

"Count of—*chose!*" growled Monsieur Patrice. It was plain that he was in a highly overwrought condition, almost beside himself with exasperation. He was a dark, sallow man, clean-shaven and quick in his movements. He wore his hair *en brosse*, unfashionably short, and was dressed very plainly in black garments of clerical cut, with a scholar's gown flung over his shoulder. Not an impressive man at first sight, thought Lady Morningquest; but what did make him remarkable was the look of lambent intelligence in his eyes, which were the dark purple-gray of a thundercloud. His mouth was thin and mobile, his brow scarred with thought.

Madame said soothingly, "Is there not an understudy, *mon cousin*? It is a pity about Ottilie, I agree, she is thinner than most of those *paysannes*, she has more the appearance of Hamlet, but still—"

"Fifine Tournon!"

Madame looked at him blankly, then remembered.

"Oh, *mon dieu*! Called away to her father's deathbed!"

"Now, do you see? It is crisis—catastrophe—chaos!"

In this extremity, Madame became Napoleonic. With

knitted brow she reflected for a moment or two, then pronounced, "There is only one thing to do. In such a case as this, *les convenances* must be put aside—as I am sure our dear friend and guest here will readily agree—"

"Indeed yes!" hastily said Lady Morningquest. "But, madame—Professor Bosschère—my dear friends, forgive me—I am shockingly de trop, and you must wish me a thousand miles off. I shall take myself away, for I have a dozen errands to perform in Brussels. I grieve to leave you in such a predicament, but I am sure that all will arrange itself in such capable hands—by the time I return this evening you will have trained a substitute—"

She might as well have spoken to the potted palm beside her. Neither of her companions paid the slightest attention.

"Marthe, I am relieved that you agree with me!" exclaimed Professor Patrice. "I knew you would see it as I do; there is only one person who knows the part, and, furthermore, can take the role and play it with intelligence at such short notice—"

"Yes, my cousin, you are right, but, *mon dieu*, there will be so much delegation of duties to arrange; let me see now—how can we manage it all—?"

"Francine!" Patrice grabbed the arm of a passing child. "Run, find Mademoiselle Paget, and bring her here."

"I will leave you for the present," repeated Lady Morningquest.

Madame was still thinking over the day's program.

"There is the collation to supervise—but old Roussel can do that; yes, and Elène can greet the parents, and preside at the prize-giving after the first few minutes—for I shall be too much preoccupied, so soon before the performance. Elène can do it—not with my polish, it is true, but ably enough. It will be valuable experience for her, furthermore, since she must learn to comport herself in polite society."

Patrice looked puzzled.

"She—Mademoiselle Paget?—greet the parents? Give out the prizes? What can you mean?"

"Why, you would not have Roussel greet them? The poor woman would die of terror and twist herself in knots. And Maury is too unpolished. No, if I am to take the part of Hamlet—and I do not see who else could do it—little Paget must manage as best she can for the first part of the afternoon."

"*You—you*—take the part of Hamlet?"

Now it was the Professor's turn to stare; indeed he received this announcement as if it had been a cannonball.

"But of *course*? What else?" Madame seemed equally taken aback. "Whom—then—did you have in mind?"

"Why, *she*—Mademoiselle Elène!"

For the first time, watching the two faces as they confronted one another, pale-cheeked, red-cheeked, Lady Morningquest thought she detected a cousinly resemblance in the square jaws, the flat cheek structure, the thin, firm-lipped mouths. But the eyes were different, hers opaque with shock, his fiery with purpose.

"*Mais—c'est une bétise—inouï—!*"

"I will leave you to your discussion," the visitor reiterated, and at last received a hurried, harried nod from her hostess, and a curt bow from the Professor. Hardly a discussion, Lady Morningquest thought with a private chuckle, as she descended the three steps from the dais, carefully lifting her gray lace skirts clear of the chalk dust and the palm spores. For Madame was saying, in a low, vibrant tone, "There can be *no possible question* of Elène Paget playing the role of Hamlet."

"But she *knows* it—she has been present as chaperon at all the repetitions—"

"Firstly, she has far too many other duties to perform during the day, from which she cannot possibly be spared. Secondly, how could I ever explain such a thing to her father in England? It would be *épouvantable*—wholly unsuitable. A young girl, in my care! All the world would consider it a gross dereliction of duty on my part. Whereas I, the Directrice, a widow and woman of the world—for me it is unusual, to be sure, but I am above scandal, and it will be an encouragement to the parents to see how I take part in the children's activities—"

"But—!"

"Say no more, Patrice! Any dispute on this matter is wholly out of the question."

As Lady Morningquest crossed the black-and-white-tiled hall, she saw Miss Paget run in from the garden, breathless and pink-cheeked. "You sent for me, madame?" the visitor heard her ask.

"Ah, yes, my child, here we have a little crisis—"

Lady Morningquest allowed herself a small ironic smile at the thought of the ensuing tripartite conversation. Patrice is no match for his cousin, she thought; Madame Bosschère will certainly have her way. Heaven only knows what she will make of the part of Hamlet—a forty-year-old Directrice! I am sorry, now, I did not manage to drag Giles to Brussels. But it's as well she won't allow Ellen to take the part—a taste for amateur theatricals is a complication we don't need at the Hôtel Caudebec.

At this point the ambassador's wife became aware of the arrival of her daughter, tiny blonde Charlotte, clad, like the rest of her schoolmates, in a calico wrapper and curlpapers.

"Mama! You are here! *Grace à dieu!* Léonore said she had seen you. Are you come to wish me luck?"

"My dearest child! Gently, I beg you—you will ruin my coiffure! And—merciful heaven—*look* at you! You are an absolute fright! If your father could see you now—and in the lobby, too—"

"Oh, nobody cares today," said Charlotte blithely. "And there is none to see, except old Philipon, and he is half blind. Still, come into the little salon."

Charlotte dragged her mother into a small reception room, stiffly furnished with gray-brocade-upholstered chairs and sofa, a green porcelain stove, glittering lustres, and a console.

"Listen, Mama!" she said. "It's so exciting. Ottilie de la Tour, who was to have played Hamlet, has broken her nose, and so Miss Paget is to have the part instead. We are all so delighted!"

"Who told you that?" demanded her mother, reflecting on the rapidity with which rumor spreads in a school.

"Oh, everybody knows. *Du reste*, who else could possibly take it on? Oh, I am so happy! I adore Miss Paget—she is my *beau ideal*! And to think of playing Ophelia to her Hamlet—Véronique and the others are all dying of envy. All of our class worship the ground she treads on—"

"Then you are a lot of very silly girls," repressively answered her mother, with the private conclusion that it was just as well Ellen Paget was to quit Madame's establishment. "And, in any case, you are quite out. Madame Bosschère is to take the part herself."

"*What?*" Charlotte's jaw dropped comically. She looked horror-stricken. "No, Mama, you can't be serious? Why, Monsieur Patrice would never, never allow it. He thinks the world of Miss Paget. He would have had her play Hamlet from the start if Madame permitted. Now she will be *obliged* to give in."

"Indeed she will not! And she is quite right. *Les convenances* would be outraged."

"But why? If it is proper for me to play Ophelia—"

"That is quite another matter. You are only fifteen. But Miss Paget is a young lady, earning her living."

"I don't see what that has to do with it. And anyway, she won't for long. Everybody says Monsieur Patrice is sure to marry her. We are all going to put our money together, as soon as he pops the question, and buy a beautiful silver epergne, with all our names engraved. Not that he is anything like good enough for her, cross old thing! But you can see he dotes on her—his eyes follow her all the time."

"Charlotte!" exclaimed Lady Morningquest sharply. "I wish you will stop talking such ridiculous rubbish. It is harmful to both parties and, I am sure, entirely without foundation."

"No, Mama, it is not. Véronique heard him, in the music room, calling Miss Paget his *chère petite amie!*"

"Charlotte, I do not wish to hear any more of such ill-judged and disgusting gossip. In any case, Monsieur Patrice would not be able to marry Miss Paget; did you not know that it is a condition of the Seminary where he is a Fellow that he remain a bachelor? It is only by special dispensation that he may come here to teach in his cousin's school."

"Well, if he married Miss Paget he could leave the Seminary—could he not?—and they could start a school together somewhere," argued Charlotte, but she looked a little dismayed by this news.

"Charlotte, I do not wish to hear another word on the subject. It is vulgar, mischievous, and, I am sure, a complete fabrication. Now I am going into town to buy lace, and I suggest that instead of indulging in addlepated speculation, you apply yourself to studying your part."

"Oh, I know it well enough," cheerfully responded Charlotte. "The part of Ophelia isn't very long, you know. And Miss Paget has been coaching me. *Au revoir, Maman, chérie, à ce soir!*" and she danced away down the hall.

Very thoughtfully, Lady Morningquest went out to her carriage and had herself driven through the leafy faubourg and along the rue Royale. She did not observe the stately houses, rosy brick or colorwashed, on either side of the wide streets. She ignored the blossoming trees, hawthorn and chestnut in their spring foliage, poplars and laurels in the park where crinolined little girls bowled hoops. She was deaf to the cheerful carillons celebrating the birthday of St. Annodoc.

Am I doing the right thing in transplanting that girl to Paris? she was asking herself.

❧

Festivities at Madame Bosschère's Pensionnat in Brussels were exceedingly lively affairs; Madame, known to be a strict disciplinarian and Argus-eyed martinet during school hours, liked to make it plain that, when her pupils had behaved well and worked with diligence, she was prepared to indulge them.

Also, it made a good advertisement for the school.

Madame's entertainments were famous. Often she had in outside performers—opera singers, puppeteers, gypsies with trained animals.

And her collations were superb; the main dishes were produced by Brussels caterers, but the school cook worked for days before preparing the Belgian patisseries, the gateaux and galettes and *pâtés à la crème* which were a speciality of the house.

Another innovation, much scandalized over by rivals in the scholastic field, was her habit of admitting to these parties youthful unmarried males, brothers and cousins of the young-lady pupils. No other school in Brussels permitted such a breach of the conventions. These dangerous masculine guests were, however, kept strictly segregated; indeed Ellen Paget often thought that Madame Bosschère's parties must be excessively boring to them, if not downright purgatorial. True, they might partake of the collation, but at a special table reserved for them alone, under the monitorial eye of Monsieur Patrice; they might watch the dramatic performance, from seats far at the back of the salle; but when it came to the ball, they were positively roped off in one corner of the large carré, and not on any account allowed to mingle with the young ladies. Still, their presence as spectators lent zest to the proceedings; the girls, dancing with each other or with fathers and married male teachers, were stimulated to a livelier grace and animation.

The forlorn squad of bachelors was there this evening as usual, penned in by a crimson velvet rope and a row of azaleas in tubs: a rank of well-dressed, well-scoured young Belgians, most of them as stolid-looking as their sisters on the dance floor, gazing, some with wistful interest, some with resigned apathy, at the frilled cloud of demoiselles provocatively twirling by in much-practiced waltzes and quadrilles.

Ellen, crossing that corner on her routine patrol, felt a twinge of sympathy for the unmarried male guests. They resembled street urchins, she thought, pressing hopeless noses against a baker's window.

Her eye caught a discreet movement of two white-clad girls drifting in their direction.

"Elfy, Eponine! What are you doing here?"

"It is so hot, Mademoiselle Elène; we wished to go into the garden for a breath of air."

"A very odd route to take! In any case, the doors are locked. You will have to go back through the salle; and if you are really going out, fetch your shawls first, from the armoire."

Crestfallen, the girls retreated, casting frustrated glances toward the row of bachelors. Ellen, glancing that way herself, was startled to observe, among all the inexpressive light-blue orbs and flaxen Flemish locks, a pair of familiar ironic dark-gray eyes fixed upon her, set in a narrow, clever, impatient face; and to be hailed in well-known teasing accents.

"Well, well, my dear Nell! At it as ever, I see! Still busy in the role of female Dragon, or is it Dragoon?

Knout on shoulder, cutlass at the ready, keeping the wolves away from your flock, eh?"

"Good gracious, Benedict!" Ellen tried to conceal her start of surprise at the sight of her stepbrother. Recovering, she gave him a cool, superior glance. It was a game they played, at their infrequent encounters; he tried to provoke her into a hot-tempered retort (or, when they had been younger, to physical violence); while she on her side, however stung she might be by his sallies, took pride in preserving an unruffled demeanor and, if possible, in some annihilating retort which would leave him speechless; only, up to now, she had never quite succeeded in achieving this.

"Why in the world have you come to Brussels?" she inquired. "Is not this your last term at Oxford? Should you not be preparing for your final examinations?"

"Oh, a fellow can't always be grinding away. Examinations are such a matter of luck," he replied airily. "Still, I don't suppose I shall be plucked. And as I'm destined for the Diplomatic, it's important that I have good languages. Dominic Arundel and I decided to give our brains a rest, to cut and run for a week or two. Our first intention is to replenish our fortunes at baccarat in Paris, but as I knew my dear mama would cut up rusty if she heard of my leaving Oxford in term time, I thought it might win her goodwill if I came round by way of Brussels to give her a report on you and your activities."

"You thought nothing of the kind," calmly retorted Ellen. She leaned for a moment on the back of a chair. The day had been remarkably wearing. During the afternoon the unseasonably hot May weather had been broken by a series of heavy thunder showers, which had driven the children and guests indoors, with consequent overcrowding and overheating. By now the atmosphere was one of wildly hysterical gaiety. Madame's performance as Hamlet, totally unexpected by most of the pupils, had added to this hectic mood; the girls were by now in a state of reckless giggling exuberance, ripe for folly. Ellen heartily wished the evening at an end. The presence of her stepbrother did nothing to lighten her weary depression. She said, "You know quite well that, so long as I am not in Petworth, and do not in some way disgrace myself, it is a matter of total indifference to Lady Adelaide whether I am in this world or the next."

"Touché, dear stepsister! You have my mama sized up to a nicety." Benedict's thin face relaxed into a swift malicious grin. "It's much the same state of affairs between myself and Easingwold. An elder brother who stands between oneself and an earldom—what a great lump of an inconvenient fellow he is! Even worse than a stepmama who won't have competition about the house in the form of a charming young stepdaughter."

"You need not waste sugary commonplaces on me, Benedict. Keep them for your female flirts."

"You must learn to accept compliments without striking out, Nell; as your stepbrother I think it my duty to give you that admonition. It is not pretty behavior. What I said was far from being sugary commonplace. Your looks have improved out of all knowledge. You have so much more countenance now. I would not have thought it possible for such a change to take place in—when was it we last met? That grisly wedding when your sister Catherine secured the hand of her nail merchant and thirty thousand a year? Eighteen months ago? You were still remarkably plain then, I assure you!"

"*Merci du compliment, monsieur,*" said Ellen coldly. "But I am afraid I cannot linger to listen to your courtesies—I have various pressing duties. I trust you will enjoy your gambling. How did you get in here, by the bye?"

"Made love to your Madame Bosschère, of course. I came along with René de la Tour. Madame was amazingly civil to us both. And I must say," added Benedict, bursting out into a spontaneous, boyish peal of laughter that made him look, for a moment, much younger and quite different, "it was worth coming, only to see Madame take the role of the gloomy Dane! It was rich! A fifty-year-old schoolma'am as the Prince of Denmark! I had never expected to enjoy Shakespeare half as much. When Uncle Harry took me and Easingwold to *Coriolanus* at the Haymarket I thought it shockingly slow. But to hear your esteemed Directrice arguing 'To bee orr nott to bee' in her Bruxelles guttural—"

"Oh, hush, Benedict! She is forty, not fifty! And someone may hear you!"

"Not with all those honest burghers squeaking away on their fiddles like demented gannets. I tell you, preserving a straight face through those soliloquies was the hardest thing I ever did."

"Indeed?" said Ellen coolly. "Excellent training for your diplomatic career, I should have thought. I am sure Madame would be gratified to learn of your efforts."

"Why, *you* could have played the part better!"

"Thank you! But I am afraid I must leave you." She started to move away. He detained her by grasping her wrist.

"Don't run away, Nell! Listen—can't you join René and me later for a cutlet at the Jardin des Lauriers?"

"Take supper with two young men? At a public restaurant? Are you mad? In any case, we shall be busy half the night, putting back the furniture."

"Oh, very well." He did not seem unduly surprised, or cast down, at her refusal. "Would you care to come driving tomorrow?" he remarked, as an afterthought.

She was surprised, but said firmly, "It is out of the question. Tomorrow is a normal school day."

"Well—then—don't tell Mama, when next you write home, that I didn't do my best to give you a treat!"

The angle of Ellen's jaw suggested that she did not

take his good intentions at a very high value; and that
her correspondence with his mother was not of a particularly warm or prolific nature. Again attempting to
disengage her wrist from his clasp, she remarked drily,
"I take it you have no news from home to give me?"

"None of any consequence," he replied in a
similar tone. "In point of fact, I have not been down
there since hunting ended—and then I only stayed a
week; the Petworth hunt is a pitiful affair. All at the
Hermitage seemed as usual then: my mama was in her
usual fidgety spirits, complaining of her uninspiring
neighbors; your young brother was meager and mum-
chance, as always; our little sister as repellently spoiled
a brat as ever; and your papa laying down the law in
his accustomed style. Nothing new. No—stay: the old
cat died."

"What?" exclaimed Ellen, before she could stop
herself, in a tone of genuine grief. "My cat Nibbins?
Why—he was not so very old."

"No, well, I believe he was caught by a fox, or some
such thing, Vicky told me. She was rather cut up about
it. Ah, there goes René, signaling to me—he has had
enough, poor fellow. Good night, Nell."

He let go of her hand, moved rapidly away among
the other black-coated young men, and was at once lost
to view.

Ellen stood staring after him for a moment, with
clenched hands and head drawn back. She took several
deep ragged breaths, as if she had been running. She felt
sore and pummeled, as always after one of her engagements with Benedict. Then, calm once more to outward
appearance, she was moving away when Madame
Bosschère, whose lynx eye missed nothing, intercepted
her. Madame had, of course, by this time put off her
scholar's gown, and was resplendent in black velvet,
russet lace, and a cap trimmed with sequins; she had been

darting about the carré like a comet, making sure that all the parents received appropriate salutations.

"Ah, *ma chère* Elène—so you have seen your brother the Honorable Benedict! That is good, that is right. Such an excellent young man—polished, well bred, thoroughly estimable. And is it true that one day he will be a vicomte?"

"No, madame," said Ellen, the touch of dryness in her tone again. "It is the elder brother who is Lord Easingwold. Benedict is merely honorable—unless his brother should die, of course."

"Ah, *bien sûr*. No matter, he is wellborn, one can see it in his look, and sure to make his way. Now, my child, I wish to hold a conversation with you on the matter of your welfare. You must come to my closet later, when the guests are gone."

"Tonight, madame? But—it will be late—after midnight, very likely."

"No matter; what I have to say is of importance. Do not forget." And the Directrice glided away, shedding affable smiles wherever she went, receiving the compliments given for her enactment of the Shakespearian role with a look of modest, twinkling satisfaction, as being no more than her due.

Ellen slipped away for a moment into a small practice room, unlit, for all its lamps had been taken to add splendor to the grand carré. For a moment weariness, of body and spirit, overcame her; she leaned against the wall, with her hands pressed against her eyes, trying to ignore the distant throb and squeak of fiddle and drum. But almost immediately her attention was caught by a closer, lesser sound: a faint, suppressed sob from a shadowy corner of the room.

"Who is there?" Ellen demanded sharply. Her eyes, growing accustomed to the dim light, now discovered a small figure crouched on a stool. "Mary-Ann Gray? Is that you? What are you doing in here? Why are you not dancing with the rest?"

"Oh, please, Miss Paget, don't send me back! The others all laugh at me because I don't know how to dance; and they say that my dress is too short, and ugly besides, and that I look a f-f-f-fright!"

Mary-Ann was the youngest and most recently arrived of the English pupils; her father, a Yorkshire wool merchant, had left her in Brussels only three weeks ago. Now Ellen, drawing her to the doorway, saw that she was half drowned from crying, her nose red and swollen, her eyes puffy and bloodshot.

"*Fi donc!* Look at you!" scolded Ellen gently. "What is all this about?"—as if she did not know very well.

"I'm so h-h-homesick! The other girls are so unkind. And"—with another burst of tears—"it's my little b-brother's birthday tomorrow. He will be missing me so!"

"Now listen, my dear," said Ellen. "This will not do." She had an impulse to put an arm round the little girl's shoulders, but suppressed it. The child must learn to manage on her own. "We have all, *all* been homesick," she went on. "When I first came here, I was no more than your age, and I was ready to die with misery at first."

A sudden piercing recollection came to her of those first hopeless days: running downstairs in the morning, early, before the other boarders, day after day, looking for a letter in Mama's handwriting, which never came. She swallowed, and said, "But you will soon get over that. We all did. And then you will find that the other girls are not so bad! Only do not let them see that they have made you cry. Why, your face is quite swelled up. Crying does not help, really; in fact it makes you feel worse. Here, lean your head over the end of the sofa— that will clear your nose. Stay like that while I run to the kitchen; I will be back directly."

She procured from the cook, who was resting and

imbibing cognac after her labors, a piece of ice and a cupful of vinegar. The ice was applied to Mary-Ann's cheeks and eyes, the vinegar was used to bathe her forehead. "Your hair needs tidying," said Ellen, and did it with a comb from her reticule. "There! Now you look fresh as a daisy, and I want you to walk calmly back into the carré and take your place with the girls in the grand chain. It is the last dance. Hark! I hear the fiddlers striking up."

"Oh, please, no, Miss Paget, I can't!"

"Most certainly you can. You look just as you ought. Nobody is going to laugh at you. It will all be over in five minutes, and then you can go to bed. Run along!"

She gave the child a little push. Obediently, almost hypnotized, Mary-Ann walked back to the ballroom, and, after a moment or two, Ellen followed, straightening her shoulders as if she, not Mary-Ann, were the new pupil expecting to be met with hostility and ridicule.

In fact nobody noticed her entrance. Guests were beginning to leave, and the large room was all in restless motion, with parties assembling together, parents bidding farewell to their daughters, final civilities being exchanged with the Directrice. Ellen wearily and dutifully placed herself where a departing parent could, if the need were felt, pause to consult her over a child's difficulties, or congratulate her on progress; she braced herself to stand upright, wishing it were permissible to sit, or to lean against the wall.

"There you are, at last!" exclaimed a voice in her ear. "I have been hunting for you, high and low. Where have you been?"

"On my duties, Monsieur Patrice."

"Duties, bah! What an occasion for duties. But I can see that is true," he went on more mildly. "Poor child, you look worn to the bone. Come aside, here, into the cabinet for a moment—I imagine you have taken

nothing at all during this whole gallimaufry." He seized
her by the arm and led her into a small office where
Madame transacted school business, and which Monsieur
Patrice used as a workroom and study when he visited
the building. "Parties—balls—festivities," he went on
irritably, pulling a decanter and two crystal glasses from
a closet. "How I despise them! False compliments are
exchanged, platitudes, inanities—there can be no sensible
conversation, no profound thought expressed in such an
atmosphere. There is only fatigue and ennui and idiocy!
Here, drink this, it is porto, it will do you good. And sit
a moment."

Obediently as Mary-Ann, Ellen sat, and sipped the
sweet powerful stuff.

"I should go back; they will begin moving the furniture," she murmured.

"And are there no hired footmen, no porters, no
menservants to do that—I say nothing of those great
bullocks of girls?"

"They will do it carelessly and all wrong; and Madame
will need me."

"So? *I* need you," he said. "*Mon amie*, listen: I have a
request to put to you; a favor to ask."

Ellen stared up at him in silence. Her face, from six
years' training, was well schooled to calm, but a great
hope grew and became luminous in her eyes.

Monsieur Patrice began to walk impatiently up and
down the small room. Although not a tall man, he had
a decision and vehemence in all his movements that
made him impressive. He was active and nervous, not
powerful, but fiery and rapid in his intelligence and quick
apprehensions. He paused and bent an almost mesmeric
look on Miss Paget.

"You, my friend, are the *one* person I can talk to in
this establishment—you are a remarkable soul—a spirit in
a thousand! And yet how often can one procure even five

minutes' converse with you? It is insupportable! Your mind clears mine, as a solvent works on a reagent; you create a path in my wilderness, order in the ferment of my crowding ideas. You are my complement; by means of your analytical aptitude my light is organized into a spectrum. You are, in effect, a necessity to me!"

"Oh, monsieur!" she murmured, overawed.

"If I had you by my side—for a week, a month—for a day, even—what might I not accomplish! This situation here is *wrong*! It is not to be endured, that you must creep about here, like a mouse in a trap, permitted to blink at the light only through bars. You must, must be free!"

A delicate color had come up into Ellen's pale cheeks. Her eyes had begun to shine. But, still wholly uncertain as to his meaning and wishes, she remained silent, breathing quickly, watching him with a faint pucker of perplexity between her brows.

"Look here!" he continued. He had on his velvet-trimmed surtout, as if he had been on the point of departure. From its pocket he dragged out a mass of papers, crumpled and crisscrossed with writing. "See, this here is my outline for a new chapter in my treatise. It deals with the subject of human love. But the writing is incoherent, loose, rambling; I find that I cannot marshal my thoughts, I need you beside me at the desk to discuss the subject."

"Human love?" she faltered.

"Passion and charity, Eros and Agape. Oh, it sounds so simple when I say it in spoken language!"

Does it? wondered Ellen.

"*Par exemple*—your love for your brother, your child, your friend, your mate, your mother," Monsieur Patrice went on, his words tumbling one over another. "Each is different in form, and how to analyze these differences?"

Ellen felt herself drifting into a strange state of shadowy lassitude. The strong, heady porto, taken on top of her deep physical fatigue, had clouded her normal vigilant wariness; instead she experienced a series of dreamlike perceptions, visiting her in flashes, like swift glimpses through moving mist. With half her attention she heard the Professor's words: "…your friend, your mate, your mother…" My love for my mother? she wondered. Long-buried recollections floated into her mind: a slight, dark-haired woman in a white dress knelt laughing under a yew tree—"Only see, Ellie, the hedgehog, see his little feet!" Or indoors, at the dining table, patiently inscribing a row of pothooks for her daughter to copy; reading Milton aloud in a clear dispassionate voice; playing hymns on the piano for Papa, changing over to Beethoven when he fell asleep, which he invariably did after five minutes; chuckling, after the visit of a formidable neighbor: "Lady Martello looks *exactly* like a heron." And that strange confidence, given once, never again referred to: "You know, Ellie, you had a twin brother, but he died at birth; poor Papa was very upset and angry about that; it took him a long, long time to forgive me—if, indeed, he ever has; though it was not my fault. But—because of that—I have always felt that *you* were somehow doubly my child." Oh, Ellen cried in her heart, and I felt so too, Mama! specially as Papa was so wholly uninterested in me. Another memory: the same figure, but with gray streaks in the dark hair, walking slowly, a hand pressed to her side. "No, I am not tired, but I have a little chill; half a day in bed will mend me." But a day had not, nor a week.

"Is this not a noble subject!" cried Monsieur Patrice with enthusiasm. "Human love! A subject requiring—demanding—thorough investigation, thorough consideration."

Ellen felt humble. To be here, alone, with this brilliant man, at such an hour, discussing such a subject—what an honor, what a felicity! Yet also, with deep apprehension, she knew that such a moment must be paid for; life always presented its accounts with merciless speed.

As indeed on this occasion. For there was Madame Bosschère in the doorway, her brow black with disapprobation.

"Mademoiselle *Paget!*" She chopped out the syllables like cordwood. "You are here? Why—may I ask—are you not superintending the rearrangement of the carré?"

"I am very sorry—I was just about to, madame—" began Ellen.

But Madame's gaze, like a lighthouse ray, had moved on to her cousin.

"Patrice! May I ask what you think you are doing? This is folly—abysmal, puerile, disgraceful folly; unworthy of you—perfidious to me! Good God! What would the world say, if it were known that you had made such an assignation, here, like this, alone, with a young girl, a teacher who is in my charge? Remember your situation—your promises—remember *who you are!*"

"Oh, pray, madame—it was no assignation, indeed it was not!" Ellen protested.

But Patrice glanced at Madame Bosschère like a caged creature. Though his eyes glittered with rebellion, he seemed brought up short by her words; he stood motionless, hands dangling at his sides, head bent, staring at his black, shining boots; Ellen, who scarcely dared breathe, began to be filled with a sickening realization that his purpose—whatever that was—had been deflected, if not wholly frustrated.

"Promises?" he muttered, half to himself. "Ay, my God, what promises, made in youth, under duress! Such promises are shameful, they are for slaves, not for men!"

Nevertheless he tucked the pages of manuscript slowly back into his velvet pocket.

"But whatever you say—more discourse with Mademoiselle Paget I *must* and *will* have!" he suddenly snarled at his cousin, who stood with her arms folded, like Buonaparte on some hard-won field, confident of reinforcements at hand which the opposing force could not possibly match.

"No! You must *not*, Patrice! Nor will you. I forbid it: now, absolutely, and entirely. You must put Miss Paget from your mind—wholly, forever, and at once!"

Now, surely, he will defy her, thought Ellen. Now his brilliance will flame out. This man I know to be a genius. Compared with her plodding commonplace talent for administration, his mind is like the sun blazing out its light into space; now—if he chooses—he can totally annihilate her.

But he did not choose. Ellen waited, breathless. The expected confrontation did not come. Patrice turned, slowly, his head still bent, his shoulders expressing defeat; the spirit seemed to dwindle inside him, like a blade sliding back into its sheath; even his eyes looked sunken and darkened, dying lamps on the brink of extinction. Without a glance at Ellen, without another word, he trudged from the room.

Ellen quivered as if she had been stabbed. The shock, the disappointment, the shame of witnessing such an unexpected transformation in somebody she had looked up to, almost with reverence, far outweighed any apprehension at what Madame Bosschère might now say to her. But, in fact, to her surprise, when she turned her eyes unhappily to that lady, she found that Madame was regarding her with a kind, even an affectionate smile.

"*Ma pauvre petite!* This is a sad business for you! Oh, how much simpler it would be if the whole race of men could be exterminated—or, better still, kept immured in a Garden of Zoology as pets, where the females could visit and feed them when they chose! I truly believe that men are too dangerous to be permitted at large among us. Consider Patrice, now, my cousin—what a charmer he is, but what a garçon, a gamin, an irresponsible child! I know, I know—you think him a genius; doubtless he is one. But, because of this great intellect of his, you, my poor child, must now leave Brussels and begin life over again in a new ménage. Oh, it is unfair! Still, perhaps, in the end, it will be for your good. It is, to be sure, time that you spread your wings a little."

"Leave Brussels?" gasped Ellen, hardly able to believe her ears. "Madame, you are not serious? You are not dismissing me?"

"*Oui! Et à l'instant, même!* You must pack up your things tonight, and be ready to depart by midday tomorrow, so that you may travel under the escort of Miladi Morningquest. Oh, don't worry, you are not leaving here in disgrace—nobody but us two shall ever know about this little incident! Indeed I am truly sorry to lose you—I grieve to part from you, my little one. But we must be practical! You could remain here no longer; it would be neither possible nor convenable for you to be meeting Patrice about the classrooms after this."

"But nothing was said—nothing took place—" began Ellen.

Madame brushed aside these remarks as if they had not been made.

"You will be going to a position of great responsibility, in a great hôtel, where you will see infinitely more of life than in this quiet little backwater. Lady Morningquest came here expressly to invite you to become companion and *gouvernante* to her husband's niece, the Comtesse de la Ferté. So observe how admirably matters have fallen out! You will depart from here with an unblemished character, my dear; indeed I fully know how good, how replete with integrity is your nature. I have already praised you to Madame in the highest terms. And, as for this little contretemps—the burnt child bewares the fire! You will be wiser in future. So do not lament that your existence here has come to its conclusion, but look forward, instead, to the enticing new sphere."

And Madame patted Ellen amiably on the shoulder.

"You appear a little pale, my child, and no wonder! The day has been full of fatigues. Run along, therefore, to your couch; all here will arrange itself very well without you. And there will be much for you to do tomorrow. Go, then!"

With a gentle push, she propelled Ellen from the room. The latter could not help glancing back wonderingly; she noticed that Madame, apparently no whit perturbed by the scene that had taken place, was carefully scrutinizing a worn spot on the piano cover, before turning to march at a brisk pace back toward the main area of the school.

It was like observing the burned area after a heath fire followed by a tempest—black, scorched, sodden, silent; one could hardly imagine the raging blaze that had traversed the same spot such a short time before.

The teachers in Madame's Pensionnat were not allotted private rooms of their own. For the purpose of surveillance, they slept among the boarders in the long conventual dormitories at the top of the house. Ellen, therefore, having toiled up the four flights of stairs, could not indulge her feelings in seclusion; she must undress in the dark and slip quietly into bed, hushing a few giggles and murmurs from pupils who were still overexcited by the day's festivities; then she must lie containing herself in silence, under the row of uncurtained attic windows beyond which lights from the city still glimmered.

Ellen did not weep. Long ago, when she first arrived in the school, the shock of leaving her intensely loved home and acclimatizing herself to this new, noisy, and hostile environment, soon to be followed by crushing, consuming grief at her mother's death, had been so complete that she had lost the power to comfort herself by tears; and now the source seemed to have dried up. Instead she hugged her arms tightly across her slight body, as if the ache within her must somehow be kept in bounds; as if her corporeal self were all she had; as if she felt that even this, her identity, might be taken from her too.

Madame Bosschère did not really need me at all, she thought. It is of no consequence to her whether I go from here or stay; she can replace me as easily as she might a withered nosegay or a torn fichu, and at equally short notice. And I—I thought I was so valuable to her!

It did not occur to Ellen that Madame might be glad to be given a pretext for disposing of a lieutenant whose power and prestige bade fair soon to equal that of the headmistress herself; might, in time, exceed it.

But he—Monsieur Patrice! she pondered wretchedly. *He* said he needed me! He seemed as if he meant it! And then—just to go—like *that*—to walk from the room without a word, without a look even. Oh, how can it be borne?

Her heart felt as if it were being slowly and painfully dragged from her body. The center of her whole being had been extracted. She could not contain the pain of it. And yet she must, and might give no hint of the anguish that was devouring her.

It was many hours before she slept.

❦

Next day, shortly after noon, Benedict Masham drove round to the Pensionnat in a fiacre. He asked for an interview with his stepsister, and was greatly startled to hear that she had left the establishment for a new position in Paris.

"It was a chance too good to be missed," Madame Bosschère told him blandly. "Indeed, *la petite* herself did not know about it until last night. Our good friend Lady

Morningquest would take no denial, I assure you—none but Ellen would do! It was her insistence that finally persuaded me to part with your *belle-soeur*—though I shall miss her like my right hand, indeed! But I greatly regret, *mon ami*, that you did not have an opportunity to bid her farewell. The whole affair was arranged with such rapidity!"

"Oh, that's of no consequence," replied Benedict. He seemed rather pale, thought Madame, acutely observing him. Up all night, no doubt, drinking and gambling. Madame knew a great deal about fashionable young men. "I shall be able to see Ellen in Paris just as well, for I am going there directly. But I have a somewhat shocking piece of news from home, just received, which I was about to break to her—"

"Ah, *tiens*—" Madame ejaculated. "Here, also, after she had departed, a *télégramme* was received for Miss Paget. I had intended to redirect it to her Paris address. Doubtless the same bad tidings?"

"Doubtless. My mother, Ellen's stepmother, has been killed in a carriage accident; and Ellen's father, Mr. Paget, severely injured in the same affair; my mother's sister, my aunt Blanche, who lives in Sussex, telegraphed to give me the information."

"Ah, *quel douleur*!" exclaimed Madame sympathetically. "In that case I am doubly grieved that Elène has quitted Brussels and must receive the sad news in a strange place. But, *hélas*, my poor friend—your mother! What a calamity! I deeply commiserate with you."

She noted, however, the ironic gleam in Benedict's eye. Cold as fishes, all the English, thought Madame; no proper family feeling.

"But in that case," she went on, "*miséricorde*, what a disaster that *la petite* has just departed to take up a new position. For naturally she will wish to return home for the funeral, and remain to care for her poor papa?"

"The funeral has already taken place, I understand. My aunt Blanche, who is the wife of the Bishop of Chichester, arranged it all. And Aunt Blanche informs me that she has already engaged a capable nurse to care for Mr. Paget, and a housekeeper for his home. No, I merely came to break the news to Ellen—and to inform her that, now her stepmother is no more, there would be nothing to stand in her way should she wish to return home. You must have been aware, madame—since Ellen has resided with you for six years—that my mother felt a—a considerable dislike for her youngest stepdaughter."

Madame shrugged.

"Such things occur in families. However, her papa, doubtless, would be happy to have her company— even if there is also a nurse? Since both elder sisters are now married?"

"I believe not," Benedict said coolly. "He is a strange man, Mr. Paget. He bore little affection toward his daughters. But naturally I thought it my duty to bring Ellen the news."

"Naturally. Poor child, she will be greatly shocked. It will seem like a recurrence. Soon after she first came here, her own mother died. In fact I believe she was sent away from home in order to make room for a nursing attendant."

"Perhaps you would be good enough to give me her Paris address, madame," said Benedict, reflecting that Madame kept herself very well informed of the affairs of her subordinates.

"*Mais naturellement*; here it is. You go to Paris now? Then you will be so good as to deliver this *télégramme* to the poor child. I shall indite her a letter with solemn condolences. But meanwhile I beg you will take her my affectionate greetings, and repeat to her, what she already knows, that she will always have a sincere, maternal friend in me."

What a pity the news did not come a day earlier, Madame reflected; then Miss Paget need not have been bundled off to Paris, but could simply have been sent home to England.

However, matters must stand as they were.

Three

SOMETIMES—MORE FREQUENTLY, IN FACT, THAN HE would allow himself to remember—Luke Paget was troubled by a haunting dream. It concerned a house—not his everyday dwelling, the Hermitage—but a house that he owned and inhabited solely in the territory of dream, that he had been visiting for the past thirty years and more. Part of this building was familiar and friendly enough, but one area—and this was where the dream became ominous, threatening, or just unspeakably sad—one area was empty, shut off, removed from the core of the house: a closed wing, a derelict suite of rooms, a disused pavilion—ruined, abandoned, wasted, desolate.

Sometimes, in his dream, he would be making plans for the occupation of this part, and its repair; sometimes he was outraged at finding unlawful settlers in possession—secret, evil beings who scurried away, mocked him, and hid in dark, dusty corners; sometimes his mood was simply one of despair, at the waste of so much useful space; sometimes he spent the whole dream in a hopeless, frustrated search for the door, passage, or many-angled stairway by which the vacant wing might be approached. But he always woke melancholy, perplexed, hollow-hearted, and possessed by the fear which had haunted him through the course of the dream, that his chances were slipping away, that soon there would be no time left in which to re-enter or restore his lost place.

Lady Blanche, parasol on shoulder, sailing majestically toward her brother-in-law over the smooth lawns of the Bishop's garden, saw that he lay sleeping in his basket chair under the mulberry tree, but that his sleep was not a peaceful one; he moaned, twitched, and whimpered; his eyelids flickered; then, suddenly, he was awake, his large pale-gray eyes were regarding her coldly. She was relieved that he had woken up; to see the chill reserve and self-control of this dour man break down in sleep had been an unsettling experience.

Blanche Pomfret, a big, self-confident woman, who shared the Bishop's straightforward piety, had never greatly cared for her sister's second husband. "Handsome— clever, I daresay—but a cold fish," she said of Luke to her husband at the time of the marriage. "It was a most unfortunate mischance that Adelaide should encounter him again so soon after Radnor died; if she had met him *before*, and come to know him rather more thoroughly, it is odds that she would never have married him. She would have settled down into widowhood, I daresay." "No use questioning God's ways, my love," said the Bishop. "No; I know; but He might have spared a thought for poor little Vicky. Imagine being left an orphan at five, with Luke for your father—and old enough to be her grandfather, at that!"

"Poor little Vicky is lucky that she has you for an aunt, then," said the Bishop blandly.

"Humph! You know how little time I have, Bishop, for family affairs. It is fortunate that I found that excellent woman to take charge at the Hermitage."

"Very fortunate, my dear!"

Now, furling her parasol, Blanche touched Luke on the shoulder.

"Wake up, my dear Luke; you were having a bad dream."

"Was I? I can remember nothing of it." Vexed at having

been caught unprepared, he ran a hand through his thick white hair, and shifted, with a grimace of pain, the leg that was still heavily bandaged and protected by wooden splints. "Is it late, Blanche? Do you come to summon me to dinner?"

"No, no, my friend; don't bestir yourself, it is early still; I am come to prepare your mind for visitors; or rather," she added, seeing a cloud pass over his brow, "to ask if you wish to receive your children, who are come, with very proper filial devotion, to inquire after you."

"*Children?*" he repeated with a look of blank incomprehension.

"Gerard, and little Vicky," his sister-in-law explained patiently.

"*What?* They have driven here—all the way from Petworth—fifteen miles? Why in the world's name did they do so? There was not the slightest occasion for it," said their father, manifesting no pleasure whatever at this dutiful behavior. "Did Gerard drive my horses? Over Duncton Hill? Has he *no* consideration?"

"No, no, they came with John coachman and Mrs. Pike."

"Who—pray—is Mrs. Pike?"

"She is your new housekeeper, Luke. Do you not recall? You did meet her, but I fear you were still in great pain at the time."

"Oh—ay. Now it comes back. Mrs. Pike." Luke Paget heaved an angry sigh, as if these names, Vicky, Gerard, Mrs. Pike, were so many feathered darts lodged in his shoulders to irritate and distract him.

"You did say," his sister-in-law calmly reminded him, "that you would prefer hiring a housekeeper than to have your daughter Ellen summoned back from Brussels. And indeed there was need to install some responsible, comfortable body without delay; and Mrs. Pike seemed eminently suitable."

"Oh, good God, yes, I am not querying your actions, Blanche; much obliged to you indeed. What use in the world would *Ellen* be—a fidgety chit of a girl, hardly out of the schoolroom? No, no, I daresay Mrs. Pike will do well enough."

"Do you not wish to see them, Luke? Since they are here?"

Quite plainly it was the last thing he wished, but, after a moment or two, with reluctance, he grunted, "I had best do so, I suppose; as they have seen fit to come all this way. And the Pike woman as well. If only to make her understand that there is no call to be taking my horses across the Downs twice a week!"

"Set your mind at rest. I have already impressed on her the need to run your household with proper economy," smoothly replied his sister-in-law, with only the slightest touch of irony. "But I understand that she had various other domestic errands in Chichester which could be accomplished at the same time. I will send them to you then—in separate detachments, so as not to overtax your strength."

She departed at a stately pace; in her massive crinoline, with parasol, gauze-and-ribbon-trimmed cap, shawl, lace gloves, and chatelaine, all in severe mourning hue, she resembled some baroque, smoke-blackened cathedral which had been set in motion and was gliding over the grass.

Luke Paget heaved another irritable sigh.

The Bishop's garden in Chichester was a charming spot. Of considerable extent, bounded by walls of rosy, ancient brick, it contained various different enclosures, contrasting formality with exuberance: here, exotic shrubs, noble trees, luxuriant foliage; there, velvet turf and carefully tended formal beds; the air was warm with the scent of wisteria, over a faint, salt tang of the sea. A mild May sun beamed down, and birds sang joyfully.

None of this had any beneficent effect upon the man in the basket chair. Luke Paget had never cared for gardens. By his reckoning, they were just places to be kept trim and productive; he had never understood his first wife's passion for planting, pruning, and tending green things. (Though, since it was a relatively inexpensive pursuit, he had not gone out of his way to hinder her activity.) Now he wished, with irritation, that he might have suffered his children's visit indoors; there was something informal and al fresco about receiving them here that did not consort with his attitude toward them.

However, as he was still unable to move more than a few paces without help, he had to remain where he was, chafing inwardly.

Often, these days, he found himself thinking of his first wife. Why? She had been dead for six years; there was no utility in such a habit; and Luke Paget was, above all things, a practical man. Yet, unbidden, exasperating, these recollections would flash out: Matilda helpless with laughter over some diverting occurrence—she had found humor in the most trivial, unbecoming sources, and loved to laugh; or thoughtful, silent, meditating some ploy in the household, which she had ordered with serene, untroubled ease. Sometimes she had laughed over her children: Kitty's follies, Eugenia's snobbery; for she had been a realist, wholly unsentimental. And yet she had loved them devotedly, and loved him, Luke, with an equal, open, uncritical attachment which, perfectly aware of his shortcomings, yet embraced him in a large, tender, humorous warmth. Why, he now wondered angrily, why had he not appreciated this happy state more while it was his? For some reason he often remembered a breakfast scene—one in particular? or was it the prototype of many?—with Mattie smiling over the coffee cups, and the girls, small then, pretty and well-behaved in their places. Gerard had been a baby in his bassinet upstairs.

Why did I not realize that I was happy then? Luke demanded of himself. What would I not give for that day back again! Furiously he now regretted, not that during the whole of their married life Mattie had received from him far less than her due, but that he himself had failed to make the most of that well-being while he had it. He was absorbed, at that time, in his ambitions—the hope of getting into Parliament, of making a name for himself at the Bar. Vain hopes! And, while he was pursuing them, the reality had slipped away from him. Now, his life offered no possibility of fulfillment, apart from some deep-seated aspirations for his son. The only immediate gratifications left were the common, accepted ones of physical taste—comfort—warmth—health; and now, since the accident in which his second wife had been rudely taken from him, even health and the pleasures of the bed were lost.

Without joy, he watched his two youngest children approach.

They, for their part, came toward him at a rather dawdling pace, as if unsure of their welcome, crossing the wide lawn at some distance apart, without addressing each other; it was plain that the occasion, not any compatibility, had thrown them together.

Vicky minced along with disdainful precision, staring frankly about her, taking in her surroundings: the battlemented brick walls, the green and flowery garden, the croquet hoops on the grass, the slender spire of Chichester Cathedral tapering above the Palace roof. Vicky was a small, round-faced, watchful child, dressed for this visit in bright tartan silk and white starched pantalettes, her wiry dark hair elaborately twisted into ringlets. She had the wary look of someone whose life produced so little entertainment that she was adept at making the very most of what came her way. Occasionally she cast a critical glance at her half brother. Gerard, the fifteen-year-old, bore a marked resemblance to his father, with the same bony build, which was gaunt in the man, coltish in the boy; and the same long lantern-jawed face, hollow eye sockets, pallor, and large reflective gray eyes; but Gerard's eyes were a darker shade of gray than his father's, and his mouth was wider, and somewhat irresolute, whereas Luke's was set in lines of rigid severity. The son's hair sprang upward thickly like the father's, but was soft and dark.

"There's not a scrap of his mother in that boy," Lady Blanche remarked once; but the Bishop, who had been fond of Luke's first wife, said, "Yes there is; just a scrap; only, will he ever let it out?"

Vicky had brought a bunch of clove pinks, tightly clenched in her hand; she laid these on the cane footrest of Luke's chaise longue and announced politely, in a flat little voice, "How do you do, Papa? I hope you are better. I have brought you these flowers."

"Mind my hurt leg," he replied. "There was no occasion to bring flowers; do you not see that I have a whole gardenful around me? I hope you had Moon's permission to pick them."

"He picked them himself and sends his respects," she said tonelessly. "Papa, how long must Mrs. Pike stay at the Hermitage?"

"Forever, I imagine," he answered. "*Somebody* has to see after the house. Well, Gerard—have you no greeting for me?"

Luke had never pretended the slightest interest in his daughters. To him, Vicky, the fourth, was simply an additional encumbrance, another useless girl for whom, in due course, a dowry and husband must be found. All his feelings, hopes, and ambitions had, for years, been centered in his son, the long-awaited heir. Yet a stranger, observing his manner toward the pair, would have detected little difference in his tone. Indeed his cold neutrality toward Vicky appeared to harden into downright disgust as he studied her elder brother.

"Your hair needs trimming, sir; you resemble a savage! And why, pray, is your cravat so untidy? May I inquire whether your tutor gave permission for this day of exeat from your studies?"

"Gerard had cramps in his chest on Tuesday," piped up Vicky. "So Mr. Newman said he had been working too hard and had best play for a change."

"Speak when you are spoken too, miss, and not before! Well, Gerard—I am waiting for your answer?"

"How do you do, Father? It is as Vicky says," Gerard replied laconically. "I took one of my breathless spells; and Mr. Newman permitted me a day's half holiday. How do you go on, sir? Does your leg pain you a great deal?"

"No—no; it is no great matter. I shall soon be walking on crutches, and hope to be at home within the week." Neither of the children appeared particularly gladdened by this information. "But as to your chest, Gerard—did not Mr. Newman think it necessary to send for Dr. Bendigo? Was it a *sharp* attack? Were you feverish?"

Gerard's bronchial and asthmatic afflictions when he was younger had been a cause of much anxiety to his family; especially to his father, who had thought it best to keep him at home with a tutor, rather than send him to Eton or Harrow. For some years a consumption had been apprehended, since the least chill or exposure was likely to bring on a severe spasm, sometimes leading to inflammation of the lungs. During the past two or three years, however, the frequency and acuteness of these attacks had greatly diminished.

"What had you been doing to bring this on?" Luke demanded sharply. "Had you ridden farther than you ought? Or been playing cricket in the park?"

"No, Father." Gerard looked mildly amused at the latter suggestion. Then he gave a sudden glare at his little sister, who had opened her mouth to speak. He went on quickly. "It was a trifling indisposition, and has quite passed off. But Mr. Newman thought a drive over the Downs in the fresh air would do me good."

"If only the scent of the hawthorn flower does not start you wheezing," Luke muttered disapprovingly. "You had better by far have remained at home in the summerhouse studying your Aristotle and your law books."

Gerard's expression did not change, but an infinitesimal shrug indicated what he thought of his father's alternative. After a slight pause he remarked, "Here comes Mrs. Pike," and, to Vicky, in a low tone, "If you wish to say your say, you had best make haste." He glanced at his young half sister with dislike and respect.

"Papa," said Vicky shrilly and breathlessly, "we don't like Mrs. Pike, not at all! Nobody does! Not Jenny, nor Agnes, nor Eliza, nor Moon, nor Tom horse boy, nor John coachman, nor anybody. Nobody likes her! She is very unjust and unkind and interferes where she has no occasion, Jenny says, and she had poor Tray whipped, and said he must not come in the house any more, and she gives me horrid medicine when I am not sick. So, please, Papa, may she not go, and sister Ellen come home from Belgium to look after us? I am sure she could do it as well—much better, Sue says."

Luke Pager's silence, as he listened to this request from his youngest child, was one of total astonishment; he was quite dumfounded; but when he did speak, his reaction was unequivocal.

"Hold your tongue, miss! And never let me hear you speak in such a way again! A fine thing—for a child of your age to be setting up in judgment against decisions made by your elders. Think yourself fortunate that I do not instruct Mrs. Pike to give you a sound whipping! Go back, now, to your aunt Blanche. If that is all you came to say to me, I am sorry that you did not remain at home!"

Vicky gasped, turned scarlet, and retreated in disorder.

Gerard made an awkward move to follow her, when his father stopped him.

"Halt, sir! I did not order *you* to leave. I trust that you had no hand in that disgraceful demonstration—that you are properly civil to Mrs. Pike, and mind what she tells you?"

It was fortunate for Gerard that he might reply to both questions together. He said, "Yes, sir," in a tone wholly lacking conviction, as the housekeeper approached.

"And your studies go on well? Mr. Newman is satisfied with your progress?"

"Yes, sir," Gerard replied with more confidence. By now the housekeeper was too close to be ignored. Luke Paget said, "Well, well"—sighing—"run along then, boy; no doubt your aunt Blanche has a nuncheon for you." Lady Blanche was not Gerard's aunt, but Luke ignored such niceties. He added, "Mind you do not take a chill on the ride home; these May evenings can be sharp. Have you a comforter for your chest?"

"Yes, Father."

"Very well, then."

Gerard walked warily away, and Mrs. Pike sent an indulgent smile after him, sharing it with her employer. She had already learned, from the servants at the Hermitage, and from Lady Blanche Pomfret, how much of the father's care and ambition centered in the son.

"How do you do, Mr. Paget? I am happy to see you looking better."

Mrs. Pike's slight, formal curtsey was indicative of the careful consideration she had given to their relative status; she might be Paget's paid employee, but she considered herself quite his social equal; an unfortunate widow, undeservedly obliged to support herself by her own exertions, but nevertheless maintaining a very proper self-respect.

Unaware of these shades, Luke Paget surveyed her

impatiently. There had not been the least occasion, in his view, for her to present herself today—or, indeed, to have brought the children; the whole visit was needless and irksome. However, since she was here it behooved him to be civil to her. And she was, he grudgingly acknowledged to himself after a minute or two, a handsome figure of a woman; in her mid-forties, perhaps, amply built, quite as stately, in her own way, as Lady Blanche, though she saw fit to acknowledge her professional role as housekeeper by wearing a less voluminous crinoline than the Bishop's lady. Her taste in dress was discreetly impressive, however; the colors of lavender and gray-blue, which predominated, served to remind of her widowed condition, but were also admirably suited to her pink-and-white complexion, large blue eyes, and abundant hair, prematurely whitened, but elaborately dressed under a lace cap with very becoming streamers and side lappets. Other laces, ribbons, and trimmings adorned her dress; too many for her situation, Mr. Paget considered.

"Good day to you, Mrs. Pike," he said rather shortly. "Why, pray, has the child Victoria not been put into black for her mother? That tartan is highly unsuitable."

Mrs. Pike took this facer without flinching. "I considered her too young for blacks, Mr. Paget. If I committed an error, I must apologize."

"Certainly she is not too young. See to it, if you please, ma'am. I trust that all goes on well at the Hermitage? Are the servants minding you as they should?"

Here she was able to re-establish herself. "Thank you, Mr. Paget. There was a little difficulty at first, with the cook and the maids. I took the liberty of giving her notice to Jenny Gladwyn, your wife's ladies' maid, since she had no duties to perform; I hope I did right?"

"Certainly."

"Otherwise, matters are going on quite satisfactorily now, I am glad to say."

Her tone suggested that Lady Adelaide had allowed the household to lapse into a shocking condition of neglect and anarchy; but, since the latter was tragically dead, convention forbade any aspersion on her shortcomings.

Looking down, as she stood by him, Mrs. Pike surveyed Luke with her indulgent smile. This was, indeed, the prevailing expression on her countenance, as if she saw much to regret and censure in the world about her, but was kindly prepared to make allowances for everybody less capable than herself.

She was too much of a lady to put her hands on her hips, but her posture suggested this attitude.

"And when shall we be seeing you back under your own roof, Mr. Paget? That day will not be too far removed, I hope?"

Her look, her tone were almost coy. He stared back at her bleakly from under his jutting brows.

"Humph!" was all the answer she received to her question; and then, abruptly, "Are those letters you have for me there, ma'am? May I see them, if you please?"

A little reluctantly she handed over his post At the sight of the letters his shaggy white brows shot up again.

"Who took it upon themselves to open these, may I ask?"

"I did," said Mrs. Pike blandly. "I saw from the superscriptions that they were letters of business, and thought they might be bills, or matters of some urgency. I consulted with the boy's tutor, Mr. Newman, and with your attorney, Mr. Wheelbird, who was visiting the house in connection with the late Lady Adelaide's jewelry and personal belongings. Mr. Wheelbird and his partner Mr. Longmore gave me permission. You will see the bills have already been paid. Mr. Wheelbird advanced me money from the housekeeping for the purpose."

She brought out the lawyers' names with a look of

considerable satisfaction, not to say triumph, but her tone remained calmly businesslike.

"Oh! Ahem! Very well. There will be no occasion to do that again, ma'am. I shall be back at the Hermitage before any other accounts fall due, and other letters you may send to me here—unopened, if you please. Is that all, Mrs.—ah—Pike? Have you any inquiries or requests?"

"No, I thank you, Mr. Paget. All is running smoothly at home."

Already, he noticed, she spoke of *home* with a decidedly proprietorial air. It annoyed him, but he could find no valid reason to find fault.

"There is nothing else then, I believe. Ah—the children—behaving themselves, I trust?"

"The little girl misses her mama—naturally. And it is plain that she has been greatly indulged; but she will soon be in a better way of behavior. You need have no anxiety about her. Your son…" Here Mrs. Pike paused. Her complacent look was replaced by an air of sour disapproval, turning down the corners of her thin mouth. "It is playing the pianoforte so much caused that nasty turn he had, any person of sense could tell," she rapped out sharply. An attentive listener might have noticed that, when she said this, her vowels and turns of speech betrayed hints of a lower-class origin, which, previously, she had been at pains to conceal.

"Playing the piano? But he had been forbidden to touch it. I had it removed to the garden room expressly."

"I don't know about that, I'm sure. But he has been playing as many hours as possible, when his studies were done. And it is a shocking extravagance with candles as well."

"Has he, indeed? You had better have him sent out to me again, Mrs. Pike, before you start back, and I will have a word with him."

"Certainly, Mr. Paget. And what would you wish done about the dog?"

"Dog?"

"The animal, Tray. It was Lady Adelaide's pet, I understand. It has been in a shocking way since—since the unfortunate occurrence; crying and whining and—and behaving itself very nasty in the house; I had to give orders for it to be kept outside in a kennel, for the maids were complaining. What would you wish to be done about it?"

Luke Paget had never cared for his second wife's toy spaniel. He said briefly, "You had best tell Moon to have the animal destroyed. But do not let Victoria know beforehand—I believe she felt an attachment to it. That will be all, then, Mrs. Pike."

"Yes, Mr. Paget." Her complacency had returned. She bestowed another graciously condescending smile on him and walked away at a deliberate pace, allowing her lavender cambric draperies to sweep behind her along the turf. Against Luke's will, his eyes were drawn after her, and he observed how her upright and buxom figure obscured, for a moment or two, the frail tapering pinnacle of the cathedral spire. It did not occur to him at once that she was hardly the comfortable, motherly body of Blanche's original description.

As for Mrs. Pike, she was saying to herself: I shall soon have him round my thumb. And he need never hear about Simon.

∞

When the Bishop, his wife, his chaplain, and his wife's brother-in-law assembled for dinner, there was a slight air of gloom over the company, and a general disinclination for light chat.

The Bishop and his chaplain, Mr. Slopesby, were continuing a conversation about the Cathedral which had been occupying them before the meal.

"This bequest of the late dean—very commendable in the dear fellow, no doubt, but why couldn't he have directed it to be used for new church plate, or vestments for the choir? Two thousand pounds will go nowhere toward structural repair—nowhere; there is so much that needs doing."

"We can raise an equal sum, Your Grace, very readily, I am positive, by public subscription."

"Yes—yes; I daresay; but once we begin to meddle with the fabric, I am very much afraid we shall discover more amiss than we have the means of setting right. Take away the prebendal stalls and the Arundel shrine and I fear—I greatly fear—that we shall discover those piers supporting the tower to be in a shocking state. Those Normans, you know—courageous fighters, but not much up here!" The Bishop tapped his round bullet head; since the aforesaid Normans had been his ancestors, it was evident he felt he had a perfect right to disparage them if he chose. "Never considered that, on a quaking salt marsh where the Romans had erected a few single-story huts, it was hardly the part of sense to throw up a hundred-and-seventy-foot stone tower weighing eighty thousand tons. No wonder there are fissures in the stonework!"

Here the chaplain, with painstaking accuracy, pointed out that the Norman work in the Cathedral accounted only for the piers and the arches over them; the vaulting above, and the tower above that, belonged respectively to the Pointed and the Geometrical periods.

"Oh, very likely—no doubt," responded the Bishop rapidly—he was a little, round, rubicund man, a head shorter than his wife, with, in general, a benign and untroubled aspect—"but those Normans must have known what would come of their activities. Build four great piers and clap round arches from one to t'other, what can you expect but that somebody will fling up a spire on top of that? Eh, Paget? What do you say?"

In his usual good-natured way he hoped to draw his wife's brother-in-law into the talk; give the lanky, lantern-jawed fellow something to think about besides his own troubles; but Paget only glowered and glared, and said, "I am ill-informed regarding church architecture, Bishop. Doubtless it is as you say," and then went back to his low-voiced conference with the Bishop's wife: "The very instant I turn my back—and with his mother not cold in her grave—"

"His stepmother," gently put in the Bishop's wife.

"Well: his stepmother; what's the difference? There he goes, flat contrary to my orders, idling away his time at the instrument—playing *tunes*. On the pianoforte! I ask you, is that the occupation of a gentleman? I had the garden room locked up; he must have procured a key from somewhere but he would not tell me how he came by it. Disobedient young dog! Wasting his time! And making himself ill into the bargain. His allowance is cut off for a month; he'll pay more heed to my orders in future. But tell me, Blanche; advise me; do you think it would be best to send him away to school?"

The Bishop's lady reflected. She did not dislike her sister's moody, inarticulate stepson; indeed she probably had a better idea of his character than either his stepmother or his own father had ever achieved; in many ways she thought it might be better for Gerard to go to boarding school. But then what would happen to little Vicky? Poor Adelaide's child, left alone with such a father?

The Bishop had suggested Vicky be invited to come and live at the Palace. But the generosity of Lady Blanche had strict bounds. A slight weakness of the heart had rendered it impossible for her to bear children and made even the exertion of looking after a five-year-old niece, she thought, ineligible. A comfortable selfishness protected the Bishop's lady from all major inconveniences or sacrifices.

"No; I do not think you should send Gerard to school," she said at length. "It is too late, now, for that course; he would be shockingly out of place, the other boys might ridicule him, and the whole experience bring on just such a physical setback as you wish to avoid. No: best wait until it is time for him to go to university. He is well advanced in his studies, is he not?"

"Yes," grumbled the father. "As to that, Newman tells me he is quite up to standard. I don't doubt of his securing a place in my own college, Worcester. But, meanwhile, what to do with him? He is lonely, too; he has no companionship of his own kind. And *that* means that he is always making undesirable acquaintances—farmers' boys, gypsy lads even!"

"If only Benedict had not gone out of reach."

"Benedict!" snorted Mr. Paget, who had no affection for his second wife's younger son.

"Benedict is a clever young man," said his aunt firmly. "I have a great opinion of his capacity. If only he had been the elder son! Poor Easingwold never had two ideas in his head. But, as I recall, Gerard used to have quite an admiration for his stepbrother."

"Benedict—that puppy! From what I hear he spends his time flitting from one card house to another all over Europe."

"Nevertheless," said Lady Blanche calmly, "I have it on good authority that Benedict is expected to take a double First at Oxford and will certainly be offered a fellowship. He has excellent prospects for a career in the Diplomatic Service."

"Well, well!" said Mr. Paget peevishly. "Benedict is *not* here, so none of this is at all to the purpose." He felt it unfair that, because he had seen fit to confide in his sister-in-law, the excellences of Adelaide's son should be dinned into his ears. However, at that moment decanters were brought to the table and the Bishop broke into their conversation.

"Come, Paget! I know you'll not refuse a glass of the '41. A capital year! That should help your fractured leg to mend, better than doctor's medicine."

"Thank you, Bishop," said Luke with a wintry smile.

Lady Blanche seized the chance to retire to her own parlor. There, presently, she was joined by Luke Paget's eldest daughter and her husband, Sir Eustace Valdoe, whose heavily mortgaged manor lay not four miles from Chichester. Having come from a political meeting (Sir Eustace was the Member for Chichester), they had seized the opportunity to call and inquire after Eugenia's father.

"Here comes Mr. Paget now," Lady Blanche presently remarked, hoping that the '41 port would have put her guest in a better frame of mind.

"Dear Papa!" And Eugenia hurried to greet her parent with much affectionate fluttering of laces and cap strings. Eugenia, thin and anxious-looking, might have been ten years older than her actual age of thirty-one. Her pale hair dangled in unbecoming bands on either side of her long, chalky face; she was dressed in a faded silk gown whose fussiness only drew attention to the angularity of her figure. For some years she had been her father's despair; he had feared she would never be off his hands. And now that she was married to Sir Eustace, Luke was in constant apprehension that his son-in-law would try to borrow money from him, or that Eugenia would appeal to him for assistance. He fended off her embrace now with a wary arm.

"No need to unbalance me, Eugenia—fetch me a chair, that would be more to the purpose! Good heavens—you look more like a wisp of hay than ever. The air this side of the Downs has finished off what complexion you ever had. Well, Valdoe! I wonder that you should be taking out your horses at this hour of the evening; young folk never consider economy; but I should have thought that you, placed as you are, would do so."

Despite this snubbing, Luke's daughter and son-in-law hung around him solicitously, bringing his cup of coffee and offering him a muffin, which he rejected with scorn.

"Maudling one's insides with such stuff at this hour. Do stop hopping round me like a wagtail, Eugenia, and sit down, for the Lord's sake."

"Dearest Papa! So stoical!" said Eugenia with a wan smile.

Valdoe, seeing that this did not please, made inquiries as to the condition of his father-in-law's horses.

"One of them had to be destroyed. And I gave instructions for the other to be sold. Wretched, unsound pair. If Adelaide had not been so bent on purchasing them, the accident need never have occurred."

Adelaide's sister pressed her lips tight together. But Valdoe said tentatively, "Should you be requiring another pair, sir, when you return home? If so, I think I might be able to put you in the way of—"

"No, Valdoe, no—none of your choosing, thank'ee! I'll look about and suit myself in my own time. I have two steady carriage horses, that is sufficient."

Luke despised his thin, nervous, congenitally debt-ridden son-in-law. It was no mitigation that the debts had been incurred by Valdoe's father. And the fact that, through family and influence, the unimpressive Eustace had achieved the position as Member of Parliament which had been Luke's consuming hope and dream for so long, did nothing to sweeten the relationship. Valdoe was at least a Tory; so much could be said for him; but almost certainly, thought Luke, his agents had resorted to bribery of the electors; and he was a beggarly, whining sort of fellow, always on the scrounge; the match had been of Lady Adelaide's making but if the pair thought they were entitled to any expectations or assistance from Eugenia's father, they were mistaken indeed!

"What was your estimate of the new housekeeper,

Luke?" inquired Lady Blanche, carrying her coffee cup to sit by her brother-in-law. She had observed that the Valdoes' efforts to conciliate Luke were having an adverse effect. Eugenia was a fool to hang around her father's neck so, Blanche privately considered. She went on, "Does Mrs. Pike seem satisfactory? I understand the Fothergills were quite delighted with her. Did I make a wise choice?"

At another time, in another situation, Luke might have said roundly that the woman seemed a deal too complacent and self-confident, odiously pleased with herself indeed, one of the forward kind whose pretensions must be continually depressed, that she was officious, encroaching, and a tattletale, but as Eugenia, lingering near, needed putting in her place, he replied, "Why, yes, Blanche, I am very much obliged to you. I think you have made a capital choice. Mrs. Pike seems thoroughly capable and amiable; a most ladylike person as well; and, what is more," he added, noting with relish the looks of dismay at this unexpected peril that passed between Eugenia and her husband, "what is more, far from disagreeable in her appearance; in fact, a fine figure of a woman!"

In the silence that ensued—even Lady Blanche appearing a little startled at such a tribute—Luke's words, spoken with no intent but to annoy his daughter, somehow sank back into his own mind and remained there like a pungent phrase which, once heard, passes into the language.

❧

The trio driving back over the Downs in the Paget family carriage were silent also. Gerard's silence was that of rage. The looks he was directing at Mrs. Pike should have shriveled her where she sat, but, regrettably, she hardly noticed them; they did not scratch the surface of her complacency. If I play my cards carefully, she was reflecting, I've a snug billet for life. Paget's a touchy, difficult man, anyone can see that, but I've handled worse than him before. If I can keep the daughters from meddling while I make my position secure…

Vicky glanced sideways at her half brother with a mixture of pity and contempt. Gerard was always running into trouble! And that in spite of the fact that he was really quite timid. He had shuffled onto his little sister the business of speaking out about Mrs. Pike. Yet this timidity was not enough to make him consider in advance the consequences of his actions. Time after time he came into conflict with his father over his passion for music. Vicky, quite as self-willed, would have pursued her ends in a devious, undercover manner. It was true, however, she did not want to play the piano! She could not imagine why Gerard should wish to sit pounding away at the keys as he did, hour after hour.

Beginning to feel sick—she hated riding backwards—Vicky raised her eyes appealingly to Mrs. Pike, and said, "May I come and sit by you, ma'am?"

"Very well, child. But don't fidget."

Mrs. Pike's voice was absent. Six months, she was thinking. He looks like a man who thinks he has a right to his comforts. I know that big, bony kind. They get hungry. And there's nowhere he could go in a small town…

"Why," said Vicky, looking ahead out of the window—they were on top of the Downs now— "there's Dr. Bendigo in his dogcart. He's stopping at Dogkennel Cottages; someone must be sick there."

Gerard glanced round, brought from his gloomy meditations by the doctor's name. No allowance for a month, and forbidden to touch the piano! It was too hard! But maybe he could enlist the doctor on his side.

"Pull up, John," he called to the coachman. "I want a word with Dr. Bendigo."

Mrs. Pike bridled. "You should have asked leave of *me*, young man!" she said.

Gerard gave her a stare of contemptuous dislike. "I wish to ask the doctor about my cough," he said, and jumped from the carriage before she could raise any objections.

After a few moments Dr. Bendigo—a weather-beaten, white-bearded man, very active in spite of his seventy-odd years—put his head in at the carriage window. "I'll drive young Gerard home, Mrs. Peak, Puke, whatsyername, Pike—I'm going round by Barlton and Crouch, the second hour in the fresh air will do him nothing but good. He needs to get out more."

"I don't know—I'm sure—" began Mrs. Pike, displeased.

"Pshaw, ma'am, I've known the boy since he was born, brought him into the world! I'll engage he comes to no harm. Why, I was used to drive his sister Ellen all over the country, week in, week out, when her poor mother was ailing. Well, Vicky, my dear, no more trouble from those chilblains now, eh?" And the doctor bustled away to his dogcart without waiting for an answer.

Four

ELLEN AND HER GODMOTHER DID NOT ARRIVE IN PARIS until after dark. The journey from Lille onwards had been made by train. It was the first time that Ellen had traveled in this manner, for on her trips to England she had used the cheaper diligence and stagecoach; so all should have been absorbingly novel and interesting. Lady Morningquest had bespoken a private compartment, supplied with every luxury—foot warmers, eyeshades, traveling rugs, and reading matter; her maid and footman were next door, ready to provide luncheon baskets and tea baskets as required; Lady Morningquest herself carried a sherry flask in her dressing bag, and a supply of biscuits; yet in spite of these amenities Ellen found it a miserable journey. She still felt bruised and shocked to the core of her being.

That morning she had risen early and packed her possessions. They were not many, so the task did not occupy her for long. What proved more difficult was accommodating the dozens of last-minute gifts pressed on her by two-thirds of the school—by the cook, the gardener, the portress, the maids, the window cleaner, the other teachers, and her tearful pupils. Fruit, nosegays, handkerchiefs, bead purses, geraniums in pots, homemade cakes, lavender water, scented soap, jasmine essence—several of these offerings were so bulky they had to be left behind; others were packed into a large rush basket, since there was no room for them in her portmanteau.

Even harder were the explanations.

"You are going to Paris? But, Mam'selle Elène, why? And why so suddenly? Yesterday we knew nothing of this—and I do not believe you did either?"

"Somebody needs my services very badly," Ellen had to keep repeating. "My godmother, Lady Morningquest, made a special application to Madame to allow me to go. And Madame very kindly permitted it. So now I must say good-bye to you, my dear, dear friends. But I will never forget you, and how happy I was here."

Strangely enough, though she had hardly realized it before, she found this to be the simple truth. She had been happy in the rue St. Pierre; she loved this big, clean, lively school with its trampled fragrant garden, its not too intelligent pupils, its atmosphere of tolerant mediocrity. Though at first it had seemed terrifying and hostile, in six years it had become a haven. She grieved to go from it—and not only because of Monsieur Patrice. I shall remember those years for the rest of my life, she thought mournfully as she waited in the lobby for Lady Morningquest's carriage. She looked through the glass doors at the bright classrooms, restored to everyday order, with children scurrying to lessons that she would not be teaching. While this place was my home, she thought, I still believed that life could be regulated by will; that, so long as one worked hard and behaved with prudence, it should be possible to attain one's hoped-for ends—if they were within the bounds of reason and decorum. But I am not certain that I believe that any more.

All morning she had hoped for a glimpse of Monsieur Patrice—that he might return to say he had argued Madame out of her decision, that Ellen was not, after all, to go, that all might be as before. Or, at least, that he would come to say good-bye, and promise to write to her in Paris, say that he would be in touch, would not forget her! But he had not come.

"No one has left a note for me?" she inquired of

Mathilde the portress, and hastily added, "My step-brother is staying in Brussels."

But there had been no note. Could she herself leave one? She could not possibly entrust it to Mathilde—the portress's office was the main source of school gossip. Slip one in a book he had lent her, which she had entrusted to Charlotte Morningquest to return? Far too risky; Charlotte meant no harm, but her tongue ran like a mill clapper. Besides, even if she wrote a note, what could she say in it? Merely good-bye. She could express no hopes, no regrets; convention held her tongue-tied. Perhaps—her heart rose momentarily at the thought—perhaps she could write him from Paris. Merely a short descriptive letter—just to remind him of her new milieu. He went, she knew, sometimes to visit friends, colleagues at the Sorbonne; was it not conceivable that he might come to call at the Hôtel Caudebec? But that impulse died also; she could not address a letter to him at the school, where her handwriting was so well known and would cause instant comment; and she did not know his address at the Seminary where he was a Fellow.

I must put him out of my mind, Ellen resolved; and so, for an hour or two, she did, as first the carriage and then the train carried her farther and farther away from Brussels, across the flat willow-and-poplar-studded levels of Belgium and northern France. Instead she thought of her home. How inferior were these monotonous plains—even when, as now, stippled by pink-and-white blossoming orchards—to the infinite beauty and variety of Sussex, where she had been born and brought up. Wistfully she remembered the high grassy Downs, nibbled smooth by innumerable generations of sheep, crisscrossed by ancient trackways, Saxon, Roman, earlier still. On the lower slopes, now, the beech trees would be unfurling their silky light-green leaves; primroses would breathe fragrance in shady corners of hedge and woodland. The clear brooks running down from the chalk slopes would be flanked by watercress and celandine and glossy kingcups. Cuckoos would be calling…

When Ellen's mother became bedridden, Dr. Bendigo had acquired the habit of taking the little girl out with him, sometimes for whole days at a time, as he drove about in his dogcart, visiting patients all over the countryside.

"Pshaw, ma'am," he said to Mrs. Paget, "she's no trouble, not the least in the world. Indeed the lass is a decided help to me—her learned and elevating conversation keeps me from falling asleep at the reins. You are doing me a favor in allowing me her company, I promise you!"

And to Mrs. Paget's day nurse, he had commented, "A house of sickness is no place for a growing bairn. It would be wrong for the child, at her age, to be a witness, day in, day out, of so much suffering. Hard for the mother too—there's a strong attachment there. When the child's out of the way she need not make so much effort to conceal her pain. Besides, the child's of use to me with my more superstitious patients."

Here he spoke no more than the truth. The fact that Ellen was the survivor of a pair of twins was, of course, well known in the district—her infant brother's grave was there in Petworth churchyard as evidence—and, in consequence, quite a number of Dr. Bendigo's rustic patients attributed supernatural curative powers to her, calling her a token maidy, or healer. Over and over again little Ellen, aged six, seven, and eight, had been invited into damp cottages, had stood by coughing children or rheumatic old men, or had sat gravely in the dogcart while more able-bodied sufferers limped out to touch her small grubby hand.

"For I wd not wish to expose her to Unnecessary Infection," Dr. Bendigo confided to his medical journal. "Tho' I congratulate myself on the Improvement of her own health, and her increased robustness since she has been receiving the benefit of so much time spent in the Fresh Air. And there can be no doubt as to her healing effect on some of my patients—Faith is a wonderful restorative! Old Ruffle has greater remission from pain after she's been by him, than from any of my boluses or eclectics."

Subsequently Dr. Bendigo earned a certain quiet renown from his paper published by the British Medical Association on "Faith-healing and Homeopathic Cures in a Rural Area of Southern England"—which success increased his fondness for Ellen. He was indeed greatly attached to the child and she to him; they conducted endless conversations as they rode about; she asked him all the questions she would never have dared put to her own father (who, absorbed at that time in his political aspirations, was hardly aware that his youngest daughter was spending thirty or forty hours a week with the doctor). Indeed, Ellen later felt that she owed the whole groundwork of her education to Dr. Bendigo, who was never too busy, tired, or preoccupied to answer her questions as fully and honestly as possible, whether they concerned plants, birds, and country lore—on which he was an authority—medical or legal matters, or more complicated moral problems. To these rides with the doctor Ellen also owed her extensive knowledge of every road and track for twenty miles around Petworth, and her friendship with a range and number of country people—farmers, laborers, woodsmen, gypsies—that would have startled even her mother and shocked her father to death.

It was due to Dr. Bendigo's robust exhortations that—in due course—Ellen was able to muster up sufficient fortitude to accept her exile to Brussels, and endure the severance from her mother without utterly breaking down.

"Pay attention to me, now, my dearie!" the doctor told her. "It's for your own good I'm advising you! Heaven knows *I've* no wish to lose your company. But that's a good school; we know as much from your sisters and your godmother. You'll learn enough to make you an accomplished woman—able to make your own way in the world—which you'll not do here at home, let me remind you. Moreover, your mother deeply wishes it, and she'll fret herself miserably if you do not go with a good grace. You'd not wish *that*? Ah, no, I thought not. So just bite on the bullet, will ye, and let's have no tears or tragedies—show your mama a smiling face when you go to say good-bye, and then I'll take the day off and drive ye to Newhaven."

What the smiling face had cost, only Ellen and the doctor knew, but she was glad she had managed it, for that was the last time she saw her mother.

Around Petworth now, she thought, the oak trees will be covered with a gold-pink mist of buds, the pear tree outside my window may be coming into flower, the garden will be full of birdsong. She thought mournfully of her old tabby cat Nibbins, the only creature at the Hermitage that she had missed since her mother died—but no, that was not quite true, she loved her young brother, Gerard, if only he would *let* one love him, if he were not so prickly and unapproachable.

Why, she wondered again, did Benedict trouble himself to come all the way to the Pensionnat just to tell me that Nibbins had died, to bring me that trifling bit of unhappy news? Out of pure spite? For what other reason could he have come?

He'll be surprised to find me gone, thought Ellen; that is, if he should return to the Pensionnat—which is not too probable.

Her mind drifted away from Benedict. She knew very little about his life these days; he spent his university vacations in London, or traveling on the Continent; his friends were drawn from the circle in which he moved, that of his own father, Lord Radnor, dead seven years ago. His mother, Adelaide, in choosing Luke Paget for her second husband, had married to please herself and had disgusted her first husband's family, who thereafter ignored her and discouraged her two sons from paying her more than the briefest visits.

Easingwold, the older, now the new Lord Radnor, had never in fact set foot inside the Hermitage, and Benedict's visits had become less and less frequent. And Lady Adelaide, Ellen thought wryly, had not even succeeded in pleasing herself for long; heaven knew what she had expected of Luke Paget, but whatever that was, it soon became plain that she was not finding it, as her discontented looks began to proclaim. She lost no time in urging Luke to arrange matches for his two elder daughters, and dispatching the youngest back to school in Brussels; she ran her household with querulous extravagance, and took her place in the best local society as, from her own birth, and having previously been married to an earl, she was entitled to do; but all this seemed insufficient to please her. She had been in love with Luke Paget at the age of sixteen, obliged by her friends to marry more advantageously; now, too late, she seemed to have proved the truth of Lady Morningquest's oft-repeated maxim that love matches never prosper.

…Poor Adelaide, thought Ellen, who had at first bitterly disliked and resented her stepmother. No one could possibly have replaced Ellen's own mother, but Lady Adelaide—shallow, self-centered, and of a peevish, lachrymose disposition—had been peculiarly ill-equipped to do so. However, her situation at the Hermitage had soon begun to seem so lonely and uncomfortable that her stepdaughter, home for the weddings of Eugenia and Kitty, could feel no more than a mild dislike and tolerant compassion. *Who* would want to be married to Papa? Not I, for sure, thought Ellen. It is true that his looks are striking; I suppose that was what caught Adelaide's fancy when she was a girl; but he is dryer than a sack of sawdust She has her carriage and her household and her little girl; but as Dowager Countess of Radnor she would have been better established, had far more consequence—and Vicky is a secretive little spoiled minx! I love the Hermitage—probably I love it more than any house I shall ever enter—but I could not live there happily in such company. Gerard detests Adelaide, Vicky is over-indulged, Papa is cold and dry and wholly wrapped up in his own concerns. All he wanted was somebody to manage his house, and now he is assured of that, he will not trouble to speak more than three sentences a day to the wretched woman for the rest of her life. I sincerely pity her, and I am glad not to be in her position.

For the first time it occurred to Ellen to be thankful that Lady Morningquest, arriving in Brussels yesterday, had rescued her goddaughter from this possibility. Suppose Madame Bosschère, in her wrath, had dispatched Ellen back to England? I do not think she would have done so, decided Ellen. That would have meant explanations to Papa—which is not her way of dealing; she prefers quiet maneuvers, secret manipulations. She is a schemer, and that is why she always appears so successful; nobody hears about those plans of hers that go awry.

Perhaps she intends one day to marry Monsieur Patrice herself?

Ellen's thoughts had run back into their old, painful groove, and, without realizing that she did so, she drew a long, unhappy sigh, clasping her gloved hands tightly in her lap.

Lady Morningquest, who was writing letters on a small rosewood desk, glanced up and laid down her pen. "You look fatigued, child, and no wonder!" she said.

"I daresay you were up half the night restoring order after Madame's fete. It is hard on you to be obliged to set out for a new position today. Fortunately in Paris your duties will be less exacting; and your surroundings by far more luxurious!"

"I wish, ma'am, that you would be so good as to tell me a little about the Countess de la Ferté and her family?"

"Certainly I will, child. I had that intention." Lady Morningquest put away her pen. "Louise, as you may recall, is my niece by marriage, my husband's sister's daughter. She used to visit us at the Embassy in Paris, and attended the Couvent des Anglaises with my elder daughter, Dorothea; and they shared a coming-out ball. At this she met Raoul, Comte de la Ferté, and both of them fell head over heels in love. I am very greatly opposed—as I have often told you—to young persons contracting love matches." She paused to look frowningly down her long, thin nose at her thin, knobbed, patrician hands. "I sincerely hope that *you* will never contract such an alliance, child. Matches arranged by a young person's friends are by far more satisfactory in *every* way. What can a young girl, straight from the schoolroom, know of such matters? However, in this case all seemed satisfactory enough; Raoul comes from one of the wealthiest and most ancient families in Normandy, Louise had a small competence of her own; perhaps he was a little wild, but no more than may be expected of such a young man, born with a gilt spoon in his mouth. Louise was received into the Catholic Church, no problem there, and the young people appeared to be devotedly attached. Her parents died within a short time of one another; they contracted the same putrid fever a year after the marriage."

"Poor girl," Ellen murmured. "She must have felt very isolated."

Lady Morningquest raised her brows. "You think so?

But she had Raoul's family, which is extensive; he has, I believe, nine younger brothers and sisters; and his parents appeared content enough with their daughter-in-law. But now all has gone amiss; Raoul conducts himself scandalously—I need not particularize about this to a girl like you, but his misbehavior is notorious. And although he inherited a large estate when his father died, he is apparently in process of dissipating it all by gambling. He frequents the worst establishments in Paris, and has set up a gaming room in his own hotel."

"Good gracious," said Ellen rather inadequately. "And there are children? Who will be my pupils?"

"One only—which is the crux of the matter. Raoul's aunts and uncles have come to me in distress many times. There is only a daughter, Menispe, now four or thereabouts, and no sign at all of a male heir. It is said that Louise and Raoul pursue wholly separate lives— she does not confide in *me*; as for the child, she has a quite disastrous existence, pampered by either parent when they remember her, and at other times left to run wild."

"Menispe will be my charge?"

Ellen's heart sank even lower. Two warring parents and a spoiled child—what a prospect! Of what value would her qualifications, her faculties, her intelligence, be here? She said doubtfully, "It seems to me, ma'am, that they need someone with twice my age and experience."

"Just what I said to Madame Bosschère," said Lady Morningquest. Did you indeed? thought Ellen. "But, as Madame reminded me, someone with twice your years might not have the energy and resilience required to deal with the situation at the Hôtel Caudebec. And Madame was most vehement in expressing her confidence as to your sagacity and presence of mind."

Well she might be, in the circumstances, was Ellen's internal comment. And little will her high opinion avail

me where I am going. Why did I allow myself to be
catapulted into this situation?

She glanced restlessly round the railway compartment.
Its mahogany and plush and brass fittings began to seem
like a prison—a trap. The poorest peasant girl, out there
on the plain hoeing beans, had more freedom.

"Don't look so doleful, child," said Lady Morningquest.
"Here we are at Clermont. I will tell Markham to make
tea; that will put you in better spirits."

"Thank you, ma'am."

"You will have ample opportunity to acquire interesting new acquaintances in Paris," pursued her godmother
briskly, as the maid lit a small spirit stove and boiled
water. "Louise, I understand, conducts quite a salon—
she has become acquainted with philosophers and poets,
playwrights and politicians. In her house you may come
across Ponsard, who wrote the tragedy *Lucrèce*; Mérimée;
Flaubert; Meilhac, the author of those charming operet-
tas; and Monsieur Dumas—not to mention some less
desirable persons such as that Baudelaire, and a whole
nest of Russian writers who prefer Paris to the snows and
barbarities of St. Petersburg."

"Indeed?" Despite her dejection, Ellen felt a prick of
interest. "And does the Comte de la Ferté also cultivate
these literary personages?"

"Quite the contrary! This is one of the difficulties.
Louise has a female friend—" Lady Morningquest's face
lengthened into austerely disapproving lines. "Germaine
de Rhetorée, who was at school with her in Bonn, and
whose tastes are even *more* literary—indeed I understand she has published some writings herself—like
that disreputable Dudevant woman who calls herself
George Sand. Germaine passes a great deal of time with
Louise—far too *much* time, in my opinion. I cannot
think her influence a wholesome one. If you can wean
my husband's niece from *that* friendship, I believe it

will be an excellent thing, and will remove one of the principal grounds for the union's failure to flourish and bear fruit. After all, why should not you become a friend to Louise? You are a sensible little thing, and, I am informed, have excellent understanding."

"The Comtesse is hardly likely to make a confidante of her governess," Ellen observed dubiously. She felt that altogether too many responsibilities were being laid on her.

"Tush, child. Your birth is every bit as good as that of Louise Throstlewick; the Pagets need humble themselves to nobody, I believe. Your father is an English country gentleman (if he *is* a blinkered, bigoted, stiff-necked ass)," Lady Morningquest added, but she added this to herself. "Your great-uncle was a bishop, one of your great-aunts was married to a cousin of Mr. Pitt, and another was a great friend of Lord Egremont. Your connections are unimpeachable."

"But I am still a governess."

"It doesn't signify. On the Continent, English ladies who teach are considered quite entitled to a place in society—if they come of good family, that is; matters are more liberal here than in England."

"That was why I managed to persuade Papa to permit me to teach in Madame's school," agreed Ellen.

"I was surprised he allowed it, I confess. No doubt Lady Adelaide advised it."

"There was really no room for me at home. Lady Adelaide finds it necessary to have more servants than Mama used—and the Hermitage is not a large house."

If Lady Morningquest had not been so highly bred she would have sniffed. "Adelaide ffoulkes is a shallow-minded, headstrong, selfish woman. In marrying her, your papa made a shocking mistake! However, that can't be mended. Nor can the fact that she has hustled your sisters into a pair of very ill-judged marriages."

"Good gracious, Lady Morningquest!"

"I daresay Kitty has got thirty thousand a year, but what use is that to her married to a man with a name like *Bracegirdle*, and living where she does? And I am told he is a sad miser, won't let her have a penny over her pin money even if she goes on her bended knees; so what use are his millions to her? While as for Eugenia—I don't say that Valdoe is disreputable, but the man hasn't two farthings to rub together, or enough energy to remedy the case, and Blanche Pomfret says that Valdoe Court is falling down."

"I hope matters are not as bad as that, Lady Morningquest."

"Quite as bad, child, if not worse. So I trust you won't allow Adelaide ffoulkes to push *you* into such a regrettable alliance."

Ellen reflected that, not five minutes since, her godmother had pronounced on the undesirability of young persons choosing for themselves; but she said, "So long as I remain away from Petworth and don't trouble her, I don't believe that Lady Adelaide will concern herself about me at all."

"True enough. Well, child, try if you can to set matters on an even keel at the Hôtel Caudebec. Do, pray, discourage Louise from seeing so much of that Germaine de Rhetorée. *Camille* and *Arsinoë*, they call themselves," Lady Morningquest added, and this time her sniff was audible. "After two mythological heroines who suffered ill treatment at the hands of men; though what ill treatment Germaine has to complain of, except not being left so much money by her father as she hoped, I am sure I don't know. But if you can civilize that wretched little child, and establish a better relation between Louise and Raoul, I confess I shall be greatly obliged. I am speaking to you now, my dear, as if you were a much older person, because I know you have a good head on your shoulders and can be trusted."

"Thank you, ma'am."

But Ellen, sighing as the dusky suburbs of Paris crept out like a gray tide to meet the train, felt neither wise nor capable. The ménage in the Hôtel Caudebec sounded dauntingly sophisticated, downright terrifying, indeed; how shall I ever be able to justify Lady Morningquest's confidence in me? she wondered. How I wish I were back in the Pensionnat, about to supervise the evening's lecture, with Monsieur Patrice on the estrade.

I wonder what he said when he discovered that I had gone.

Blinking away tears, she turned to gaze at the high, slate-roofed houses.

"Ah, there is the Sacré-Coeur," said Lady Morningquest. "Now we shall soon be home. I shall tell my coachman to take you on to the Hôtel Caudebec, child, after he has driven me to the Embassy. It will be much better for you, in your dealings with the servants, if you arrive in a private carriage—they are an ill-regulated crew, and in any case the status of a governess in a private household must always be defined by herself. If you do not establish from the start that you are a lady, and to be treated as one, the domestics are sure to take advantage."

"You are very thoughtful, ma'am." Ellen's spirits sank still lower.

"That's right, Markham; put my papers away in the secretary… And then, child, when you have righted matters in the la Ferté household, we must see about finding a respectable parti for you," said Lady Morningquest, taking her feet from the foot warmer so that Markham could hand it to the manservant.

Ellen reddened, embarrassed at having her future so casually discussed in front of servants. She said hastily,

"I beg you will not trouble yourself about my affairs, Lady Morningquest."

"Highty-tighty, child! Someone has to, since your father has virtually cast you off. And your mother was my dear friend; remember that."

"I do, ma'am; and I am obliged to you; but I am sure I shall be able to make my own way in the world."

"Humph! Well we shall see."

The Embassy carriage was waiting at the station, and took them speedily to the ambassadorial residence in the rue St. Honoré. Here, however, Lady Morningquest's careful plans received a check. It appeared that, not five minutes previously, her high-spirited youngest son, Thomas, escaping his tutor to run to the hall and look for Mama's arrival, had slid down the marble stair rail, fallen onto the stone floor below, struck his head, and been picked up senseless. The household was in uproar; Monsieur l'Ambassadeur was from home; a doctor had been sent for but had not yet arrived; and the tutor, Mr. Culpeper, a gentle, scholarly man, was wringing his hands, not knowing what to do for the best.

Lady Morningquest had the whole situation organized in a trice; the boy carried to his chamber, hot and cold compresses called for, and a messenger dispatched to find Lord Morningquest and bring him home. In due course the doctor arrived, and was closeted in the boy's chamber, with his old nurse and Lady Morningquest, for a long, anxious period. Meanwhile Ellen waited in the large cold formal drawing room, feeling decidedly out of place and unwanted, much tempted to order the Morningquest coachman to drive her on to the Hôtel Caudebec, but reluctant to go without taking leave and thanking her godmother for all her kindness and consideration, however undesired.

At last the conclave in the bedroom broke up; the doctor came downstairs looking grave. He issued a whole series of instructions to the nurse and Lady Morningquest.

"And let me be sent for at once if he shows any alarming symptoms. I bid you good night, my lady. I will be here again very early tomorrow."

Only after he had gone did Lady Morningquest recall her goddaughter.

"Ellen! My poor child, this is a sorry arrival for you. In all the commotion I am afraid I had forgotten you."

"It was of no consequence, ma'am," said Ellen. "Indeed I would have asked for a fiacre and taken myself off, only it would have seemed so discourteous after all your kindness; and I wished to inquire after the little boy. What does the doctor say?"

"Wretched imp!" Lady Morningquest frowned and smiled. "The doctor says he has a head of solid mahogany, and may well be none the worse when he comes out of his swoon. That we shall have to see. But you, my child—I think, as it is so late, you had best spend the night here, and I will have you driven to my niece's house tomorrow morning."

"Oh, no, ma'am!" The last thing Ellen wished was to wait, dangling between two worlds; if she must commence a new phase of existence, she had a violent urge to make the change as soon as possible. She said, "If it is not inconvenient, pray, pray let me be taken to the Hôtel Caudebec directly. I believe you said, ma'am, that they keep odd hours? So perhaps it will not put them out if I arrive rather late."

"Oh—very well, my dear, if that is your wish. Certainly it is no inconvenience to me; I shall hardly be stirring from home until Tom is in a better way. Wait, then, and I will indite a note to Louise."

She disappeared into her boudoir and soon returned with the note. "There. And I shall call myself to see how matters are going directly Tom is pronounced out of danger. Good night, child; I hope you will be comfortable, and I trust that you will do your duty."

"Good night, ma'am, and I thank you most sincerely."

The carriage ride to the Hôtel Caudebec was rapid, for the la Ferté residence was located in the rue de l'Arbre Vert, off the new Boulevard Haussmann. In ten minutes the coachman was knocking at the outer gate, and presented Lady Morningquest's note to the porter. After a somewhat lengthy interval, Miss Paget was requested to come in. Her shabby portmanteau and the rush basket were handed to a couple of impassive-faced footmen in black velvet knee breeches, and she herself was led across a cobbled inner courtyard where a fountain played, through a lobby with painted ceiling and gold-encrusted furniture, and up one side of an imposing double flight of stairs. From here she was hurried along through an interminable series of reception rooms, where her eyes were dazzled by a succession of Florentine bronzes, Venetian chandeliers, Japanese lacquer screens, velvet-upholstered chairs with bronze sphinxes for arms, huge Chinese porcelain jars, Boulle cabinets, and Pompadour carvings. The impression received was of extreme opulence, unguided by the discipline of good taste, or, indeed, of any taste at all.

Turning into another wing of the house (which seemed enormous), they entered a suite of rooms much more elegantly and sparsely furnished, and then passed into a silent, scented boudoir which appeared to Ellen's bewildered and weary senses like the inside of a large, pale-gold bubble. The delicate fluted chairs were upholstered in straw-colored damask, an immense expanse of velvet carpet matched them in color, as did the brocade window curtains. A Venetian candelabrum, a gold inkstand adorned with cherubs on a delicate Régence desk repeated the same pale, cool brilliance. There were few ornaments in the room, save a gilt clock representing the nine Muses, and some paintings by Greuze of diaphanously clad ladies.

At a small round marble table, its top inlaid with checkered squares of black and white, two girls sat silently playing chess, occasionally pausing to refresh themselves by sips of ice water from crystal glasses. They were dressed identically—and very unfashionably, was Ellen's first thought—in delicate severe gowns of flowing vestal white, over primrose-colored slips. They resembled actresses in a play when the curtain has just gone up; only, Ellen wondered, who is there to admire them, apart from me?

She could not help admiring them very much as she moved doubtfully in the footman's wake; compared with their cool elegance she felt dreadfully clumsy, travel-stained, undersized, and dowdy, in her plain stuff traveling dress, merino cloak, and the beaver bonnet which she had trimmed herself. It seemed probable that these scornful swanlike girls might rise up, preen themselves, and then peck her to death.

Both had pale-yellow hair which glistened like fine corn silk; it was drawn austerely from their brows, taken smoothly upwards, and dressed in Grecian style to fall in clusters at the back of their necks. They seemed much of a height, but one was more slenderly built than her companion; her hair was a paler gold, and her features in a thinner mold. This one, glancing up as the footman bowed, remarked, "You may wait outside, Gaston... So you are Miss Ellen Paget, sent me, it seems, as a species of Easter gift by my energetic aunt Paulina?"

"How do you do?" murmured Ellen, but the Comtesse, without paying attention, went on, "How that woman delights in seeing herself as a *dea ex machina*; it would be diverting, if there were not the fatigue of having to thank her for her unsolicited good offices."

"Are you obliged to accept them?" inquired her

friend. Ellen had little trouble in guessing this to be the Germaine de Rhetorée considered an undesirable influence by Lady Morningquest. She looked intelligent, strong-willed, and fascinating, Ellen decided: blunt-featured, with a long, round neck, a wide-lipped mouth, dark-gray eyes, beautiful brows, and that kind of biscuit-pale skin, rather thick in texture, which never varies in color.

"Oh, what can one do?" yawned Louise de la Ferté, glancing up carelessly at Ellen. She added with a shrug, "Doubtless, Miss Paget, if you are such a paragon as Aunt Paulina will have me believe, you will be able to set us all to rights in very short order."

"Is there so much, then, that requires doing?" Ellen inquired rather tartly. She was discouraged by this chilly reception.

Louise appeared vaguely surprised at such a reply, and murmured, with another shrug, "Ah, who is to decide?"

But Germaine's heavy white eyelids flew up, she accorded Ellen a full, intent scrutiny, then smiled, displaying magnificent teeth.

"Perhaps, after all, Miss——?"

"Paget."

"Perhaps Miss Paget will be an addition to our circle, *ma chère* Arsinoë. Do you know Greek?" she asked Ellen.

"A very little."

"And Latin?"

"A little more. I was used——" Ellen checked herself. To help Gerard, a slow beginner, she had studied Latin and Greek for four years with him and his tutor—but why volunteer information to this coolly patronizing catechist, who was not even her employer?

"Oh well…" Louise yawned again, delicately closing her mouth with two thin fingers. "Doubtless it will be all for the best…" And she turned her eyes back to the chessboard, apparently forgetting her new employee.

Ellen stood wondering what she should do; aching with fatigue, she longed to retire, yet was not certain if the interview was over. She did not think she was going to like her new situation at all, and heartily wished that Lady Morningquest had not seen fit to interfere in her affairs.

Germaine remarked, "Miss Paget probably wishes to leave us, my dear."

"What is that you say?" Louise glanced up again. "Oh, are you still there? You wish to retire? But it is not particularly late? Had you not best enter immediately upon your duties?"

No inquiry about her journey, her luggage, her room, or whether she had dined.

"Certainly, Countess," Ellen said. "I shall be glad to do whatever you wish—if you will be so good as to tell me what that is?"

"Why, I suppose you should find my tiger kitten and put her to bed."

"Your—?"

"The little countess. My daughter Menispe. Your pupil," replied Louise, raising her fine flaxen eyebrows. Her lashes were remarkably long and sweeping, over large gray-green eyes; and they had the interesting peculiarity of a narrow dark-brown stripe across their silvery pallor.

The strikingly similar looks of the two girls must, Ellen thought, have been one of the original factors causing their alliance. There must—surely?—have been more than a touch of self-interest in an association that so underlined and emphasized the appearance of the two friends.

She began to find in herself a strong curiosity about the Comte de la Ferté. What did *he* look like? And where did he fit in?

"Your daughter is not in bed yet?" she inquired politely, and felt justified in raising her own brows.

The hour was now eleven-thirty at night, high time, one would have thought, for a four-year-old child to be asleep.

"Oh, I imagine she is with her father. She spends what time she can with him—*when* he chooses to visit his own home, which amounts to about four hours in four hundred," replied Louise in a fatigued manner, her hand suspended over a knight on the board. "Check!" she added, and then sharply struck a little gilt bell. Gaston the footman reappeared.

"Conduct Mademoiselle Paget to wherever Menispe is with Monsieur le Comte, Gaston. Oh, and instruct Marmoton to see that a room is prepared for Mademoiselle; adjacent to that of Mademoiselle Menispe."

"Miladi." He bowed, and turned to lead Ellen out. As she trod behind him across the endless expanse of soft pale carpet, Ellen heard Louise murmur, "What a little field mouse. Well, at least Raoul won't fall in love with her."

"I would not depend on that, *chérie*. You know his unexpected habits."

"Undiscriminating, you should say."

One of them laughed, a cool, unamused sound. Then Germaine said, "I like her eyes. And her voice."

"Oh—if you care for that kind of pert self-confidence. I find it presumptuous and *ennuyante*."

"You have placed yourself *en prise, ma chère*," Germaine said gently, just before the door closed.

Seething with annoyance, Ellen followed the footman.

She was not sure what she expected. There had been something a little touching, to her mind, in Louise's description of the small Menispe insisting on being with her father during his brief periods in the mansion; it had called up an image in her mind of the child curled up asleep by the young man as he sat, perhaps, signing papers in some library or business room.

The reality proved otherwise. Gaston conducted Ellen down another flight of stairs, paused to confer with a gray-haired steward, then took her along a wide corridor paved with white and gray marble, which led round two sides of yet another courtyard, to an opposite wing. Here she entered an opulent suite of four rooms, interconnected, hung with purple and gold silk, lavishly heated by warm air from underground vents, and furnished with marquetries in copper and brass, horn and tortoiseshell, by Boulle and Bérain. On the walls hung superb paintings by Ruysdael, Van Dyck, Titian, Rembrandt, and Teniers in gold frames. All the rooms blazed with light from Boulle lustres and candles in silver-gilt sconces. And they were filled with company, fashionably dressed men and women, strolling, drinking, talking, and playing cards. The contrast to that distant room where the two girls sat over their chess game, sipping ice water, could not have been more complete. A buffet was set with elaborate dishes, from scalloped oysters and ortolans to ices and sorbets. Footmen hurried about with trays of iced punch and champagne, tea, coffee, and liqueurs.

Why, thought Ellen, looking about her in amazement, Lady Morningquest was quite right. It is a regular gaming salon.

She had never expected to enter such a place.

Distributed about the rooms were a number of green-baize-covered tables, at which players sat engaged in games of whist, piquet, écarté, Boston, and baccarat-à-deux-tables. Other guests strolled between the tables. A hum of talk filled the apartments.

Some of the guests turned to stare in mild surprise at Ellen, plainly dressed and travel-soiled, as she doggedly followed behind Gaston to the farthest extremity of the suite. She heard murmurs in well-bred voices:

"Who can that be?"

"The housekeeper? Some indigent relative? An old flame?"

"A burnt-out flame in that case, surely?"

It occurred to Ellen that Lady Morningquest's description of the Comte's associates had been quite wide of the mark. These people looked like the cream of Paris society. They were all handsome, beautifully dressed, and, to judge by their demeanor, highly bred. Most of them appeared also to be extremely rich. Ellen noticed, in passing, a magnificent gown of black satin brocade with flounces of English lace, a necklace of diamonds large as hazelnuts that must be worth 150,000 francs, a lady with twelve rows of huge pearls on each arm.

At the extreme end of the farthest room there was a roulette table, and toward this Gaston made his way.

The banker at this table was a man younger than most of the company.

"*Faites vos jeux, faites vos jeux, mesdames, messieurs,*" he was calling cheerfully.

A professional croupier? thought Ellen. He was thin, active, light-limbed; although correctly enough dressed, like the other men, in black and white, he seemed very untidy; his cravat had gone awry and, from the cigarillo which dangled between his lips, a trail of ash had fallen on his collar. His hair, which he wore rather long, was rumpled, his lids, half closed to keep the cigar smoke out, sometimes flashed up to reveal deep-set eyes of a curious light-gold color. Then, with a shock of surprise—though why in the world should she be surprised?—Ellen saw that he had, beside him in his massive carved chair, a little girl in a cream-colored frock who was dancing up and down with excitement and calling out numbers as the wheel spun: "*Sixaine, Papa! Douzaine! En plein! À cheval, à cheval!*" Good God, thought Ellen, that must be the Comte. But he is so young! Younger, surely, than his wife? And she is not at all old!

There was indeed something startlingly youthful and vulnerable about his face; though the sculpture of its bones was strong—tragic, even—his expression was still that of a boy, laughing, wary, excitable, sensitive. The look of youthfulness was increased by the darkness of his jaw; like many black-haired men, he plainly needed to shave more than once a day, and had not done so.

The wheel spun to a halt. Amid screams of joy and cries of self-congratulation or mock despair, new chips were distributed. Then Gaston ventured to approach the banker and whisper in his ear.

"Milord—there is a—a demoiselle here who comes from Madame la Comtesse—"

Surprised, the Comte turned round. His eyes held a flash of momentary emotion—surprise, certainly, hope, perhaps which faded when he beheld the prosaic figure of Ellen. Yet he greeted her with cool politeness.

"Mademoiselle? How can I serve you?"

"Monsieur le Comte de la Ferté? Good evening." The only thing, thought Ellen, would be to carry off the situation with firmness and dispatch. "I am your daughter's new *gouvernante*, Ellen Paget," she told him. "I was informed by Madame la Comtesse that the little girl was here. I am come to take her to bed."

The Comte looked utterly astonished. "Menispe? To bed? What new caper is this? She never goes to bed before three on nights when my friends come to play with me. Indeed, I cannot afford to part with her—she is my luck! Without her, the bank is certain to lose!"

The child at his side set up a clamor. "Papa! I am not to go to bed, am I? I do not wish to go to bed. I *will* not go to bed!"

She was a flaxen-haired little creature, resembling her mother in that, but not in her features, which were strongly marked, more like those of her father. It seemed probable that she might, in time, become a striking woman, but at present she was an ugly child, bony and scrawny, like a fledgling bird.

"Oh, la-la," Ellen heard the lady with the pearl bracelets murmur. "It seems that Madame Mère plays a new tactic in the domestic campaign."

"The new tactic must have been carefully chosen not to upset Raoul's susceptibilities. Do, pray, observe the prunella boots!"

"And the gray stockings!"

"The bluestocking has sent him a gray stocking."

"Hush! The poor dear will hear you."

"*Eh bien, mon cher* Raoul, it seems that you are to lose your talisman. The lady wife has put her foot down."

"Ah, come, my dear miss; let the little one remain just another half hour. What difference can it make?"

Ellen reddened, but held her course.

"I am afraid I must trouble you to accede to the Comtesse's request, monsieur; it is not at all healthy for a child of her age to be up so late, and in this hot, smoky atmosphere. Furthermore—"

"What can you know about it, mademoiselle?" he retorted. "You appear to be hardly out of the schoolroom yourself."

"On the contrary, I am an experienced teacher, Comte, and even if I were not, it does not take an acute observer to see that the child is greatly overtired and overexcited. Come, little one."

And with a swift movement, Ellen picked up little Menispe, grasping her firmly, and turned to Gaston, saying, "Conduct me, if you please, to the child's bedchamber."

She caught an expression of blank amazement on the footman's face, which was immediately replaced by one of startled respect.

"Very good, mademoiselle."

"I will bid you good night, Monsieur le Comte," said Ellen, as well as she could above the kicking, threshing, and screaming of little Menispe, who was carrying on like a demented fury.

The Comte shrugged resignedly, and called, "*Bonsoir, mignonne, bonne nuit!*"

"*Mon dieu!*" somebody muttered. "What a little spitfire. It is true that child is disgracefully overindulged. One cannot help pitying the *gouvernante*."

"I do not envy her," the pearl-braceleted lady was heard to remark.

"I hate you, I hate you, I hate you!" screamed Menispe into Ellen's ear. She twisted, she kicked, she scratched, she bit. Ellen, however, was wiry, though small in stature, and she was also well accustomed to dealing with brawny young Flamandes, who had been known, on several occasions, to offer physical violence to their preceptresses; this skinny little scion of French aristocracy was no match at all for her. And the child was, indeed, overtired; by the time that Ellen had left the gaming rooms, traversed two more lengthy corridors, and climbed another flight of stairs, the small flaxen head was already lolling against her shoulder. And when they entered a very pretty child's room furnished with rosewood and blue chintz hangings, little Menispe was three-quarters asleep. She opened her eyes to mutter again, "I detest you, I shall never love you, never!" then sank into profound slumber, as her bonne, a pleasant-looking Norman girl in red petticoat and printed cotton gown started forward to receive her.

"Ah, *la petite! Elle est bien fatiguée.* It is not well done of Monsieur le Comte to keep her up so late. *Merci, mademoiselle.*"

"I will bid you good night," said Ellen, who could scarcely keep awake herself.

"Your chamber is close by here, mademoiselle," Gaston said, eyeing her with even more respect. And he conducted her to the door of an equally pleasant room with a chintz-canopied bed, velvet-upholstered easy chairs, lace curtains, and a Pompadour glass on the dressing table. A fire blazed in the grate, and someone had already unpacked her trunk and laid out her nightdress, which looked skimpy and poverty-stricken spread out on the satin quilt.

"Thank you; good night," said Ellen, digging in her reticule for the pourboire which he undoubtedly expected. With a little irony she wondered whether life in this lordly household might not cost more than she could afford.

"'Service, mademoiselle," and he was gone.

She found hot water in a porcelain jug, and rose-scented soap in an alabaster dish. What a contrast to the rue St. Pierre, and Madame Bosschère's institutional dormitory with the rows of narrow white beds, thought Ellen, sponging little Menispe's bite marks, some of which had drawn blood, on her arms and wrists. And to think that last night at this time I was talking to Monsieur Patrice...

Shall I ever see him again?

The day had been too long and too confusing; her last thought, as her head sank into the opulent, down-filled pillow, was a vision of home: the bluebells like gray lace under the orchard trees, the cuckoo calling in the valley; then she slept.

Five

ELLEN HAD ASSUMED, FROM WHAT LADY MORNINGQUEST
had said about the Comte de la Ferté, and from his wife's
scornful allusion to "four hours in four hundred" that she
would not be seeing much of her pupil's father.

She was somewhat astonished, therefore, halfway
through her first morning at the Hôtel Caudebec, when
he appeared in the schoolroom. Since it was to be inferred
that he had entertained his guests in the gaming rooms
until an advanced hour of the night, or morning, it might
reasonably be assumed that he would still be asleep, rather
than vigorous, alert, healthily glowing, *tiré à quatre épingles*,
in an elegant dark-green riding costume, apparently
having been up and about for several hours.

Ellen felt herself at something of a disadvantage. She
had been greeted with such hostility by little Menispe
when she presented herself that morning that she saw
there could be no progress made in teaching the child
until time had improved the relations between them.
Accordingly Ellen had at first appeared entirely to ignore
the glowering Menispe, and had occupied herself instead
with beguiling activities, involving the use of silver paper,
wax, artificial flowers, feathers, cardboard, and scraps of
satin and gauze, which she had procured with the assistance of the bonne. When these occupations failed to
ensnare Menispe's interest—though Ellen noticed one or
two inquisitive glances—she resorted to simpler tactics,
building a large baroque structure on the table with a box
of child's building bricks which she had discovered in a

closet; their chipped and battered condition suggested that the set was in frequent and favorite use. Menispe had not been able to withstand this lure.

"Those are *my* bricks!" she indignantly shouted. "*Not* yours!"

"I know they are yours," calmly responded Ellen. "And I am building you a beautiful palace with them."

"It is *not* beautiful!" And with a sweeping gesture of fury Menispe ran to the table and destroyed the elaborate edifice with a blow of her fist.

Content at the result of her stratagem, Ellen proposed, "We will see how quickly I can build another tower before you can knock it down."

"No we will *not*!"

But the child could not resist the destructive pleasure of demolishing Ellen's ornamental creations—often before they were half completed—and, despite herself, she was being drawn into a kind of hostile partnership in this make-and-break game, when her father unceremoniously entered, tossing his riding whip onto a chair.

"Papa!" Instantly Menispe ran and clung to his leg like a squirrel.

"Well, *mignonne*? Are you working hard with your new teacher?"

"No, I am not! I hate her! Tell her to go away, Papa!"

His eyes met those of Ellen over the child's head, and she realized that her first impression, only a moment before, had been a false one. The brief glow from riding in the fresh air had already left him; his eyes were set in hollows, and his thin features were pale.

"No, *mignonne*, I will not do that," he said, tousling the child's flaxen head. "Mademoiselle is here to make you into a clever lady, like your mama. Soon you will be doing all kinds of pleasant things with her." And to Ellen he said, "Though I must confess, Mademoiselle—?"

"Paget."

"Ah yes, Paget, forgive me; I must confess that when you appeared last night like one of the Erinnyes, and bore off this *fillette*, I was apprehensive! I feared you might deal hardly with her, and wear out her little life with severe disciplines. But I see my fears were groundless. *Au contraire. Tout va bien.* May the good work continue!"

And he smiled at the scatter of blocks over the table and floor, retreating as rapidly as he had come.

"Papa, stay! Do not go!"

"I cannot stay, *petite*. I have business affairs to attend to."

"Can I come and be your *bonheur* when you play at the tables?"

He glanced guiltily, laughingly at Ellen, who kept her face blank.

"Not tonight, *chérie*. Maybe I do not play at the tables tonight. *Au 'voir!*" And he was gone.

❧

Naturally, after this very correct paternal visitation, Ellen expected that the Comtesse would also appear in the schoolroom to discuss hours of work, methods of tuition, curriculum, and so forth. Or that she would summon her new employee for such a purpose. But during the next two days neither of these things happened.

When she woke on her first morning in the Hôtel Caudebec, Ellen had congratulated herself on the comforts of this new existence. Her bruised and sorrowful heart might have been left in Brussels, but at least her body had its creature comforts: the fire already lit in the hearth, the cup of chocolate brought to her bedside by a chambermaid, the charming, luxurious room.

But she soon realized that these solaces were going to be dearly bought.

After three days of battle against the hostility, willfulness, inattention, screaming fits, utter ignorance, and frenetic

overactivity of little Menispe, Ellen sought an interview
with the Countess. When, after considerable difficulty, this
was achieved, Ellen came bluntly to the point.

"Has your daughter ever been examined by a doctor?"
she asked.

Louise glanced up with an air of slight irritation from
a book which she had been studying with absorbed
concentration as Ellen approached her. She seemed
intending to make it clear that, since a governess for her
child had been thrust on her without reference to herself,
she was absolved, thereby, from any further concern
regarding the educational process.

"A *doctor*? No, why? She is not ill? Quite the contrary,
in fact, rudely healthy." She raised her blond brows and
gave Ellen a cold smile. "Last time I attempted to take
her out in the carriage she kicked my shins, wore me
out with her wriggling, and completely ruined a yellow
jaconet walking dress."

"Of course Menispe is not sick. That was not what
I meant." Ellen reined in her patience as best she could
in the face of this willful non-comprehension. "But I
wonder if such unbridled energy is normal in a child her
age? And—although in some ways she is quite forward—
her vocabulary is excellent, for example—in other areas
her aptitude seems oddly poor. Of course—"

Of course, that might be because she has been almost
entirely left to her own devices, Ellen had been on the
point of saying, but stopped in time. This might quite
possibly be the explanation, however. Such of the household as had, at one time or another, been moved to try
and impart a little basic instruction to the child, had soon
given up in despair, it was plain, daunted by the impos-
sibility of persuading the mercurial little creature to sit still
and pay attention for more than two consecutive minutes.

Louise said haughtily, "You are suggesting that my
daughter is wanting in her wits? Mad?"

"Of course not, Countess. I would not dream of making such a ridiculous suggestion. On the contrary; in many ways she is unusually advanced." In her grasp of the game of roulette, for instance, Ellen thought. "But she has an almost complete lack of ability to concentrate—"

"Oh, my *dear* Miss Paget—what do you expect in a child of four?"

"And unusually poor physical dexterity," Ellen persisted doggedly, "which, coupled with her nonstop, tireless, almost hysterical activity, makes me wonder if there might be some slight maladjustment of the nervous system—which a doctor might be able to help—"

"Oh, *mon dieu*, my dear creature! If you come here and find fault with us in this way, I shall begin to regret that Aunt Paulina—however excellent her intentions— ever imported you into our household."

Again Louise gave that brief, unamused smile, the corners of her pale mouth turning down, not up, her eyelids drooping to disguise the chill in her eyes. "And— do forgive me—but what can you know of such matters? You are, after all, *quite* young; your experience is necessarily limited—"

"I have taught children of all ages in a large school for a period of four years—" Ellen countered stubbornly.

"—And, moreover, you are judging the poor little angel on a basis of—what? Three days? Is not that a *trifle* premature?" Louise glanced sidelong at her charming gilt clock with the nine Muses. "Dear me! How very late it grows. I fear I must ask you to withdraw, dear Miss Paget, for I have the Nicomachean Ethics of Aristotle to commit to memory; I am to conduct a discussion on them in my salon this evening. So, pray, my dear creature, do not burden me any further, just now, with nursery matters."

Germaine de Rhetorée, who had been absorbed in writing at a distant escritoire, now stood up, stretched, and strolled toward her friend. She had apparently passed the night in the Hôtel Caudebec; she wore a primrose-colored velvet negligee with fetching falls of lace.

"What is vexing you, my tigress?" she inquired.

"Oh, it is nothing, dear Camille—nothing at all." Again the disdainful smile flickered briefly as Louise glanced at the governess. "Miss Paget here finds my tiger kitten too active."

"Active? Surely a four-year-old should be a bundle of activity and curiosity?"

Ellen shrugged and withdrew. She did not intend to embark on a discussion with Mademoiselle de Rhetorée. Curiosity, though, she thought, returning to the nursery wing (which was situated at a considerable distance from the rooms occupied by the Comtesse)—curiosity is just what seems signally lacking in the child; she overturns objects, she empties drawers, she causes chaos and confusion, she interrupts, she contradicts, but she *does not ask questions*; she shows no wish to learn.

But perhaps that is due to the atmosphere in the Hôtel Caudebec?

As Ellen crossed the golden boudoir she heard Germaine remark, "After all, perhaps the poor child takes after her father—who, we must admit, must we not, has himself never grown out of the schoolroom?"

Louise merely laughed in reply. The laugh was unexpected: a warm, conspiratorial bubble of sound, wholly unrelated to her sour smiles.

I don't blame Lady Morningquest for mistrusting such an influence on her niece, thought Ellen; I would imagine that Mademoiselle de Rhetorée is about as helpful to the marriage as a hyena in a hen coop.

Sighing, she once more addressed herself to her struggles with little Menispe.

At first Ellen had assumed that a child who seemed to have received so little adult attention might, in the end, be wooed by the sheer unaccustomed pleasure of being the object of somebody's full-time care and attention. But after several days she was obliged to admit that she had been mistaken. Menispe was not to be won by anybody's solicitude. She did not want attention. At all times she wanted to be doing, and she wanted the results of her actions to be as visible and far-reaching as possible. She was an unselfconscious child, often hardly aware when she was under scrutiny; but when she did become aware, the attention focused on her was a cause for annoyance, not gratification; she would charge head-down like a little bull at any grown person who bothered her with questions; she would kick shins, bite, or throw whatever article was to hand. If she felt that too much pressure was being put on her she would react by a screaming fit, lying on her back, drumming her heels, becoming first red, then blue in the face; after these convulsions she would be limp and sick for several hours, needing treatment with ice packs and tisanes.

Toward two people only did she display any feeling: her father, whom she patently adored, and her bonne, Véronique. The latter came in for a fair number of bites, thumps, and kicks, but also for some rough careless affection; by Véronique, Menispe would allow herself to be tucked in bed at night and kissed without instantly hitting out or struggling away. For her mother she evidently felt a bewildered kind of awe, regarding her as she might a fairy or some mysterious spirit who had come to take up habitation in the house; but this reverence was not enough to prevent the child from exasperating Louise every time they met by her fidgets and clumsiness; she was seldom permitted to remain in her mother's boudoir for longer than five minutes. It was plain that Menispe had a strong dislike for Germaine de Rhetorée, at whom she invariably scowled and put out her tongue; but some of the awe she felt for her mother extended to her mother's friend; Germaine was not in danger of physical assault. The latter, on her side, evinced a cool interest in the child, and would watch with dispassionate pity as Menispe committed some act of folly or disobedience and was dragged kicking and screaming from the room.

Ellen possessed an unladylike gift of which Lady Morningquest was quite unaware; it would have scandalized her to know that her goddaughter could whistle like a bird—or like a boy. Quite by chance one afternoon, a few days after her installation at the Hôtel Caudebec, when Menispe, made even more restless than usual by rainy weather, had overturned a chair, spilt a pot of ink, and torn some engravings in her urgency to get away from the table where her governess was trying to encourage her to draw, Ellen discovered the power that a simple tune held over her wayward charge.

Putting down sheets of blotting paper to soak up the spilt ink on the green baize table cover, Ellen had commenced an absentminded whistling. To her amazement Menispe, who had darted away to the farthest corner of the room, now came creeping back, eyeing her preceptress with wonder.

"What tune is that?"

"It is called '*J'ai du bon tabac*.' Do you not know it?"

The untidy flaxen head was shaken vigorously.

"Oh! Well, I will sing it to you sometime."

"Now!"

"No, not now. *Now* I am busy mopping up the ink that you knocked over."

"Sing it now. Now!"

Ellen shook her head, smiling a little, guessing that here, possibly, she might have a lever, by means of which good behavior—or at least cooperation—might be achieved.

"Another time. When you have done something to please me."

At this moment the schoolroom door opened. Unexpectedly, Germaine de Rhetorée strolled in. Ellen had encountered her several times by now—she seemed a constant visitor in the Hôtel Caudebec; but she had never approached the nursery wing before. This afternoon Ellen was startled and somewhat shocked to see that she was wearing men's clothes—or at least a replica of a man's costume: the strapped trousers, redingote, high stock, had all been copied in rough, cream-colored silk. She had metal-heeled boots and carried a stylish top hat; her hair was tied back by a bandeau. Tall, supple, with her firm chin and strongly marked brows, she looked like a handsome boy.

Little Menispe, at sight of her, furiously thrust out her lower lip and retreated to a corner, where she set to work energetically stripping the wool off a toy sheep set on rockers. Ellen had already decided that there would be no purpose at all in continual prohibitions; let the child fulfill her bent for destruction, if she must, on objects that were of no particular importance.

"You do not forbid?" Germaine inquired, indicating the activity with raised brows.

"I reserve my fire for major engagements," Ellen replied coolly.

Germaine smiled. Ellen, as on the night of her first arrival, was struck by the immense charm of this smile. It seemed to light her face, her whole being, the room itself, with warmth and friendship. Her large dark-gray eyes opened wide, revealing greenish lights in their depths.

"So quickly you are learning to deal with the poor little flibbertigibbet! It would certainly require more patience than I possess!"

"How very good your English is, mademoiselle," said Ellen politely—they were speaking in that tongue.

Germaine laughed—a free, infectious boy's laugh.

"Tactful Miss Paget! You do not intend to discuss

your employers' child with a third party. But—*en effet*—I did not come here to discuss *la petite*."

"No?"

Germaine sauntered to the window. With a movement of her hand, as she stood looking out, she invited Ellen to join her. The room looked south onto the large formal town garden which lay to the rear of the Hôtel—a pleasant place at this benign season, with its clipped trees in tubs, paved walks, and glowing beds of tulips, though in winter it would be gray and dreary enough.

Although the sky today was dark and threatening, the Comte de la Ferté and his wife were to be seen there, standing halfway along a graveled allée; even from this distance the antagonism in their bearing was unmistakable. He appeared to demand, and she to refuse; his gestures were wild, beseeching, and angry, hers cold, restrained, and implacable.

"Poor things," said Germaine, glancing at them, shrugging. "A disastrous match. The sooner he accepts that, the better for all."

Detachedly, Ellen wondered if Germaine's motive in coming here had been to observe the couple from this point of vantage. Averse, herself, to a kind of eavesdropping—though words could not be heard at this distance—she walked away from the window, and asked, "How can I serve you, Mademoiselle de Rhetorée?"

Unexpectedly, Germaine said, "Have you ever tried your hand at translation?"

"Of what nature?"

"Ah, there! I see you have not. But I am wondering if you might not discover in yourself a decided talent for it…whether you might consent to become my collaboratress? Any dolt can see that your work here, attempting to subdue that little monster, will only employ a twentieth part of your intellectual powers—"

"You are too good, mademoiselle," said Ellen coldly, but Germaine only laughed.

"Oh, I have been listening to you, believe me, since you arrived among us! You have a mind of your own. And indeed, that old dragon, Lady Morningquest, had reported you as a *jeune fille à caractère* of considerable intellectual endowments! One must always take the aunt's opinions with a grain of salt. But I find that in this she did you no injustice."

Ellen's few days in Paris had by no means inured her to the loss of the Brussels life. She continued to feel desperately lonely and disoriented. The occasional cold civilities of Louise de la Ferté and the daylong company of little Menispe were no compensation for the continual energetic use of her mind that the Brussels school had demanded; and her salary proved to be somewhat less than she had been receiving there—though, to be sure, her circumstances were more comfortable. But she still pined for the big carré, the noisy spotless classroom, her blunt, friendly colleagues at the Pensionnat, and the daily chance of an encounter with Monsieur Patrice. This offer of what sounded like interesting work and the necessary interaction that it would involve with a lively and stimulating personality was a temptation not lightly to be dismissed.

She replied with caution, however.

"Anything I might undertake would have to be acceptable to the Countess."

"Oh, my dear girl! You are not her slave! And Louise is no slave driver. What you do in your spare time is of no concern to her."

"Besides, I may not have the necessary capacities. What is it that you are suggesting?"

"Oh, *quant à ça*, I have already observed that both your English and your French are fluent and pure. Why should not you be the one to achieve an ideal rendition of my work? I do not know if Lady Morningquest informed you that I have written various *nouvelles* and feuilletons?"

Ellen murmured that the Countess's aunt had mentioned something of the kind.

"Ha! And I can imagine what the old Gorgon said about them. Well, it is true," admitted Germaine, "that I did begin by writing terrible rocambolesque rubbish for *La Presse* and *Le Siècle*—one has to commence somehow, after all! But now, my romances are quite *intellectuel*, and have been published in *Le Constitutionnel* and *La Revue de Paris*—after all, even *Madame Bovary* was first serialized there! So there is no need for old Recherche-matin to look down her long nose at me. And nothing I gave you would bring a blush to your cheek."

In talking about her work, Ellen noticed, Germaine seemed younger, less poised and more spontaneous.

"You wish your romances to be translated into English? Have any of them been, already?"

"No, none! And it is in England that the money is made," said Germaine with greedy cheerfulness. "Why—of Monsieur Guillaume Thackeray, it is said that he lives in the style of an aristocrat, that his footmen are turned out in silk stockings! *Le Cricri du Foyer* earned Charles Dickens *un million*!—and that is by no means one of his major works. Balzac was consumed with envy for Dickens. Rates of pay here are wretched—that poor Flaubert received only eight hundred francs for the book version of *Bovary*. Imagine it!"

This seemed like a handsome sum to Ellen, whose entire salary was nine hundred francs a year—but at least she could be certain of it; writing must be a terribly chancy occupation. She was impressed by the glibness with which Germaine ran off these sums and well-known names.

"I am sure that I should greatly enjoy reading some of your work, Mademoiselle de Rhetorée," she ventured civilly. "And I imagine I should soon be able to decide whether translating it lay within my capacity."

"Oh, I feel certain it will," said Germaine firmly. "And then, among your English connections, you are, perhaps, familiar with some publisher?"

Ellen was obliged to confess that she had no personal acquaintance in such circles.

"No matter. The Société des Auteurs et Compositeurs will furnish me with addresses—however, I look too far ahead. Tomorrow I will bring you *Ondine* and *Corombona*—those are my two best novels—and you shall give me your opinion of them. How I look forward to that!"

Threading her arm through that of Ellen she went on in a cajoling tone, "But my selfishness is outrageous. Here I am, pressing my concerns upon you, boring on with my own business, when, in point of fact, I am dying of curiosity about *you*. Tell me about yourself. I know that you are 'born,' as we say—both Louise and I are acquainted with your brother Benedict. What a charmer! So I think it very gallant of you to earn your bread abroad as a free woman, rather than remain at home to submit to a *mariage de convenance*. How in the world does this come about? You English are so independent. Let me hear all your history!"

"Oh," Ellen demurred, slightly taken aback by this sudden burst of interest, "I am not really as 'born' as you seem to imagine, mademoiselle. True, my mother was an earl's granddaughter, but my father is only an English country gentleman; and Benedict Masham is my stepbrother, not my real brother. My father married Benedict's mother after my own mother died." Ellen stopped short.

"Your own mother's death? That was a great grief to you?" pounced Germaine with an acute look.

"Yes!"

"Lucky girl—to have been fond of your mother! Mine I virtually never saw; I was an only child, sent off to be brought up on a farm in the country while Maman lived in Paris; then I went to the Couvent des Anglaises, where I met Louise; then we both attended a lycée in Bonn."

"You have been friends so long?"

"Since we were fourteen. We vowed to spend our lives as close to one another as we could," said Germaine with her conspiratorial grin. "But your father? What kind of man is he? And do you have sisters—brothers—of your own?"

"My father? A dry, disappointed man. He read for the Bar; but never practiced law. He had a great ambition to go into Parliament, but after contesting three elections and failing to be returned, had spent most of his inheritance, and was obliged to relinquish any hope of a political career. So for years he has been merely a Justice of the Peace, and occupied himself with local affairs. He has two passions—not spending money, and thinking himself better than other people."

"You paint a devastating portrait, *ma chère*. Sisters?"

"Two, both married, unhappily, I am afraid, pushed into hasty matches by my father and stepmother. There is also a very much younger half sister, Vicky, a little older than Menispe. And a brother, Gerard, aged fifteen."

Recalled to thoughts of her charge, Ellen turned to the child, who was looking abused and mutinous. She had tired of her assault on the wooden sheep, and was irritably tearing up some fashion plates which had been given her to color with crayons.

"Your stepmother: is she unkind to you?"

"Not unkind; but we are not compatible."

"Describe her."

Why am I spilling out all these personal details to a total stranger? Ellen wondered. But she could not help being disarmed and attracted by Germaine's apparently eager and genuine interest.

Giving a brief description of Lady Adelaide, Ellen walked over to Menispe.

"If you do that, then you will not have the pictures when you wish to color them," she pointed out.

"You are supposed to play with *me*, not her," grumbled Menispe, scowling at Germaine.

"Oh, la-la! Children's convenience must give way to that of adults," Germaine told her airily. "And who would wish to play with a sulky-faced maggot such as you? I am sure your sister Vicky is not such a one," she said to Ellen. "And your younger brother? Is he *sympathique?*"

"He is a musical genius; he has little time for human relations. In a way, he is very like Papa."

"*Tiens!* Are you, then, musical too?"

"A little, but not to Gerard's degree. I was wondering, though, if Madame la Comtesse would consent to a pianoforte in the schoolroom. I suspect that our friend here might benefit."

"You will have to apply to Raoul; he holds the purse strings. It is a daily aggravation to my poor Louise. Married to one of the richest men in Normandy, and she must apply to him for every sou. Moreover—when you consider those gaming rooms, and what he does with his millions—"

Ellen considered that the subject had moved outside her scope, and she picked up a pair of blunt-ended scissors, as a hint that she had neglected her duties for long enough.

With a flashing smile Germaine said, "Enough of the la Ferté problems! And I must go and robe myself for Louise's salon. Why do you not attend, one of these afternoons? She holds them every Tuesday and Thursday. You would find them amusing, I believe. My Arsinoë knows how to attract good company, it is her gift—the brightest wits in Paris gather here on those days.

Halévy—Baudelaire—Flaubert—the Goncourt pair—
even sometimes Madame George, who is our heroine."

"Baudelaire?" Ellen was caught by the name. "Is he
not very scandalous?"

"Tah! He was ordered to remove six poems from *Les
Fleurs du Mal*; he removed them; propriety is satisfied.
His literary and artistic judgment are masterly."

"But would Louise permit me—?"

"Oh, *mon dieu*, yes! Anybody who has read, and
can talk, is welcome—particularly a personable young
female, to offset all those old witches whose husbands
are members of the Académie. You could, perhaps, be
dressed a little more in the mode. Gray merino, my dear
child, is not quite the wear! But you are much of a height
with Louise; she has half a room filled with garments that
she never looks at. I daresay her maid Michon would
soon alter something—"

"Thank you, mademoiselle," Ellen said with hauteur,
"but I believe I need not trouble the Comtesse or her
maid. I am accustomed to look after my own wardrobe,
and feel confident of achieving some suitable apparel
when I have had time to study the Paris costumes."

"Well, well, don't ruffle up at me! I meant it kindly.
Arsinoë and I wear classic dress, but that won't do for you,
you are not sufficiently *maigre*; current fashion will be best,
a restrained draping, swept-up line, and military *jaquette*."

"Thank you for your advice," Ellen said, resolving to
follow none of it.

Germaine laughed at her. "Eh," she said in French,
"you are as prickly as a *châtaigne*—fierce as a bear. I think
I shall call you Callisto! And now good-bye—I have
vexed you long enough."

Kissing her hand to the sulky Menispe, she was
on the point of leaving when a footman knocked,
entered, and proffered a card to Ellen on a silver
salver. Ellen's heart leaped, then sank again. Germaine,

glancing sidelong at the pasteboard with her keen eyes, exclaimed, "The Honorable Benedict Masham. *Tiens*, but how charming. Your *beau-frère* comes to seek you out in this nest of hornets. *Eh bien, à demain, mon amie—*" and, flickering her long supple fingers at Ellen, she strolled from the room.

"I left the young milord in the small blue salon, mademoiselle, while I came to ascertain if you wished to see him," said Michel the footman, in whose eyes Ellen's status had evidently soared as a result of this very eligible caller.

"Yes. I will see him. Véronique?" Ellen put her head through the door into the nursery, which was next the schoolroom. "Will you bring your sewing, please, and sit with Mademoiselle Menispe for ten minutes? I have a visitor."

"*Bien sûr*, mademoiselle." The bonne good-naturedly gathered up her things, and Ellen reflected that one, at least, of Lady Morningquest's warnings had not proved valid; the servants in this house seemed disposed to be friendly to the governess, probably because they were glad that somebody else had to grapple with Menispe. But as for the rest of the warning... What would her godmother say if she knew that Ellen had agreed to translate Germaine de Rhetorée's novels? Ellen was supposed to be doing her best to discourage the frequency of Germaine's visits, not entering upon a relationship of her own with the undesirable confidante.

Well, perhaps I shall discover that I am incapable of undertaking the translation, she reflected. Or that I don't like the books and don't wish to do it. Or perhaps Germaine will not like what I do... But if I do it, and do it well, and we become friends—then perhaps it will be possible for me to drop a word of advice in her ear.

She smiled to herself at the improbability of her

finding it possible to counsel the assured, not to say swaggering, Germaine. Admit, she told herself, that you have been bowled over by her charm. And also by the chance to embark on a new career—an interesting, distracting occupation.

Endeavoring to banish Germaine from her thoughts, she turned her mind to Benedict. How strange it was—more than strange—that he should have sought out his stepsister like this, twice, in quick succession. What could be his reason? He did not need an entrée to the Hôtel Caudebec—Germaine had said Louise knew him; and in any case he would not achieve it by way of the governess. Not Benedict! He and the Comte probably attended the same gaming halls.

Michel stood aside, bowing, and she walked swiftly into the small blue salon. Benedict came forward to greet her. She was startled at once, and made anxious, by the unbroken black of his clothes and the unwonted gravity of his expression.

"*Benedict?* Is something wrong? You look so—"

He took her hands and said rapidly, "Do not be under any apprehension! I have bad news, but it does not closely concern you; or at least—"

"Oh, what is it?" she cried in affright. "Pray tell me at once—do not try to break it by degrees!"

"My mother has been killed in a carriage accident," he said. "And in the same occurrence your father was injured, but not fatally; he suffered a concussion and a fractured hip, but is now said to be going on well—"

"Oh, Benedict! I am so very sorry. Your poor, poor mother—what a frightful thing!"

"It was that peacocky pair of matched chestnuts she insisted on buying from Curtis," he said gloomily. "I *warned* her about them—so did your father, times out of number. A wholly unsuitable team for a lady to be driving round those narrow Sussex lanes—but my mama, as you know, was resolved on cutting a dash and pursuing her own course, come what may."

"Poor Benedict," she said again. "I am so very sorry."

But his narrow clever face appeared somber rather than grief-stricken. Ellen was aware that in fact most of Adelaide's shallow affections had been concentrated on her elder son, Easingwold.

"Where is my father now? And how did you obtain this intelligence?"

He told her about the message which had arrived in Brussels just after she left.

"This was followed by a letter from my aunt Blanche Pomfret. Doubtless your sister Eugenia has written to you, to Brussels. Your father was in the Infirmary in Chichester, but is now removed to the Bishop's Palace, where your sister Eugenia visits him daily."

"He won't be too pleased at that. Poor Papa! How will he manage now? He is bound to consider that Fate has dealt him a most unjust blow—just after he had settled down so comfortably with your mother."

"*Comfortably?* Humph! My aunt Blanche writes that she has hired a housekeeper who is presiding at the Hermitage, and will no doubt take care of your father when he is fit to return home."

"Oh, heavens! I wonder if I ought to go back?" Ellen wrung her hands rather distractedly. She could well imagine people in Petworth—her sisters—Madame Bosschère—Lady Morningquest—saying, "Without doubt it is the duty of his unmarried daughter to return and take care of Luke Paget."

"Why? He wouldn't say thank you." Benedict was blunt and unflattering. "What could you do that a housekeeper could not do as well?"

"But poor little Vicky? And Gerard?"

"Poor little Vicky—that spoiled brat—has two adoring maids and a Mrs. Somebody who comes in daily to give her instruction. As for your young brother—he needs no one, as you are aware. They will do well enough."

Ellen reflected that this was true. And—for that matter—her efforts on behalf of little Menispe de la Ferté had not been signally successful. Why should she be likely to do better with Vicky? She thought: supposing I had received this intelligence before I left Brussels? I would have gone straight to England. Would that have been for the best?

Oddly enough, she could not feel so. The idea of England, so nostalgic and beguiling as she sat in the train, now struck with a strange chill. To be there, in the depths of Sussex, cut off, with an angry, resentful invalid, an orphaned little girl, and a moody fifteen-year-old boy—what a dreary prospect! But I would go, of course, if it seemed my duty, she thought with a shiver.

"Just the same," observed Benedict—now there was a look of decided disapprobation on his fair, clean-cut face—"a fine *galère* you have got yourself into here, my dear sister! Why the deuce could you not have stayed at Madame Bosschère's? There, at least, you were out of harm's way."

She was immediately irritated—the more so, because he seemed so much more adult in his manner than he had done in Brussels. She said in a measured tone, "Lady Morningquest made a particular request that I should leave my duties in Brussels to come here. The child"—she lowered her voice, though they had the room to themselves—"is in urgent need of instruction and a firm guiding hand."

"Indeed?" he said sardonically. "But why, my dear Ellie, should the hand be yours? Are you also intended to regulate the household and govern the activities of the parents—not to speak of their friends? As you had occasion to do with me—for example? Shall you be able to prevent Raoul from gambling? And persuade Louise to dispense with her *persona grata*?"

"I do not know in the least what you are talking about." Ellen's tone was cold, but her cheeks reddened. She was hurt and deeply mortified by his reference to an incident in their past; she had hoped that by now it was forgotten.

"Surely you must have met the fascinating Germaine? I understand that she practically lives here."

Ellen had been wondering where, recently, she had come across the phrase "hornets' nest"—now she recalled that Germaine herself had used it when speaking of Benedict. "*Il va vous chercher dans cet guêpier—comme c'est charmant!*" she had said; at the time Ellen had wondered whether there had not been a touch of irony in her tone. Now it seemed certain there had been.

"Naturally I have met Mademoiselle de Rhetorée." Pricked by Benedict's needle-sharp look, Ellen added, "She seems very agreeable."

"Agreeable! That young lady would make Cesare Borgia seem like Ethelred the Unready. She is the most ruthless person you are ever likely to meet."

"I must make allowance for your present distress of mind, Benedict," Ellen said primly. "But I beg you will not come here and discuss my employers or their friends with me. It is not at all the thing."

"Oh, don't be so self-righteous, you little blockhead! You may be green still, but you are not *stupid*!" said Benedict, suddenly losing his temper completely. "Can't you see that you have come innocently tripping into the middle of a highly explosive situation? And may precipitate the most shocking imbroglio in any number of ways?"

"I see nothing of the kind!"

Infuriatingly, she felt her eyes swim with tears, and had to steady her chin to prevent her mouth from trembling.

"Go away, please, Benedict," she said in a moment, with dignity. "I am grateful to you for bringing me news

of the accident—and—and very sorry about your poor
mama—but you must not come and make trouble for me
in my new position. I—I was certainly unhappy to leave
Brussels—but I believe it was for the best—and I intend
to try and do my best here—"

Benedict strode angrily about the room. His lean, mus-
cular body seemed ill at ease in the formal black clothes.

"*Women!*" he muttered to himself. "Managing, inter-
fering, conniving, pigheaded, bigoted, thick-skinned,
despotic—"

Ellen recalled Madame Bosschère's remark about how
much easier life would be if men were all confined in
zoological gardens. She managed a cool indulgent laugh.

"My dear Benedict—pray do not put yourself in a
passion on *my* account. I shall bear your admonitions
in mind—I promise you—and I daresay I shall do well
enough. And if I don't," she added crossly and childishly,
"I fail to see what concern it is of *yours*. After all now—
now poor Lady Adelaide has died—there is really no
connection between us. I daresay we shall not meet once
in a dozen years. So you need not worry what becomes
of me."

"Oh, confound it!" exclaimed Benedict, in the tone
of a man goaded beyond endurance, and he strode
toward the door, pausing to say, "You forget that we
have a small half sister in common." Then he left the
room, without the least attempt at a polite farewell—or,
indeed, any farewell at all.

Ellen, more shaken than she cared to acknowledge to
herself by the suppressed violence of his manner, waited
a few moments to make sure he had really gone before
making her way slowly back to the schoolroom. She
recalled again Germaine's teasing voice: "Your stepbrother comes here? Ah, how charming that is!" and had
to suppress an idiotic sob which would rise in her throat.
I'm homesick, she thought. It is all so strange here. And

it was upsetting, seeing Benedict like that. I wish he had come to take me out to tea at Tortoni's!… Oh, if only Monsieur Patrice were here, to talk to me about Virgil's poetry, or Plato's philosophy.

She sat down wearily in the schoolroom and began to draw a simple picture for Menispe to copy. Véronique, with a smiling curtsey, took herself off. Menispe, for a wonder, was perched quietly by the window, watching the raindrops trickle down the pane, and following their course with her finger. But soon she tired of this activity, and turned to gaze at her new teacher, stationed so unwontedly silent and pensive at the table, with chin propped on hands. Without a word, Menispe uncurled from the window seat and came to stare closely, almost accusingly, at Ellen's face.

"Why do you cry?" she demanded.

"Was I crying?"

"*Mais oui! Regardez!*" Menispe extended a small dusty finger, touched Ellen's cheek, and followed the course of a tear. "Just like the rain on the pane."

"*Tiens!* So I was. You were quite right. Well, I will stop. And, look, the rain has stopped too. We'll go out, shall we, and drink some chocolate at a patisserie?"

Six

SOME UNEVENTFUL WEEKS NOW PASSED. ELLEN RECEIVED two letters from her sister Eugenia, one relating in detail the tragic accident which had ended the life of their step-mother. This had been forwarded from Brussels. Ellen replied to it, and in due course heard again.

"Papa is still suffering from a severe depression of the spirits," wrote Lady Valdoe. "He remains in the Palace, where Lady Blanche and the Bishop care for him with the most solicitous attention; but you know Papa! He considers that his misfortunes are wholly undeserved, and he is not to be placated. Fortunately, all goes on well at the Hermitage; I asked Caroline Penfold to call in once or twice, and she reports that the housekeeper Lady Blanche found seems to be a capable woman enough. (Gerard hates her, of course.) I believe Great-Aunt Fanny occasionally bestirs herself to ride down in the doctor's pony cart, but her visitations, as you may imagine, are of little import." Ellen smiled at that. Great-Aunt Fanny was a particular favorite of her own; but Eugenia had never been fond of this relative, finding her too indifferent to the usages of polite society. "Little Vicky and Gerard go on as well as may be expected," Eugenia continued. "Lady B. reports that they called on Papa at the Palace. So do not, sister, be thinking that it will be needful for you to give up your new position and return to Petworth, for I assure you it will not. You had far better lose no chance to contract useful connections in Paris while you are there. How I wish I might join you! But

Valdoe says he must spend this year's rents on renewing the mortgages. It is dreadful to be so grovelingly poor."

What Eugenia really means is that she would like me to marry a rich, well-connected Frenchman, Ellen reflected, and then I could invite her to visit me. She smiled at the unlikely idea. And even if I was married to the rich Frenchman, he would probably not be at all anxious to welcome fretful Eugenia and her brood of whiny children for long visits!

Ellen had communications, also, from various of her affectionate pupils in the rue St. Pierre and a formal letter of condolence from Madame Bosschère, but not a word from Monsieur Patrice. If she hoped, day after day, to see his small, difficult handwriting on one of the letters Gaston brought her, she knew in her heart that the hope was delusive. He would not write.

But he might come.

Germaine had made careless inquiry, when she turned up with the two slim paperbound novels: "You were in Brussels before, *ma chère* Callisto, so Arsinoë informs me. Did you have interesting acquaintances there? Some of these heavy Flamands possess a kind of granite intelligence, even if they are lacking in wit."

"Some even have wit as well," Ellen said defensively, and Germaine, with her swift pounce, had drawn out the connection. "Aha! Le Professeur Patrice Bosschère? Why yes, I have read his *Traité de l'Orphée*—a quite brilliant work! And you know him well? Famous! Does he never come to Paris? Why should we not invite him to attend one of Louise's disputations? If *les convenances* prevent *you* from inviting him, they certainly will not hinder *me*! I shall obtain his address from a friend at the Sorbonne."

And she floated off, leaving Ellen with a feeling as if the wind had blown by, scattering her possessions far and wide, until she was not sure where they had got to. Was

that how Germaine had used Benedict? Was that why he
so patently detested her?

⤷⤶

Out of doors Menispe was easier to manage; her wild
energies could be canalized with less risk to persons
and property; so, as the weather continued benign,
Ellen formed the habit of spending many hours with
the child in the garden, or in the Parc Monceau or
Tuileries Gardens, talking, singing, and attempting to
play games, which generally ended in a rough-and-
tumble, as Menispe's impatience overthrew the rules.
Out of doors, too, her screaming fits were not so likely
to occur; her attention was more engaged by what was
going on all around.

One sunny morning they were in the Hôtel Caudebec
garden when Ellen, endeavoring to teach Menispe a
singing rhyme for *sauter-à-la-corde*, saw the Comte stride
across a stretch of grass and enter a little classic pagoda
that stood in the distance.

"Papa! There is Papa!" joyfully shouted Menispe,
flinging away her skipping rope so violently that it
snapped off the heads of half a dozen tulips. "I will go
and say *bonjour* to him."

Ellen had rapidly discovered that Louise's angry
estimate of the amount of time passed by her husband
at home was not far short of the truth; he was highly
elusive, seldom in the hotel, often out of Paris entirely,
on his estates in Normandy. Since her first morning she
had been unable to obtain an interview with him, and
was reluctant to write him a note over so trifling an affair
as a piano for the schoolroom.

Now, therefore, she did not discourage Menispe,
but followed the child along a graveled path that led
to the little pavilion. It was only when they were just
outside the building, which was smothered in jasmine

and honeysuckle, that she realized the Comte was not alone in there.

Angry voices could be heard.

"Louise! For God's sake be reasonable! Is what I am asking such an unheard-of thing? If anyone could hear me—your *husband*—I should feel so ashamed—to be petitioning in this way—"

"For the thousandth time, I tell you no! No, and no again! I risked my life for you once, and once is enough. You can have no idea—you are so thick-skinned and insensitive—you have no *conception* of what I went through—never in the world would I endure that a second time—"

"But my aunts say—"

"Your aunts, every one of them, can go to Gehenna for all I care!"

"But the succession—"

"I hate your family, and all this to-do about the succession! You and your jointures and trusts, your muniments and estates and title deeds and progenitors and quarterings and dowries, all your fuss about male and female issue! Let one of your brothers succeed! What do you think I am—a brood mare? The very sight of your child makes me ill—gives me a migraine—when I look at her and remember what she cost me—"

"Menispe, come away," whispered Ellen. "We must not trouble your parents now—"

She tried to draw Menispe out of earshot. But the child did not heed her words, which, in any case, came too late; Louise, white with anger, swept out of the summerhouse, brushed past her child and the governess, sparing the latter only one cold, surprised glance, and hurried across the garden, huddling her fine white woolen shawl around her shoulders.

Menispe, without waiting an instant, bounded into the pavilion.

"Papa! Come quick, and see how I can skip with my rope!"

Ellen's heart warmed to him, for it seemed that even after such a distressing scene, he could greet his daughter without too obvious strain and irritability.

"*Holà*, is that you, my chaffinch? But I am busy just now, I fear, so you must run back to your *gouvernante*."

"But, Papa, I wish you to come and see what I can do."

"Menispe," called Ellen, "Menispe, come to me, I beg!" Nervously she presented herself in the doorway, saying, "Excuse me, monsieur, if you please. Menispe loves you so dearly, it makes her so happy when she sees you—"

"It is of no consequence," he replied. His tone was heavy, he looked white and exhausted, with a set to his mouth that was painful to see in so young a man. Absently he fondled the child's head and said, "Another time, *chérie*. Run along now—I have business affairs to arrange."

"But there are no papers here? And Pondicheau has not brought your account books."

"The business is in my mind, little one."

"Come, Menispe," Ellen repeated.

Something perhaps in the gentleness of the way she spoke succeeded in penetrating the child's consciousness; she turned slowly, and took Ellen's outstretched hand. Ellen's tone of voice seemed also to make contact with Raoul, despite his wretched preoccupation; he raised his eyes to hers and inquired, with an effort at lightness, "How are you prospering in your efforts to civilize this wild character, mademoiselle? I hope she does not tire you to death?"

"Oh—our progress is slow—but I think perhaps there has been just a little, monsieur," answered Ellen with a faint smile, all the time gently drawing Menispe away along the path. "And you are comfortable? You have all that you require?"

"Might there be—a pianoforte—in the schoolroom— would Monsieur le Comte sanction the expenditure? I believe that your daughter may have the germ of music in her—"

"A piano? But of course. Tell Pondicheau the kind you prefer—you shall have one this very day. I imagine there are half a dozen about the place. *Au revoir, mademoiselle—'voir, mignonne.*"

"He didn't want to see me skip," said Menispe, with drooping mouth.

"Another time, *chérie*. We will go and ask M. Pondicheau to find us a piano, and very soon you will be able to dance like Madame Vestris. Then you can invite your papa to a performance!"

⁕

By midsummer, Ellen was quite habituated to life in the Hôtel Caudebec. She had not seen her godmother again. Lady Morningquest was still wholly preoccupied with the condition of her son Thomas, who had developed a brain fever as a result of his fall on the marble stair, and whose life, for some days, had been despaired of; he was now, happily, on the mend, and about to be taken off to Etretat for a period of convalescence; his mother, during this anxious period, had had little time to concern herself with affairs in the rue de l'Arbre Vert. She had sent affectionate messages to her goddaughter, expressing hopes that all was going as it should. Ellen replied punctiliously to these, and made inquiries as to Tom's progress.

But although she tried to write encouragingly about the la Ferté household, she felt, with some guilt, that if Lady Morningquest knew how matters really stood, she would hardly approve.

Some progress had been made. Little Menispe was

no more amenable, but she was, at least, better disposed toward Ellen. The importation of the piano had been a decided help; so long as Ellen would play on it, Menispe was happy to dance about the room, and, by the end of a couple of hours passed in this manner, would be sufficiently tired to be prepared to sit down and listen to a story for ten minutes. Her capacities, as Ellen had guessed, were considerable; although appearing to take in nothing, she had a quick grasp, and after several days of apparent noncomprehension, would carelessly bring out some piece of information as if she had been born with it. But she was an exhausting pupil. Four hours with her left Ellen drained as she had not been after coping all day with the turbulent *deuxième classe* in Madame Bosschère's Pensionnat.

"You need a respite," Germaine de Rhetorée told her firmly. "You cannot spend all the hours of daylight with that little *diablesse*, or you will be *à bout*."

Ellen realized that this was true; she asked and received permission to invoke the assistance of a music master and a dancing master. These were two aristocratic old gentlemen, lucky to have escaped with their lives as children during the Revolution, who, having lost all their family wealth, made a living by passing on the graces of the ancien regime, now much in vogue again. Their attempts to teach Menispe musical notation, or how to curtsey, retrieve a dropped fan, sit gracefully, or withdraw from the presence of royalty, would have made an angel weep, but, as Germaine said, "They deflect a little of her energies from you, Callisto, and so, I hope, leave you more strength for translating my foolish romances."

The translation, in point of fact, was going rather well. Ellen had been impressed by Germaine's feuilletons, simple but witty tales of ordinary people and their lives, cross-purposes, and problems, in Paris of the present day.

"*Réalisme* is the fashion now," Germaine said. "Art must be an impersonal, unidealized picture of life.

Champfleury and Duranty set the vogue, and M. de Balzac. And, above all, Madame George, our heroine. She is the epitome."

"Madame George?"

"George Sand." Germaine opened wide her huge gray eyes. "You have not read her yet? Well, her latest, which came out this year, *Elle et Lui*—that tells all about her affair with Alfred de Musset, it is very entertaining—oh, what a wretched, wretched character, that man! You must certainly read it. However, Arsinoë is in the middle of it at present, so I will lend you *Le Marquis de Villemer* and her play *François le Champi*."

Ellen recalled some scathing remark from Lady Morningquest about "that Dudevant woman."

"Is she not wicked? Madame Dudevant?"

"Wicked, why? To leave a husband who was not her equal, who was unfaithful to her? To take lovers as she chose? Men can do so, why not a woman?"

Ellen was not sure why not. The question alarmed her, as much as if the assertion that two and two made four were to be disputed. Suddenly a boundary appeared ahead of her, and, on the far side of it, anarchy and chaos.

"But to write novels about her lovers?" she said doubtfully. "Is that kind? Or right?"

"Kind? Right?" Germaine laughed at her. "What a little English pedant you are! What has rightness to do with the case? What other subject would one write about, if not one's lovers?"

"Does she often come to this house—Madame Sand?"

"Not very often. She prefers to work in the country, in her château at Nohant. She says of herself that she is unsociable, a savage. But when she does visit Paris, then she comes here. You must meet her. She is wonderful—a strong, wise, untrammeled being. But now, leave that nonsense—" Ellen was making pictures of horses for little Menispe to copy, having discovered that this subject, of all others, had power to hold the child's fickle attention. "Leave that nonsense," repeated Germaine, "and come out for a promenade about the city. I will be your cavalier."

"I must bring Menispe, then. She has not been out today."

"Oh—! Very well." Germaine screwed up her handsome face in an impatient, lightning grimace. "What a stickler you are for duty. Is not my English excellently idiomatic?"

Menispe having been arrayed by Véronique in bonnet and pelisse, the trio set out.

"Just like a good bourgeois family," said Germaine, who was, as usual, wearing a man's redingote, trousers, and a top hat. "We will walk along one of the new boulevards and drink pastis at one of the new family cafés. Or I shall drink pastis; I suppose you and Menispe will take *eau sucrée*."

"We certainly shall."

Despite some doubts as to the proprieties, Ellen greatly enjoyed these promenades about Paris with Germaine. They climbed to the top of Notre-Dame to watch the sunsets; they browsed along the stalls on the quais by the river; on wet days, for as long as Menispe would endure it, they strolled in the Louvre and Luxembourg picture galleries and looked at works by Titian, Tintoretto, Rembrandt, and Rubens.

Ellen had stayed in Paris before, visiting her godmother, and had been taken for heavily chaperoned, carefully supervised outings; but there had been nothing like this heady freedom to stroll and gaze, to observe and discuss. What would Papa think if he were to see me now, she sometimes thought. Or Eugenia? Or Kitty?

"Of course, this is academic stuff," said Germaine, dragging her away from Rubens. "All those gods and goddesses! Realism is the coming thing in art, as in writing." And she insisted on taking Ellen to someone's atelier to look at two enormous paintings, one of a village funeral with a crowd of stolid peasants all in black, the other of an untidy studio with a painter and his friends. "Everyone laughs at this man now, but he will make a name for himself, you will see." The name was Courbet.

Sometimes they drank sirop or lemonade at the Café Riche, which, Germaine told Ellen, was frequented by all the literary lions of Paris; it was a sumptuously decorated place, all white, gold, and red velvet. The customers all seemed to know one another, and there was such a brisk interchange between tables that Ellen felt almost stunned by the noise and the rapidity of the conversation, which seemed mainly concerned with literary fees and royalties, and the faults of somebody called Ponson. "He is the only writer in Paris who rides about in a dogcart," shouted a cadaverous, bearded man. "And why? Because he has sold his soul to the devil—or, in other words, to popular taste. He tells his editor, 'Give me notice a few days ahead, and, if the readers are getting bored, I'll finish the book at the end of this chapter.' Imagine that!"

On one occasion they visited a famous fortune-teller in the rue Fontaine St. Georges. "I have sold my new novel to *Le Siècle* for three hundred francs," said Germaine. "I will buy us all a good fortune!"

The walls in the fortune-teller's dimly lit dining room were all covered with hands cut out of white paper, framed on a black background. Famous hands were there—Napoleon and Robespierre, Madame de Pompadour and the Empress Eugénie, all marked with dots and annotations in ink. The seer was a silent, solemn man with a large square head and a huge mustache; he wore a black velvet gown and smelt strongly of snuff. First he asked them questions: their day, month, and hour of birth, favorite flower, animal, and color; they were invited to choose a card from an outsize pack in which the cards were a foot high and the pictures were of Eastern gods.

"Arsinoë does not believe in all this," said Germaine gaily. "She is not at all superstitious. I tried to make her come last month—she laughed me to scorn. Well, monsieur, what fate have you in store for me?" as he peered at her hand.

"Prison," he replied unexpectedly. "I see you in a cell. I see you shut up—a long period of incarceration, inactivity."

The light came feebly through stained-glass windows, but Ellen thought Germaine paled a little—though, with her biscuit skin, it was hard to be sure.

"*Eh bien!*" she said drily. "Many I know have been imprisoned for their political opinions. Madame George nearly was, two years ago, when she wrote *La Daniella*; the newspaper that published it was suspended, until Madame herself appealed to the Empress, begging for the poor newspaper workers to have their jobs back. If I must go to prison I shall be in good company, and at least it will give me new material for my writing."

The fortune-teller now turned to Ellen and studied her palm.

"You have a brother?" he asked her suddenly. "The same age as yourself? *Un jumeau?*"

Startled, she nodded.

"I see an old man—the father. And two hungry women. They open their mouths like cormorants. The father carries a great stone. It is his heart—cracked in two. On one half 'salvation' is written, and on the other, 'hell'! That half holds a mass of writhing devils. The old man raises the stone—he is going to crush your brother with it. No—he is going to crush *you*. You must escape—as your brother escaped—or free him from the stone—"

The seer seemed to be in a kind of trance; he was sweating freely and swayed from side to side.

Little Menispe broke the tension by starting to fidget

nervously and knocking a china vase, which fell to the floor. A large white owl which had been perched on the mantelpiece—stuffed, they had assumed—silently spread its wings and coasted down onto the back of a chair.

"*Oh! L'hibou!*" Menispe shrieked. "*J'ai peur! J'ai peur!*"

"Quiet, you little imbecile!" scolded Germaine, but the spell was broken; the seer glared at them and said angrily, "How can I foresee the future amid such disturbance?"

"*My* hand, look at my hand now?" Menispe demanded, holding out her small sticky palm.

The man took it, then threw it down angrily.

"I cannot predict the future of a child. There is nothing to work on. You are too small. You must come back in five years, seven years."

Yet, Ellen thought, he *had* studied Menispe's palm for a moment.

"That is all, that is quite enough," he informed them curtly. "I can tell you no more. I have another client. Good day."

"Brrrr!" exclaimed Germaine when they were in the street. "What a dismal, churlish boor! And what a worthless pair of fortunes he has sold us! I have a mind to ask for my money back. Prison for me—and all that rigmarole for you about the old man and your brother. Do you have a twin brother? You never told me about *him*?"

"I had one," said Ellen, "but he died at birth."

An odd, cold silence held them for a moment. "Oh well," said Germaine, "I daresay the man could tell that easily enough from your hand. It shows he is not wholly a charlatan. But I am disappointed! Come, let us go to Tortoni's and eat an ice."

From Germaine, Ellen learned facts about the la Ferté ménage that shocked her profoundly.

"We made a pact, Arsinoë, and I," Germaine explained.

"An alliance—how do you call it?—an offensive and defensive alliance."

It was a sunny afternoon; they were sitting on the stone seat by the fountain that played in the courtyard.

At Ellen's suggestion, since Menispe was so fascinated by horses, a tiny New Forest pony had been procured for her, and, mounted on it, breathless with excitement, she was about to undergo her first riding lesson, under the tutelage of the old coachman.

"Watch me, Mademoiselle Elène!"

"I am watching, never fear!"

Ellen had brought out a translated chapter of Germaine's novel *Ondine*, to discuss with the author. But the sun was so pleasant and the play of the fountain so lulling that they had fallen, instead, into a lazy conversation, interspersed with long stretches of silence.

"It is such a pity that Menispe was not a boy," Germaine remarked, watching the child as she valiantly grasped the reins.

"I agree that her character would have sat more comfortably on a boy. But I think I am surprised to hear you utter such a sentiment, mademoiselle? Since you advocate the equality of the sexes, what difference should it make?"

"Always ready to debate a point, you English logician!" Germaine said, laughing. "But I was thinking of it as related to the greatest good of the greatest number. Raoul passionately desires an heir. If only Menispe had been a boy, he would be content. But Arsinoë was so disgusted by the process of childbearing that I greatly fear she will not capitulate a second time. And then, only think what trouble to us all will ensue."

"It is an unhappy situation, I agree," Ellen said thoughtfully. She remembered her own mother, a small, delicate woman, badly injured by the births of Eugenia and Kitty, both of whom had been unusually large infants; weakened still more by carrying twins, of which Ellen had been the sole survivor; after the birth of Gerard, another large child, she had contracted a fever of the womb from which she never fully recovered. "One would think," Ellen went on slowly, "that, since childbearing is such a risk to women, they themselves should be the arbiters. And yet—if an heir is needed? Louise must have known that when she married? And Raoul is her husband, and she loves him?"

"Not she," said Germaine.

Ellen opened her dark eyes wide. "But my godmother told me it was the most romantic love match?"

"On his side, *bien sûr*. But on hers, no. He happened to be the first that offered; the first suitable, that is to say. It was our pact, you understand."

"Pact?"

"Our business partnership." Germaine grinned her urchin grin; then she enlightened Ellen. "Arsinoë and I were two poor girls with our way to make in the world. Both wished to become writers. But we had no money; my mother died bankrupt, my father left me a pittance only. And Louise was in the same case. The career of a female *écrivain* is far from easy, you must be aware; if you are Madame George, even! The men hate us. Jules Goncourt and his brother loathe women. Imagine it— Jules said, 'Women have never done anything remarkable, except for sleeping with a man, absorbing his moral fiber. And a virgin has never produced anything.'"

Ellen gasped, partly from shock at Germaine's freedom of expression. But Germaine, for once, was not studying Ellen's reactions. She went on vehemently, "And that artist Gavarni—whom one must admire, because he is a genius—but he, the monster, said, 'Woman is impenetrable, not because she is deep, but because she is shallow.' I repeat, the men hate us—the world is run to suit *them*, and we are beginning to threaten their ascendancy. Who controls the finances, who makes the laws, of inheritance, for example? *They* do. Why should Menispe not inherit? Because she is not a boy. But so it is—and so it will be, I daresay, for decades to come. Therefore I, and Arsinoë, decided that in this life-and-death struggle, all is fair; or, rather, that women have been used to such outrageous injustice for so long that we are entitled to any means we can find to redress the balance. We agreed—we made a pact when we were fifteen, signed in blood—that the first who could marry advantageously must do so, and then support the other on her husband's money."

"*What?*" Ellen gasped.

"It was too bad that Raoul turned out to be so unexpectedly miserly," Germaine added drily. "He seemed such an open-handed creature at first—Louise thought he would be as clay in her hand.

"But then she, as I say, is proving tediously obdurate in this matter of the heir. One should keep to one's bargains, I think. If only she would make a second attempt! Do you not think *you* might be able to persuade her, dear Callisto?"

Ellen looked at Germaine in stunned astonishment. There she sat, quite at ease, today wearing a severely simple white cashmere robe bordered with ornamental Persian work in black, and with a black velvet ribbon round her supple neck. She leaned her ash-fair head against the carved stone seat back; she looked like an angel.

With some irony, Ellen thought: And, in fact, Germaine's wishes in this matter are exactly those of my godmother. How surprised Lady Morningquest would be to hear this conversation.

"If *you* cannot persuade Louise—is it likely that *I* would be able to do so? She does not like me at all."

And Ellen was obliged to admit—but to herself, not aloud—that the lack of liking between herself and the Countess was mutual. She found Louise cold, self-centered, superior, languidly irritable, and unkind to her child; also something of a *malade imaginaire*. But, knowing now that she had been maneuvered into this marriage by her charming, dominating friend, Ellen began to feel some tinge of sympathy for the unfortunate girl. Most probably she had not in the least realized what she was taking on. Without malice, glancing at Germaine, Ellen wondered if the latter had played fair with her "business partner." Or had she taken care that Louise would be the one to accept the first eligible offer? Had she remained silent about marital chances of her own, if they did not appeal to her? Behind her apparent candor and captivating charm there lay a calculating brain.

"Oh, you are wrong there, *mon amie*; Arsinoë likes you well enough," Germaine said easily. "It is just that she is a true intellectual; mathematics, history, philosophy are to her of far more importance than personal relations. Ideas, and her own writing, have more value for her than people."

Louise's own writing, Ellen had gathered, was a theoretical work depicting a Matriarchal Age which was believed by some savants to have prevailed from 2500 BC to 1500 BC, benignly presided over by a Mother Goddess. Even the misogynistic Goncourt brothers, said Germaine, who had been privileged to see some chapters of this work, had been greatly impressed by its scope and profundity.

"Though whether she will finish it in the next twenty years…" Germaine shrugged. "There is yet much to do. But I have pointed out to her that childbearing need not affect her work. If she feels tired, she can always lie on her couch and dictate. Has not your Mrs. Gaskell produced both children and novels?"

"Yes—but—" Ellen could not feel that the cases were comparable. "If she refuses to bear Raoul another child— what can he do? Could the marriage be dissolved?"

"Possibly. But—he loves her. That would not be a desirable solution for him. And it certainly would not be for me!" She laughed ruefully. "Then *I* would be obliged to put my head into the matrimonial noose. And I assure you, my dear Callisto, that is the last thing I wish. Males are to me, as a tribe, objectionable; I have never met one whom I could consider as a mate—not even your charming Benedict! But, in any case, matters are not come to that pass yet. I daresay the la Fertés will presently hold a *conseil de famille*, and try to bring pressure to bear on my poor Arsinoë."

Raoul clattered into the courtyard in his dogcart, and, seeing Menispe, radiant on her pony, went to praise and admire her. Then he approached Ellen and Germaine. His bow was polite, but Ellen thought she detected a chill in his manner toward Mademoiselle de Rhetorée. Having heard the history of the marriage, Ellen could not find this surprising. How much about the "pact" between the two friends did Raoul know, or guess?

"Where is Louise?" he asked Germaine.

"She had one of her migraines; she was lying down. I will send to inquire how she does... Thank you for this, Callisto; it begins most promisingly. I will read it through and let you have it back tomorrow." She tapped the bundle of manuscript and strolled away with her long, leisurely stride.

"You are a writer also, Miss Paget?" Raoul asked. He sounded surprised, and far from delighted.

"No, Comte; I am merely translating some of Mademoiselle de Rhetorée's work into English for her."

"I hope she pays you," he commented rather drily.

Ellen reflected that this point had not been raised.

"I imagine that, if the work is brought out in England, I will have a share of the proceeds."

"You are no businesswoman, Miss Paget. Myself, I

would enter into no such arrangement without a hard-and-fast agreement beforehand."

"Thank you for your advice," Ellen said stiffly.

His somber face flashed into its sudden surprising smile. "Hoe your own turnips, Monsieur le Comte, is what you wish to say! But now *I* have a request to make on my own behalf. I am at present reading a novel by your Charles Dickens. Here and there my English is not adequate to understand his phrases; especially with the humorous characters; would you have the goodness, and the time, to spare me a little assistance?"

"But of course, monsieur; I shall be happy."

"You should demand payment for your time," he pointed out reprovingly.

"Why? You already pay me," said the literal Ellen.

"And I am beginning to think that you are worth considerably more than I pay you! I must confess, mademoiselle, at first I was not overjoyed at the officiousness of Lady Morningquest in foisting upon my household a *gouvernante* of whom I knew nothing—"

You thought she would be another ally for your wife, Ellen thought. But what, in fact, am I? she wondered. She began to feel decidedly sorry for the Comte. Elegant, self-assured, keen-witted—yet, visibly, young, perplexed, and vulnerable, he stood rubbing his boot toe with his carriage whip.

"Your doubts were entirely natural," Ellen assured him politely. "Indeed they did you credit."

"They are now wholly dispelled. And I think already my daughter shows signs of improvement."

Ellen could hardly agree. He had not been a witness of yesterday's screaming fit. "At least her energies are canalized," she said. "Menispe is a child of unusual—capacities, monsieur."

"Can you wonder that she is not as other children?"

he exclaimed bitterly. "Her mother has hated her from birth. If only she had been a boy!"

Ellen doubted whether this would have made the least difference to Louise's feelings. Matters might have been even worse. But she kept her opinion to herself and admonished the Comte: "Now do not you be upbraiding the poor little creature for what is none of her fault. I myself know how hard *that* is! My father never had a word or a look for me, because I was not the boy he had hoped for, after two older sisters."

"You, Miss Paget?" He looked at her with surprise. "But you are so intelligent and—forgive me—charming in appearance—how could a parent not love you? Whereas my poor little one is like a half-fledged sparrow—she will never win hearts by her looks."

He turned toward Menispe, who had been lifted from her mount and now came unsteadily toward them. She was grubby, red-faced and shiny from exertion, her flaxen hair hung in untidy wisps over her eyes. But the light of triumph shone in them. "I rode, I rode, Papa. I rode twenty times round the courtyard!"

"So you did, *chérie*! Soon we shall be out galloping together in the Bois de Boulogne!"

The child leaned contentedly against his leg and he tousled the untidy hair still further, saying, "I think you had best go in to Véronique, *ma mie*, and have her make you clean." Over her head he said to Ellen, "But indeed I do not blame the little one for what is not her fault. I—I have an affection for her. Unlike *your* father, Miss Paget—if he is really so unfeeling!"

Seven

LADY BLANCHE POMFRET HAD BECOME DECIDEDLY TIRED of her uncongenial guest. She was a woman who derived her principal pleasure from management; when her only sister was killed, and the sister's husband injured, it had been some consolation to be able to busy herself in selecting a housekeeper to look after Luke Paget's orphaned family, procuring the best surgeons and nursing attendants to care for the injured man, and arranging for his convalescence to be passed under the roof of the Bishop's Palace. But Blanche's generosity and good nature had definite limits, once the first period of activity, negotiation, and arrangement was gone by; and it quite frequently occurred that these limits had been reached before the necessity for her help was finished—as in the present case.

"It is a great trial that Luke must remain with us until the end of the month," Lady Blanche told the Bishop. "I have had quite enough of his gloomy face and surly ways, I can tell you! No wonder poor dear Adelaide was becoming so moped latterly."

"Adelaide was a feather-pate," said the Bishop. "I cannot imagine a more incompatible pair. It was characteristic of Adelaide's self-willed foolishness to marry him—a man for whom she had had a partiality at the age of sixteen!"

"But do you not think, Mr. Pomfret, that Luke might go home a few days earlier? I am sure he is well enough. And there is no doubt that he looks as if he wished himself a thousand miles from here."

"No, Blanche, he is not well enough to go home," said the Bishop firmly. "I am certain there is something holding up his recovery—he appears so haunted and hag-ridden at times. But I fear he will not confide in me. In any case, Dodd the surgeon still visits him every day—the poor man could hardly ride fifteen miles to Petworth and back. But I will take Luke off your hands this afternoon; I intend driving out to visit old Canon Fordyce at Lavant; Luke can ride with me in the carriage."

This was self-denying of the Bishop, who enjoyed his rare solitary excursions into the countryside, and would otherwise have driven himself in his gig; now he was obliged to go in the landau and take the coachman, so as to accommodate Mr. Paget and make him comfortable on the cushions. Nor did Paget seem particularly grate-ful. He made brief, perfunctory replies to such remarks as were addressed to him, and sat gloomily gazing out of the window the rest of the time.

The pastoral visit to Canon Fordyce did not take long; the aged canon was bedridden and fast becoming senile; but the visitors were then invited to partake of cake and currant wine and sit talking with the old gentleman's almost equally aged sister before they could proceed on their way.

In order to lengthen the outing, the Bishop next ordered his coachman to drive northward toward the Downs, so as to inspect a boundary of some glebe land which was under dispute; then he inquired if Luke would wish to call in on his daughter Eugenia and her husband, since Valdoe Court was only half a mile away.

"Good God, no!" replied Luke, almost grinding his teeth in the vehemence of his refusal. "Why, they are forever coming to the Palace as it is! I cannot endure Eustace Valdoe—he is such a shambling, mewing pitiful fellow. And Eugenia goes along with his shilly-shallying ways, instead of making him pull himself together."

"Oh come, come, my dear Paget," said the Bishop. "Valdoe isn't such a bad sort, you know; I like him very well. And he has had a hard time of it, setting that place to rights; his father was a shocking wastrel, I believe he left debts to the tune of fifty thousand. Whereas I hear that by retrenching and improved methods of land use, Valdoe is getting the estate into better heart."

"God knows why I ever let Adelaide arrange the match. If I had been properly informed as to his father's position I would never have sanctioned it," muttered Luke, conveniently forgetting that he had been glad to get Eugenia off his hands.

"And as our Member I believe Valdoe is beginning to make his mark," said the Bishop, unaware that he was touching on a very sore spot.

"Every time I see them, if I give her half a chance, Eugenia is on at me to let them have a little capital. Capital! As if money grew on trees!"

"I imagine that Adelaide's fortune was tied up for her own children?" inquired the Bishop delicately.

"Well; yes; most of it."

Now they passed Valdoe Court, a big old-fashioned house, flint-built, half manor, half farm, which lay on the flat fertile land halfway between Chichester and the Downs. It was surrounded by quite a little township of barns, farm buildings, and estate cottages nestling under massive old elm and ilex trees; seen from the road it looked snug and prosperous enough.

"Valdoe Court; I only wish *I* could afford to live in such style," snorted Luke. "Both my elder daughters did well enough; very well, in my opinion."

"And how does your third daughter go on—Ellen?" inquired the Bishop, measuring with his eye the sun's distance from the horizon. Blanche would not thank him if he brought Paget home before dinnertime.

"Ellen? Oh, she is residing with some count's family

in Paris; Paulina Morningquest saw fit to remove her from the school in Brussels; I daresay she will be too proud to speak to us soon."

"Should you have any objection if we passed the Cathedral on our way home?" inquired the Bishop, as they re-entered the quiet, pleasant streets of Chichester. "As you know, we intend to use the Dean's bequest on enlarging the nave, as soon as sufficient funds have been acquired by public subscription to provide all that is needed. Recently I asked my architect, Mr. Slater, to remove a part of the prebendal stalls, as a preliminary step, to discover what condition the stonework behind may be in. I fear that a great deal of repair work may be necessary, and we must know how large an outlay may be required, before making our appeal to the parishioners."

If this had been intended as a gentle hint to Mr. Paget, who was understood to be very comfortably off, it fell on deaf ears; Luke, though a punctilious churchgoer, had never been liberal in his donations, and was not about to begin now. However, he raised no objection to going round by West Street, and sat in silence as the carriage rolled over the cobbles.

A cart, with some mason's tools, was stationed on the green outside the Cathedral, and when they halted they were greeted by Mr. Slater, the architect, a thin enthusiastic young man, who led them in, along the nave, and through a litter of dismantled woodwork to where a couple of workmen were waiting.

"I am so delighted Your Grace came just now!" said Mr. Slater. "You could not have arrived at a better moment. Come and see what we have discovered: it is a Resurrection Stone! At some time it must have been removed from the west front, and built into the pier— see, there it is—doubtless in some attempt to reinforce the crumbling stonework."

"Dear me! A Resurrection Stone! What a singular misuse of such a fine piece of carving."

"No doubt they would have had to go a long way to find a slab of equal size. There is no rock in this part of the country. And, of course, at that time, the stone would have been visible here, not concealed by the choir stalls."

"Just the same, it is singular, very singular," said the Bishop, studying the bas-relief with interest. "You say it would originally have been sited outside the west door?"

"Without doubt."

"When do you suppose it was moved to its present position?"

"In the twelfth century, I would guess—see this early English string course—"

"Perhaps those early builders, in their simplicity, believed there to be some special virtue in the stone which would protect the tower from further subsidence," suggested the Bishop.

"Very possibly. But I fear their hopes were vain. Look here—and here! I do think, though, do not you, my lord, that this interesting and remarkable piece of carving should be shifted from its present position, where no one can see it, and restored to the original site?"

"Oh, by all means. Yes indeed."

"What is a Resurrection Stone?" inquired Luke, who had been listening to this exchange with some irritation and very little interest; his hip was paining him and he wished that he had sat down on one of the benches at the far end of the nave.

"Why—this is one! Come and look at it, Mr. Paget, it is really most skillfully carved"—and the enthusiastic Mr. Slater lit a couple of rush dips to illumine more clearly the corner behind the woodwork that had been exposed.

Luke Paget saw a stone slab set into the tower wall. It was perhaps five feet high by four feet wide, and was covered with elaborate carving in deep relief. The scene represented was evidently the Day of Judgment—blessed spirits, at the top of the slab, were drawing up the souls of the righteous, who were abandoning their scattered bodies like so many suits of clothes on the ground, and rising joyfully with outstretched arms to meet the angelic hosts above. Many of the faces were depicted with great liveliness and fidelity.

"In a number of ancient churches," explained the knowledgeable Mr. Slater, "there would be two slabs like this, set on either side of the west entrance, facing into the churchyard. That on the right would show the resurrection of the virtuous, and that on the left the damned being dragged down to the infernal regions. So the right-hand one was called the Resurrection Stone, and that on the left, the Doom Stone. In the days before the generality of the populace could read, the carvings would have served as salutary reminders of man's latter end, and the fate of sinners."

"This, then, is the Resurrection Stone." Despite himself, Luke was beginning to be interested. "But where is the Doom Stone?"

"It is odds but we'll find it somewhere behind there," said Mr. Slater, waving a confident hand at the prebendal stalls. "Where one is, very likely the other is not far off… Very well, then, Your Grace, I will give orders for this slab to be removed; and then, in the course of time, we will restore it to its original position by the west porch."

"Axing your pardon, sir, and Your Lordship," said an elderly workman who had listened to this exchange with a disapproving expression. "Axing your pardon, but you didn't ought to do that."

"Oh, and why not, Hoadley?"

"You ought to leave that-urr stone where 'er bides. To my way of thinking, 'twill bring larmentable bad luck if you goo shifting 'er. 'Tis an unked thing to shift a Heaven Stone; and do 'ee remember the owd saying now: 'If Chichester Church steeple do fall, In England thurr'll be no king at all!'"

"Why, you silly old man, I am quite shocked to hear you voice such superstitious nonsense—here in the Cathedral, too!" said the Bishop cheerfully. "And you might as well keep your breath to swing your crowbar, for I am resolved the stone shall come out. Besides, who says the steeple will fall? That is just what we intend to prevent, by initiating these repairs."

"The stonework certainly is in a shocking state," put in Mr. Slater. "You may see here how it has settled— look at this great crack. Subsidence has plainly been going on for at least five hundred years."

"Well, as yet no harm has come of it; we must hope and pray that the problem can be solved."

"'If Chichester Church steeple do fall, In England thurr'll be no king at all,'" reiterated Hoadley doggedly.

"Well, we haven't got a king *now*, my dear fellow—we have our excellent Prince Albert, and the dear little Queen!"

"Ill 'ull come of it—mark my words," said Hoadley.

The clock overhead chimed the third quarter.

"Good gracious me!" exclaimed the Bishop. "Lady Blanche must be wondering where we have got to. We shall be late for dinner. Good-bye for the present, my dear Slater. It is a capital thing that you have discovered that stone, and I shall look forward with interest to your unearthing its companion."

⁂

That night Luke had another of his unearthly dreams.

He was still subject to intermittent pain from his healing hip, and found it hard to lie comfortably in any position for very long. His slumbers were therefore light and broken. Moreover, the food at Lady Blanche's table, which he privately considered most unsuitably rich and indigestible, was another factor contributing to broken repose. Dreams came to him many times during a night.

On this occasion he dreamed that he saw his own heart.

He seemed to be outside himself, detached from his body, a tiny helpless witness; he saw his heart, massive as some piece of industrial machinery, towering above him, with all its workings exposed to view like a surgeon's diagram: its auricles and ventricles, its valves, sinews, ducts, and blood vessels. The valves were opening and closing, the heart pumped, the blood coursed up one side and down the other, from heart to lungs, and from lungs back to heart. Luke watched, awestruck at discovering the working of this immense complex structure laid bare to his gaze.

But then he began to observe that there was something wrong: or perhaps the heart began to change; he saw that it was made of stone, and that the stone was crumbling, was full of holes, like a great fossilized sponge. And the holes, when he looked closely, were the mouths of faces; the heart consisted of two enormous semicircular slabs that were fitted together and carved all over with images of people; on the right the people were soaring heavenward, on the left they were perpetually falling, falling, with expressions of despair and terror; he could not hear their voices but he knew they were crying out in agony. Their shrieks and wails were drowned by the thud of the great engine itself.

"But it is foretold that it must be so!" he gasped, as if somebody had uttered a protest. "The righteous shall be saved, and the doomed shall perish. The virtuous *must* be rewarded, and the sinners sent to prison. The offenders *must* be punished; they must be sent away from the presence of the righteous. But supposing the machine breaks down! It is so old! What can be done?"

He woke himself by shouting these words aloud, and

lay gasping for breath, in a strange passion of grief and terror; its cause he hardly knew. His face was wet with tears; his pulse raced; and he could not expunge from his vision the final terrible moment of his dream when the stone heart, all eroded away by time and weather, cracked clean in half, and the two parts, cascading blood or dust, had fallen away from each other.

He lay hugging his arms across his chest, as if in a desperate effort to hold himself together against dissolution.

"I am not well!" he groaned aloud. "I am not well. That confounded woman's food is bad for me. I must go home; I must go home tomorrow. I should be in my own household. This is no place for me."

He thought of his son Gerard, his life's last hope, his only bright spot. Gerard must be taken in hand without delay, he needed the utmost discipline and surveillance, for he was liable to terrible waywardness and self-indulgence, outrageous whims and starts: piano playing, natural history, reading all manner of unsuitable trash, instead of bending all his energy toward the career his father had chosen for him.

Suddenly, unaccountably, Luke remembered his other son: the son who had died at birth. Such a beautiful infant he had been! When the distraught father had been summoned to see his child, as was thought proper, before the infant Luke had been sewed into his tiny shroud, the sight had been almost unbearable: the little perfect waxen creature, lying motionless in its cot, had seemed like some calm Egyptian godling with its strangely elongated head (due to the process of birth), its face dispassionate and remote, as if the refusal to engage in life had been a moral choice, not a physical failure. The anguish of that moment, the intolerable frustration, the excruciating disappointment, had never really left him; he could still feel it as fiercely as when first experienced.

The birth of Gerard, six years later, had come almost as an anticlimax.

How old would the younger Luke have been now? he wondered, and it was not for several minutes that he recalled that the boy was Ellen's twin; she was now twenty-one, so would her brother have been. At University, doubtless, or reading for the Bar; and there would have been coming-of-age festivities. The birthday was in April; it had passed unregarded because of Luke's accident. In any case, who would wish to celebrate *that* date? For with hindsight he saw that, after the birth of the twins, Matilda's slow decline had set in.

Once, beforehand, she said to Luke, laughing, with no premonition at all, "Imagine it, *twins*! How extraordinary! It seems so bizarre to produce human beings in pairs, like socks."

"Mattie! How can you speak so?"

"How can I not?"

"But what you are saying is so—so frivolous—almost irreverent! As if you disputed the ways of Providence, Who has seen fit to bless us with two children, instead of only one."

Two sons! he had been thinking. Perhaps it will be two sons.

"Oh, no, my dear, I wouldn't dream of disputing with Providence. What would be the use? Providence always has the last word. No, I was just thinking about the twins. There they lie inside me, poor little dears, cuddled together so lovingly; no one will ever be so close to them again as they are to each other now. Do you suppose that one will be very good, and one very bad? I do hope they are *quite* different from each other—it would be rather stingy if Providence fobbed them off with one character between the two."

She had held up her clasped hands, smiling at them thoughtfully. When she smiled at very small children, or animals, or plants that she had grown herself, Mattie had a wonderfully serene, amused expression, as if she were in the confidence of the creative mind that had planned this delightful absurdity.

Later on in the day Luke had been rather scandalized to find on Mattie's dressing table a copy of a medical diagram showing the position of twins curled up in their mother's womb. Who could have supplied her with such dangerous rubbish? If it were Dr. Bendigo, he would speak a sharp word in that gentleman's ear. Just looking at such a picture might be enough to make the over-imaginative Mattie become downright morbid.

Luke cut the engraving into small pieces and carefully burned them. He did not mention what he had done to Mattie, and she never alluded to the loss of the picture.

But sometimes, strangely enough, the image of that diagram came back to him, as clearly as the one of little Luke, motionless in his cradle. Forever embraced, the embryonic twins clung to each other, like the two halves of his heart in the dream.

Eight

ELLEN SOON FOUND THAT HER TIME AT THE HÔTEL Caudebec was very fully occupied. She worked on Germaine's manuscript, she read with the Comte, she taught, as best she could, little Menispe, and took her for outings. The only person, in fact, with whom she had very few dealings at all was her pupil's mother, who continued aloof, and, Ellen thought, somewhat hostile.

"You are growing quite a literary character, Miss Paget, I gather," Louise remarked acidly one afternoon, discovering Ellen at work on Germaine's manuscript in the sunny courtyard while Menispe took her riding lesson. "My husband has nothing but praise for your rendering of Dickens. For him, it is like looking into Chapman's Homer." Fleetingly Ellen wondered why the Comte had not asked his wife to elucidate the difficulties of Dickens. "Raoul is becoming quite a changed character," Louise went on. "We see so much more of him these days!"

She did not sound gratified by the change; indeed the irony in her tone was unmistakable. For a moment Ellen, overwhelmed by irritation, was on the point of snapping at her: I am not neglecting your wretched child! She is probably receiving more attention than ever before. Nor am I flirting with your husband—though I can't imagine why you should object if I did.

But, restraining herself, she recalled that one of Lady Morningquest's reasons for introducing her into the house was to be a friend to Louise; in which aim so far she had signally failed. Unfortunately Louise did not appear to require her friendship, though it took no perspicacity to see that all was not well with the Countess. She was paler, frailer than ever; elegantly dressed for walking in black-and-white muslin and a straw hat with yellow roses, she looked wraithlike; the hand holding the lace parasol was pitifully thin, and shook slightly. Despite her annoyance, Ellen could not help feeling sympathy toward the poor girl. She had, after all, involved herself in the pact with Germaine when still a child; and she was still very young, and in far deeper waters than she had reckoned on.

I must try harder to win her confidence, Ellen resolved, not for the first time.

She said gently, "Menispe does not suffer because of the other things I do, Countess. Indeed, I think if you were to visit the schoolroom, you would be impressed by her gift of moving to music, and her drawings of horses—"

"Oh, very likely—I daresay—" Louise, impatient, distrait, glanced up at the clock tower over the stable archway. Its hands pointed to three o'clock. "I am sure you do your best with the child—I don't criticize you. What can have become of Mademoiselle de Rhetorée, I wonder?"

Ellen, as she continued to wait and to fidget, said, with a good deal of diffidence, "Countess, if I made sure that Menispe was happily occupied at the time, would it be permissible, perhaps, for me to be present at one of your salons? Ger—Mademoiselle de Rhetorée's descriptions have, I confess, given me a great curiosity to hear some of the disputations—"

Louise glanced her way in surprise. For an instant the mask of ice appeared to crack—a human being looked out. Then she replied in a colorless tone, "Why, certainly, my dear girl—if you are so interested? Come when you choose. The child can be with Véronique, having her *goûter*—I daresay it makes little difference—"

"Thank you, Countess." Mastering another upsurge of annoyance, Ellen turned to meet Menispe, who had just dismounted.

"If you are going into the house," Louise said, "and should encounter Mademoiselle de Rhetorée, perhaps you would be good enough to remind her that she and I had arranged to go to Mrs. Clarke's this afternoon."

"Of course," Ellen said.

Germaine was easily discovered in the library. This was a handsomely appointed ground-floor room, which had been stocked with rare books by Raoul's father, and was now devotedly looked after by an elderly cousin, the Abbé Grandville. It was one of Germaine's favorite haunts; indeed she had once said to Ellen, with a wicked grin, "As soon as I heard about this collection I told Louise that she *must* marry into the la Ferté family."

Raising her head from a magnificently illustrated *Decameron*, she said pettishly now, "To Mary Ann Clarke's? That dowdy old Englishwoman who thinks she conducts a salon? What a bore! Why cannot Louise go on her own?"

"She is waiting for you," said Ellen.

"Oh—pfui!" Then she glanced sideways, laughing. "Now, if it had been *you* who asked me—"

Leisurely, she picked up her hat and removed herself from the room.

❧

Ellen had learned to swim at the age of eight. This was a rare accomplishment, shared, she found later, by none of her colleagues at the Pensionnat. It had come about—like many other blessings—from her friendship with Dr. Bendigo. In warm Septembers the family of a gypsy named Pharaoh Lee would come and settle for a month on the sunny side of the Downs at Eartham, whittling hazel wands for clothes-pegs. Dr. Bendigo, on cordial terms with the tribe, would borrow little Selina Lee, who was the same age as Ellen, and take the two children to the sea, where he encouraged them to race on the sands and splash in the still-warm water. Selina seemed to have been able to swim since she was born; she and Dr. Bendigo rapidly taught the art to Ellen.

Remembering those days, she sometimes wondered which she missed more: the affectionate, unfettered dialogue with the old man or the physical bliss of running free on the sands, swimming in the buoyant water. In dreams she found herself riding on the cracked leather seat, lulled by the regular clip-clop of old Dobbin ahead, putting some question to the doctor, waiting for his thoughtful measured reply. Or she would be in the sea-green swell off Selsea—where she and Selina might swim only on calm days, for there was a dangerous undertow—drifting up and down between smooth glassy rollers, effortlessly floating.

Now—unexpectedly—in the white-and-gold music room of the Hôtel Caudebec, Ellen found herself reminded of both her happiest memories. The exhilarating lift and flow of the talk that surged about the room seemed akin to the joy of swimming, of running barefoot.

How in the world could she ever have guessed that she would owe this to Louise de la Ferté?

The Thursday salons at the Hôtel Caudebec always opened with a formal discussion on some elevating theme, ethical or technical: Why should moral suffering be considered more interesting than physical? Which should be of paramount importance to the writer, the thought or the phrase? Sometimes a work, classic or contemporary, would be read aloud, and then discussed by the assembly.

This first, organized, part of the evening was, by some

of those present, considered a shocking bore, but Louise deemed it essential to establish a dignified tone, break the ice, and put the guests in the right mood, lively but not malicious, for the general conversation which then followed. The change to the latter stage was signaled by the handing round of refreshments—which were always extremely modest, due, it was whispered, to the Comte's parsimony—tea, wafers, and sorbet.

Then, after a few hesitating moments, the real business of the evening would start; talk would break out, sporadic, becoming torrential; voices would grow louder (though never loud to the point of ill-breeding— the room was too large, and too beautiful, to encourage any raucousness); faces became intent, gestures liberated, groups divided, re-formed, and split again, as friends and rivals observed and sought each other; talk ran like a river, ideas bounded like drops of spray, and through the midst of it all Louise de la Ferté, in command of all this animation, moved about, calmly enjoying and directing it like the master of ceremonies at some great firework display.

Who would ever have thought it? Ellen wondered, watching Louise in amazement; she seemed less to participate than to enjoy her power as directress, escorting learned old ladies to meet ethereal young poets, introducing cynical, careworn critics to aspiring playwrights, listening with every appearance of sympathy to earnest talkers while her eye roved, ceaselessly, capably, round the room, making certain that nobody felt left out or slighted, that arguments did not become rancorous, that no vulgarity or personal vendettas were allowed to cloud the atmosphere.

I don't believe Louise will ever be a writer, Ellen said to herself (for Germaine had showed her some pages of the *Treatise on the Golden Age of Gynautocracy* and, unlike the Goncourt brothers—perhaps they were just being polite?—she had found it turgid, over-romantic, and muddled), but for this kind of thing she certainly has a genius. It is plainly what she was made for.

In no time Louise had noticed Ellen lingering diffidently near the entrance, and had, like a hard-working sheep dog, rounded her up and introduced her to a dowdy old lady, the Duchesse de Quelquechose, who had a piercing eye, a bristling mustache, a priceless cap of Mechlin lace; this lady rapidly turned Ellen's brain inside out, analyzed and rearranged its contents, before drawing into their conversation a large undistinguished-looking man with prominent eyes, red weather-beaten face, and drooping mustaches, who just then drew near.

("It is M. Flaubert," she rapidly confided to Ellen. "He is a very unsociable fellow, he hates coming to these affairs, but he comes, nevertheless, because he can't resist talking to me about writing; he knows I will enlarge his ideas.")

M. Flaubert appeared mulishly reluctant to be subjected to this process, but he was no match for the Duchesse; she soon had him involved in a rattling discussion with a tall, well-built, gray-haired man in a trim frock coat who turned out to be the cartoonist Gavarni, so much detested by Germaine de Rhetorée for his opinion of women. "Just the same, a man of genius," Germaine said irritably, and Ellen could only agree, as the talk leaped exuberantly from Cartesian philosophy to higher mathematics—"the music of numbers"—and back to writing. Could this, Ellen wondered, be the Flaubert who wrote *Memoires d'un Fou*? He seemed so very rustic, unlike her idea of a writer. But yes, it was he.

"The *plot*," he was saying, "is of no interest to me. When working on a novel, my aim is to produce a tone, a color. My Carthaginian novel, for example, will be purple. In *Madame Bovary*, I wanted a dove-gray mole color. I didn't give a rap about the story. Why, just a few days before I began, I still thought Emma was going to be a pious old spinster. But that would never have done for a heroine. *Would it?*" He rounded on Ellen, fixing her with a bulbous, bloodshot eye, and she surprised herself by replying, "Possibly not for you, monsieur, but I fail to see why such a character might not serve as the subject for another writer. The obstinacy of some saintly old lady might easily drive a whole community into difficulties."

"Very good, child," said the Duchesse. "Saintliness can be a much more troublesome attribute than wickedness. Everybody knows, in theory, how to deal with sin. Whereas saints are nothing but a nuisance."

"My God, yes!" remarked Gavarni, with a sour look at Ellen. "England is full of them. It is a wonder that any fiction may be published there; especially when you consider the national drink. Le gin du pays!"

They were joined by a heavy-faced, weary-eyed man, who kept yawning and interrupting Flaubert in his discussion of style, to say, "Pardon me, *mon cher*, but form *inevitably* gives birth to thought."

"Isn't that what I was saying?"

"I have always, always hated writing. It is so useless! Ahhh! Excuse my yawns, I have been at my desk since six-thirty this morning. But writing now…I never think what I am going to say; I toss the phrases into the air as if they were kittens; and they always come down on their feet—"

"And then you give them a saucer of cream, my dear Théo," said the Duchesse.

The talk bounced to Edgar Allan Poe, a writer unknown to Ellen.

"Marvelous! A marvelous innovator!" Gavarni was saying. "He is something wholly new—you mark my words, this will be the literature of the twentieth century! Science at last embodied in miraculous prose—the fabulation of A plus B—"

"But *objects* in his writing play a greater part than humans," objected Flaubert. "That cannot be right."

"That *is* good, that *is* right! Humans have had their day—emotions should now give place to statistics."

"But if you listen only to the brain, never to the heart," objected the Duchesse, "the human race will die out."

"And a good thing too!"

Ellen resolved to procure the works of Poe. Almost certainly Germaine would have them.

At this moment Germaine herself strolled up and drew Ellen away.

"Good that you have found your way here at last, *mon amie*! (And that blue becomes you excellently, you look like a wild hyacinth.) Now come and meet Matilde, whom you will love; she resembles everybody's kind aunt."

Ellen went a little reluctantly. Matilda had been her mother's name; she was not sure that she wanted to meet another. And she had been enjoying the conversation of the Duchesse's group.

But the Matilde in question, at the center of another lively circle, greeted Ellen with the utmost friendliness. She was, just like her description, a dumpy woman with a broad, sweet, kindly smile and a peering, shortsighted expression. She asked innumerable questions about the writings of Mrs. Gaskell, Currer Bell, and George Eliot. The latter Ellen knew to be female—"I believe she was the assistant editor of the *Westminster Review*, and has just produced a new novel, *Adam Bede*"; about Currer Bell she was not so certain, save that she believed the writer to have died some three or four years ago.

"And was it this Bell who wrote *Les Hauts de Hurlement*?"

No, Ellen understood that to be another, related Bell.

"For my part," said Germaine, "I am sure they are

both women. Who but a woman could write *Jane Eyre*? And I admire her with my whole heart."

Ellen's attention wandered a moment; she heard Flaubert exclaim, "Theatre criticism? It's easy. You swallow a couple of absinthes in the foyer bar, then write, 'The play isn't bad but needs cutting.' Every play does. Last time I went to the Comédie, I sat next to two women who were telling each other all the way through what would happen next. Of course that's what's wanted, in boulevard theatre—for the audience to be able to guess what's coming."

Madame Matilde said very kindly to Ellen, "I shall hope to see you at *my* house. Camille, here, will bring you: Wednesdays, every alternate week. I shall tell my friend Madame de Fly to send you a formal invitation."

"Thank you, madame," murmured Ellen, impressed by the mix of authority and grace in her manner; who could she be? "I shall be happy—that is, if the Comtesse de la Ferté can spare me."

With a smiling salutation the lady took herself off.

"Who is she?" Ellen asked Germaine.

"Princess Matilde, the Emperor's cousin; she married Prince Demidoff, a Russian nobleman, but the marriage failed, and they separated."

"That was Napoleon's cousin? The daughter of the King of Westphalia? Why in the world did you not warn me?"

"Oh, she makes nothing of her rank; she is quite *du peuple*; and her house is the most comfortable, informal place in the world. We'll go there sometime and listen to Madame de Fly reading aloud."

Soon after this, Raoul de la Ferté came into the room. The company had thinned after the Princess's departure; a number of the men left, murmuring about a meeting at Magny's; and the arrival of the Comte, like a hawk drifting over a chicken run, was enough, it seemed, to disperse the rest of the guests. Yet why? Ellen wondered. He did not appear formidable; in fact he seemed quite sorry to see everyone go. Germaine was among those departing; she kissed her hand to Ellen, and called, "You made a great hit with Théo Gautier! He called you Mademoiselle Myosotis! *A bientôt, mon vieux*—" and she drifted out.

Suddenly the temperature in the round room shot down. Ellen, exhilarated, confused, depressed, made haste to express her thanks to Louise, who looked fatigued and distrait, curtsey to the Comte, and take herself away to the solitary but exquisitely served meal which would be brought to her in her own quarters.

She wondered how the la Fertés would spend the rest of the evening.

&

Ellen did not attend all the soirees in the round music room. Whether she did so was contingent on three factors: her own conscience, little Menispe's behavior during the preceding days, and the demeanor of Louise. Sometimes, if Menispe had been noticeably troublesome, or Louise especially unamiable, she judged it best to stay away. If the domestic climate in the Hôtel Caudebec were particularly acrimonious, Ellen felt it more prudent to keep within the bounds usually ascribed to a governess.

During the month of July, however, the domestic climate remained mild. Raoul held far fewer gambling parties. "All his friends are out of town, that is why," said Germaine. Louise applied herself with zeal to the history of the Era of Matriarchy, passing whole days in the library, where she kept the disapproving old Abbé Grandville hard at work looking up references and taking down dusty volumes. Not infrequently, though, she paid for this diligence by migraines, which were spoken of with awe throughout the household.

"*La pauvre*," said Véronique. "When she is thus afflicted she can hardly see—and she is in such pain! I have known Michon spend whole days putting ice on her brow. *C'est affreux*. But what would you? *Le bon dieu* did not intend ladies to study so hard at books."

Intermittently attending the salons in the music room (writers, it appeared, were not so prone to leave Paris during the summer, since, unlike Raoul's fashionable friends, they had no money and no country houses), Ellen became better acquainted with, and more irresistibly fascinated by, the literary panorama that was spread out before her. And not only literary—representatives from the worlds of music, drama, and art also made their appearance in the Hôtel Caudebec. Pauline Viardot, the ugly bewitching singer, currently using her "bitter orange" voice in Gluck's *Orphée*, was to be met there; and Ivan Turgenev, a huge, good-looking, untidy Russian writer, Pauline's faithful adorer, who followed wherever she went; the composer Gounod; the critic Sainte-Beuve, a little, round, cheerful man, dressed in rough country clothes, his large bald forehead and bulging eyes counterbalanced by a wide, smiling, kindly mouth; there was the poet Baudelaire, an extraordinary-looking individual with hair cropped short like a convict's, always shabby, in threadbare clothes without cravat or vest—he had haunted eyes and a voice like a musical saw; there was Teresa, singer of burlesques at the Alcazar; Madame Allan, the chief comedienne at the Comédie-Française, who had a loud croaking voice like a frog; Natalie, actress at the Gymnase; Jeanne de Tourbey, a woman of extremely doubtful reputation, who held a salon of her own, was witty, fascinating, and a great friend of Germaine; there were dozens of other writers—the younger Dumas, Feydeau, Xavier Forneret, Lassailly the journalist, Aurélien Scholl, and a quiet bearded man, Dr. Philippe

Ricord, who seemed to know everybody, and to have critical opinions about everything.

"He knows all the men here intimately," whispered Germaine, pointing out the doctor, "because they all have social diseases for which he treats them. He is a syphilis specialist."

Here was another word to be added to Ellen's rapidly growing vocabulary, and another startling concept for her extending range of ideas. Germaine added, "All these men sleep with prostitutes, of course; why, it is said that Baudelaire and Sainte-Beuve regularly meet on the same stairway; so I strongly advise *you*, Callisto, not to go to bed with *any* of them; unless you adhere to Edmond Goncourt's theory that mental perceptions, like the pox, can never be acquired by a woman save through contact with a man."

And she strolled off among the guests, leaving Ellen almost paralyzed by shock.

That such things could even pass through people's minds, let alone be freely expressed in words!

But she was beginning to be accustomed to this astonishing freedom of thought and expression, so different from the atmosphere at home. Possibly in London there might be found sections of society where such opinions as could be heard here were current, and permissible; but in the small English country town where Ellen's childhood had been passed, characters like Flaubert, Sainte-Beuve, and Baudelaire would be hardly conceivable; they would be regarded with outrage and horror as emissaries of the devil himself. Nor had the propriety of Madame's Pensionnat in any way prepared Ellen's mind for what she was to encounter in Paris. Notwithstanding which, this liberal, free-thinking climate suited her wonderfully well; she could almost feel her faculties expanding, day by day.

George Sand, when she finally visited the rue de

l'Arbre Vert, was something of a disappointment; after Germaine's enthusiastic descriptions, Ellen had expected a kind of fiery Muse, something much more dazzling than this sober, homely lady in gray serge gown and jacket with plain linen collar and sleeves, who talked, slowly and pontifically in a flat monotonous voice, about politics and the conditions of work among the 150,000 female operatives in Paris. She had, moreover, a double chin, a sallow complexion, and muddy eyes. Ellen remembered Baudelaire's vitriolic comment the week before: "She is heavy, stupid, garrulous; she has about as much depth of judgment as the average concierge. *Sapristi!* I can't even *think* of the stupid woman without a shudder—she's one of those aging ingénues who refuse to leave the stage. If she is coming, I shall stay away—I couldn't refrain from throwing a basin of holy water at her head."

Ellen wondered that the author of *Elle et Lui* should be so very prim, so very sedate; now if *she* appeared in Petworth, Sussex, everybody would take her for a wealthy brewer's widow.

Nevertheless, one must acknowledge that Madame Dudevant's writing style was superior; far superior to that of some other frequenters of the la Ferté salon, such as Lassailly, who had the hero of one of his stories kill his mistress by tickling her feet; or Forneret, whose hero committed suicide by swallowing his mistress's eyeball.

If *I* ever write a novel, thought Ellen—for at some point the idea had become lodged in her mind—if *I* wrote a romance, I should take George Sand for my model rather than that rocambolesque rubbish.

But of course I would have to acquire a great deal more experience before I wrote anything...

Lacking experience she might be, but she often went to bed, after these evenings, so dazzled and ablaze with ideas that it might be hours before she slept. Phrases would recur; Flaubert shouting: "A publisher

may exploit you, but he has no right to *judge* you!";
Sainte-Beuve making some devastating pronouncement:
"Balzac may have been a man of genius but he was also
a monster!"; Théo Gautier, lit up at the end of a lively
evening, dancing a ridiculous pas seul, "the dance of
the Creditor"; Flaubert arguing with Feydeau about
repetitions in writing: "Tautology is to be avoided *at all
costs*—even if you have to spend a week searching for a
synonym"; Baudelaire telling some extraordinary story—
the man who fell in love with his friend's mistress, and,
so as to avoid any risk of engaging her affection, shaved
off his hair, beard, mustache, and eyebrows—"*There* is
true, disinterested friendship for you!"; or a strange game
the company played sometimes when Turgenev and
Pauline Viardot were present, in which Turgenev, who
had unexpected talent as an artist, drew little portrait
heads on bits of paper, and everybody present wrote
analytical descriptions of the imaginary persons depicted.

"Paris is certainly changing you, Callisto," said
Germaine one day. "Not so much the new plumage,
though it is charming—"

"How, then?"

"When I look into your eyes now, I think they are
like deep, deep wells; I gaze and gaze, and it is like a road
without an end; the distance is concealed in mystery.
There are hidden depths—you are expanding inwardly!"

"Perhaps I shall explode." Ellen met the smiling intent
scrutiny more composedly than she would have a month
ago; she was learning to keep her feet in this new life.

"When the explosion comes, it will be interesting.
Are you about to take Menispe for her outing?"

"Yes, she has to go to the dentist, poor child."

Raoul's mother, the Dowager Comtesse, had come
from Rome, where she lived because of her health. She
was staying in Paris for a week, to take part in the *conseil
de famille* regarding the marital situation of Louise and

Raoul which was shortly to be held. The Dowager was a formidable little lady, small, of the utmost icy elegance, with an eye that missed nothing. At first she had viewed Ellen with considerable suspicion and reserve, but after twenty-four hours this had given way to a qualified approval; Menispe had, she conceded, learned a few things in the past months and appeared to be a fraction less ungovernable. But the poor child's teeth were shockingly irregular; what could Louise be about, to let them get into such a state? Her granddaughter must immediately attend a dentist in the rue de Rivoli. Thither, accordingly, Ellen and her charge were bound, Menispe cooperative only because she did not understand what was in store for her.

"I will accompany you," Germaine said. "I have to go to my apartment, for I left there a story by Allan Poe which Arsinoë wishes to read. You may come with me, if you wish?"

Ellen had never been to Germaine's apartment. She had had the intention of remaining to keep an eye on Menispe at the dentist's; but the latter said that he and his nurse could manage the child better on their own; they were quite accustomed to dealing with patients of a tender age, and Menispe would be completely safe and happy. Doubting this, Ellen had, however, no option but to agree. She ordered the coachman to return in an hour's time, and set out to walk with Germaine to her apartment in the Passage Langlade.

Familiar with the opulence of the rue de Rivoli and its handsome shop fronts, Ellen was startled to find what a sinister and shabby network of small streets lay so close to this center of industry and fashion. Dark, ill-paved, and muddy, even at this season, stinking from household refuse, the neighborhood seemed like the exposed viscera of a live body that has been slashed open; things were exposed to view that should have been concealed.

As the two girls picked their way over irregular cobbles—"I don't suppose you expected that I would live in a place like this?" Germaine remarked mockingly.

The house in which she dwelt was formidably high, but lacked depth; a narrow stair climbed back and forth inside the street wall, feebly illuminated by a minute window at each landing. Every floor held a two-room apartment; that of Germaine was the attic, five floors up. One room had a bed, one was the kitchen, and for water she went down to a sink on the floor below. Ellen gazed appalled at the worn, broken red tiles, half covered by a threadbare carpet; at the single armchair upholstered in greasy canvas; at the wooden cot over which was thrown a stained calico coverlet; the dirty wallpaper; the cracked windowpane plugged with a folded issue of *Le Siècle*; the bundle of firewood, the dirty pots in front of the fireplace; the clothes hung on a nail; the dingy mahogany table littered with papers.

"Can you wonder that I spend as much time as possible at the Hôtel Caudebec?" demanded Germaine with a wry mouth, picking up a manuscript and a folded newspaper from the table. "Oh, don't worry! You are not likely to contract some disagreeable infection—so long as you stand perfectly still in the middle of the room and don't breathe too deeply... There—that is all we came for, now we can pick our way back to civilization. Oh, but just one instant, let me make certain—"

She pulled up a loose floorboard and removed from the cavity underneath an object that turned Ellen pale with fright.

"A pistol!"

"Yes, it is one of those new revolving pistols with six chambers," Germaine informed her with nonchalance. "See, the lock works like this, and the barrel rotates so. Do not worry, I will not point it at you, *ma chère!*" She restored it to its hiding place.

"But—good God—how do you come to possess such an article?"

"Well, you see, this is not a very respectable house. And the lock on my door got broken, and the landlord is extremely negligent about repairing it."

In fact it was plain that the door had been smashed in at some time; there were deep gouges on the outer surface, and it hung by one hinge.

"Are you not afraid to stay here alone?"

"Not a bit; but naturally I prefer the rue de l'Arbre Vert," said Germaine, briskly going ahead of Ellen down the dark stone stair. "Take care—it is quite slippery just here where the water escapes from the basin—"

She nodded amiably to the concierge, a terrible toothless old woman who sat mumbling in a kind of niche at the stair foot, and again to the wine merchant who kept the ground-floor shop. "I would offer you a glass of wine here—it is not bad, and exceedingly cheap—but I daresay you would rather return to the rue de Rivoli."

As they emerged from the doorway, Ellen, glancing along the sordid street, saw a young man who looked remarkably like Raoul de la Ferté turn in at yet another of the dark entrances. *Was* it Raoul? But Paris was full of such handsomely dressed young men. She did not mention the matter to Germaine.

"Can you not afford better quarters?" she demanded bluntly as they turned into a wider and less fetid-smelling thoroughfare.

"You are thinking of that novel I sold to *Le Siècle*? The three hundred francs? But you see, alas, I was obliged to borrow from a moneylender when my family cut me off"—Germaine, Ellen knew, had been brought up by an uncle after her parents died—"and the man's rates of interest are quite extortionate. So I am still in debt—what a nuisance it all is! Still, don't look so horrified. That ridiculous little man Ponsard was last year awarded a government pension of 25,000 francs; why should some such windfall not come my way?"

She grinned at Ellen. They had by now arrived at the dentist's, and the carriage stood waiting. "You are such a sweet innocent, Callisto. Don't look so troubled! I manage well enough... Do you know, I had thoughts of making love to you just now—but I saw that it would not do. In my poor little chamber you seemed too incongruous. You have such a perplexing charm, you woodland nymph—no wonder that poor Benedict is so *bouleversé* about you—wayward, provoking creature that you are!" She raised her brows mockingly at Ellen's expression, and added, "I think I will not accompany you back to the Hôtel Caudebec just at present. I must find— never mind! And I have a disinclination for the company of Menispe—who, I daresay, will be in a very *mauvaise humeur* after the tooth-puller's attentions. Do you, my dear Callisto, give these to Arsinoë. I will see you later on at the soiree—where I have a surprise for you. *A bientôt!*" And she gave Ellen the papers, then sauntered off into the crowd, kissing her hand airily as she went.

Wholly disconcerted, Ellen stared after her. Could those remarks have been serious? Surely not. She had been teasing—but why? More and more, latterly, Ellen had the impression that Germaine was trying to manipulate her in some way; was making use of her; that every action, almost every word was calculated to a particular end. This trip to the wretched apartment in the Passage Langlade—what was the purpose of that? To make evident to Ellen the real and desperate need that Germaine had for the help she received from Louise? To enlist Ellen's sympathy and support before the la Ferté family council? But what use will that be? thought Ellen. I shall not be present at the council; my opinion certainly will not be sought... How can she bear to live in that stinking den? It was not only squalid, it was *frightening*.

Surely—however poor she is—she could find better quarters than that?

Little Menispe, after her ordeal at the dentist's, proved unwontedly subdued; apparently the surgeon and his nurse had been a match for her. Tearstained, taciturn, she huddled against Ellen in the carriage like a small wild animal which has only just managed to elude pursuers and reach its burrow. Ellen had planned a visit to Tortoni's, for consolatory ices, but saw this would not do, so told the coachman to drive straight home.

As they bowled along the handsome streets, and the mild summer air blew against them, Ellen looked about her with a different vision. She was becoming more and more attached to Paris; its glitter, its gaiety, its angular antique beauty, its modern elegance, the superb style of its fashionable women, and the free-ranging intellects of its men, had answered a deep need in her. Yet now she realized her view of the city had been a superficial one— as had been her first notion of Germaine de Rhetorée. There were subterranean regions under the bright surface. If I am to understand Paris thoroughly, thought Ellen, I must know the dark as well as the light.

❧

Waiting at home was a letter from her middle sister, Mrs. Bracegirdle.

Imagine it! Miserly old B. had to attend a conference of manufacturers in London, so actually brought me with him, in order not to forgo a chance of my acquiring household linen cheap in summer sales. I was able, therefore, to go down into Sussex and pass a night at the Hermitage, for I had received alarming accounts from Eugenia regarding Papa's new housekeeper. My dear Ellen—matters are quite as bad as E. represents—if not worse! The woman,

Mrs. Pike, is odious—*encroaching, sly, sickeningly condescending, with an eye like a fishhook and a voice like a ratchet! Papa permits her to deal with all household affairs, and she is undoubtedly feathering her own nest as fast as she is able. Pa continues stingy as ever (it is no wonder that he and Lady Adelaide found me a husband like B.). The household accounts cd be written on thread paper. Pa seems well enough recovered from his Accident, tho' he still has a decided limp. He is morose, taciturn, and more disagreeable than ever; also— which he never was before—afflicted by a strange, visionary fancy, somehow related to a stone that was dug up in Chichester Cathedral, and his past activities as a Justice of the Peace in judging criminals. I confess I did not make much effort to understand it. This Maggot in his Mind makes him no easier to live with—he and Gerard were at continual odds. Gerard had been taking pianoforte lessons from old Gotobed the church organist—which put Pa in a passion—since Ld Chesterfield said piano playing was no occupation for a gentleman, an observation quoted by Pa at every meal. Also, Gerard has struck up a friendship with Dr. Bendigo and, through him, made the acquaintance of some wholly undesirable personage, a shepherd, or gamekeeper, or some such. Naturally, Pa forbade the association, but G. is excessively hard to control; he slips away like quicksilver. He is just as sullen and uncouth as ever. School wd do him a World of good, but the Dr. still thinks it wd impair his health.*

I called on Aunt Fanny but she was not at home; out, I was given to understand, at some Cottager's bedside. She and Gerard are two of a kind.

But, my dear Ellie, the main burden of my letter is this: Eugenia and I are seriously apprehensive

*of the possibility that Pa will take this odious Mrs.
Pike for his third wife! There are but too many
indications of this.*

You know Papa's nature [before "nature"
another word had been many times scratched
out; evidently Kitty had had second thoughts
about some attribute of her father which Ellen,
as an unmarried girl, could not be supposed to
comprehend]—*he is not a man to live patiently
without connubial connection* [Kitty went on
more confidently]. *His glances, his gestures, demonstrate a growing infatuation all too clearly. And,
Ellen, it wd be a shocking misalliance! The woman
is far from being a lady, it wd sink our family in the
estimation of every person of quality in the county.
She is vulgar, low-natured, and scheming. Gerard
and Vicky both detest her. Further, there is a story
that she has a child, or children (so Eugenia says);
where they are is not known, but you may imagine
that, once she had Pa in her toils, they wd soon be
installed. And consider the inheritance! It would be
outrageous if Mama's fortune were to be willed away
from her own children to this Hateful woman and
her low Brood. Yet, if she got her clutches on Papa,
that might well happen.*

*Therefore, my dear Ellen, it is your plain Duty
to give up this position in Paris and return to
Sussex. In any case you are best away from such a
disgracefully licentious city. Benedict Masham (who,
by the bye, passed his final examinations with great
credit) lately visited the Radnors at Matlock Chase,
and rode over to pay his respects. He gave me to
understand that the household in which you reside
leaves a great deal to be desired. What can Aunt
Morningquest have been thinking of, to place you
there? But such great folk consult only their own*

convenience. *Do, pray, Ellie, leave Paris at once
and return home—I truly believe that the future
comfort of our family depends on you! And Paris is
no place for a girl your age—you will never find a
respectable man to marry you once it is known that
you have made any considerable sojourn there.*

Yr affec. Sister,
Catherine Bracegirdle

Ellen could not withhold a smile as she read this artless
missive. It was plain that Kitty, married to a parsimonious,
Dissenting ironmaster, living in a small Derbyshire manu-
facturing town, strongly begrudged her younger sister's
freedom and independence in Paris, and wished to deprive
her of the pleasures pertaining to such an existence. Ellen
was not swayed in the least by Kitty's argument about their
mother's money. Matilda had wished this to be portioned
out between her three daughters after their father's death,
but there were no legal bonds constraining Luke to do this.
Kitty and Eugenia evidently placed considerable dependence on the future acquisition of their mother's fortune;
Ellen, now that she had been put in the way of earning
her own living, gave it less importance. Still, she thought,
sighing, perhaps it is selfish in me not to make some push
to rescue Kitty and Eugenia's portions. Only how could
I set about it? If I did return to the Hermitage—where I
should be wholly unwelcome—how could I make any
attempt to detach Papa from this female, if he is set on
marrying her? I am indeed sorry for Gerard and Vicky,
if they are unhappy, but I have no power to dismiss Mrs.
Pike, unless she be caught in any actual wrongdoing. And
to conduct a kind of inquisition into her dealings would
be most repugnant. Besides, I cannot keep guard over
Papa forever. If he is resolved on marriage, he is certain to
achieve it, sooner or later.

As for Benedict, she thought, glancing at the final paragraph of the letter once more, as for Benedict, I hope he is soon dispatched to Pernambuco or Trincomalee! What gives *him* the right to meddle in my affairs? Household in which I am living leaves much to be desired! Insufferable impertinence! Odious interference! I daresay it is due to that officious call of his that Kitty paid her visit to the Hermitage; otherwise I am sure she would prefer to remain in London while she had the chance. And what moved Benedict to call on Kitty? He always detested her.

Now Ellen recalled again Germaine's astonishing comment: "No wonder that poor Benedict is so *bouleversé* about you." Could that, conceivably, be true? But no, Ellen knew better—she and Benedict had been on such hostile terms for so long—since that unfortunate affair of Dolly Randall—that she could not possibly be mistaken in the matter. Germaine must have spoken ironically.

Feeling decidedly ruffled, Ellen consigned the tearful, sleepy Menispe to her bonne for early supper and bed, then carried the feuilleton of Poe's story to Louise in her golden boudoir, where she reported that the trip to the dentist had been successfully achieved.

"*Très bien*," yawned Louise indifferently. "No doubt my *belle-mère* will be delighted. Thanks, Miss Paget... You will be attending the soiree tonight?"

"Is there to be one?" Ellen was surprised. "I had thought—while the Dowager Comtesse was in Paris—"

"That old trout? I do not intend to let my intellectual activities be curtailed by *her* presence. Of course there will be a soiree, as usual. (Fortunately the old Comtesse will be dining with a whole concourse of stuffy relatives in the rue St. Honoré. Raoul wished me to go, but"— she shrugged—"I said it was out of the question.) No, I asked if you would attend this evening because I am given to understand by Camille that an acquaintance of yours, from Brussels, may be there—a Professor Bosch, de Bosch, some such name?"

To her own astonishment Ellen felt a wave of heat sweep over her, from toes to scalp; she almost fainted at the intensity and suddenness of the sensation. Murmuring some brief acknowledgment, she got herself out of the room; Louise, absorbed in the Poe story, hardly noticed her going.

Back in her own room Ellen attempted to analyze the surprising turmoil of her own emotions. If she had been able to weep, she would have done so now—and yet she hardly knew why. She had imagined that the strength of her feeling for Monsieur Patrice was gone by; dwindled to a mere affectionate regard, overlaid by all the new impressions that occupied her mind. She had indeed thought about him less; there had been so much to distract her. Yet, all the time, the suppressed feeling had, it seemed, been growing; fed, not stifled, by these new perceptions. She felt herself suffused by a fierce longing to see him. And yet how could she bear to, so briefly, and in a room filled with other people, strangers? It would be torture. How could she bear to watch him conversing, making himself agreeable, to others—to Louise, Germaine, Princess Matilde, Madame Viardot? He was a great devote of opera, doubtless he would have seized the opportunity to hear Viardot in her current role of Orphée. Sudden fierce jealousy, an emotion hitherto unknown to Ellen, almost overwhelmed her. What *can* be happening to me? she asked herself in despair. These feelings are disgusting— uncalled for—it is ludicrous that I should entertain them for a single minute.

Yet she felt them; and felt, too, a deep resentment against Germaine de Rhetorée for having, like Benedict, seen fit to meddle frivolously in her affairs; why did Germaine take it upon herself to lure Professor Bosschère to the Hôtel Caudebec? Did she do it for Ellen's sake, or for some devious purpose of her own?

I won't attend this evening's soiree, resolved Ellen suddenly and fiercely. I am not a puppet, to be manipulated for Germaine's amusement. It would afford me no pleasure—in fact it would be pure pain—to see Monsieur Patrice in such circumstances, to be obliged to greet him under Germaine's observant eye. In any case, he will hardly notice my absence, in his pleasure at having gained the entrée to such a circle.

Fleetingly a memory came back to her, of some similar occasion: "Won't you come with us, Ellie?" and her own reply, haughty with resentment: "No, thank you, I don't choose to!" because she had not been the only one singled out for an invitation. When had it been? Benedict had been connected with it somehow…

Instead of changing, after she had eaten her dinner, into her new dark-blue cashmere, and going down to the music room, Ellen remained, therefore, in her own chamber, working on a chapter of Germaine's novel. But then it occurred to her that she might be summoned; the Professor might express a wish to see her. She had best find another refuge. Seizing a pen and a bundle of manuscript, she hurriedly made her way toward the library, approaching it by a circuitous route, in order to avoid the risk of encountering the arriving guests, and entering by a small outer door, used by servants who brought coal for the fires.

The library was dimly lit, but from the adjoining music room, where the soiree was already in full flow, a blaze of light streamed into the courtyard, and, even through the closed double doors, a gale of conversation and laughter could be heard. Perhaps *he* is already there, thought Ellen, settling herself at a small table; perhaps among those voices the notes of *his* are mingled.

By degrees she realized that she was not alone in

the room. A quiet step could be heard in the gallery overhead, and presently somebody descended the stair. Glancing up, expecting to see the old Abbé in his snuff-powdered cassock, Ellen was a little embarrassed and surprised to find that it was Raoul de la Ferté.

"You here, Mademoiselle Paget?" He, too, sounded surprised. "I thought that you would be next door—attending my wife's gathering?"

"I felt no inclination for it this evening," said Ellen. She gave no explanation; she was a little disconcerted by this encounter. "Does my presence here incommode you, Comte?"

"No, not in the least. I shall be going out directly, to my aunt's dinner party." Indeed he was dressed for the occasion, and carried a silk hat. Ellen wondered again if it could possibly have been Raoul whom she saw that afternoon in the Passage Langlade.

He seemed in no hurry to leave, despite his words; he lingered, turning over the pages of a journal. Ellen quietly applied herself to her work.

"It is a strange sound; is it not?" he remarked after a while, inclining his head toward the roar of talk from the next chamber. "The greatest intellects of this nation—or so my wife would have me believe—engaged in bawling out light chat at the tops of their voices."

He spoke so acidly that Ellen felt bound to dispute, or at least qualify, his view.

"You do not, then, approve of conversation as a recreation, Comte?"

"Oh—" He spun his hat moodily on his finger. "It is probably because I am no adept myself; doubtless you would say that was sour grapes! I like to read, to ponder on what I have read, but I have no skill at expressing my opinions aloud. Sometimes I sit in here, of an evening, listening to all that chat next door—like parrots screaming in the forest—and ask myself, what is the point of it all? No record is left of what they say. Who will recall it—or be one centime the better for it?"

Ellen felt a pang of pity for him, sulking in here alone like an unwanted child, listening to the sounds of animation from next door.

"But I think you converse very well, monsieur," she told him gently. "You express your thoughts with clarity and sense; what more is required?"

His melancholy face lit in its rare smile. "Nothing more, perhaps, by you, Miss Paget! But then, to you I find it easy to talk. Perhaps you should be giving me conversation lessons, as well as teaching Menispe her letters." He glanced at the watch on his fob. "It is time I went. Have you sufficient light for your work? Ring for more candles if you require them." He walked toward the door; hesitated; came back. "Miss Paget—has my wife—has Louise expressed any opinion to you about this—this family council that is to be held?"

"I am afraid not to me, monsieur; the Comtesse and I are hardly on confidential terms."

"I regret that," he said. "I think you would be more likely to give her good advice than—"

At this moment the intercommunicating door to the music room swung open. Louise walked through, her head turned to call a remark over her shoulder.

"I will find it in the dictionary. You will see that the Duchesse is right—"

Then, facing forward, she discovered the presence of the other two. Her evident surprise was instantly replaced by a haughty composure.

"Oh! I beg your pardon. I had not the least intention of interrupting a private conference—"

"There was nothing in the least private about our conversation," Raoul said irritably. "The encounter was accidental—Miss Paget was working here and I—" but Louise had already picked up a volume and withdrawn, shutting the door with exaggerated caution as if not to disturb them. Raoul uttered a smothered malediction and left the library.

Much later, long after the uproar of talk next door had died down and the guests had departed, Ellen returned to her own chamber. There she found two notes, delivered in her absence. One, from Germaine:

"What became of you, Callisto? I longed to see you in the salon, entertaining your Bruxelles bear. What mysterious English mood can have kept you away? Pique, because it was my invitation, not yours, that brought him? Chagrin? Or simply ennui? But he is most amusing—a truly clever man—a most entertaining conversationalist! Though *not*, I think, a genuinely creative mind—and, *mon dieu, ma chère,* he certainly has a conceit of himself! I think I was able to cut him down a little. He expressed sincere disappointment at not seeing you—all the appropriate regrets—made all the proper inquiries—sent all the most correct messages. But, Callisto, I warn you, he is not a man to possess! You might as well wish to appropriate the river flowing by. Dismiss him from your heart—if not your mind. There are others more deserving! *Tout à toi*—Camille."

The other note was the Professor's, in his tiny, cramped, intelligent hand, expressing, as Germaine had said, all the appropriate regrets, proper inquiries, and correct messages. "It is a cause of great disappointment not to see you, for I return to Brussels tomorrow early, being obliged to deliver a lecture at the University tomorrow evening. I shall hope, however, during next year, to send you a small but sincere token of my enduring regard. P.B."

Ellen tore up both notes and dropped them in the fire.

The family council at the Hôtel Caudebec was a formal affair. It lasted several days, each member of the family, apparently, being entitled to a lengthy expression of opinion. Elderly representatives of the la Ferté tribe had traveled in from Rouen, from Lyons, from Orléans, from Caen, even from Italy, where one aged uncle was a cardinal. Another was a bishop, two were marquises, and an elderly duc had promised to attend but had been prevented at the last moment by gout. But even without him the assembly was formidable enough: elderly ladies in rusty black with necklaces worth 150,000 francs round their scrawny necks; snuffy old gentlemen, their sparse locks carefully smoothed with bandoline, their whiskers dyed and waxed, their stays creaking under leather waistcoats. A duchesse who was the second cousin of Raoul's mother had a mahogany ear trumpet, which she waved menacingly, like a trident, at anybody who came near her.

Ellen was privileged to get a brief glimpse of the assembled family, for Raoul asked her to bring Menispe to greet her relatives at the opening of the formal discussion. Fortunately Ellen was able to plead, truthfully, that the child's jaw was still sore and swollen from her visit to the dentist so that she could hardly speak, and the exposure was a short one.

"Just curtsey to the ladies, that will be all you need do," Ellen encouraged the child, when Véronique had put her into a silk dress and done her best with the wispy flaxen hair which fell out of curl two minutes after it had been under the tongs. The pair of them went into the great salon, where all the old trouts, as Germaine called them, were assembled, and Ellen led Menispe round the wide horseshoe of elderly personages, who variously patted her head, told her to be a good girl, or exclaimed that she did not look in the least like her father. Then they were able to withdraw, Ellen sighing with relief that her charge had not thrown a tantrum or in any way disgraced herself. But, poor Louise! Fancy having to face such a tribunal!

The fourth day of the council was concluded by a dinner party. Who had made the arrangements for this, Ellen did not know; she had heard Louise declare that nothing would persuade her to order an elaborate dinner for all those old monsters. But somebody had evidently attended to it, for the great dining room was set out with gala splendor; Ellen allowed Menispe to peep in at the gold dinner service, the elaborate epergnes piled with fruit, dishes encircled by wreaths of roses, and the Venetian chandeliers casting rainbow sparks from their colored pendants.

"Why cannot I stay up to see the dinner?" Menispe demanded.

"You would become bored soon enough. Besides, with your sore jaw, you can only eat gruel," Ellen reminded her. "Your turn to sit here will come later, never fear! You will be having your coming-out ball in this room, doubtless."

"But when? How long to wait?"

"Not long. The time will soon pass."

Staring at the huge, white-shrouded table, the double row of empty damask-backed chairs, Ellen suddenly shivered; in spite of its festive furnishings, the silent room seemed somber, oppressive, as if laid out for a wake.

"Come, little one; it is high time you were in bed."

But when Véronique arrived to undress her, Menispe clung to Ellen with unwonted tenacity.

"Do not leave me, mademoiselle. Stay, don't go!"—boring her flaxen head into the crook of Ellen's arm.

"It is all the strange folk about the house," said Véronique, looking down at the child compassionately. "Young ones are like animals, change upsets them." And indeed Menispe seemed like some small, only half-domesticated creature that would never be wholly accustomed to human ways.

"I will come and play cat's cradle when you are in bed," promised Ellen, and on this understanding Menispe allowed herself to be borne away. But later, when Ellen went into her bedroom, she was already asleep, curled up like a dormouse under the blue quilt.

Ellen was still standing, meditatively regarding the child, when Goton, Louise's maid, came in search of her.

"Mademoiselle Pagette, Monsieur le Comte has sent a message that he will be greatly obliged if you can come to the Comtesse's chamber and give your advice. Poor Madame has one of her bad migraines; she is in shocking pain."

"Well, I will come, of course," said Ellen. "But I don't know what Monsieur le Comte expects me to do. I am no doctor."

Following Goton through the lengthy passages to the other wing, Ellen reflected that it was hardly surprising Louise had a headache; such a battery of distinguished relatives-in-law would be enough to afflict anybody.

Arrived at the bedside, she realized that "headache" was a completely inadequate term to describe the condition: ghastly pale, with black circles under her eyes, writhing, sweating, moaning, retching, Louise was plainly in acute agony. Two scared-looking maids were taking turns to apply ice packs to her brow and smelling salts to her nose—which operations were rendered difficult because she continually threw herself from side to side in the beautiful Régence bed.

"Has her doctor been sent for?" demanded Ellen, appalled at this spectacle.

"*Bien sûr*, Dr. Ricord has seen her; he says it is merely one of her usual spells, perhaps a little worse than usual; he has prescribed ergot of rye."

"But—poor lady! It is atrocious that she should suffer so!"

The maids shrugged. "It is God's will," said one.

At this point Raoul, already in evening dress, hurried into the room. From the vaguely surprised, observant glances he threw about him as he crossed the room, Ellen guessed that he seldom entered this apartment. At the sight of his wife's affliction he turned pale; it was evident that he had suspected her illness to be a mere pretext for avoiding the family dinner, but now realized he had misjudged her.

"Ah—poor Louise, my poor girl," he muttered hoarsely.

At the sound of his voice, Louise opened her streaming bloodshot eyes and glared at him through the slits.

"You brought this on me!" she gasped vindictively, and thrust herself away from him to the far side of the bed, moaning, "Oh, God! I feel as if men with axes were splitting my skull!"

"She must have laudanum—something to dull the pain!" exclaimed Raoul.

"The doctor said it was not necessary," objected Goton.

"Well, the doctor is a fool. I am sure she should have it."

"Oh, go away, you brute!" shrieked Louise. "I do not care what you think. Only get out of my room."

As the maids, too, were giving him hostile looks, Raoul withdrew to the doorway, summoning Ellen to him with a gesture of his head.

"Do you think you could persuade her to take some laudanum?" he asked when she joined him. "Ricord is such a pigheaded ass—I believe he thinks it is woman's role to suffer; and I am very much afraid that Louise is bent on extracting all the suffering she can from her situation."

"I doubt if she will listen to me—perhaps Mademoiselle de Rhetorée—?"

He shook his head. "Goton tells me that she and Louise have had a violent quarrel. I am afraid this also must have contributed to her condition."

"Well, I will try to persuade her," said Ellen doubtfully. "But I am afraid that my words do not carry much weight with her. She ought not to suffer like this, though—it is dreadful."

"Poor girl," he murmured again. "It is all too hard on her. I thought she might have been feigning an attack to avoid the dinner—but I see it is not so. Now I am without a hostess—well, it cannot be helped." Impulsively, diffidently, he turned to Ellen. "I suppose you would not aid me in this impasse, Miss Paget—act as hostess for me, just for the evening?"

She was utterly astonished.

"No, *indeed* I would not, Comte! It would be wholly ineligible. I am not acquainted with your family—and they would be utterly scandalized, I am sure, to find your governess presiding. Think of the speculations it would give rise to," she added, blushing. "Put the idea out of your mind! But I will be glad to stay with the Countess and help her in any way I can."

Without looking to see how he received this rebuff, she left him and returned to the bedside. She noticed that Goton, who had been near enough to hear the exchange, gave her a measured, frowning glance, and was noticeably cool in her manner for some time thereafter. But since Ellen's practical wit and experience of sick-nursing in the rue St. Pierre made her a much more useful assistant than the two maids, who were scared, clumsy Norman girls, they were presently dismissed, and Goton's attitude to Ellen gradually thawed. They took turns in applying the ice packs to the sufferer's head, warming her feet with a hot brick, and employing what means they could to relieve her agony. At last, when Louise was almost fainting from pain, it was found possible to administer a few drops of laudanum, and by degrees she sank into a heavy sleep, frequently disturbed by moans of distress, or muttered broken exclamations. "Oh, it is infamous!" she gasped. "They are choking me! They are starving me!"

"No, no, my lady, they will not do that!" soothed Goton. "Now, try to sleep, and forget all about it—see, old Goton is here to look after you."

When Louise had sunk into a deeper slumber and slept for half an hour without disturbance, Ellen softly suggested that Goton should try to get some sleep on a divan. "For I am afraid she may wake later, when the effect of the drug has worn off, and then you will be needed. Meanwhile, I will sit beside her."

Reluctant at first, Goton finally agreed, and retired to the dressing room.

Ellen picked up a copy of Dumas's *Le Fils Naturel* which lay on the inlaid marble dressing table, and sat quietly down at the bedside.

Time passed. Very distantly, as if from another planet, she could hear when the dinner party broke up, and the carriages of the departing guests clip-clopped away into the night. Shortly after midnight, Raoul scratched at the door and cautiously put his head round to ask how his wife did.

"She has slept now for a couple of hours," whispered Ellen. "Let us hope that her pain is abating. The longer she sleeps, the better."

He crossed to the bedside and stared somberly at the sleeping figure.

"Regrettably," he murmured, "the situation that caused her pain will still be there when she wakes."

Ellen could have slapped him for his thoughtlessness. He had spoken softly, but some echo of his voice seemed to penetrate his wife's slumber. She opened her eyes and regarded him. Her features composed into a mask. The faint thread of voice in which she spoke was filled with malice.

"Still here? Enjoying your triumph?" Her gaze shifted to Ellen. "Ah, I had not observed you, Miss Paget. How stupid of me not to realize that it was a conspiracy. You were in league together to replace me. What could be more natural? Camille was right…" For a moment her face contorted in a grimace of pain, of grief. Then she said acidly, "Kind Miss Paget, so obliging, so feminine—and poor deserted Raoul, with his penchant for les Anglaises—"

"Take no notice, she is half delirious," muttered Raoul. And, to his wife, "Be silent, Louise, pull yourself together, you know that you are talking mischievous rubbish. Miss Paget is nothing to me, nor I to her. If you were not—"

"Oh, hush!" whispered Ellen urgently. "She is feverish, do not try to argue with her now. Her face is all flushed—wait, madame, while I refill the ice pack. And now, try to sip a little water. Ah, here is Goton—"

She was startled at the maid's closeness, and wondered how much she had heard. But her face remained impassive and she merely said, "Do you go and rest now, mademoiselle. I can see that my mistress has passed the crisis. Thanks to you I have now had sufficient sleep, and can now nurse her alone."

Ellen was dubious.

"You are certain, Goton? You will send word if you want me again?"

"Assuredly, mademoiselle. If I want you—I will send." Goton's black eyes remained unreadable. She added drily, "Good night, mademoiselle. Good night, Monsieur le Comte."

Thus dismissed, Ellen and Raoul quitted the room. He went with her as far as the main stairhead and, hesitating there, suggested, "Would you not care for a cordial? Something to make you sleep? I am afraid this has been a most trying vigil for you—"

"No, no, it was nothing. And no cordial, I thank you," Ellen told him hastily. "I am well used to sick-nursing. At the school in Brussels—"

"As for my wife's accusations—I am more sorry than I can say—"

"Please, Comte, I beg you! Think nothing of it. She was in a fever, she rambled—when she wakes, she will probably have forgotten what she said. At such times, people speak nonsense."

But, Ellen thought to herself, at such times people tend to say what they secretly believe.

"She was deeply distressed, you see, by the outcome of the family council. It was decided that she must give up these literary salons—and must retire to my chateau in Normandy, for a year at least—lead a life of domesticity—"

Ellen gasped. *Poor* Louise, she thought in horror; no wonder she was half distracted by pain and frustration. And a quarrel with Germaine, as well. But what tyranny, to impose such a restriction on the wretched girl. How can she ever bear it? And how can he condone it?

She raised perplexed eyes to Raoul, who said, "Yes, I know what you are thinking. It is a kind of despotism. But I am subject to it also. Ours is a large, wealthy, and ancient family, you see; we have the line, the inheritance, to consider, not merely our own selves." He added miserably, "I should never, never have married her. English—Protestant—it was utter folly."

Since Ellen heartily concurred in this view, she could think of nothing to say, except "I will bid you good night, monsieur. You need rest too."

"Let me at least thank you for your kindness and forbearance." He held out his hand; a little reluctantly, Ellen put hers into it. He looked so young, distracted, and forlorn—not in the least like the tyrannical head of a wealthy, ancient, and noble family—that her heart was wrung for him.

"Good night, then."

But to her utter dismay he drew her close and, before she could pull herself away, rested his head, like an exhausted child, on her shoulder. His arms went round her.

"Oh, how tired of it all I am," he muttered. "Oh, how much I wish those things she was thinking were true!"

"Monsieur, you forget yourself," said Ellen. Gently but firmly she disengaged herself from his embrace, and slipped away in the direction of her own room. Not far away, she heard a door close softly. She could not escape the uncomfortable conviction that someone had been watching them.

❧

Next afternoon Ellen was occupied in teaching Menispe to press flowers when a maid came to say that Madame la Comtesse intended driving out to pay a round of calls, and wished her daughter to accompany her. Amazed at this summons, Ellen went downstairs to the courtyard with a hastily tidied Menispe. Louise, looking wax-pale and heavy-eyed, but elegantly dressed in creamy muslin and a huge hat smothered with white and gold roses, sat already in the carriage, impatiently tapping her card case on the leather armrest.

"Are you really well enough to go out, Countess? And to take charge of Menispe—after last night?" began Ellen, troubled at her appearance.

"Oh, do not *you* begin now, my dear creature." Louise gave an irritable trill of laughter. Her voice was high and forced. "I am always in fine fettle after one of my attacks; quite another person, I assure you. And I am anxious to ask the advice of my dear Clarkey about this exile the la Fertés have seen fit to inflict on me. Clarkey is always demanding to see Menispe, she dotes on children. If Aunt Paulina were not still in Etretat I would consult her too—"

"You will not keep Menispe out too long? She is still not quite the thing after that visit to the dentist." Really it was of Menispe's mother that Ellen was thinking; she was dismayed by Louise's appearance.

"Don't fly into a fuss, I will take the very best possible care of her. I *am* her mother, after all!" Louise's mouth curved down in the familiar unamused smile. "Come, child," she said. "Miss Paget deserves the afternoon off—no doubt she can find many pleasant ways of employing herself!"

Deeply troubled at the sound of that high-pitched laughter, Ellen waited while the reluctant Menispe was lifted into the carriage and the horses trotted out of the courtyard.

Because she did not wish to sit indoors with her thoughts, she, too, put on a hat and set off to stroll about Paris. The afternoon was gray, sultry, and oppressive; thunder muttered over the heights of Montmartre. Ellen bought a scarf she did not need at the Bon Marché, and a fifteen-franc novel at a circulating library, where she read for a while in the *cabinet de lecture*; she drank a *citron pressé* in the rue de la Paix, and watched the workmen erecting triumphal arches, huge golden Victories garlanded with crowns of laurel. These were to celebrate the termination of the Franco-Austrian War; but, as Ellen had gathered from articles in the *Revue des Deux Mondes*, there was little cause for rejoicing. Disraeli, in England, had ironically called the war "a magnificent spectacle, which only cost a hundred thousand lives and 50 million sterling."

Who starts a war? Ellen wondered. Are wars planned deliberately? Does some statesman sit down, with pencil and drawing board, deciding, "At this point, a war will be to our advantage; we will spend so many lives and so many francs"? Are there rules to be followed? Men seem to feel the need for rules. They are never comfortable without them—rules for the government of nations, of families, of wealth, of inheritance, of wives.

I am not sure that I wish to marry, mused Ellen, sipping her *citron pressé*; from what I have seen of it, I doubt if marriage would suit me. But then—averting her eyes from the flirtatious glances of two young dandies idling past her table—the lot of a female on her own is so difficult. What sharp, hard faces Frenchmen have, she thought, as the ogling pair once more strolled by: long, bony cheeks, stiff beards, sharp mustaches—they all seem to be trying to look as much like the Emperor as possible. Hardly a lovable race—yet there is no denying their intelligence.

To live alone, thought Ellen, you need the courage of Alexander, the cunning and circumspection of a Jesuit. To live without love—is that possible? Madame Dudevant does—but she has it both ways, the love *and* the independence. Am I as brave as that? Would I have the courage to reject love—if I felt that it involved too much servitude?

She recalled Patrice Bosschère saying so urgently, "I need you beside me. If I had you, what might I not accomplish!" But was it love he had in mind? She thought of Raoul de la Ferté, last night, leaning his head exhaustedly, confidingly, on her shoulder. When they had talked in the library, or about Dickens, she had felt for him a kind of comfortable, easy warmth, as she might for a dear friend, a dear brother. Not, however, as she felt toward Benedict! But last night that warmth had quickened to a dangerous urgency of tenderness, frightening her, giving her a wholly unexpected glimpse of her own capacity to feel.

God knows, thought Ellen, that Louise, poor

thing, had no grounds for her spiteful suggestions; but from now on I must be on my guard. The very fact of her having made such an accusation is enough to lodge the idea in one's mind. No more tête-à-têtes with the Comte. But, presumably, if Louise is to be exiled in Normandy, Menispe and I will accompany her. And doubtless Raoul will remain in Paris, leading his own life.

Ruefully she acknowledged to herself how much she would miss the Paris life. And how in the world would Louise fill her days among the cows and apple orchards? Working at the *Treatise on the Golden Age of Gynautocracy*? Would that suffice for the loss of her salon?

The two young men were passing at ever more frequent intervals, becoming bolder in their glances; Ellen stood up, opened her parasol as a screen against them, and walked briskly away. None too soon: warm heavy drops of rain, large as sous, had begun to fall on the pavement, and the purple storm clouds were almost overhead; she would hardly reach the rue de l'Arbre Vert before the storm began.

Greatly to her surprise, when she reached the Hôtel Caudebec, she found that Louise and Menispe were not yet back from their visit to Mrs. Clarke. It was after Menispe's bedtime—and unlike Louise to tolerate the child's company for more than a couple of hours. But perhaps she had decided to wait for the end of the storm before quitting the rue du Bac—rain was now falling in torrents, lightning kept the sky in a purple flicker. Nonetheless, Ellen felt very uneasy; she kept looking from her window into the courtyard, hoping to see the carriage return.

Presently Véronique the bonne came to the room, somewhat agitated.

"Mademoiselle Pagette—I have just seen Jules, and he says he did *not* drive my lady and la petite to Madame Clarke's house!"

"He did not? Where, then, did he take them?"

"My lady said she had shopping commissions to execute; she told Jules to set her down outside Crista, the modiste, and said she would take a fiacre to the rue du Bac when she had done—a fiacre! My lady! Never has she done such a thing. Jules asked, should he not come to fetch her home from Madame Clarke, and she said no, she would return in that lady's carriage. But she has not done so yet. And it is so late!"

"Does Monsieur le Comte know this?"

"Mademoiselle, no, he is not at home."

Ellen thought, hurriedly and anxiously: Was this some tactic on the part of Louise—a ruse to escape the family network? A threat, using Menispe as a lever? Had she ordered Jules to set her down in the middle of Paris so that no one would know where she had gone?

Then reason reasserted itself.

"Have Jules take the carriage to Madame Clarke's house; the storm is so severe, perhaps other guests are stranded there. The Comtesse will probably be glad to have her own conveyance. And you had better put a warming pan in Menispe's bed—poor child, I hope she does not take a chill from this long outing. And she hates thunder—"

"I have already put a pan in her bed, mademoiselle," said Véronique loftily, and retired to give the order to Jules.

Troubled, Ellen paced about her comfortable room. If only Louise had not committed some folly—

After another half hour, with no sign of the returning carriage, Ellen's eye was caught by a light in the library. It would be the old Abbé de Grandville; he might have sensible or soothing advice; and his calm company would be better than her own. Ellen flung a shawl round her shoulders, for the storm had brought chill to the air, and took a circuitous way through passages to the other side of the house, since crossing the courtyard was out of the question.

In the library she found not only the Abbé but an elderly

great-aunt of Raoul on his mother's side, a lady who bore
the title of Princess Tanofski, since she had in youth briefly
been married to a Polish nobleman. She was exceedingly
poor and, having exerted herself to make the journey
from Périgord, where she lived in a small pension, had
announced her intention of staying in Paris for three weeks,
so as to make the most of her great-nephew's hospitality.
She was snugly ensconced in a velvet armchair with her
feet on a footstool, her puce merino dress tucked round
her, sipping a cup of tisane, and engaged in a theological
argument with the Abbé. Both their wrinkled old faces
displayed mild irritation as they turned to gaze at Ellen.

"I beg your pardon, Princess—Monsieur l'Abbé—"
Ellen was a little embarrassed. Could she conceivably,
she asked herself, have been hoping to find the Comte in
here? But no, perish the thought. "I am a little disquieted
in my mind about the Countess and Menispe—" She
explained the situation.

Princess Tanofski shrugged; evidently no folly on the
part of Louise would surprise her; but the Abbé suggested, "May not the Countess have gone to take counsel
with her aunt at the Britannic Embassy?"

"But no, monsieur; Lady Morningquest is still out of
town, at Etretat."

"Might it be possible that Louise, on the spur of the
moment, decided to go there and see Miladi Morningquest?"

Ellen accepted this idea with relief.

"Thank you, monsieur. Perhaps that may be so. If—if
the Countess does not return soon, do you think we
should telegraph Lady Morningquest?"

"Where is Raoul?" demanded his great-aunt. "Out
gambling, I suppose, or at a bordello, when he should be
at home watching over his affairs."

Ellen felt this was a hard judgment, and the Abbé
shrugged, evidently sharing her sentiment.

"I do not think we should wait for the Comte's return

to telegraph," Ellen said. "When—if Jules returns without them—if the Countess has not been at Mrs. Clarke's—"

"Perhaps she has gone to that terrible demon girl of Lesbos—what is her name? Justine? The de Rhetorée chit," suggested Princess Tanofski.

Ellen thought this hardly probable. Would Louise take refuge in Germaine's squalid den—Louise, who was so fastidious that she would not touch fruit or even flowers unless they had been washed? And the Abbé shook his head.

"They had a bitter quarrel," he said knowledgeably. "I do not think we shall be seeing so much of Mademoiselle de Rhetorée—"

At this moment Véronique tapped and entered the room, her pleasant face deeply distressed. As she curt-seyed, Ellen reflected how involved the servants were in all that concerned the family—witness the speed with which Véronique had tracked her to this spot. Nothing that passed went unobserved.

"Madame la Princesse—Mademoiselle—Jules has returned, and he reports that my mistress never went to Mrs. Clarke's house! Mrs. Clarke had not been expect-ing her!"

"*Tiens*," said the Abbé. "This begins to look serious; it has the air of a flitting. Miserable girl!" His pale, pouched old face was extremely condemning.

"Well, if she has run away," said the Princess cheer-fully, "that will make it easy for Raoul to divorce her."

"Are you mad, Séraphine? The la Fertés do not divorce!"

"But, Théodule, consider the succession!"

The ensuing argument was cut short by the entry of Ernest, the majordomo, who looked excessively shocked. He was accompanied by two men in frock coats and top hats.

"Monsieur l'Abbé—I do not know if I do right to come to you—but Monsieur le Comte being from home—these two gentlemen are from the Police Department—"

"Oh, *mon dieu*, what now?" demanded the Princess shrilly.

But the Abbé, with mild dignity, said, "Certainly you were right, Ernest. What can I do for you gentlemen?"

Stiffly the two men explained their errand. They had been summoned by a hysterical concierge in a tenement off the rue de Langlade, who declared that she had heard pistol shots in her attic apartment.

"Oh, *no!*" whispered Ellen.

Mounting to the top floor, the police had effected entry, and had discovered two bodies, that of a lady and a child, both well dressed, persons of quality. The terrified concierge had told some garbled story about her attic tenant being acquainted with a wealthy lady, the Comtesse de la Ferté.

"And where, meanwhile, *was* the tenant?" demanded the Abbé.

"She was not there, monsieur. Accordingly, lacking positive identification, we made bold to come here—"

The Abbé was already rising painfully to his feet, tightening the fringed sash about his cassock. He took a heavy cloak from a peg under the gallery, and said to the policemen, "Messieurs, who is more fit for a deathbed than a priest? If that is what you require, I am ready to do what is necessary."

"Oh, Théodule, you will catch some dreadful illness, or an inflammation of the lungs. Hark how it rains! And the rue de Langlade is a most infamous quarter!"

"Be silent, Séraphine," said the Abbé firmly. "It is my duty to go." Addressing Ellen, he added, "Perhaps, mademoiselle, you had best come too. If by any chance either of these unfortunates—supposing them to be whom we think they are—were found to be still living—"

"There is no question of that, Monsieur l'Abbé," said the senior officer.

But Ellen, shivering, said, "Of course I will accompany you, monsieur."

❧

The journey through the glossy, dark, dripping streets was a silent one. By Parisian standards the hour was not late, but the rain had driven most people indoors. The Abbé told his beads as they rode along, Ellen huddled silently in her corner. All too soon they arrived in front of the tall, narrow house, where Ellen recognized the wine-shop, the portress's niche, the greasy stairs. Trembling, she followed the three men up the dark flights.

Germaine's bare rooms looked very different now, glaringly lit by gas flares and a number of lanterns. Two more police stood mounting guard while a third prowled about making notes. On the dismal bed lay something covered with a sheet from which Ellen averted her eyes, but not before she had seen the pool of dark liquid which had dripped onto the boards below. A flounce of creamy muslin dangled to the floor, its hem dabbled and stained dark brown.

"Wait by the door if you please, mademoiselle," said the senior officer.

Ellen felt she could not have moved; she stood trans-fixed as the Abbé walked quietly to the bedside, lifted the sheet, and glanced at what lay beneath. Then he replaced the soiled calico and stepped back, his eyes meeting those of the senior officer.

"It is the Comtesse de la Ferté and her daughter," he said.

"You are certain, monsieur?"

"No doubt whatever."

"Then I need detain you no longer. I am sorry that you should have been obliged to come to this wretched place, mademoiselle," the man said to Ellen, who replied mechanically, "It did not matter. But—are you *certain* they are dead, monsieur? There is no possible chance that—"

"None, mademoiselle."

"Oh, how dreadful. Oh, *poor* Monsieur le Comte!"

"Come, my child," said the Abbé. "We had best return to the Hôtel Caudebec to break this sad news to him… I infer," he said to the police, "that the bodies will be brought there, when you have taken such measures as you think fit?"

"Certainly, monsieur."

All the way home in the carriage the Abbé was murmuring the Office for the Dead. Ellen did not like to interrupt him to ask questions. But Princess Tanofski, when they were back in the Hôtel Caudebec, instantly demanded, "Well? Was it Louise? And the child?" The Abbé bowed his head. "And they were dead? Both dead? Oh, what lunatic folly! What had the poor sacrilegious idiot done—taken poison?"

"No," said the Abbé. "They were both shot through the head."

"Oh, *mon dieu*! How shall we break it to Raoul?"

"You do not need to do that, Tante Séraphine," said Raoul's voice. They all whirled round to see him standing in the doorway. He was ashy pale, and held a half sheet of paper. "I found this letter from Louise on my desk," he said, and read it aloud. "'You and your family have driven me too far. So I plan to escape from you all and I shall take Menispe with me. I know you pretend to love her—but I know, too, that if she grew up, you would condemn her to the same grotesque slavery for which you destined me. Perhaps the thought of *her* may cause you an instant's regret. I know you had no pity for *me*. Louise.'"

Raoul's voice cracked with misery as he read the letter. He cried at them, "We killed her, among us! Do you deny it? Poor, poor wretched girl. All she wanted was to read and write and talk about philosophy—now she is dead and gone to hell! She was only twenty-two! And Menispe was four. And it is our fault."

"Nonsense, Raoul," said the Princess sharply. "She was a silly, selfish, hysterical girl. *No* blame attaches to you—or to the family. Good heavens, you gave her everything in the world—"

"It is true, my son," said the Abbé. "You have no cause to blame yourself. We are all fallible, *le bon dieu* knows—but you behaved with generosity and restraint in very trying circumstances. Why should Louise take it upon herself to find fault with the normal lot of women?"

Why should she not? Ellen thought. But she did not speak this thought aloud. Raoul had sunk miserably onto a velvet couch, his head in his hands; she felt she had no right to be there, witnessing his grief and remorse.

"I will return to my room, Princess," she whispered. "Unless I can do anything for you?"

"Yes; you can escort me to *my* room," said that lady. "We will leave Monsieur l'Abbé to console my nephew. Give me your arm, child," and, leaning heavily on Ellen, she hobbled upstairs, and sank into a fauteuil by her own fireside.

"*Asseyez-vous, mon enfant*," she ordered Ellen, "for there is much to discuss. We shall all need to proceed with the utmost discretion, if there is not to be an atrocious scandal after this disastrous act. Louise was, after all, well known in society, and in literary circles—it cannot be hushed up. Thank heaven she at least left a note admitting her intentions—otherwise the police and certainly the public would assume that Raoul had done it."

Ellen was horrified.

"Do you really think so, Princess?"

"Indeed yes. If the press can make matters worse, they always will. Or maybe they will say the de Rhetorée girl killed Louise, out of jealousy. Or"—the shrewd, prune-brown eyes raked Ellen's face dispassionately—"they will say Raoul was conducting an amour with you, Miss Paget, and Louise discovered, and so made an end of herself."

"Madame!" Ellen felt herself flush crimson, and hoped the firelight disguised it.

"Oh, they will say all those things, you may be sure. For Raoul's sake, you had best be out of this house tomorrow. Or—wait—there will be all the funeral notices to dispatch; it is most unfortunate that Raoul's mother had to return to Rome, silly woman; perhaps you had better stay till that is dealt with. My presence in the house will lend propriety to the situation, I daresay. But after that you had better take refuge with Lady Morningquest."

"Oh, she will be so dreadfully distressed. I must telegraph her tomorrow."

Ellen felt a pang of horror and guilt as she remembered her godmother saying, "Why should you not become a friend to Louise?" I *did* make the attempt, she told herself, but the voice of conscience retorted, "You could have tried a great deal harder. The truth is, you did not like her." I tried my very best with little Menispe, she argued—and then, realizing fully for the first time that she would never again have Menispe's waywardness and inattention to battle against, she broke down and cried bitterly, for the first time in many years. The tears surprised her as much as they did Princess Tanofski, who exclaimed, "*Tiens*, you were so fond of Louise, then? I had not remarked it."

"No, but of that poor little child," Ellen sobbed, trying to master herself.

"So? But I had thought she was almost imbecile, no great loss," remarked the Princess callously. "*Tant pis*. But now Raoul may marry again, and, we hope, get a male heir. Ring the bell, if you please, Miss Paget; I am an old lady and must have my *goûter du soir*."

Chilled by the old lady's ruthless practicality, Ellen did so, then took her leave and went to her own room; she did not feel as if she could ever eat or drink again. The image of the two recumbent shapes under the sheet in Germaine's dirty room returned to haunt her; and for the first time, she thought: Where is Germaine? Why was she not there? Why did she not try to dissuade Louise from doing what she did? Or—a touch of icy grue—perhaps she was there? Did she have some hand in the business? Could her lack of sympathy, her displeasure, or her cynical attempt to persuade Louise to conform to family pressure have been the last straw?

But Germaine could hardly have wished Louise dead, for now she had lost her goose that laid the golden eggs.

Nine

Next day the Hôtel Caudebec was hushed and stricken, as servants crept dolefully about, emissaries from the police came and went, unfeeling callers who had got wind of the affair left cards with inquisitive or commiserating messages, and Ellen, at the Princess's direction, wrote innumerable cards, summoning back the members of the family who had just left Paris. The two bodies had been released by the police, and the funeral was fixed for the following Wednesday. But apparently police inquiries were still proceeding; the officers had read the letter left by Louise for Raoul and were not satisfied that it denoted an intention to make away with herself.

At about noon a note came which was addressed to Ellen.

From Lady Morningquest, was her first thought; but Lady Morningquest would never send any communication on a grimy, torn half sheet of paper sealed by a greasy wafer. She slit the paper and read:

"I presume you will be going out to take the air, or to buy black gloves? I shall be choosing a cravat in the Bon Marché at 1:00 and will hope to see you. G."

The black spiky handwriting was very familiar; in fact Ellen still had a half-translated manuscript of Germaine's in her possession. She wondered whether to take it with her to this assignation; then decided not. That would look—wouldn't it?—as if she intended to break off the association.

The Bon Marché was, as usual, crowded with bourgeois

matrons taking advantage of the large display of wares at low prices; it was some little time before Ellen recognized the unassertive young workman in belted blouse and corduroys, his black cap pulled forward over his eyes, who stood, hands in pockets, gazing doubtfully at a table covered with neckerchiefs.

His gaze moved to Ellen at last, he gave her a slight nod, or jerk of the head, and sauntered casually toward one of the exits.

Just outside the door: "Where shall we go to talk? Down by the river?" said Germaine.

"On the quai? Good God no," Ellen objected. "We should be drenched."

Last night's storm had dwindled to a steady, penetrating summer rain which appeared likely to continue all day.

Germaine shrugged. "*Eh bien*, then let us go to the Café Thiémet; if you have some money on you, that is. I have none."

Ellen had money and agreed; she did not like the Café Thiémet, a large, crowded, noisy place, but did not wish to stand arguing in the rain with Germaine, who looked haggard and hollow-eyed; her normal bisque pallor had turned to the damp yellow-white of fishmonger's marble.

They walked the few blocks to the café, both sheltered under Ellen's umbrella, Ellen devoutly hoping that no one would see and recognize her apparently promenading with a young ouvrier; but she herself was wearing an old black mantle and hat remaining from her months of mourning for her mother, and could have been mistaken for any shabby dressmaker or ladies' maid.

But who, on this dismal day, would give them a second glance? The streets were full of dispirited horses slipping on the wet cobbles, and impatient coachmen lashing and swearing; no one who could help it was on foot in such weather.

The Café Thiémet was packed with steaming, dripping customers; but Germaine, with her customary vigor and tenacity, thrust a path to the back and secured a table under the noses of two affronted matrons, who shrugged indignantly and moved elsewhere.

"Deux café cognacs," she ordered the garçon.

"No cognac for me," said Ellen, but he had gone.

"*Alors*, I will drink them both," said Germaine impatiently. "You, I daresay, had breakfast; I did not; I have been walking about the streets all night."

"Germaine—what happened?" burst out Ellen. "Did she—did you—was it an accident?"

"Hush! Not so loud! The flics are certainly looking for me, and I daresay this place is full of their informers. No—how stupid you are! Of course it was no accident. She was bent, poor idiot, on self-destruction. I came home last night and found her there, with the child, my pistol beside her, writing me a letter full of condemnation and commination. I argued with her—naturally—did my best to dissuade her—but she was crazy—imbecile—quite beyond reason. Her only retort was to threaten to shoot *me*. And I value my life, I assure you! I had no intention of being snuffed out by such a poor-spirited creature."

Germaine lifted her head arrogantly. In the shabby workman's clothes she looked young, rough, and intractable; her nostrils spread, her wide mouth tightened.

The boy returned with their two cups of coffee, and she gulped one down hungrily.

"Ah! That's better. I was hollow as a drum."

"So what happened?"

"So—despite all my arguments—she carried out her threat; shot first the child, then herself." Ellen shuddered, her imagination flinching from the scene. "Well, what could I do?" said Germaine. "I could not prevent her. She had the pistol. I removed the letter she had written— which uttered all sorts of idiocies and blamed me for every ill in her life. Bad enough she should be found in my place, no need to have it all spelt out for the popular press. Then I climbed out of the window onto the roof, for I knew old Madame Pelletier downstairs would have raised the alarm when she heard shots; I dared not go down the stairs. Luckily Madame had not seen me come in—she was in the wineshop. I crawled along the roof and in through Matthieu Rotrou's attic window; he always leaves it open and is dead drunk by that time of night. And I walked the streets till morning, as I told you. By bad luck there was no cash in my room. Only afterwards I thought that *she* probably had some on her; I could have kicked myself."

Ellen shivered at this ruthlessness.

"But, Germaine—"

"Hush! Not so loud!"

"Why do you not go to the police? If—if your story is true, they will believe you. Show them her letter."

"I tore it up." Germaine's lip curled. "Whining, self-pitying—it disgusted me."

"But you cannot live like—like a fugitive—for long. It will only make them suspect you. And they are bound to catch up with you."

"You talk folly. I would make the perfect scapegoat. Why should Louise de la Ferté—with everything in the world—make away with herself? What a shocking idea! No, it is by far more likely that I—hungry, jealous, disappointed—dispatched her in some fit of passion and despair. Think what a fine headline that would make for *Le Siècle* on the railway bookstalls! A Sapphist murder!"

"What do you plan to do?"

"Oh, I will go and live quietly in the country for a while, in the Bocage, maybe, or the Camargue— somewhere they'll never think of looking—till the brouhaha is over. But I shall need cash, and this is where you, my dear Callisto, can be helpful."

"I am afraid I have no more than two hundred francs on me," said Ellen, beginning to dig in her reticule.

"Thanks—that will be useful." Germaine took the money without demur. "But what I really need is for you to act as emissary for me. Will you take this letter to my publishers? I can't go myself, the flics may be watching the place. Villedeuil owes me four thousand francs, and I'll ask him to give you the money; on that I can live for months, till the furore has died down. If they can't get hold of me, very likely they will fall back on Raoul and arrest him. The idea of a husband killing his wife is always popular, specially if he is young, rich, and handsome. The public love that."

"How can you be so heartless?"

"Oh, you are such a self-centered little English prig." Germaine gulped down Ellen's coffee and ordered two more; she had an unerring knack of catching the waiter's eye. "Will you go to Villedeuil for me?" she demanded. "His office is in the rue d'Aumale."

"Yes; very well; I will go." Ellen was not at all sure that she ought, but she had been stung by that "self-centered English prig"; she had failed Louise, but she wanted to demonstrate to somebody—herself perhaps—that she could be useful to *somebody* in this tragedy.

"Good. In that case I'll be obliged if you will go directly; the sooner I leave town, the better. I should like to set off tonight."

"Will the publishers be able to obtain the money so fast?"

"Certainly; old Villedeuil does excellently out of my work; he will not want me sent to the guillotine. I have explained the whole matter in this." She handed a letter to Ellen. "Now, where shall we meet? We should not return here. I will see you at the Sainte Chapelle, upstairs, at four o'clock. Now you had better run along—but stay, you will need a little cash for a fiacre. There—that should be sufficient. By the bye, have you finished translating my *Contes Tristes*?"

"No, I am only halfway through."

"Well, we will talk about that later; adieu for the present."

Rather indignant at being thus coolly dismissed, Ellen took a fiacre to the publisher's office (not without difficulty, the wet weather had rendered transport very scarce); during the twenty-minute drive she had leisure to reflect on Germaine's story. Was it true? It had an air of probability—but that, for a practiced storyteller, would be easy to contrive. Still, what benefit would there be for Germaine in killing Louise? She had just demonstrated—if demonstration were needed—her total, cold-blooded practicality. It seemed wholly improbable that she would commit a crime of passion or impulse—or kill a child who meant nothing to her—let alone perform the deed in her room, where suspicion would instantly fall on her.

No, it had been the last vengeful act of Louise, who intended that the finger of blame should point at her heartless friend.

More in charity with Germaine after arriving at this conclusion, Ellen alighted at the publisher's office, and asked the cab to wait. She sent Germaine's letter in to the editor, who soon appeared looking alarmed. He was a short, fat man with a sallow complexion—the last person, Ellen thought, in whom one would have expected to find an appreciation of literary merit; but he seemed genuinely appalled at Germaine's predicament.

"Such a remarkable talent! Such a terrible blow!" he kept repeating. "I have sent my head clerk to the bank for the money, mademoiselle; he will be back very soon. Oh, it is deplorable that a writer such as our friend should be subjected to such shifts and difficulties. I think she bids fair in time to rival Madame Sand—if only she had the income to support herself while she writes, if she did not lead such a hand-to-mouth existence! What a disaster that the Comtesse is dead—the papers are full of it—where will our friend find such a patron again?" He glanced nervously out of the window. "Is that a police agent across the road?"

"I have no idea," said Ellen.

"If only they do not come to question me! Ah, here is Charpentier, at last, with the money; and I have given Mademoiselle double what she asks; her new novel, *La Religieuse*, is just printed; the clerks are doing up the bundles now; I have printed six thousand, and with the publicity over this case, I am certain to have demands for another six thousand, very likely more! It will be a *succès fou*! Tell our friend, when she has an address in the country, to write to me—not here, but at an accommodation address"—he gave Ellen a card—"and I will keep her supplied with funds."

"Thank you, monsieur."

Ellen left the office, glancing warily at the man leaning against a lamppost—who did resemble a police spy—and told the driver of the fiacre to take her to Notre-Dame. There she paid him off, went into the cathedral, and knelt in prayer in the candlelit dimness. She felt troubled, confused, and grief-stricken; for whom, she could hardly have said; for all the parties in this tragic affair, herself not least.

What will become of me now? she wondered.

The cathedral clock struck the half hour and she rose stiffly from the chill stone floor. Leaving by a side door, she walked slowly in the direction of the Sainte Chapelle, glancing cautiously about her. Nobody seemed to be taking any interest in her movements. The rain had stopped at last, and walkers thronged the streets.

At the Sainte Chapelle she climbed to the upper floor, which was dusty and deserted, except for one slight, shabby figure.

"You got it without difficulty?" said Germaine eagerly. "Thanks, Callisto!" For the first time that day she smiled—her full, fascinating smile. Already she looked revived—less haggard, her eyes brighter.

"What do you wish me to do about the translation?"

Ellen felt her sympathy sink, in inverse ratio to this recovery; she spoke rather coldly.

"Let me think! Why do you not send it, when it is finished, to the English publisher Longman? I have the address—here." Germaine scribbled on a small tablet she carried. "If they like it—if they wish to print it—tell them to send any moneys to M. Villedeuil; he can act as my agent. He is an honest fellow—as publishers go."

"Very well," said Ellen. "And—I wish you luck."

"Thanks, *mon amie*, I wish you the same," said Germaine absently. "I suppose you must now be looking for another situation? It is a pity. If Raoul is not arrested, you could do worse than marry him." She tossed off this suggestion carelessly, as a joke, but then, struck by her own percipience, added, "Yes! Marry him, why don't you? He has a penchant for English girls, he is quite ready to fall in love with you; I have seen it in his eyes. And you are everything *she* was not: rational, gentle, kind. *She* had seen his interest too—that contributed more fuel to her melancholia. Accustomed to his helpless devotion, she was quite shocked to see it withdrawn and conferred on another—even though she despised him." Germaine spoke rapidly and authoritatively, as though she had already made notes on the matter, for fictional purposes. She went on, "But if *you* were married to Raoul, I am sure you could handle him a thousand times better. In fact we might—"

She grinned almost her old urchin grin at Ellen, who broke in, utterly scandalized, "Oh, hush! How can you say such things at such a time. If you could have seen that poor man! Has he not been cheated enough? Leave him alone, you have done him enough harm already. He is not a fit subject for jokes."

Germaine raised her classic brows.

"Oh, oh, touchy, are we? Mademoiselle Fine-Airs considers herself above such tawdry calculations, eh? Well, let me tell you, my dear"—her lips drew back, her tone was suddenly guttural, vicious, hostile—"*I* may do harm, as you put it in your censorious way, but I do good too, to my friends; I live, I love, I create, I give devotion and admiration where they are deserved. But what do *you* do, you coldhearted hypocrite? I used to watch you, nose in air, at those salons. You think yourself so much above us low-class writers! Nor did you make the least push to befriend or advise Louise— though I daresay you could have done so. You did not comfort Raoul, though if you had given him the least encouragement he would have turned to you and left off pestering Louise. All you did was walk about with your chin up, studying only what impression you were making on other people, or dreaming of that narcissistic professor in Brussels. You have no red blood in you. You work so hard at perfecting yourself that you never turn aside to look at other people. Your veins are full of fish glue!"

"Oh," exclaimed Ellen, hurt and outraged at this tirade. "How dare you?"

But Germaine had spun round on her heel and, with her free, supple stride, walked to the end of the chapel and ran down the stair. By the time Ellen had followed to the lower room, the cap, blue blouse, and black corduroys were nowhere to be seen.

Ellen made her way into the street. Her cheeks stung as though she had been slapped. Numb, shocked, bitterly wounded, she turned her steps mechanically in the direction of the rue de l'Arbre Vert.

The worst part of her pain consisted in the

consciousness that there had been a good deal of justice in what Germaine said.

⚜

When she reached the Hôtel Caudebec she was thunderstruck to find waiting for her a hostile reception committee composed of Princess Tanofski and Lady Morningquest.

"Ma'am!" exclaimed Ellen, curtseying and then embracing her godmother. "I am so relieved to see you—but oh, in what dreadful circumstances."

Lady Morningquest did not waste time in greetings and exclamations. Her face was ravaged by grief, and ominously severe.

"Where in the world have you been? Why did you choose, on this day of all days, to absent yourself for such a period of time? The Princess has been in great anxiety about you—as indeed have I—"

"I—I am exceedingly sorry, ma'am. I—I went out—"

"To buy black gloves, I can see that. You might have considered that the Princess would have occasion for your services. Now: she and I have been taking counsel together about you. Since the wretched Raoul has been arrested—"

"*What* is that you say?" gasped Ellen. "They have arrested Monsieur le Comte?"

"Oh, it was bound to happen. They always arrest the husband in such a case. They will probably let him go again, by and by; his high-placed relatives are all at work pulling strings. At all events, he has been taken off in police custody. So there will be no impropriety in your remaining here for a few days more, while you can make yourself useful to the Princess; her *dame de compagnie* cannot get here until Tuesday. After that you must, of course, come to me, until we can decide what to do with you."

Lady Morningquest spoke drily; it was evident that she regarded her goddaughter's predicament as nothing but a nuisance.

Ellen could only repeat, "They have arrested Monsieur le Comte? But how could they? Surely they can have had no reason for supposing that he had anything to do with—with the deaths? Let alone evidence? It is complete injustice."

Lady Morningquest's face became even more disapproving. "That is as may be. Apparently Raoul was in the habit of visiting a *maison*—a house of assignation in the street close to where the murder took place."

"Oh, heavens—"

"And last night, it seems, he was there; actually there, in the same street, he admitted it himself. So naturally the police assume that he committed the murder."

Shocked, crushed, Ellen muttered, "But he did not do it. Louise put an end to her own life."

"How do you know that?" pounced Princess Tanofski.

There was nothing for it—specially after Germaine's accusation of selfishness and hypocrisy; Ellen could not stand by and see Raoul charged with a crime she knew he had not committed. She said, "Germaine de Rhetorée told me. She was there, she saw it all. Louise came to her room in the Passage Langlade, reproached her bitterly, then shot herself and—and Menispe—"

"*You have seen Germaine de Rhetorée?*" exclaimed both ladies together. "Where?"

"I met her at the Sainte Chapelle. I brought some money for her, from her publisher."

Her interlocutresses threw up their eyes to heaven.

"And where is the miserable creature now?" demanded the Princess.

"I do not know. She said she was going a long way off—into the country."

"You will have to tell all this story to the police," said

Lady Morningquest, very sternly. "Merciful heaven! What the papers will make of it all, I shudder to contemplate."

⚜

The next few days were exceedingly unpleasant for Ellen. She was subjected to endless interrogations by the police, who treated her with marked suspicion and hostility when they discovered that she had had clandestine dealings with one of the parties in the tragedy who had now disappeared.

For a whole day, Ellen was not even certain whether they believed her, and it seemed highly possible that she, too, might be taken into custody like Raoul. Luckily Villedeuil the publisher substantiated her story and was able to produce Germaine's letter to him; and the servants at the Hôtel Caudebec bore witness that Ellen had been within doors during the evening when the death of Louise had taken place; this was sourly confirmed by the Abbé and Princess Tanofski. Ellen's connection with the British Ambassador and his lady also stood her in good stead.

But there were endless unpleasant insinuations in the press. "What part does the charming young English lady residing at the Hôtel Caudebec play in this marital disaster?" disagreeably inquired the *Globe*. "M. le Comte de la Ferté was married to one Englishwoman; could it be that he enjoyed a *ménage à trois à l'anglaise*?" *Le Monde* asked why Ellen had not been arrested; *Le Siècle* suggested that she be deported without delay. There were sinister rumors, apparently emanating from some of the servants at the Hôtel Caudebec—suggestions of late-night assignations and long confidential interviews between the Comte de la Ferté and the mysterious young English lady.

Ellen had to suffer, besides this unpleasantness, the continuous irritable faultfinding and disapproval of

Princess Tanofski, who, though fully prepared to make use of Ellen in a secretarial capacity, made it plain that she considered the latter's dealings with Germaine disloyal and reprehensible. And Lady Morningquest, who spent a great deal of time at the Hôtel Caudebec, occupied most of it in scolding and reproaching Ellen.

"I brought you to Paris—introduced you to a life of interest and luxury—gave you such opportunities as will never come your way again—and what is the result? Without lifting a finger to prevent it, you allow this disaster to take place!"

Ellen felt some of these reproaches to be unjust. Part of the blame, she thought, must at least rest with Lady Morningquest, who had permitted her niece to make such an unfortunate alliance. But of course one could not say this; it was impossible to defend herself; and Ellen was so miserable that she made no attempt to, simply bowed under the storm of commination and waited numbly for it to die away. Indeed, she was still too shocked and distressed to have very clear opinions about it all. And she felt horribly lonely—she missed little Menispe; willful, teasing, difficult, the child had been, but it was a challenge to catch her wayward attention, and she had not lacked the capacity to feel: witness her devotion to her father. Of Raoul, what his grief and wretchedness must be like, Ellen hardly dared think. She missed his friendly presence too, and Germaine's quick-witted lively company. While the memory of poor Louise—antagonistic, despairing, trapped—was almost too painful to be borne.

On the day before the funeral, Raoul was unexpectedly released. This was due to the fact that another letter from Louise, written to Lady Morningquest at Etretat, came back to Paris, forwarded from the hotel where the latter had been staying. This letter, like those to Raoul and Germaine, was a disjointed stream of angry accusations, blaming her aunt for not allowing her the freedom to escape from marriage and choose her own way of life; and making her suicidal intentions perfectly plain. "My lost friend Camille has a weapon which is the only remedy for such ills as mine; if she will accompany me, we will journey to the Elysian fields together; in any case I intend to take with me my wretched child, who shall never be made to endure the miseries that I have suffered."

Ellen, reading these lines (which had been released by the police and were printed in *Paris-Soir*), could not help reflecting that to some people the miseries endured by Louise might seem like the height of comfort—but it is impossible to assess other people's feelings, she thought, next moment, more justly; Louise did suffer, there could be no doubt of that.

She was appalled by the appearance of Raoul after his return from police custody. Chancing to look from the window in the schoolroom—where she was packing up Menispe's toys to be sent to an orphanage—she saw him standing in his garden, outside the little pavilion where he had quarreled with Louise. His shoulders were stooped, his head sunk, he looked like a person who has received such severe punishment that his mind has collapsed. His expression was lost, bewildered, anguished. In three days he had aged twelve years; his cheeks were hollow, his brow furrowed, over his black hair lay a broad stripe of dusty gray.

Aghast, Ellen stepped back from the window, feeling it had been an infringement of his privacy even to witness such desolation. She did not see him again that day; he had gone to the library, Princess Tanofski reported, and shut himself up there.

"I think it best you do not attend the funeral, Mademoiselle Paget," that lady added tartly. "Your presence might cause further unpleasant comment and speculation; there are bound to be representatives from all those disgusting newspapers. You may employ the time in packing up your possessions; I understand that your godmother will return here for the collation after the ceremony, and she is then prepared to carry you back with her to the Britannic Embassy."

Ellen concurred, but with a sore heart. She had not relished the prospect of the funeral, where no doubt she would be exposed to cold or malicious scrutiny from all the members of the de la Ferté family; but she had felt it to be the last, least thing she could do for Menispe and Louise. She had no intention, however, of intruding where she was not wanted.

Her packing did not take long. As she folded garments, sorted books, and laid sheets of music together, she was reminded of her departure from Brussels. I always seem to leave in disgrace, she thought dejectedly. But at least when I quitted Madame Bosschère's Pensionnat, I had a destination ahead of me; I was traveling to a place where I was wanted and needed. Where am I going now? What lies ahead of me?

The clock of St. Etienne chimed eleven. This was the time at which the funeral service was scheduled to commence, and Ellen had resolved to spend the next hour in prayer and meditation; but Gaston the footman knocked and entered to tell her, respectfully, that a lady had called and wished to speak to her.

"Not Mademoiselle de Rhetorée?" asked Ellen in astonishment.

"Oh, no, mademoiselle; an English miladi." And Gaston proffered a card on a salver. Hardly able to believe her eyes, Ellen read: *Mrs. Samuel Bracegirdle, Maple Grove, Burley, Stoke-on-Trent.*

"Good gracious! Of course I will see her, Gaston. Where is she? The lady is my sister."

The reunion between the two sisters began in a burst of affection. They had not much in common, but Kitty, shallow, lively, and pretty, had always been carelessly kind to the little Ellen, seven years younger, and felt sincerely sorry for her now. While Ellen, lonely and wretched, was spontaneously delighted to see a representative of her own family.

"Kitty! I am so rejoiced to see you! Is Mr. Bracegirdle here too? What on earth are you doing in Paris?"

"Good gracious, child! Your looks have improved out of all measure! I would not have believed it possible! And your dress! That dark color don't suit you—however, mourning, of course, it can't be helped—still, that line is far and away smarter than anything I saw while passing through London. How much was that rep a yard, pray tell me? And the needlepoint? Did you buy it ready-made, or have it made up? The piping is beyond anything! Ah, if only I could take you back with me to Maple Grove—"

"But, Kitty, do tell me how you come to be here? Is your husband in Paris on business? I thought he never traveled? Are you staying with Lady Morningquest?"

"That old meddler? I should say not! If *she* had not thrust in her oar, you would still be earning an honest living in Brussels. No, I passed the night at an hotel—B. will have a fit when he hears what it cost—no matter. How do I come to be here? Why, to take you home, of course, silly child! You must not pass another night under *this* roof."

"No," said Ellen mechanically, "I did not intend to. My things are all packed. I was waiting—"

Kitty interrupted. "Your things are packed? Why, that's capital. Here—you—" She turned and addressed Gaston in French which, considering the years she had spent in Brussels, was hardly a credit to her. "Have my sister's boxes taken down to my carriage."

"*Très bien, madame.*"

"But, Kitty—how can I? I am supposed to go to my godmother—"

"Psha! Where's the sense in that? She don't want you, I'll be bound; and the sooner you are away from here, the better. Indite a note to Paulina Morningquest—the servants can give it to her—and let's be off."

Kitty had put on weight since her marriage. At twenty, round-faced, rosy-cheeked, with curly dark hair, she had been a lively, bonny girl. Now solidly built, high-colored, clad in matronly fringes and velvets, she had become a presence of some authority. Despite this, Ellen resisted a moment longer; but then she thought: After all, why should I not go with Kitty? It's true, Lady Morningquest will be glad to be rid of me. She only takes me in from a sense of duty; I shall be a horrible reminder of her failure to avert the tragedy—she will scold me all the time I stay with her. And Raoul? I should not have seen him again in any case. In a week's time he will have forgotten my existence and that will be best for him. Should I write him a note? No, that would be neither prudent nor proper.

Again, she had a sense of events repeating themselves.

She did pause to say good-bye to the Abbé de Grandville, who, stricken by violent gout, had not been able to attend the funeral service, but was reading his breviary in the library.

"I am leaving now with my sister, Monsieur l'Abbé—so I will bid you farewell."

He greeted this news with gloomy approval and surprised her by saying, "I shall miss you, mademoiselle. But doubtless it is for the best. And so you return to England?"

"I—I really am not sure," said Ellen. The whole thing had happened so fast that she had not paused to consider whither Kitty was whisking her.

"M. Grandville, will you—will you please give my—my best salutations to the Comte, your nephew, and say that I hope—I hope time will bring him solace and a new happiness."

"Thank you, mademoiselle. I will do so." The pouched, weary old eyes briefly surveyed her, he gave a slight nod, then returned to his murmured orisons.

Ellen left her note for Lady Morningquest with Gaston, and went out to the carriage, where she heard Kitty tell the driver to go straight to the Gare du Nord.

"But, Kitty! You intend quitting Paris so soon?"

"Of course. I only had leave from B. to stay one night—or as long as it took to extricate you from those Frogs. Benedict will be waiting for us at the station. He undertook to reserve a compartment."

"Benedict? Did *Benedict* accompany you?"

"Certainly he did; since nothing would persuade Mr. B. to cross the Channel. Benedict has, I must say, been of the greatest possible assistance. We have much to thank him for."

"I might have known it," muttered Ellen. "Tell me, Kitty: what made you so determined to come and rescue me?"

"Why, child—we could hardly stand by and leave you in such a scandalous situation; there were even stories about it all in the English newspapers. Mr. B. was quite disgusted that such things were being said about some-body connected with his family."

"So he gave you leave to come and fetch me?" suggested Ellen with curling lip.

"Yes; but only after Benedict had agreed to escort me. It has all fallen out quite conveniently," said Kitty, digging in her reticule for coins to pay the driver, "because, of course, it is your duty to come home in any case, and prevent Pa from marrying that odious woman; but I could see that so long as you were snug in a fine situation, you would be hard to drag away from Paris. But now you have got to shift, so it is really just as well that silly Louise Throstlewick made an end of herself; I remember her well; she was at Madame's for three terms when I was there—a haughty, peevish creature who would speak to nobody."

To this, Ellen had nothing to say.

Ten

THE JOURNEY BACK TO ENGLAND WAS LONG, TEDIOUS, and remarkable only for a violent quarrel which took place on deck between Ellen and Benedict Masham; Kitty, who was a wretched sailor, having retired below to the ladies' cabin with her smelling salts and her maid.

"I would be greatly obliged, Mr. Masham, if you could see your way to desist from meddling in my private affairs!"

"Your affairs, my dear Ellen, are hardly private when they are reported in *The Times* and the *Morning Post*."

Ellen could have slapped him. She felt—with fury, with despair—that she was being treated like a naughty child, snatched away from misdoing, scolded, given no right to exercise her own will or choose her own course. She, who had been earning her own living for years, while Benedict was still at college! And why, of all people in the world, should Benedict and Kitty assume the right to judge her? Kitty, who had married a disagreeable man twice her age for his money—who lived in a hideous Midlands town, whose husband manufactured nails and talked with a Bradford accent—how dared she venture to lay down rules for other people's conduct? Let alone Benedict—Ellen stared at him with real hate.

Having addressed his remark to her in a cool, measured tone, he was leaning on the rail and gazing at the ominously large waves as if there were no more to be said. He looked, as always, trim, composed, and elegant, in gray trousers, dark broadcloth coat, beautifully cut, and fine, soft black ulster; he held his hat in his hand, for the wind hummed menacingly in the shrouds, but his thick corn-colored hair remained annoyingly unruffled; the fashionably jutting beard he had recently grown and his travel-bronzed skin gave him a somewhat buccaneering appearance.

Whereas Ellen felt herself to be blown about, blowsy and untidy; she had not dressed for a sea voyage; her bonnet threatened every minute to lift off her head, her shawl and skirts tugged and fluttered (and she had much ado to keep the latter from flying up in a most undignified and improper manner—she was glad at least not to be wearing a crinoline, for she noticed that the English ladies still adhering to this fashion were in even worse difficulties); her hair was being whirled over her face, and a huge lump in her throat prevented her from giving Benedict the setdown he deserved. Women had the worst of it in every possible way, she thought resentfully; considered incapable of making sensible decisions for themselves, treated as if they were mentally deficient, and obliged to dress in clothes that curtailed or prevented any active life and left them at a hopeless disadvantage.

Clutching at the rail to keep her balance, she, too, stared at the humpbacked, slate-colored waves, each with an ominous curdle of foam bristling against the dark sky.

"Had you not best go below?" inquired Benedict coldly. "It appears likely that we shall run into a severe squall."

"Thank you, I would rather remain here." The deck was, in fact, infinitely preferable to the hot, crowded ladies' cabin, filled with retching, lamenting figures, all in competition for the horsehair couches. Benedict can get wet mounting guard over me, Ellen thought vindictively, and serve him right.

However, it soon began to be plain that Benedict's clothes were better adapted than Ellen's for keeping out the weather.

"You will be soaked," he observed censoriously.

"It is of no consequence, I don't regard it." She tried not to shiver. The weather in Paris had been sultry and she had only a thin muslin dress and cashmere shawl.

"Where are your other things?"

"Packed away in the baggage hold, no doubt."

Benedict went off, and shortly reappeared with a ladies' macintosh cape which he had procured from a stewardess.

"Thank you," she said with stiff hostility. "That was not necessary."

"Don't be an obstinate little fool. What use will you be to your family if you return home only to succumb to a feverish cold?"

"Benedict: will you tell me why, just why you and Kitty—and Eugenia, too, I suppose—think you are entitled to drag me from Paris like—like a child—and make me return to a place where I am not wanted, and have no wish to go?"

He removed his gaze from the heaving sea, set it on her dispassionately, and replied, "My dear Ellen. We are not dragging you from Paris—as you put it. You are a free agent. Come, consider! You are highly educated, and reputed to have superior sense—do not, I beg, behave like a ten-year-old. You *must* be aware that your situation in Paris was highly undesirable, and might soon have become notorious. They—we all—wished to prevent you from making a fool of yourself."

"Thank you! I would not have done so."

He ignored this, and went on in the same measured manner. "Also—a fact which you seem to have over-looked, or choose to ignore—you can be of real use to your sisters at this juncture. Their anxieties about your father are not idle. *He* is in danger of making a far *greater* fool of himself; of falling into a wholly unsuitable entanglement, from which it is extremely urgent that he be rescued. I have met this housekeeper—this Mrs.

Pike—and can only say that her employment was a most unfortunate piece of bad judgment on the part of my officious aunt Blanche—her excuse must be that it was done in haste, at the time of your father's accident."

"And why should you, Kitty, and Eugenia set yourselves up to be arbiters of my father's actions?" demanded Ellen hotly. "Perhaps he is truly fond of this Mrs. Pike—how can you know his state of mind? Why should you feel yourselves entitled to meddle in the matter?"

"Oh, come, my dear Ellie, you are not lacking in sense—don't pretend to be stupid out of willful obstinacy! You know your father. Like you, he is obstinate as a mule, won't look a step out of his way, once he is set on a thing—despite the fact that he is learned in the law and a Justice of the Peace. He is selfish, pigheaded, narrow-minded, bigoted, and wholly intent on securing his own comfort, cost what it may. I had ample opportunity to observe this while he was married to my mother."

A sharp retort sprang to Ellen's lips concerning Lady Adelaide, but she suppressed it. Instead she replied in a trembling tone, "Thank you. And I suppose I resemble him?"

Benedict gave her a glance full of exasperation.

"In your self-centeredness and pigheadedness, I begin to think you do! Can you not see that your father is to be pitied? I believe he truly loved your mother—"

"He never showed it! He sent me away from home—who would have been a comfort to her when she was ill—and, and he married *your* mother before the grass had grown on her grave—"

"Oh, my dear girl! Use the sense your creator gave you. My featherbrained mama was on the catch for him, because she had once felt a girlish attachment for him and believed him to be a hero—a Phoebus—something quite other than what he was; a notion of which she, poor fool, was rapidly disabused once she was married to him! And *he* was lonely; was simply looking—blindly and precipitately—for someone to replace your mother; which he still is."

"And why should Mrs. Pike not be that?"

He gave a short laugh.

"Mrs. Pike! Just wait till you see her!"

"If—if she is so undesirable," went on Ellen doggedly, "and if your aunt Blanche and the Bishop and my sisters have not been able to convince Papa of the fact, why should you believe *me* capable of doing so? You do not—seem to have much respect for my other abilities."

"I know nothing of your other abilities! The point is that you will be on the spot. There is almost certainly something discreditable about the woman, which you will be able to discover."

"In other words, you want me to be a spy?"

"In order to keep *your* hands clean, you would allow your father to become ensnared in a disgraceful alliance?"

This had an uncomfortable echo of Germaine de Rhetorée. Benedict went on, in a milder tone, "Oh, I am aware that it may be disagreeable, returning to the Hermitage; your father will be surly, Mrs. Pike is an odious woman—and you have been used to earn your own living, it will be hard to be once more in a position of dependence. But can you not consider your brother and your little sister, how glad they will be of your company?"

Determined not to be mollified, Ellen said, "I doubt that! Vicky hardly knows me, she has not seen me above four or five times in her life. And Gerard is always wrapped up in his own concerns. Had you considered, moreover—Papa will very likely not permit me to remain at home for long. He will be expecting me to find another situation."

"It is more likely that you will find a husband," remarked Benedict. "I don't doubt all the local beaux will be clustering round, now you have acquired such a Parisian polish. I believe Wheelbird, the attorney's clerk, still calls regularly to inquire for news of you—"

Here he made a tactical error. Ellen hit back savagely. "Indeed? And does pretty Dolly the dairymaid still inquire after *you*, I wonder?"

Benedict's expression became blank. He replied with glacial calm, "Dolly Randall has been happily married to a young farmer at Lickfold for five years. His name is Tom Barren and they have three children."

"How satisfactory," said Ellen with equal calm.

They eyed one another like gladiators.

"If I were to accept some Petworth suitor," said Ellen after a pause, "I should hardly be in a position to prevent Papa from marrying Mrs. Pike, should I?"

"Oh, I don't imagine it will take you very long to send Mrs. Pike packing," Benedict replied blandly. "Remembering the rapidity of your action over Dolly, I credit you with some skill in a campaign of that kind."

"And then—having established Papa with a more respectable housekeeper—have I your leave to return to Paris?"

"Why should you wish to return to Paris? To get into another scrape?"

"*I was not in a scrape!* I love Paris. I have friends there."

"Who, for instance? That snaky de Rhetorée girl?"

"People of intellect! Why should you feel free to catechize me? Writers, men of letters, whom I talked to at Louise's salons. People who are capable of conversing intelligently!"

"Oh, I see. Minds of true elegance and refinement! Of course, we poor English rustics can't be expected to converse intelligently."

"Do you think you are doing so now?"

"Come, Ellie! Don't let us quarrel!" His tone, his expression were coaxing, but then he added fatally, "I daresay your head has been a little turned by all the attention you may have received—English young ladies are not so common in Paris, after all. No doubt Raoul de la Ferté, poor fish, went out of his way to be polite, but still, I fancy—"

Ellen said in a shaking voice, "It may interest you to know that I passed last night with Raoul de la Ferté!"

The silence that fell between them then was like the blank pause while a duelist stares at the blood pouring out of him, before he realizes that he has a mortal wound.

"You did what?"

"You heard what I said."

He had gone very white, under the bronze; after a moment or two he asked, "Do you propose to marry him?"

"Certainly not."

"Then I shall take the next boat back to Paris and go after him with a horsewhip."

"You will do nothing of the sort. You would be making a great fool of yourself." With angry joy, Ellen realized that she had gained the ascendancy in this painful battle. What it had cost would take some time to assess. "You would be creating just the kind of scandal you seemed so anxious to avoid. And for what? He and I will never see each other again."

Benedict stared at her for several minutes. At last, swallowing, he said hoarsely, "It seems I have been mistaken about you. I believed that, despite your obstinacy, you had high principles. You are not the person I took you to be."

"Evidently not!"

Benedict muttered, "And he—he—I knew his reputation as a rake and a gambler—but I could never have imagined—" His voice died away, he stood gripping the rail with white knuckles, staring out over the whipped-cream breakers.

Ellen thought, wearily, dreamily, of the hours she

had spent last night in the ice-cold library, while the candles guttered, and the ashes of the dead fire crumbled in the hearth, as Raoul, crouched on the floor, his head in her lap, had wept out his wretchedness and remorse, and talked, endlessly talked, about his troubled relations with Louise, and about his little lost daughter. "Menispe—Menispe—how could she? I would never—never—Oh, what have I done? How can I possibly atone for this guilt?"

Ellen said levelly to Benedict, "Perhaps you should give up trying to interfere in other people's lives. To do that advantageously, some kind of rapport or sympathy, I believe, is necessary…"

"Pray say no more, Miss Paget. I am *indeed* sorry that I ever meddled in *your* affairs."

The rest of the crossing was passed by them in silence. The air became bitterly cold as they neared England, and Ellen began to feel chilled to the bone and rather sick as well, partly from the motion of the ship, more from the bitterness of the quarrel. Fortunately the cliffs of Dover were now in sight—their progress had been hastened by the force of the following wind. The Kentish coast appeared unutterably damp, gray, and dismal; Ellen began to feel as if she were returning, not to another kingdom, but to another planet.

❧

The last stage of Ellen's journey was taken alone.

She had not spoken to Benedict again after the quarrel on the boat; at Dover station he had silently escorted the two sisters to a ladies-only compartment on the London train, installed Kitty's maid next door, and then taken himself off to a divan car, where he could smoke. There had been time to telegraph Mr. Bracegirdle, so at the terminus, as soon as Benedict had ascertained that the ladies were in safe hands, he removed himself at speed, courteously raising his hat to Kitty, bestowing on Ellen not a single glance.

At the time of his wedding to Kitty six years earlier, Mr. Bracegirdle had been a thickset Yorkshireman with reddish hair, a florid complexion, and protruding blue eyes. He had then been forty (a first wife had died in childbirth) but had looked considerably more than eighteen years older than his bride. Now the age disparity seemed to have lessened, due to Kitty's matronly appearance and stout girth. Ellen was obliged to acknowledge to herself that the couple seemed well matched; their greeting was calm, but they appeared to have a good understanding. Bracegirdle's hair was now brindled with gray; otherwise he looked much as he had done at the wedding. The protuberant eyes turned upon Ellen, surveying her person and her blue Parisian costume with a complete lack of enthusiasm.

"Well, miss. Seems ye ha' got yourself into a right pickle over there in Frogland. Lucky for you I could spare Kitty to step over and fetch ye back, or ye'd have ended up in a Frog jail, happen."

"I do not think it would have come to that, Mr. Bracegirdle," Ellen said, restraining an impulse to tell him to mind his own business. "But I am obliged to you and my sister, naturally, for your concern on my behalf."

"Humph! Well, get in, get in"—for he had a cab waiting. "We'll discuss it at dinner. Brown's Hotel, cabman, and look lively."

Kitty, however, declared that she was still suffering from the effects of mal de mer, and insisted on dining off a tray in her bedroom; it was easy for Ellen, similarly, to plead fatigue and avoid the threatened discussion. But Mr. Bracegirdle pinned her down next morning in the hotel coffee room.

"Now, see here, miss—I've invested a fair bit of capital and time in this business—sending Kitty off to France, kicking my heels here in London waiting for her—I joost want to make certain that investment's repaid."

"I am not fully certain that I understand you, Mr. Bracegirdle," replied Ellen coldly.

"You onderstand me perfectly well, miss! Let's have none of these finicking, Frenchified manners, if you please. Kitty and I—and Eugenia too—want you to put a spoke in that woman's wheel. You know who I mean—the Pike woman. Your pa's a well-found man—a bit clutch-fisted, but there's nowt wrong wi' that, I'm the same road meself, all the more to put by for a rainy day; I married your sister Catherine in the reasonable expectation of a share of his brass by an' by, an' I don't aim to see it all squandered on some fly-by-night widow. A—no argufication, now!" as she opened her mouth to protest. "I've met the woman—lady, *she* calls herself—an' I could tell, as soon as look at her, that she's out o' the wrong basket—bent as a buttonhook, or my name's not Sam Bracegirdle. You ain't a fool—you've been about the world a bit—you'll soon see what I mean."

Kitty now slowly descended the stairs—her plump face still imbued with a waxen pallor—and at once added her arguments to those of her husband.

Deciding that dispute would be a waste of breath—though she found Mr. Bracegirdle detestable, and her sister hardly less so—Ellen said simply, "My opinions carry no weight with Papa—why should my presence affect the matter?"

"Pooh, pooh! You're a canny lass—I daresay there's a hundred and one ways ye can discourage the business. Show the woman oop a bit—open his eyes to her faults. Find out all ye can about her—there's bound to be summat shady. And, if necessary—send for us. At least ye'll be on t'spot, and your presence will prevent your pa compromising himself—or the woman saying he has."

Resolving privately that she would do none of these

things, Ellen, for the sake of peace, at least let it be understood that she would watch the situation and keep the Bracegirdles apprised of how matters stood at the Hermitage. Then it was time for her to catch her train at the Pimlico station while they went north.

"Mind an' remember what I've said, now!" was her brother-in-law's parting injunction as he saw her into her cab. "It ain't convenient for me to keep stepping down into Soossex, so we're relying on you!"

❧

Sitting in the small local train between Pulborough junction and the new Petworth station, Ellen meditated wryly on the difference between earned money and the kind that comes by gift or bequest. Earned money, honestly come by, did nothing but good; while the other kind seemed instantly to poison or vitiate the relations between donor and recipient. Louise had hated her husband, because his wealth had supported her; Germaine, straightforward and self-respecting in her dealings with journals and publishers, became a ruthless parasite on Louise and Raoul, exploiting them without remorse or pity. Kitty and Eugenia, brought up on strict Christian principles, seemed to throw all these principles to the winds at the mere possibility of losing any part of what was not theirs by right, but was merely what their father might choose to bequeath to them.

It is his own fortune to dispose of as he pleases, thought Ellen, gazing at the pale stubble fields as they slipped by. Thank heaven I have a little money saved, so that I need not be dependent; thank heaven I have the means of earning my living again in the future. Making up to someone for their money is so odious!

But then—with some discomfort—she thought of how Germaine would sneer at this sentiment, and call her a self-satisfied English prig. It was easy to be virtuous if one was secure. And the thought of Germaine led on to Benedict's accusations, which were too painful to be reviewed just at present. Attempting to put them from her mind, she turned her eyes again to the landscape. It was seen from a new angle, for she had never returned home by train; the railway had reached Petworth only two years before. A somewhat unsettled aspect of the country close at hand made this evident: the banks were still raw-looking, covered with willow herb and thistles, fields had been oddly divided, and the hedges had not yet grown back. It made Ellen mournful to see well-loved copses and meadows thus mutilated; yet, she reflected, it is wonderfully convenient to be able to travel down from London in little over an hour! Now the South Downs were in sight, a bare undulating line of hills beyond the Arun marshes; now, in the Rother Valley, copses on the gentle hillsides closed off the more distant view. The trees were dark green, dull with the tarnish of summer's end, the land lay tranquil in mild hazy weather, a pause of silence and recollection before the winds of autumn.

Here every tree, stile, and thatched cottage was a well-known friend. It is queer, thought Ellen, that the sight of the country makes me so happy when my heart is charged with misery, and there is nobody ahead to welcome me, no one I love or wish to see except Dr. Bendigo and Aunt Fanny—dear Aunt Fanny!

She climbed out onto the short wooden platform and found that she was the only person there.

"Has Mr. Paget's carriage not come to meet me?" she asked the porter as she handed him her ticket.

"There's been no carriage here s' arternoon, missie. The omnibus'll be waiting yonder, though, if ye want to get into Petworth."

He took Ellen's bags, and she followed him toward the Railway Inn, wondering if this was a deliberate

snub from her father—or had he not received Sam
Bracegirdle's telegram?

As she neared the inn—built since her last visit—
Ellen's spirits were revived by the sound of music, played
on flute, fiddle, and tabor. On a patch of green before
the public house, twelve men were practicing a morris
dance. It was only a rehearsal, Ellen could see, for they
did not have on the traditional bells or ribbons; but they
danced well and seriously, with great spirit, weaving in
and out of an elaborate figure. The music was provided
by two men, a little shriveled grasshopper of a fellow and
a white-haired elder, who sat on a bench by the open
inn door, and a boy, who stood behind them and played
the fiddle. The tune—a lazy, teasing, seductive lilting
rhythm called "Merry Milkmaids"—had been long
familiar to Ellen; she smiled unconsciously at the sound,
quickening her pace. She could see the horse bus waiting
by the green, and the driver leaning against the shaft.
Evidently he was in no hurry, and watched the dancers
with a critical eye, sometimes shouting a comment. As
Ellen reached the bus, the figure came to an end. The
dancers, smiling and panting—for the day, though gray,
was sultry and warm—flung themselves on the trampled
turf. Several, including the boy fiddler, went into the
inn, and reappeared with mugs of cider. The boy did not
return. The cider was passed about the group; also pieces
of fruitcake.

A fair-haired young man came up to Ellen and solemnly offered her a piece of cake. He looked a little like
Benedict.

"Morrisers' cake—for luck, missie!" he said, smiling.

Sweet fruitcake was the last thing she wanted after a
hot journey, but Ellen took a piece.

"Welcome back from furrin parts, missie," he said as
she nibbled it.

"Why, you are Ted Thatcher—I hardly knew you!

You have grown so tall. How is your mother? Does she still have trouble with that hand?"

Now several of the men came up and greeted her—diffidently, offhandedly but she knew there was genuine warmth underneath. Long-buried memories returned, and she was able to address each by name.

"Mr. Goble—Penfold—Gatton— Pullin—"

"Reckon your dad'll be pleased to have you home, then. 'Twas a bad business when his lady got herself killed. Not far from here, just up the hill, 'twas. And now he's found hisself a 'countable proud-stomached house-keeper from Wiltsheer. Fair put the wind up my wife's cousin Sukey at the Hermitage, that Mrs. Pike do!"

"Hush thy mouth, Tom Gatton; Missie Paget 'on't want to hear thy tales—"

At this point the driver intimated that he was ready to set off. Ellen, the only passenger, gave him her six-pence and climbed on board the bus. As it started on its mile-long journey (Lord Leconfield, owner of Petworth house and park, had not wished the railway to pass too close and disturb his guests, or deer)—"I admire that your brother didn't ride back into town with you," said the driver.

"My brother? What can you mean?"

"Warn't that Mus' Gerald I see goo into the pub?"

All the country people called Gerard Gerald, Ellen remembered. She said, "My brother? That boy who went inside? Surely not?"

"Ah, I reckon as 'twas," the driver persisted. "Since owd Doc Bendigo died, he do spend a deal of time down thurr."

"Dr. Bendigo has died? Oh no—when?" A pang of pure grief transfixed Ellen; the world suddenly seemed a gray, dusty, impoverished place.

"Took sudden lars' month; eighty-two, 'e were. A fine owd fellow; you 'on't get 'em like that no more."

Trying to master her grief, Ellen wondered if the driver could possibly have been right about Gerard. If it was he, she thought, either Father's attitudes have changed amazingly or the boy is courting disaster. At the very least, a shocking scene is in store for him if Father finds out.

The tall church steeple came in sight as they breasted a slope.

"'E must be wearying for home, Mis' Ellen," said the driver.

Ellen automatically agreed, but she thought his words hardly described her feelings. Such a contradictory weight pressed on her heart that, perversely, she wished the road were twice as long, wished it would never end. The insidious tune of the men's morris dance wound through her head; now it seemed wholly sad. The kind greeting of Ted Thatcher, who looked like Benedict, had stirred up yet again the memory of their miserable quarrel. And—supposing that had indeed been Gerard at the inn—had he recognized her and coldly, warily, chosen not to make himself known? Did he think she would betray him?

She thought of Raoul de la Ferté, alone in his huge mansion, and of Germaine disguised as a peasant somewhere in the French countryside. All that former life seemed to have exploded—like a seed-pod, she thought, half consciously noticing the downy filaments of willow herb floating over the road; probably I shall never see those people again. Time moves on and we move with it. There came to her a strange, fatalistic conception of the irreversibility of time; as the horse plodded up the gentle hill, its hooves seemed to rap out the words: Never more, Never more, Never again.

"Your dad found the Doom Stone yet?" inquired the driver chattily.

"Doom Stone? What in the world is that?"

"Why, they're a-mending the Cathedral, over to Chiddester, and they found a 'dentical big slab of stone, called a Heaven Stone, that did by rights oughta be set up by the right-hand side of the main door. But the Bishop he say there did oughta be another stone—that be the Doom Stone—to goo on the left-hand side o' the doorway. And your dad be main keen to have it found. Twelve mortal pound, he promise, to the man as'll bring him a true tale of where it be."

Ellen was amazed to hear that her father, usually so frugal with his cash, should have offered so large a sum for such an object. "Why is it not in the Cathedral now?" she asked.

"Ah, who can tell? Mebbe owd Mus' Cromwell he took it away, in they bygone wars. Or thieves—there've been aplenty rapscallions since that church were builded. 'Ere we be at the Half Moon, missie. And no one to meet you, by the look of it."

There was not, and Ellen, hurt, but by now unsurprised at the omission, paid a boy another sixpence to carry her bags up the hill to her father's house.

The small town of Petworth did not seem to have changed in the slightest particular since she had last been there. The houses, mostly of soft old red brick, looked small, comfortable, trim, and rural, compared to the grandeur and squalor, the palaces and tenements of Paris. The cobbled square and narrow street smelt of hay and horse dung, and of the late roses and asters in little gardens half seen through arches and up alleys. There were few people about at this time of early evening; a couple of women with vaguely familiar faces glanced curiously at Ellen in her dark-blue Parisian dress.

The orchard in front of her father's house was heavy with a handsome crop, not quite ready for picking. Ellen had a brief memory of sitting with Lady Morningquest in the train crossing the flat Flemish plain covered with orchards and poplars, wondering what Paris held in store for her. How full of hope I was, in spite of all, she thought.

Then Sue, the elderly housemaid, was opening the front door, and breaking into a wide smile of welcome.

"Miss Ellen! Well, I'll be jiggered! No one said ye was a-coming! Daze it, ye'll be as welcome as flowers in spring. Well, I *am* pleased to see ye!" And she gave Ellen an unaffected hug of joy, which was warmly reciprocated.

"But did Mr. Bracegirdle's telegram not arrive?"

"Not as I knows on, Miss Ellen. Never mind; I'll have your bed readied up in a trice. You dad'll be dumbfounded with joy to see you, I reckon," she added with less certainty.

"Where is he, Sue?"

"Such a hot afternoon, he's out in the garden, him an' that Mrs. Pike." An expressive grimace indicated her opinion of the latter lady. She leaned close and whispered, "Things has gone badly since ye were here last. Lady Adelaide warn't a mucher, but she were better nor *her*. Do you go out and make yourself known, now, I'll take these up."

Ellen walked into the well-loved garden. The house looked across a deep grassy valley, but from the downstairs windows, or on first walking out, a visitor would never have guessed this; a massive yew hedge, twenty feet high, enclosed the rose garden immediately next to the house. The hedge was so high and thick that the plot it bordered was like a room, warm and quiet and sweet-smelling. Ellen lingered to sniff a late lily and pick a sprig of rosemary; then, hearing voices, she went on through an arch in the yew hedge, to the path beyond, known by the family as the Valley Walk. This was a grassy ride, a hundred yards long, running between two summerhouses. The yew hedge bounded it on the garden side; on the other, a low stone wall permitted a wide view over the valley and the distant northern weald.

Ellen believed she would never tire of this prospect; seeing it now, she felt that a thirst, of which she had been almost unaware, was suddenly, aboundingly satisfied; she could have remained leaning on the wall and looking out for the rest of the afternoon.

But at the west end of the grass walk, in front of the larger summerhouse, she could see three people: a man in a top hat seated on a garden bench, absorbed in a book— her father; a little girl in straw hat and white dress sitting on the grass—that must be Vicky; and, with her back to the serene view, ensconced very upright on another seat, a handsomely dressed lady in voluminous satin brocade, with ringlets, embroidery frame, and elaborately ornamented cap—a rather sharp-featured lady who must be Mrs. Pike.

Eleven

VICKY PAGET WAS AN OBSERVANT LITTLE CREATURE. Neither of her parents had ever loved her; Luke took no interest in a fourth female child, and Lady Adelaide was far too dissatisfied with the outcome of her impulsive second marriage to expend much energy on its sole product.

Vicky had to make do, during her nearly six years, as best she could, with the random affections of servants, who, under Lady Adelaide's fretful regime, came and went with unsettling frequency. In consequence, her nature, though it held the capacity for feeling, was wary, skeptical, and ready to retreat at the first rebuff. She made overtures to nobody, had no friends, and managed to contrive her own amusements out of very little. She did possess a knitted doll, presented to her when she was three by her aunt Blanche. This object, now somewhat worn and raveled, was her chief treasure. But since the advent of Mrs. Pike, Vicky, realizing with unchildlike shrewdness that the housekeeper, who had a very punitive nature, was likely to seize the doll as a hostage, kept her plaything concealed in an earthenware jar under the yew hedge. It was better to have a hidden toy than none.

Instead of games, Vicky therefore employed her powers of observation to the full, and had lately developed a passion for recording her visual discoveries on any scraps of paper she could beg from the servants, steal, or acquire by vigilant attention to wastebaskets. She hoarded morsels of crayon, charcoal, and pencil stubs.

Although still unable to read, her constant practice had instilled in her a remarkable facility in portraiture; many a citizen of Petworth would have been startled if he had guessed with what accuracy the small, secretive-looking, dark-haired child who stared at him in the street was later able to record, not only his features and posture, but even some passing expression or grimace, on a torn sugar bag or soiled piece of shelf paper.

This habit of watching had also made Vicky very attentive to behavior. Today, from early in the morning, she had been aware that Mrs. Pike was on the lookout, that something unusual must be liable to occur. Vicky's vigilance had been especially aroused by the housekeeper's unwonted amiability toward her. In the morning she had been allowed to help make quince jelly and lick the spoons. Then, midway through the afternoon, Mrs. Pike had smoothed and twisted the child's dark ringlets and told her to bring a plate of biscuits while she herself carried a jug of lemonade to Mr. Paget, who sat reading on the little terrace by his garden room. It was such a hot afternoon! said the housekeeper; Vicky's father must be in need of refreshment. At this, Vicky's suspicions mounted sky-high. She was never, in normal circumstances, permitted to venture into her father's presence. To be told that she might sit on the grass by her papa and eat a biscuit made her even more mistrustful. Mrs. Pike, meanwhile, established herself nearby with an air of condescension, as if graciously deigning to snatch a few moments from her pressing duties for social intercourse.

She looks as if she were sitting for her portrait, thought Vicky, nibbling a caraway biscuit very slowly; and her fingers itched to pull a torn scrap of paper from its hiding place in her waistband and record the housekeeper's complacent yet expectant air as she sat sewing, from time to time casting a glance toward the yew arch.

As for Papa, after his initial air of vague wonder and

irritation, he had immediately returned to his book, and ignored his unwanted companions. Vicky sat quiet as a leaf; she knew that any fidgeting would incur instant dismissal, and she wanted another biscuit; also she was curious to see what Mrs. Pike was up to.

At long last her patience was rewarded.

A voice from the yew arch said, inquiringly, "Papa?" and a young lady emerged, walked across the grassy ride to admire the view over the wall, then came, with a certain diffidence, toward the little group. Though not tall, she was, Vicky thought, very pretty. Her face was faintly familiar—like the portrait of Papa's first Mrs. Paget in the dining room. Her dress would be far more interesting to draw than Mrs. Pike's bulbous crinoline, since it had so much more shape: draperies and swathings, an overskirt looped smoothly across the front and drawn up to a gathering at the back of the waist, with two rows of buttons on the bodice and a frill at the throat; while her tiny round blue hat was ornamented with a cockade of the same blue. Her pale face wore a slight, questioning smile.

"Good God!" said Mr. Paget, lowering his book and staring over it.

He did not look at all pleased.

"Why—goodness gracious me!" exclaimed Mrs. Pike in artless astonishment. "Who can this be?" She addressed the young lady. "I cannot understand, miss, why the maid did not announce you. Pray, did nobody answer the door?"

Her tone rang false in Vicky's ears; I don't believe she's really surprised, thought the child, watching the three faces.

The girl's tone was absent as she replied, "Why yes, thank you; Sue let me in. She said you were in the garden. Were you not, then, expecting me, Papa? Did you not receive Mr. Bracegirdle's telegram?"

"Telegram? Bracegirdle? Certainly not. Why the deuce should that fellow be sending me telegrams?"

"To tell you that I was coming."

"Mrs. Pike? Was any telegram delivered, ma'am?"

"Dear me no, Mr. Paget," said the housekeeper. "I should of course have informed you at once. Am I to understand that this is Miss Ellen? But what a charming surprise!"

She's lying, thought Ellen instantly; she knew I was coming, and she wanted it to be a disagreeable surprise for Papa. Meeting Mrs. Pike's cold china-blue eyes and hostile smile, she understood in a flash why Eugenia, Kitty, and Benedict had been so uncharacteristically unanimous in their dislike of the housekeeper.

"But I do not understand," Luke Paget was grumbling. "Why should Bracegirdle send a telegram about you, Ellen? Why did you not send it yourself? One can never rely on young persons to do anything in a planned, rational manner, showing consideration for others; it is all flibbertigibbet, here one minute, there the next. Why—pray—are you not in Paris?"

"Did you not read in the papers about the poor Comtesse de la Ferté?" began Ellen, but at this juncture Vicky piped up.

"But a boy *did* come with a message, Papa!" She was not going to see Ellen unfairly blamed. Rashly, she went on, "Do you not remember, Mrs. Pike, you were looking at the pippins in the orchard when he came through the gate, and you took the paper from him?"

"What moonshine is this, child?" said the housekeeper, a spot of color on either cheek, and Mr. Paget rapped out, "Speak when you are spoken to, miss, not before!"

Vicky, scarlet and silenced, hung her head. But she had impulsively pulled a torn paper from her belt. Ellen gently took it from her and saw that it was, in fact, the text of the message that Bracegirdle had dispatched.

"Wicked, wicked little girl!" exclaimed Mrs. Pike. "So *you* took the message, and, I suppose, proposed to do some more of your eternal scribbles on the paper, and leave your poor papa in ignorance?"

"I didn't! I did not! *You* tore it in half and threw it into the hall basket—I saw you—so I took it from there."

Mrs. Pike cast up her eyes to heaven.

"I know somebody who needs a good dose of malt and brimstone to cure her of telling untruths and prying, poking underhand ways. I am sure your papa agrees?"

"Yes," said Mr. Paget irritably. "It is very unladylike, Vicky, to go rummaging in wastepaper baskets. And if you took the paper from the boy and did not deliver it, that was exceedingly mischievous."

"I didn't! I didn't!"

Vicky was removed, tearful and struggling, by the housekeeper, who appeared to have considerable strength. Ellen looked after the pair, deeply troubled. She had a strong impulse to exclaim, "I am certain that Vicky was telling the truth and that woman was lying!" but restrained it. To embark at once on overt warfare with Mrs. Pike would be rash tactics, though she felt distressed for the child; and it would be likely to antagonize her father. She had best keep quiet, until she had a stronger case.

Meanwhile she continued to answer Luke Paget's impatient questions.

"But I fail to understand why you are come home. Why, if there was trouble in the house where you were employed—no, I never read news items about Paris—why did not Lady Morningquest find you another situation?"

"Oh, Papa! Poor Lady Morningquest was in great grief over the death of her niece—she was in no case to be finding me situations. Besides—do you begrudge me a brief holiday? I had hoped that—that you might be pleased to see me?" She refrained from saying *since the death of my stepmother*, which might annoy him further. Besides, there had been something alarmingly cozy—almost conjugal—about that garden scene with the jug of lemonade and Mrs. Pike's embroidery tambour, which quite banished any image of Luke Paget as a lonely disconsolate widower.

All at once Ellen began to feel a certain sympathy for Eugenia and Kitty.

❧

When Ellen went in to unpack and change her dress for dinner, she heard, as she climbed the stair, unmistakable sounds of sobs and retching. They came from the attic floor, where there were two small bedrooms.

Sue the housemaid, setting a jug of hot water on the washstand, listened to these with tight-pressed lips and a crease between her brows.

"That Pike," she muttered. "Pike her name and Pike her nature. Always dosing the poor child with brimstone or castor oil, or Gregory's powder, acos Master say it be his affair to slipper her if she's bad, but dosing the child *she* can do any time, and say 'tis for her good."

"Vicky sleeps up there?"

"Ah. Her in one attic, Mus' Gerald in t'other. Mrs. Pike, she have the big guest room. See to her own comfort, that one do."

Having slipped on a dress of silver-gray tarlatan suitable for such a warm evening, Ellen stole up to the stuffy attic floor, carrying with her a bundle of fashion magazines which Kitty had purchased in Paris and packed into one of Ellen's bags, where they had been forgotten. Kitty would be annoyed when she found she had lost her Paris modes, but they might be put to better use here. Ellen was sorry there had been no time to buy her small half sister a toy before leaving Paris, but perhaps the magazines might prove better than nothing.

Indeed, Vicky received them with rapture.

"Oh!" she breathed. "What *beautiful* ladies!"—studying the wasp-waisted giantesses with rosebud mouths and tiny extremities. Matter-of-factly, she added, "It seems almost a pity to draw on all these pages."

"Is that what you wish to do?"

"Of course. May I not?" Vicky asked anxiously.

"Do just as you wish," Ellen reassured her. The child's face was pale, still streaked with tears; she hiccupped from time to time. Her expression strongly tempted Ellen to promise that in any future confrontation with Mrs. Pike she would take Vicky's part; but she had best, she told herself, begin with discretion; such a promise might prove impossible to implement.

"Are you truly my sister Ellen?" Vicky was asking. "I don't remember you very well."

"You were only three when you saw me last, at Eugenia's baby's christening."

"I think you were not so pretty then? You had a pink gown."

"So I did."

"It had a collar like this." Vicky dragged a scrumpled page from under her pillow and drew a careful outline on it. Ellen noticed that the paper, an advertisement for Patent Soot Remover, was covered with drawings.

"Why, that is Papa!" she said, surprised. "And Mrs. Pike! These are very good, Vicky."

"I can do better now," said Vicky carelessly. "Those were done weeks ago. See, here is Sue—and Mr. Wheelbird—"

Ellen had to laugh, the expressions had been caught so shrewdly, the maid frowning with lower lip thrust out, the young lawyer open-mouthed in conversation, his eyes bulging and Adam's apple almost bursting from his tight collar. Vicky had a cartoonist's knack of seizing on the salient characteristic.

"I have more—" Vicky said, beginning to delve under

her mattress; but at this moment a step was heard on the stair, and she hurled herself back into bed.

"Mrs. Pike! She'll be in a rage when she finds you—"

"Don't worry," began Ellen; but fortunately the step proved to be that of Gerard, who put his head round the door, remarking, "Is that you, Sue? You won't half catch it if La Pike hears you in Vicky's room." Then he saw his sister and his jaw dropped. "*Ellen?* Nobody told me you had come home."

He was undoubtedly the boy who had played the fiddle at the Railway Inn, but Ellen realized now that he had simply not recognized her in her Parisian finery. She gave him a sisterly kiss, which he took defensively, backing away with a nervous air.

"Then it was you, playing for the morrisers!"

"For the Lord's sake—*hush!* Papa would just about—" He pantomimed a wild explosion, then rapidly disappeared into his own attic, from which sounds of hasty ablutions could be heard. Then he put a wet head back round the door to beg, "Whatever you do, don't mention that!"

The dinner gong boomed downstairs.

"Good nighty Vicky." Ellen hugged her small half sister. "There is more drawing paper in my box, which you shall have tomorrow; and some French crayons."

She could not help smiling at Vicky's awed expression as she retreated down the attic stair; though there was not much to smile at in this household, she could see.

Supper was a gloomy meal. Gerard did not mend matters by arriving late, which earned him a seven-minute reprimand from his father and continued subsequent rumblings throughout the meal. Ellen tried to enliven the conversation with descriptions of Paris and the boat trip, but Mr. Paget had a depressing habit of slapping down any idle remark, made to fill an awkward silence, with some withering rebuttal.

"French ladies all seem to have English terriers this year—"

"*All?* How can they *all* have? There would not be sufficient breeders in the Kingdom to satisfy such a demand."

Mrs. Pike, who, it appeared, ate with the family, did not help by letting fall numerous disparaging remarks about Paris and the French; these Ellen parried as good-temperedly as she could, although their ignorance irritated her even more than their evidently spiteful intention. Gerard, who had always been a silent boy, applied himself speechlessly to his plate, with shoulders hunched and eyes cast down. Luke, too, ate mainly in silence, apart from various snubs to Ellen and some animadversions as to the folly, laziness, and inconsiderate habits of the younger generation. Ellen recalled that it had always been impossible to please him. He always expected that people would prove to be idle, bungling, and unhelpful. If, contrary to expectation, they were skillful, handy, and anxious to please, it irritated him; and if his pessimism was proved correct, he was equally annoyed. In consequence, his gloom and displeasure were continuous; all that he saw appeared to depress and exasperate him.

Mrs. Pike made it her business to agree with all he said, emphatically nodding her capped and ribboned head up and down at each of his strictures.

The food was plain, tasteless, and served in penuriously small portions; Ellen, who had been hungry after her journey from London, rose at the end of the meal feeling almost as hungry as when she sat down.

After the dessert Mr. Paget remained in the dining room drinking a small glass of port. Mrs. Pike went down to the basement kitchen to reprimand the cook for putting too much sugar in the blackberry pie.

"Psst! Come out here a moment," murmured Gerard to Ellen with a sideways jerk of his head. She followed him into the garden, which was beginning to fade into dusk, and he dragged her away through a pair of wrought-iron gates and down a tree-lined way known as the Glebe Path, which led into the valley below the house.

"Can't talk within doors, that woman has ears like a bat," he explained. Then he came swiftly to his point. "I say, Ellen, did you bring any music with you from Paris? It is *devilishly* hard to buy sheet music here—I can't order it from Arnold's, or Pa would twig, and I can't invent pretexts to go to Chichester above once every six weeks or so."

Ellen had brought a little music, but at most of her catalogue of names he groaned.

"Liszt! Czerny! How could you? Mendelssohn is just tolerable. Oh, if only I had known you were coming. I could have asked you to bring me some Beethoven quartets."

"But how could you play a quartet? Do you have companions? And since when have you been learning the fiddle?"

"Oh, for a few months—don't tell Papa! Tom, at the Railway Inn, teaches me. Anyway, I like to read the scores. Beethoven is so tremendous, Ellie! I believe he is the greatest genius who ever lived."

Gerard would have gone on at length about Beethoven—Ellen saw he was just the same moody, self-absorbed creature as ever—but she interrupted him.

"Gerard, do you not see a great change in Papa?"

"He is worse-tempered than ever," agreed Gerard. "Forever harrying me about my Latin and law work—and I do work hard, he has no reason to complain, but he does. If he had his way I would never lift my nose from Blackstone's *Commentaries* and Mowbray's *Jurisprudence*. He's surly as a bear—though La Pike butters him up all she knows how—but that's nothing new?"

"He is so haggard and gaunt-looking! And his eyes,

when he is not speaking, have a—a kind of inward glare. And his voice is so hollow—as if he spoke from a pit."

"Oh, pho! I do not know what you are talking about. He is getting older, that is all. Will you ask him for the key of the garden room, Ellie?"

"Whatever for?"

"He has had the piano moved out there. You could say that you wish to play it—he will allow *you*. It is all right for girls. And he never goes there after dinner."

"But, you absurd boy, I don't wish to play. I am tired, after traveling, and intend to go to bed."

"Will you give me the music, then?"

"Oh, very well!"

As they returned, she asked, "Is there a piano at the Railway Inn?"

He nodded with a half grin. "If I play tunes for the customers, Tom lets me practice on it. And he pays me a shilling an hour. I slip out in the evenings—that's how I make money to buy music."

"You are *mad*. If Papa found out! Someone might easily tell him."

"No," Gerard said. "No one likes him in the town."

"Suppose Mrs. Pike heard?"

"Ah. She's a troublemaker, to be sure. But she's from Wiltshire—has no friends here."

"Where in Wiltshire?"

"I haven't a notion. She'd been looking after some old gentry who moved to Chichester—she came there with them, I fancy—Aunt Blanche hired her because they died and she came free at the time of Pa's accident."

Ellen resolved to try and find out more about Mrs. Pike's antecedents.

The housekeeper sat in the drawing room, working at her embroidery by the light of a parsimoniously small lamp. She received the news that Ellen proposed to retire with a small, cold nod. She did indeed already appear to regard herself as mistress of the establishment.

Ellen, glancing about the room, was saddened to see that most of her mother's plain graceful Hepplewhite and Gillow furniture had been replaced by heavily ornamented, plush-upholstered articles which took up a great deal of space and made the room seem small and overfull. No doubt these things had been acquired during Lady Adelaide's period as chatelaine. One or two of the discarded pieces had found their way upstairs to Ellen's chamber, which was otherwise, mercifully, unaltered. Lying in her narrow bed, listening to the owls in the orchard, she remembered how often she had longed to be here.

But now all was changed. She felt a desolation of sadness.

And Father, she thought. There is something dreadfully wrong with him, I am certain; beyond the pain of his mended hip. Can he be grieving over Lady Adelaide? I had not thought he loved her much.

He looks—he looks as if he owed somebody a debt, and does not know how he can ever pay it.

❧

Word rapidly spread through the town that Mr. Paget's third daughter had come home, and people soon resumed their habit of bringing sick children for Ellen to touch. This custom was probably augmented by the recent death of Dr. Bendigo; his replacement, young Dr. Smollett, had not yet gained the confidence of his patients.

"Shocking, vulgar superstition!" sniffed Mrs. Pike. "Carrying their nasty dirt and diseases to the back door— *I'd* soon put a stop to it."

But to her annoyance Mr. Paget would not take a stand on the matter. "My wife always permitted them" was all he said.

"*Lady Adelaide?*"

"No, no. Mrs. Paget, Ellen's mother. And Bendigo condoned it."

Dr. Bendigo had been one of the objects of Luke's reluctant, half-hostile respect.

"Well," said Mrs. Pike, "don't blame me if you find half the apples or all the poultry stolen away. *I* never *heard* of such a thing."

The rebuff did not ameliorate her relations with Ellen.

"Can you let me know how much longer you intend to stay, Miss Paget? With so much more to do, I fear I will need to be asking your papa for an increase in the housekeeping—which will not please him, I promise you!"

"He will probably feel better about it when he hears that I intend to undertake Vicky's tuition," calmly replied Ellen.

"What? And deprive poor old Mrs. Socket of her only paid occupation?"

"She wishes to give up teaching and go to live with her married brother." Ellen did not add that old Mrs. Socket had said she only continued coming because she felt so sorry for the little girl, and was delighted that Vicky's sister had come home to take her part.

The news that he need no longer pay Mrs. Socket for her daily visits did, in part, reconcile Luke to Ellen's presence in the house; though he continued to ignore her and rebuff any attempts at conversation. He had a gift for making people feel that they were in his way; this, though apparently unconscious, was remarkably powerful. Moreover, when he looked at Ellen, which he did as little as possible, it seemed to be with the utmost dislike. Did he resent her youth and health? she wondered. Did they aggravate the indignity of his limp? Luke had always been an active man, but the accident had aged him rapidly, and it was plain that he was far from reconciled to his disability.

Mrs. Pike did her best to exacerbate the situation by continual allusions to Ellen's appearance.

"It is such a pity, Miss Paget, that your clothes are so out of fashion," she would remark with tolerant contempt. "In those queer flounces I fear you must seem a regular figure of fun to Petworth society. But I daresay *that* will not worry you—such a clever young lady as you are, more interested in books than style. If you were going to stay here for long, you might contrive to put two of those gowns together and make one decent crinoline. However, I daresay your visit will not last above a week or two longer—a young lady accustomed to Paris will soon tire of our little backwater—will she not, Mr. Paget?"

"On the contrary, I intend to stay until Vicky is able to read," said Ellen cheerfully, "which may prove a long business."

Vicky, insatiable at drawing, was no scholar.

Mrs. Pike shook her head sadly. "One sister teaching another never answers. There can be no proper discipline in such a case."

⁂

Soon after her return, Ellen received a note, handed in by a small boy at the back door.

> *My very dear Ellen: I am Rejoic'd to hear of yr return to Petworth & write to beg the Pleasure of an Early Visit from you. No doubt you have a Thousand things to occupy you, but, as soon as Convenient, do pray step up for a Dish of Tay with Yr,*
>
> *Always Affctnt*
> *Great-Aunt Fanny Talgarth*

Ellen smiled with pleasure as she read these lines. Great-Aunt Fanny Talgarth was, in fact, no blood relation. She had been married at sixteen to Luke's great-uncle Thomas Paget, who had died when Fanny was barely twenty, and their only child had also died as an infant. Fanny then made what was at first considered a shocking misalliance—she had married Andrew Talgarth, a landscape gardener and improver; but the marriage, which lasted forty-five years, had been very happy, and her husband, whose services were in demand by such eminent persons as the Duke of Wellington, Lord Melbourne, and even the Queen herself at Osborne House, had died a successful and prosperous man. Aunt Fanny had now outlived him by some fifteen years and was well into her eighties; she missed her husband deeply, but, as she often said, kept so busy that the time until their reunion in the next world was passing wonderfully fast. Their marriage had not been blessed with offspring, but Fanny was held in affection by all the humble people round about, and her time and energy were invariably at their disposal. Eugenia and Kitty had always tended to look down on her, because of her very modest way of life—at her husband's death she retired to a small gamekeeper's cottage in the woods east of Petworth—but Ellen had always loved her dearly.

As soon as Vicky's morning lessons were finished next day, she accordingly walked off down the Glebe Path, descended the steeply sloping pasture below, crossed the brook by a cattle bridge, and climbed the other side of the valley where the sheep nibbled dry September grass and blackberries dangled in the hedges. On the hilltop, a ten-mile stretch of woodland began, known to locals as the Dillywoods because of the wild daffodils that bloomed in spring, and threaded with bridle paths in all directions; Aunt Fanny's little house stood by one of these, about a quarter of a mile into the wood. It had originally been erected as a folly, or viewpoint, to be visible from Petworth House on the opposite elevation; it was crowned with a row of battlements on one side and

had a small absurd turret. The trees had crowded about it
to such a degree that its original function was now obvi-
ated, for it could not be seen twenty yards away.

Ellen thought, as she approached, how unlike Fanny's
practical and self-effacing nature was this fanciful piece of
architecture. The small garden was, however, crammed
with useful herbs, vegetables, and sweet-smelling shrubs;
a loaded vine scrambled all over a small summerhouse,
and the boughs of apple and fig trees were heavy with
fruit. Fanny herself was to be seen reading at a table in
the summerhouse; she sprang up and came to greet Ellen
with a brisk step that gave no hint of her advanced age.
Always small in stature, she had become tiny; she looked
like some little brown dryad with her sheaf of snowy hair
skewered in a careless knob on top of her head.

"Dearest child!" She embraced Ellen warmly and
admired her dress with unaffected pleasure. "What a
treat to see you in all your à-la-modality! Such an elegant
change after those grotesque crinolines—more like the
Empire styles when I was a girl. Sit down in the arbor
and tell me every single thing that has been happening to
you. But first some grape juice. I have it hanging in the
well and it is cold as ice."

Ellen sat, observing that among the books on the
littered table were Plato's *Protagoras*, Dante's *Purgatorio*,
a Greek grammar, *Lois the Witch*, by Mrs. Gaskell, and a
New Testament in Greek.

Fanny followed her eyes.

"I have decided to give Andrew a surprise." She
chuckled. "I have been learning Greek since I saw you
last, so that I shall be able to read Plato aloud to him in
Paradise. But it is quite difficult—oh, not the Greek but
the Plato; so from time to time I have to fall back on the
Bible. You laugh: you think me conceited to have such
confidence in Paradise; but, for Andrew's sake, they will
have to let me in. And he is certain to be there."

"Pooh, Aunt Fanny—if anyone is to be received there, it will be you. But are you so certain that Plato will be there?"

"Oh yes, I think so." Fanny tilted her head to one side in birdlike consideration. "After all, he *meant* well, poor man. But now, tell me all. You are very thin, child."

So Ellen told. Fanny listened intently, her mouth curved into a childlike pucker of concentration; at the end she said, "More has happened to you, I daresay, in the space of three years than to many people in the course of a whole lifetime. Your task will be, not to grieve wastefully, not to brood, but to *make use* of this experience, my love; to plough it back in, and enrich your pastureland."

"Yes," Ellen said doubtfully. "I am sure you are right, Aunt Fanny, for you always are—but how, in what way, shall I do this?"

"Why, you need not worry your head about *that*; life is sure to give you plenty of opportunity soon enough. Now tell me about them at the Hermitage; is Gerard still bent on being a composer?"

"I am afraid so. It is going to cause a terrible breach with Papa, who is so ambitious for him; he expects Gerard to become Lord Chancellor at least."

"The breach will have to come. Luke can't turn the boy into a substitute for himself. Gerard has real musical talent. He used to find his way up here, sometimes, and play on my tuneless old clavichord. He has not been so often of late. And little Vicky? Was she much distressed by her mother's death?"

"Not too greatly, I think; I do not think Lady Adelaide ever devoted much time to her. My father's housekeeper is very hard on her."

"Ah, the redoubtable Mrs. Pike. I have not met that lady. And your father—how does he go on?"

Luke Paget had always disliked Fanny. To him, she

represented all that was flighty, wayward, and unpractical; her husband's profession had affronted him, and her retreat into the woods, after Talgarth's death, had seemed to him frivolous and inconsiderate.

"Suppose she became ill, what then?"

More annoying still, there had been a strong and devoted friendship between Fanny and Ellen's mother, despite the age disparity between the two women; while well enough to do so, Matilda Paget walked up into the wood to visit Fanny every couple of days; and after she took to her bed, Fanny rode down to see her with equal regularity, often employing some conveyance that insulted Luke's sense of dignity: a farmer's hay wain, a butcher's trap, whatever happened to be going her way.

Now, studying Ellen, Fanny observed, "You have a remarkable look of your mother. Luke may find that troubling, I imagine?"

"*Something* is troubling him sadly, Aunt Fanny. He—he is very strange."

"Unlike himself?"

"No—*like* himself." Ellen found it hard to put her father's state into words. "He is more—more careful with money, parsimonious, rigid, suspicious, puritanical, than ever—if I laugh with Vicky, he glares at me, if Gerard whistles a tune he earns *such* a scold—all this is hard to bear, and yet, often, he has such a careworn, distressed look that I cannot help feeling sorry for him. He is very selfish—he is continually making little plans for his own comfort, and if they are overthrown by mischance, he is utterly outraged and dismayed; he does not realize that I notice this. Poor man! He is dreadfully disagreeable, and yet, somehow, I feel for him. I do not think it is grief for Lady Adelaide that distresses him so; I cannot tell what it is."

Fanny nodded her little brown wrinkled face as if none of this surprised her.

"He is beginning to guess what he has lost."

"And what is that, Aunt Fanny?"

"That he won't discover until he has found it! But now, child, what are your plans?"

Ellen hesitated to mention the somewhat ignoble mission that had been thrust upon her by her sisters. In Fanny's company it seemed even more distasteful.

But Fanny said, "I imagine, if Mrs. Pike is making Vicky and Gerard miserable, that your first task must be to find somebody more suitable; or to take over the housekeeping yourself?"

"Yes," Ellen said cautiously. "But Papa dislikes having me at home. And, it is true, Mrs. Pike seems to make *him* comfortable enough. He would have very strong objections to any change."

"Mrs. Pike may give him the wrong kind of comfort," said Fanny. "Perhaps a little discomfort would be better for him."

"Tell that to Papa! I must acknowledge that it troubles me not to be earning my own living; I have become used to that."

"Aha," said Fanny. "In that respect—some people might not approve of my telling you this, but you are a sensible child and I do not believe it will lead you into folly; in two years' time, my love, you will come into a very respectable competence, amounting, I understand, to about one thousand pounds a year; so if you can contrive to manage until then, you need feel no anxiety about the future."

Ellen gaped at her great-aunt in a very unladylike manner.

"I shall? But how can this be? Aunt Fanny, are you certain?"

"Oh yes," Fanny said comfortably. "I arranged it with your mother long ago. I once had a dear friend, cousin of my first husband and distant relative of yours, named

Scylla Paget, who became Mrs. Cameron; she left me, when she died, a large sum, which I first proposed to give to your dear mother. But she asked me, instead, to tie it up in a trust for you. 'Ellen will have little enough affection, I fear, when I am gone, until she grows up,' Mattie said to me. 'Let her at least be provided for on reaching her majority, so that she may follow her bent, if she has one.' I fancy Mattie thought you might share her passion for music, but that, unfortunately, seems to have come out in Gerard."

Ellen was absorbed in wonder at this new, astonishing vista that stretched ahead of her. To be able to choose her own path; why, she thought, now—like poor Louise—I could help Germaine—without being obliged to make a wealthy marriage; I can take time to discover if I myself have any gift for writing; this is freedom indeed!

Rapturously she hugged Aunt Fanny.

"I can hardly take it in! Dear, dearest Aunt Fanny, what amazing, what truly extraordinary news! I could share the money with Gerard—if there should come to be a breach between him and Papa— "

"Wait, now!" cautioned Fanny. "I would ask you, Ellen, not to be telling Gerard about this. Keep it to yourself. The boy has enough to unsettle him. And, if he can comply with Luke's wishes and hopes, at least until he is through college, the discipline will do him no harm at all, and will make Luke happy. The poor man is so besotted over that boy! Gerard is all he has in the world."

Ellen saw the force of this.

"So, for the moment, keep the news to yourself. Even your father does not know about it. But I hope the knowledge may serve to keep up your spirits in what sounds like a trying situation at home."

"Indeed it will!" said Ellen.

And—she thought, walking homeward—the news that her own future was secure had somehow done more than anything yet to put her on her sisters' side in the matter of Mrs. Pike. The fact that she was now comfortably provided for must make her more mindful of her obligation to see that *they* did not lose what they looked on as their right.

~⁂~

Several weeks later, the lawyer Mr. Wheelbird came to call on Ellen. When Sue announced him, Ellen was sitting making polite conversation with Mrs. Pike, while waiting for Vicky to finish a row of pothooks.

"Dear me!" said the housekeeper with her small, tight smile. "Our young lady from Paris is continually in demand. Poor folk all day long at the back door—and now a smart young attorney! Let us hope that some rich uncle has died and left you a handsome fortune!"

Her guess came so close to Aunt Fanny's piece of news that Ellen cast her a startled glance. But the housekeeper's expression remained blandly impenetrable. She rose, folding her embroidery into a napkin. "*Pray* do not think of receiving Mr. Wheelbird anywhere but here, Miss Paget! I have a thousand errands to perform, and will leave you undisturbed use of the parlor. I—alas—am *not* on holiday!"

And she trailed with dignity from the room.

Ellen hardly shared Mrs. Pike's opinion of Mr. Wheelbird. She could not think him smart. Her first acquaintance with him had been long ago at a time when he, as a gawky young lawyer's clerk, had shown a disposition to come dangling after the fifteen-year-old Ellen, and had been smartly sent about his business by Luke Paget. Now in his thirties—for he was some ten or twelve years older than Ellen—he had filled out a little, but was still the same bony, scrubby-looking individual, with a stiff brush of hair so liberally plastered with bear's grease that it was almost impossible to guess the color;

his large Adam's apple sat uncomfortably on top of his
high collar, as if trying to make do for the lack of chin,
and his cod-like mouth had a tendency to hang open. He
had grown a fashionable pair of whiskers since Ellen saw
him last, but they seemed to bear no relation to the rest
of his face. Above the ineffectual mouth, however, a pair
of pale, shrewd eyes made careful, admiring inventory of
Ellen's appearance.

"How do you do, Mr. Wheelbird?" she greeted him
civilly. "I am to congratulate you, I believe? You have
passed your examinations, I understand, since I met you
last, and are now a partner?"

"That is so, Miss Paget, that is so indeed."

He accepted her words with calm gratification.
"And may I likewise congratulate you, ma'am—upon
the transformation from caterpillar to butterfly? You
shed radiance upon the town of Petworth like a—like
a meteor."

Ellen thanked him gravely, without troubling to point
out that few ladies enjoy being likened to caterpillars,
and inquired the purpose of his visit. She had assumed it
must have some connection with Aunt Fanny's legacy,
but, to her surprise, he said, "You may find the communication which I am to hand you, Miss Paget, is of
a kind to agitate, discompose, and distress. I am aware
that ladies have—ah—ladylike dispositions, and are easily
overset by such a thing as—as a communication from
the dead. I think you should be seated before I hand you
this document."

"From the *dead*, Mr. Wheelbird? What can you possibly mean?"

Her knees did begin to tremble, and she sat down
by a round table covered in layers of plush and lace.
Mr. Wheelbird solemnly presented her with a stiff legal
envelope, upon which was written: "To be handed to
Mfs Matilda Ellen Paget, if she should at Any time return

for a Protracted Sojourn under her Father's Roof at the Hermitage, after the date of her Achieving her Majority."

"I believe, Miss Paget, that your twenty-first birthday fell in April of this year?"

"Why yes—that is so, Mr. Wheelbird."

"I took a little time," he said with a complacent smile, "to ascertain—to make certain that your stay in Petworth *was* more than a brief visit. Young ladies are volatile birds of passage, I know! But since your residence has now continued for some weeks—Allow me to open the communication for you, ma'am."

"Thank you, I already have it open."

Inside the large envelope was a smaller enclosure, which consisted of several pages folded together and sealed with wax. On the outermost sheet was written simply: "For Ellen." The handwriting caused Ellen to gasp and turn white.

"From my mother!"

Mr. Wheelbird inclined his head. She broke the seal and, at the top of the first page, read: "My dearest Child…" There were several pages of handwriting.

Ellen looked up at the young lawyer, whose eager pale eyes were regarding her somewhat avidly.

"This is a private letter, it seems, Mr. Wheelbird. I am *exceedingly* obliged to you for bringing it to me and—and for keeping it safe all these years. I—I believe I need not trouble you to remain while I peruse it."

He looked very disappointed. "You are quite certain that you feel strong enough for the ordeal, ma'am? Should I not ring for sal volatile? Are you sure you would not prefer that I remain—at a suitable distance—in case you should faint?"

"*Quite* certain, thank you."

"Very well." Somewhat crestfallen, somewhat offended, he retreated to the door, but turned to say, "If the communication should require any—any legal action

taken, ma'am—or any kind of consultation—you know
that you may depend on me to give you my very best
assistance and advice."

"Thank you, Mr. Wheelbird." Her voice was absent,
her head was bent over the paper. She hardly heard him
close the door.

July 1852

My dearest Child:

*You will be a woman grown when you receive this
letter. What a strange notion! At the moment you
are still my little Ellie, in gingham pinafore and
blue stuff dress, freckles on your nose, a bandaged
knee, and hair falling into your eyes. Soon you
must go to school in Belgium, and then I shall never
see you with my corporeal eyes again. (Though I
love this house and garden so much, I cannot help
believing that some part of me will remain here, at
least for a time, and may keep watch over you when
you come back.)*

*As I said to you once, you have always been
my special child; your poor father grieved so terribly
over the death of your twin brother that he had no
love to spare for you—and therefore, by some lucky
dispensation, I was given double!*

*I can feel my strength fading, and know that I
have not many months to live. Perhaps not many
weeks. For myself, I am not sorry to go, if I am
called, because I have been so very happy in this
life, I cannot help believing in the possibility of
happiness everywhere.*

*But I cannot help being anxious for you, Ellie.
Your father will take the greatest care of little
Gerard, I know; poor man, he was so happy to*

have a son at last. Eugenia will soon be married to her Eustace, and Kitty will always be able to look out for herself.

But you, Ellie, were always a defenseless child; you never had the confidence of Kitty or Eugenia. I have—with dear Aunt Fanny's help—made practical provision for you, about which you will soon learn. (I would leave this letter with Fanny too, but fear she might not survive to give it you, so I will entrust it to the lawyers.)

Ellie, if you return home on leaving school, I fear it will be very disagreeable for you at the Hermitage. Poor Papa will not be able to manage very well without me. [Humph, thought Ellen; he did his best to manage, at all events, by marrying Lady Adelaide.] I beg you, therefore, my dearest child, to look after him for me. This will be no easy task. I truly love Luke, but I am aware that most people find this surprising. He is not an easy man. And he has been so often disappointed. He was so promising when young! Many people—knowledgeable, important people—expected great things of him. Ellie, try to use your imagination (with which I know you to be well endowed; there, too, unlike Eugenia and Kitty). Try to imagine Papa's state of mind. If you can do this—if you can learn to love him—if you can teach him to love you—this may be his salvation. I am asking a great deal of you, I know. How can I tell what plans, what connections, you may have formed by this time? But you have a large heart and I know that, for the sake of the strong feeling that you and I had for one another, you will be ready to put aside your own projects for a time, and enter into mine.

See what confidence I place in you, Ellie! While

*I write this, you are out, riding with Dr. Bendigo in
his dogcart, growing brown and happy and strong.
How I wish that you were here with me now, at
this moment, to make me chamomile tea, and read
aloud some of our favorite Cowper poems, and have
one of our long conversations! Instead, I ask you to
think of love as a torch, that must be passed on from
hand to hand. Do not grasp it—give it away freely.*

*Good-bye, my treasure, my dearest child; a
strange good-bye, this, for I shall see you again this
evening. But some part of me, some part of you, is
now locked away, a legacy for when you are older.*

*Your loving
Mother*

*P.S. It has just occurred to me—Papa may not,
of course, be living when you receive this. In which
case you are, of course, absolved from responsibility!
But somehow, I think he will be. The Pagets are a
tough race! In which case, give him my dear love.*

By the time she had reached the conclusion of this
letter Ellen was so bathed in tears that she could only lay
her head down on the plush tablecloth and abandon herself to sorrow. Her aching, profound, continual sense of
loss—for the life of Brussels, Paris, for Patrice Bosschère,
for Menispe, Germaine, Raoul—all this had rendered her
especially vulnerable to her mother's words.

She felt almost awestricken at the appositeness of the
letter's arrival.

The door opened softly. Mrs. Pike! thought Ellen, aghast,
but it was only Vicky, with her copybook of pothooks.

"Oh—*poor* Ellen—have you a bad pain?" The child
came close and stared at Ellen, round-eyed; she had
never seen a grown-up person give way to such woe.

"Shall I ask Sue to make you some chamomile tea? She brings it to me, sometimes, secretly, after Mrs. Pike has given me a dreadful dose. It takes away the pain. Shall I?"

She stood regarding Ellen doubtfully, finger in mouth. But Ellen reached out an arm and pulled the child to her.

"Never mind the chamomile tea, thank you, dear." Chamomile tea! she thought. "Just—just wait here a moment. Then we'll go for a walk." She laid her head against her small sister's pinafored shoulder. It smelt of clean cotton and grass. Vicky stood quietly by her, solemn and solicitous. Ellen suddenly remembered little Menispe, after Benedict had been to tell her of Lady Adelaide's death—there had been rain on the windowpane. The memory made her weep anew. But at last she drew a long, shaky sigh, wiped her eyes, and smiled at Vicky.

"There, I've finished. I expect my face is as red as a beetroot. I had better go and bathe my eyes before Mrs. Pike sees me."

"Oh, *she's* in the garden talking to Mr. Wheelbird," Vicky reassured her.

"Then I'll run up quickly. Wait here—I won't be a moment." As she carefully put together the pages of her letter, Ellen's eye fell on the open copybook Vicky had laid down. "Why, these are excellent, Vicky—the best you have done yet."

❧

At dinner later that day Mrs. Pike was heavily playful about visits from handsome young lawyers, until even Luke Paget came out of his gloomy abstraction long enough to inquire, "Lawyers? What is that you say, ma'am? *Wheelbird* has been to see Ellen? Why, pray? There is to be none of that old nonsense, I trust. What can he have had to say to Ellen that should not properly have been addressed to me?"

"It was nothing he came to say, Papa," Ellen said, blushing and wishing Mrs. Pike at the bottom of the sea. "He had a letter to deliver to me."

"A *letter*? From whom?"

Ruefully, Ellen reflected how free and private her life had been at the Hôtel Caudebec. She could receive letters or callers, go out, pay visits, and no one questioned her activities; while here, every moment of the day was subject to scrutiny.

She said slowly, "It was a letter from Mama. One that she had written me before she died."

"From your *mother*?" Luke was so startled that he went perfectly white. "From *M-Matilda*?" After a moment he added slowly, "What can she have had to say to you? You must have been a mere child—twelve? thirteen?— when she wrote it."

"Yes," said Ellen. She wished this conversation need not have been held under the calmly observant eyes of Gerard and the frankly inquisitive stare of Mrs. Pike, but went on, "That is why Mama entrusted the letter to the lawyer's office—so that I should be certain to receive it after I grew up."

"I wonder that she did not leave the letter with *me*," remarked Luke in a mortified tone.

"Oh, Papa! It was not—not that she did not trust you. But human life is so uncertain! Her own was fast drawing to a close. Whereas a lawyer's office will always have *somebody* in it."

"Well; well. And what did your mother have to say in the letter?"

"She—she asked me to give you her dear love," said Ellen slowly.

"Oh." Luke was silent for a while. His long, hollow-eyed face stared over Ellen's shoulder; out of the window behind her, to an immense distance. Then he brought his gaze back to demand, "What else did she say?"

"Papa—I am sorry. It was a private letter—advising me how—how to direct my life. I cannot divulge any more of the contents."

"*What?*" Luke's wrath was sudden and violent as a lightning flash. "You say that to *me*? You defy me? You actually refuse to show *me*—your own *father*—a letter written to you by your mother—my *wife*?"

"Eh, dear, dear," said Mrs. Pike interestedly. "Fancy that!" She shook her head commiseratingly.

Gerard gazed at his sister in fascinated alarm. Prepared whenever possible to circumvent his father by subterfuge, he never mustered the courage for direct disobedience.

"I am sorry, Papa," said Ellen steadily. "The letter was written by Mama for me alone; it would be betraying her intention—disloyal to her—if I were to show it to anybody else—even to you." Particularly to you, she thought. But she could not help pitying him; poor man, he did so long to get a sight of that letter! And he was not used to being thwarted.

"Disloyal? What about your loyalty to me, pray? I have a right to oversee your correspondence."

"Please, Papa, do not make an issue of this. You would—I *assure* you—be going against Mama's wishes in the matter."

"What could she have to say to you that I might not read?"

"I cannot answer that, Papa."

He stared at her, fulminating, for a moment's silence. Then he said, "Leave the room. You have not heard the end of this."

"I will leave the room," agreed Ellen, "but only because I have finished my dinner. You cannot force me to show you the letter, Papa; I am of age now, and not subject to you."

"You certainly are, miss! So long as you are under my roof and I provide for you."

"I have savings. I can pay for my own board."

"Hoity-toity!" said Mrs. Pike.

"And," continued Ellen, ignoring the housekeeper, "if necessary, I shall ask the advice of Mr. Wheelbird. He said he would be glad to counsel me over any legal action that might arise from the letter."

After which broadside she went out, and gently closed the door behind her. But she was far from happy as she climbed the stair to her room and stood gazing out over the orchard to the red-tiled roofs in Angel Street. This was a most wretched outcome of her mother's request that she should learn to love Luke—the last thing Mattie would have wished, or intended.

Plague take that Mrs. Pike!

After a moment, Ellen's eyes fell on her mother's letter, which she had left on her little bureau. She sat down and read it again—slowly, calmly, carefully. Then, with a heavy heart, she lit a candle and burned it in the flame. Certain slight rearrangements of objects and papers in her drawers from day to day had already convinced her that some alien hand made free with them. Sue, an old and faithful servant, was above suspicion; Cook and the kitchenmaid never came upstairs; Vicky had no opportunity and Gerard would not be interested. All indications pointed to Mrs. Pike. That woman shan't read it and report to Papa on its contents, vowed Ellen—or what she chooses to suggest as its contents; this way it will be safe.

For some days after this scene Luke's manner to Ellen was lowering and charged with gloomy disapproval. But—to her considerable surprise—he did not allude to the letter again. Perhaps Mrs. Pike had told him of the ashes in the bedroom candlestick. Or perhaps he had decided that he could only lose dignity in pursuing the matter.

Twelve

DURING THE NEXT FEW WEEKS ELLEN SOMETIMES FOUND herself wondering who, precisely, she might be. Her own personality seemed to be overlaid by those of her two parents. Besides being herself—solitary, sad, hungry for the companionship, the cheerful sounds, the talkative voices of Paris—she seemed to feel with the senses of Luke and Matilda, to hear with their ears.

The Hermitage was a silent house. Separated from the town on two sides by orchards, overlooking the peaceful valley, it received no sound of traffic or human activity; furthermore, Luke Paget detested noise and had trained his household to respect this idiosyncrasy. The inmates were the reverse of convivial. Gerard, for some undivulged reason, had become much more withdrawn lately; taciturn and somber, he worked hard with his tutor at law and Latin all day, then disappeared on his own ploys in the evening. Vicky, under threat of retribution from Mrs. Pike, was hesitant about displaying too much friendliness to Ellen. The servants went glumly about their business; and Mrs. Pike seemed to watch and wait.

Living in this silence, Ellen came to remember her mother more and more vividly. Every tree in the garden, every corner of each room had its message. In the parlor, for instance, there still stood a little ottoman, on which, before she took to her bed, Mattie had been wont to rest, tucking a small hard bolster behind her spine.

"Are you weary, Mama?"

"No, not weary, my love, but I have a little chill in my back. Read me *The Castaway*, and it will be better directly."

During the four years before Ellen went to school, her mother had been much afflicted by toothache, and had been obliged to pay numerous visits to a surgeon in Midhurst, from which trips she would return white, exhausted, and trembling, obliged often to retire to bed. But she was always up and about again next day.

How little of her suffering, thought Ellen, I, in my childish self-absorption, ever noticed or troubled my head about. But why did not Papa take more thought for her? I do not remember his ever asking her how she did.

Luke was then, Ellen supposed, in the full current and turmoil of his political aspirations; traveling in the constituency, canvassing as prospecting candidate for Chichester; he must have been too busy to observe his wife's ill health; or it had seemed of secondary importance.

His daughter now pondered about him a great deal. She could see that he was in continual pain from his mended hip. He limped; sometimes he uttered an exclamation when rising or sitting down. Ellen wondered how he spent his time. Long hours were passed in his study, or garden room; he received and read all the London papers, besides parcels of books from Mudie's; he made notes, for sometimes when Ellen slipped into the garden room to play the piano after dinner, the table would be littered with index cards and slips of paper and padlocked files of manuscript. Perhaps he was engaged on some political treatise?

"Do you think I should offer to assist him?" Ellen asked Fanny.

"I should wait, my love, until he himself requests your services. We place a low value on what is freely offered; sad but true; and Luke is given to undervaluing other people as it is. Nor has he acquired the humility that comes from being valued by others."

"Mama valued him, Aunt Fanny!"

"Yes, but Luke is an arrogant man; he did not rate her esteem as he should. He felt it was his right. Mattie told me that once he had hoped—indeed, fully expected—that he would rise high in politics, achieve Cabinet office, even become Prime Minister. When he was a young man, he was both strikingly handsome and had a remarkable presence. He seemed highly gifted to many people of importance; Lord Castlereagh heard him speak and prophesied that he would go far; he did brilliantly in his Bar examinations; and then all this somehow petered out into nothing.

"Of course, most of us, not only your father, start out with high opinions of themselves—for a child thinks he is the most important person in the world! What gives us a truer notion is not failure, but our first successes, however trifling. When other people begin to show they value us, then, by discovering our real worth, rather than our imagined one, we learn humility."

Ellen, recalling her early blunders and small victories in the rue St. Pierre, and how, during those days, mild self-respect began to replace touchy, anxious self-assertion, realized that what Fanny said was true.

"But somehow your father has never been given the chance to measure himself against the esteem of others. He fell so far short of what he intended that his early, inflated image of himself is still the only one he possesses."

"He can't see himself as we do? No," Ellen said, answering her own question, "of course he cannot."

❧

Discharging her own duties about the house, Ellen was hauntingly aware of her father's personality; it hung like a heavy cloud. His feeling of not having received his just due, a jealousy of any happiness that excluded him, a bitter anxiety about the future, and a ravenous insistence on his rights—or what he took to be his rights—all these emotions made themselves felt as if they had been printed on the air; also his feverish ambition for Gerard. The pain from his injured hip he viewed as an intolerable imposition, since he was accustomed to enjoy health as a matter of course. To have his sleep broken night after night and wake to discomfort—this was not to be borne, it could not go on! And yet it did go on. Added to this were vexations over some new and ill-chosen associations of Gerard's—not to mention the uninvited return of his daughter—was it any wonder, Luke felt, that he was often almost beside himself with irritation?

Indeed Mrs. Pike was the only member of his household who did not afford any aggravation; she was so invariably solicitous for his comfort that the very thought of her was a cordial. When he woke in the night, his mind would at once range fretfully over its causes for discontent: there was talk of a French invasion, the Volunteer troops were drilling; besides this, there were rumors of impending civil conflict in America; Luke, whose first wife had brought as her dowry holdings in a Lancashire cotton manufactory, was concerned at the loss of income such a dispute would mean. Then there were Kitty and Eugenia, always hoping for gifts of money, if not asking for it...and Gerard, with his unsuitable acquaintance... From all these ills—and others, deeper, unexpressed even to himself, but much more afflicting—Luke would turn to the thought of Mrs. Pike with relief, as the one positive in a world of negatives. There she was, handsome, cordial, always on his side, and certain to have ordered him an excellent breakfast.

Ellen, observing all this, as well as Mrs. Pike's growing complacency, began to feel that her sisters had better resign themselves to the inevitable. It seemed almost certain that Luke would presently propose marriage to the housekeeper, if only to secure her services permanently.

And unpaid, too, thought Ellen, with a cynicism acquired in Paris. She said as much to Eugenia.

Her eldest sister, anxious to learn how the land lay, had arranged for Ellen to spend a night at Valdoe Court. "It is so long since we saw you," she wrote in a letter delivered by the penny post. "Eustace may fetch you— he is to attend a sale of yearling heifers at North Chapel. And you may return to Petworth next day by the public coach. Papa can spare you, I daresay—and Vicky will not suffer from the loss of a day's lessons!"

Luke sanctioned the arrangement (with some grumbles as to gadding about) and Mrs. Pike gave it the seal of her approval by entrusting to Ellen various commissions in Chichester.

Ellen was pleased to ride over the Downs with Eustace Valdoe in his wagonette, loaded with sacks of seed and agricultural implements. It was a delight to see through frosty dusk the beeches and spindle trees flaming out in their autumn colors. Luke thought Eustace a fumbling, ineffectual, hopeless fellow, but Ellen, little though she knew him, liked him very well.

They talked little on the road; Eustace was not an articulate man and felt shy of his smart young Parisian sister-in-law; but the minute Ellen had been set down among the decayed grandeurs and shabby comforts of Valdoe Court, Eugenia pounced on her.

"Well? How goes it between Papa and that woman?... Oh, do run away!" she snapped irritably at a small pinafored girl and two pale little boys who were hanging about her skirts. "Go to Nurse and tell her to fetch Baby and keep you all with her." She turned with a martyred sigh to Ellen. "You do not know your good fortune in not being married! I have so little help, sometimes I do not know how I contrive! Look at those curtains—faded and worn beyond repair. Sometimes my trials seem beyond endurance." She evinced no curiosity about her sister's experiences in Paris, but went on, "Does there seem to be an attachment growing—does Papa treat that woman—speak to her—look at her—with much particularity?"

Ellen gave it as her opinion that, within the limits of his unforthcoming nature, he did so, and she saw little to be done about it. Eugenia threw up her hands and turned to her husband, who entered the room just then, having changed for dinner into a tailcoat of ancient cut.

"Eustace! What are we to do? Ellen confirms that the Pike woman is setting her cap at Papa and he is becoming infatuated! If he marries her and settles Mama's money on her—our children will die paupers!"

"Oh, come, come, Eugenia! Matters are not at quite such a pass. After all—even if your father does not remarry—he is a strong healthy man, we have no reason to assume that he may not live for many years yet. You should not be placing a dependence—"

"Fiddle! Men of his age are carried off every day. There might be another cholera epidemic."

The conversation was terminated by the arrival of Lady Blanche and the Bishop, who had been invited to dinner. Eugenia had warned Ellen not to discuss Mrs. Pike in front of them, since Lady Blanche had selected Mrs. Pike, and plumed herself on her sagacity in having supplied Luke with such a treasure. Talk became general, and adverted to the possibility of an invasion by Napoleon III. Ellen, speaking with an authority she certainly would never have been permitted at the Hermitage, said she was sure the French Emperor had no such intention. "His cousin in Paris said that his main ambition is to develop the French overseas empire in Africa."

When the men had drunk their port, the Bishop brought his coffee cup and came to sit by Ellen.

"You appear to have grown into a young lady with a mind of her own," he said, beaming at her.

Ellen had always felt a fondness for the Bishop, who,

at the wedding of her father to Lady Adelaide, when she was feeling very miserable, had patted her head, talked to her with great kindness, and promised her a pony, which she had been unable to accept, since she had been on the point of returning to school in Brussels. Now he reminded her of this promise. "And I have the very fellow for you in the Palace stables, eating his head off, since my daughter Grizel was married. I shall have him sent over next week."

"Oh, sir! You are too kind! Indeed you should not."

"Indeed I should. But tell me, how does your papa go on? Would you say, my dear, that he is laboring under some nervous affliction? He writes me such very strange letters."

"*Does* he, sir?" Ellen was startled to hear that her father wrote to the Bishop at all.

"That he does! About the Doom Stone, you know, which he is so set upon finding. He appears to attach such importance to it that, I confess, I have been wondering if that sad affair sent him a little astray, you know—" And the Bishop tapped his temple.

"He seems quite rational in all his household dealings," Ellen said slowly. "Very much so."

"Ay, well, it can be so. A man can be as sane as may be, save in the one particular. Look at that fellow in the novel by Mr. Dickens. Mr. Dick—King Charles's head, you know? Capital book that. Perhaps your father is in the same way over the Doom Stone. Most improbable that we shall find it now, since it has not turned up in the fabric of the Cathedral. Found some beautiful Purbeck panels, which Mr. Slater believes to date from 1000 AD—but no Doom Stone! Pity, but there! Knocked to pieces long ago, I fear. If only we could convince your father of that."

Lady Blanche then came in her stately way to commend Ellen for showing proper daughterly feeling in returning to keep her father company.

"You did very right, my dear; a young gel is best at home. Indeed I do not at all approve of young ladies staying abroad. You do much better to employ yourself with Vicky's education. I am extremely pleased with you." Some considerable proportion of Lady Blanche's approval was also due to the termination of a tiresome guilty feeling that she ought to take some action regarding her sister's small orphaned daughter; now that anxiety was allayed, so she smiled benignly at Ellen and patted her hand.

Ellen had never cared greatly for the Bishop's lady, who reminded her of her unloving stepmother, Lady Adelaide. She therefore turned the subject, and asked, "How did you learn about Mrs. Pike, Lady Blanche? I understand we have you to thank for supplying Papa with such a capable housekeeper?"

"Is she not a paragon? Did I not furnish your papa with a treasure?"

"Usually such persons are bespoken years in advance," said Ellen, feeling a hypocrite. "How was Mrs. Pike free to come to the Hermitage at such very short notice?"

"She had been housekeeping for old Canon Fothergill and his simpleminded niece. When he died there was not enough money left to continue paying Mrs. Pike's wages, so a place was found for Miss Fothergill in St. Mary's Hospital, where, poor soul, they care for her very well."

"Miss Fothergill—I remember her," said Ellen. "Mama used to visit her and teach her embroidery."

"Very likely, child. Your mother was often lavishing time and energy on hopeless causes. Come, Bishop; it is time our carriage was spoken for."

❧

After breakfast next day Eustace drove Ellen into Chichester to execute her shopping commissions. He had various business to attend to himself, and arranged to meet her by the Butter Cross at noon.

Ellen went to the apothecary's for the oil of almonds, essence of bitter aloe, gum tragacanth, and other requirements on Mrs. Pike's list.

She was explaining to the pharmacist that the oil of almonds was a superior one, much esteemed by Mrs. Pike and kept in stock for her especially, when a little old woman who was deliberating over a display of soaps on a table by the door, catching the name Pike, glanced up and eyed Ellen with curiosity. Then she sidled over.

"Would that be Mrs. Emily Pike, now, that went over for to do for Mr. Paget in Perrorth?" she murmured ingratiatingly.

"Why yes," said Ellen. "Is she a friend of yours? Do you wish to send her a message?"

"Ah, you see, dearie, I used to be cook for poor old Canon Fothergill and Miss Phoebe. But tell me, love, is it true what they say—that Emily's to marry Mester Paget? Is it really true?"

Startled, Ellen glanced at the pharmacist. But he was out of earshot at the other end of the shop, by a rampart of brass-handled mahogany drawers, spooning powder from a black japanned canister.

Ellen said, "Is that what people say? That Mrs. Pike is going to marry my father?"

"Lord-a-mercy!" The little woman gasped with fright. "You be Mus' Paget's *daughter*? I took ye for one o' the maids, wi' your gown so skimpy-like; otherwise I'd never ha' said what I did, missie. Don't ye take no notice, now!" And, quick as a lizard, she scuttled from the shop.

Very thoughtfully indeed, Ellen completed her tale of purchases, and then made her way in the direction of St. Mary's Hospital. Something furtive and scared in the little woman's manner had rekindled all her doubts. It was all very well to say to Eugenia, "Why should not Papa marry Mrs. Pike if he is fond of her?"—but what if there were really something underhand, discreditable, about Mrs. Pike?

St. Mary's Hospital, a twelfth-century foundation, lay hardly five minutes' walk from the Butter Cross, close to the center of the town. From outside it was like a combination of a church and a tithe barn; a long, splendidly tiled red roof sloped up almost from the ground. Inside the resemblance to a church increased, for there was a nave and an east window of five lights, and an altar; but the space on either side of the nave had been partitioned off into eight tiny self-contained dwellings, each with its own front door. In these lived eight old ladies of attested respectability, devout habit, and straitened means; the only other qualifications for acceptance being that they must have been born within the parish of Chichester.

"May I see Miss Fothergill?" inquired Ellen of the matron, who greeted her civilly in the porch.

"I'll just make sure she's fit to see ye, miss; after morning chapel some of the old 'uns goes back to bed. What name shall I say?"

"Miss Ellen Paget; my mother, Mrs. Matilda Paget, used to be a friend of Miss Fothergill."

In a moment the matron returned. "Please to step this way, miss. It's the third door on the decani side. Maybe I oughter warn you," she added in a lower tone, "the poor old lady is apt to wander in her wits. She never was right sharp, and she's seventy-eight—her uncle the old Canon was just a few days short of a hundred when he passed away—she mistakes folks for those she knowed when she was young, so don't mind her, miss."

Ellen tapped on the door and was summoned by a quavering "Come!"

She had never been in one of the St. Mary's Hospital dwellings, and was charmed by its nest-like compactness. There was a tiny kitchen, a parlor, and a bedroom, all scrupulously clean, miraculously so, considering the

abundance of objects—china, glass, miniatures, pincush-
ions, framed watercolors, evidently all the old lady's
personal treasures—which clustered on every surface.
There was a little grate, in which burned a frugal fire,
and two small chintz-covered nursing chairs, on one
of which sat Miss Fothergill, erect and expectant in
tobacco-brown silk.

"Matilda!" she whispered. "Oh, Mattie dear, they told
me you were dead! Even Lady Blanche said so. They
told me I must never hope to see you more. Oh, I *am* so
delighted that they were mistaken!"

"No, dear Miss Fothergill," said Ellen gently. "I am
afraid they were not mistaken. I am not Matilda but
Ellen—do you remember Matilda's youngest daughter?"

"Nonsense, my dear, you are quite out. Ellen is only
a little thing—I have often given her bits of orange peel
to feed to Sir Walter there."

A hoarse voice made Ellen start. It issued from a cage
by the window, and remarked, "Polly wants a comfit! A
little bit of peel for Sir Walter, if you please!"

"Your parrot! I had quite forgotten him. But truly,
Miss Fothergill, I am Ellen Paget, grown up. I have been
residing in France since Mama died."

A tear crept down the old lady's cheek. "Then it was
true, after all? Poor Mattie did die? I might have known
she would come to see me otherwise—if the Shark
didn't prevent her." An anxious, melancholy expression
overspread her face; she glanced sidelong and said, "They
do not let *her* in here—thank goodness!—but I fear she
may be able to hear what we say."

"To whom do you refer, dear Miss Fothergill?"

The old lady extended a trembling hand. Ellen took it
carefully and Miss Fothergill drew her close.

"Uncle William is going to leave her all his money!
I fear I shall be quite destitute. The house goes with his
office, you know. I am in such distress about the future!"

"But, dearest Miss Fothergill—here you are, snugly established in St. Mary's—I am sure you need not have the least anxiety."

"Are you sure, my love? Is this where we are? But then—where is *she*?"

"Do you refer to Mrs. Pike, ma'am?"

"Hush! Not so loud." Miss Fothergill glanced about apprehensively. "She said her son would come and lock me in the summerhouse—but there is a hard frost! I should never last through the night. Her son is a criminal..."

The old lady was so agitated and tremulous that Ellen did not like to pursue the subject any further—though by now her suspicions were rampant. She talked, instead, about her mother, and the embroidery she had taught Miss Fothergill.

"Drawn-thread-work, was it not? And crewel-work?"

"Dear me, yes! I have many examples of your dear mother's worsted-work with me. See, here! And here!" In a moment the old lady was happily opening drawers and boxes, her fears quite forgotten. Ellen stayed with her another ten minutes, then, hearing the Cathedral bell chime the quarter, took her leave, promising to come back.

Driving to Valdoe Court with Eustace, she asked if he had ever heard any gossip about Mrs. Pike's dealings with her previous employers. He rubbed his high, balding brow, thought for a while, and said at last, "I do recall that the old Canon bequeathed a substantial sum to his housekeeper in his will. Ay, that's right, there was some talk about it, since he left his niece quite poorly provided for. I had forgotten it was the Pike woman. But nothing improper was imputed—the Canon was in his nineties, after all. Folk assumed he had grown so old that he hardly knew what money he had. The niece, being somewhat simple, was not considered in a position to contest; and, fortunately, a place was found for her in St. Mary's—though they had lived elsewhere, she had been born in Chichester; so nobody felt called upon to pursue the matter. After all, people often do leave large sums to faithful housekeepers."

"Have you ever heard a son of Mrs. Pike's mentioned?"

"Why no," said Eustace, after more thought. "I cannot say I have. But Mrs. Pike is not a native of the town, you know; she was already in the employ of the Canon when he came here from Winchester."

Ellen was puzzled at the thought of trying to pursue inquiries in a town so far distant as Winchester. But Eustace said he knew an attorney there, and would ask him.

Eugenia, fretfully darning tablecloths in the morning room at Valdoe, listened with sharp interest to the story about Miss Fothergill, and exclaimed, "There! What did I say? There is something bad about that woman, and she will terrorize Papa as she did the Canon and his niece. Now do you see that it is a good thing we brought you back?"

"*You* could have gone to see Miss Fothergill yourself, any time these five months," Ellen pointed out.

"How can I leave the house, with so much on my hands? It is all very well for *you* to go jauntering about, Ellen," complained Eugenia, and went on hastily, "You must on no account leave Papa alone with her!"

"But the Canon and his niece were aged, simple people. Papa is far from being that!"

"The Bishop thinks he is astray in his wits—because of all this to-do he makes about the Doom Stone. And he behaved most foolishly about that wretched shepherd."

"Ay," said Eustace, "that *was* an ill-judged business. It was very wrong of Paget to make Noakes turn off his shepherd, simply because Gerard had made friends with the man. People round here had a deal to say about that, I can tell you."

"Make Noakes turn off his shepherd?" Ellen was bewildered. "What can you be referring to? Noakes the farmer in Duncton? Papa's tenant?"

"Ay; it seems your young brother had made great friends with his shepherd, one Matthew Bilbo. Paget had several times remonstrated with Gerard about what he considered a most unsuitable association, and in the end, last month, losing patience, he told Noakes to dismiss the man."

"But how monstrously unjust!" exclaimed Ellen. "No *wonder* Gerard has been going about so silent and furious-looking these last few weeks. He must feel dreadfully to blame—if Papa had warned him and said what he would do. But the poor shepherd—what became of him? Is it known?"

Eugenia pursed her lips disapprovingly. Eustace said in a deprecating tone, "Well—in point of fact—felt sorry for the poor fellow—excellent man at his work—no harm in him at all—so I took him on here. My Southdowns are increasing handsomely and I can find work for a second man—there's an old tumbledown hut on Lavant Down I told him he could have. But I would be obliged, Ellen, if you'd not mention this to Mr. Paget."

"No wonder we never have a penny," sniffed Eugenia to her darning needle. "But needless to say *I* am not consulted."

"That was very kind in you," said Ellen warmly to her brother-in-law. "But why was Papa so against the man? Simply because he was a shepherd?"

"No, the story goes further back. Bilbo is in his fifties, and has been in prison for nigh on twenty years. Your father was one of the Justices who originally sentenced him."

"What was his offense?"

"Poaching. I was away at college then, but I looked up the case. Bilbo was not caught in the act, but an information was laid against him, and a poached hare was found in his house."

"So the sentence may have been undeserved?"

"It seems highly possible. Bilbo is a gentle, inoffensive, most law-abiding man. He stated on oath that he had not taken the hare. And many people came forward to speak highly of his character."

"So now it will be said that Papa, having sentenced him unjustly, is hounding him even more unjustly."

"I fear so," said Eustace.

⁕

Ellen rode back to Petworth on the public coach with much to occupy her mind. I have to brace myself to speak to Papa, she thought. Not to warn him about Mrs. Pike. I have no shadow of right to do that at present, no definite accusation to make; it would seem mere malice, and would do more harm than good. But it is my plain duty to say what I think about this wretched shepherd; and to tell Papa that he is going quite the wrong way about his management of Gerard.

She was sure that Luke never gave the least thought about how his actions might appear to others. He was hardly aware of the outside world. He had never asked Ellen about her life in Paris, or displayed any interest in the la Ferté tragedy; he seemed wrapped in a cocoon of his own weaving. Gerard was his only link with the present or the future.

And Mrs. Pike, of course.

At this moment Ellen absently glanced from the coach window. They were slowly climbing the long gentle ascent to Petworth. A clump of trees stood to the left of the road, by a track that led to Frog Hole Farm. Ellen, from her high seat by the window, had a view over the hedge, and could see two women talking in the little spinney. One, a thin young woman in black, looked to be a stranger, but the other—surely?—was Mrs. Pike herself. Her stance, her carefully tended gray ringlets, a glimpse of lavender color were unmistakable, despite the old brown mantle. She was handing the young woman a small basket—she seemed vexed, shook her head repeatedly, then walked rapidly away from the copse. Crossing the turnpike behind the coach—and now Ellen was sure it was Mrs. Pike—she took a diagonal across a stubble field which would bring her out in Petworth, not far from the Hermitage.

At dinner, Ellen did not mention this occurrence. But Mrs. Pike herself brought up the matter.

"Mrs. Standen, at Hoadley's, told me there were excellent young ducklings to be had at Frog Hole Farm," she announced. "So I went there—but it was a Banbury story, there were no ducklings, and I had my walk for nothing."

Nobody seemed very interested, but Ellen civilly commiserated with the housekeeper on her fruitless errand.

Perhaps the short absence in Chichester had sharpened Ellen's perception, or the relationship between the other two had advanced a step during her visit to Valdoe; at all events Luke's behavior toward the housekeeper did strike his daughter quite forcibly that evening. There seemed a kind of awareness—glances were exchanged—or rather, Luke glanced, Mrs. Pike wore a demurely complacent air; he went out of his way, uncharacteristically, to address various trifling remarks to her; he asked her questions, he sometimes contrived to touch her hand or sleeve as she passed him his cup. He did, Ellen was obliged to admit, bear the appearance of a man in the first stages of infatuation.

What a disastrous time to embark on an attempt to undermine his authority!

"Papa," she said quietly, after the meal, when Gerard had gone off. "I should like to speak to you, if it is convenient, about—about a matter that is troubling me."

Reluctantly Luke turned his eyes in their deep sockets away from Mrs. Pike, and fixed them on his daughter. Notwithstanding his aura of sexual excitement, he seemed to Ellen a sad and lonely figure; in her mind's eye she saw him as a great eroded monolithic image in the desert, long since abandoned by the tribe that had once paid homage—if indeed homage had ever been paid. No, she thought; Mama did truly love him. I must remember that.

"*Now?*" said Luke irritably. "You wish to speak to me *now?*"

"Yes, if you please. Or at any other time that suits you."

He glanced about in a beleaguered manner. They were in the overfurnished parlor. Vicky had long since been dispatched to bed. Mrs. Pike, by the tea tray, was stitching away at her eternal embroidery. A woman of tact and grace would at this point, Ellen reflected, have gathered her things together and made some pretext to leave; not so Mrs. Pike. Her needle snicked in and out of the canvas, her eyes moved, with equal speed, from Luke to Ellen and back.

"Oh—very well," Luke grunted. "What is it you wish to say?"

"May I not be private with you? Perhaps we should go to your business room?"

At this plain hint Mrs. Pike rather huffily folded her work and said, "If I am in the way, I shall of course take myself off!"

"No, Emilia, no, ma'am; why should you disturb yourself?" Luke demanded. "Anything my daughter has to say may be said in your presence."

Emilia! thought Ellen. Aloud she said doggedly, "I would rather be private, if it is all the same to you, Papa."

"Well, it is *not* all the same, miss. I don't choose to

move, and I don't choose that Mrs. Pike shall be forced
out of the parlor. Say what you have to say and have
done with it."

"Very well; if that is your wish. It is about this affair
of the shepherd—Matthew Bilbo."

"And what the devil business is that of *yours*, miss?"
growled Luke, surprised and not at all pleased. "I suppose
Eugenia and that fool Eustace Valdoe have been bleating
on about it?"

Ellen had armed herself against this attack. She said,
"You know what a number of people come to me if they
are sick. Many have mentioned it to me."

She had, in fact, taken pains, after her return, to
call on a number of such people and had led the talk
round to the affair. She went on, "People in Petworth
are distressed about it, Papa. They do not like it. They
say that Bilbo's original sentence was almost certainly
undeserved, but could have been sheer misfortune. His
dismissal now, though, they feel to be deliberate, vindictive hounding of a defenseless man. And," added Ellen
warmly, forgetting that she had intended to model her
manner of the cool, dégagé air of Louise de la Ferté, "I
think so too! I think it was a very mean act, Papa, to
make Noakes dismiss the man, and does you no credit at
all. It has alienated Gerard from you—so in that respect
it was a calamitous mistake."

"For shame, miss!" exclaimed Mrs. Pike. "What a way
to speak to your father!"

Luke remained silent. He was utterly astounded. Ellen
continued, "For Gerard's sake, Papa—but even more for
your own, to reestablish yourself in people's minds as a just
man—you should tell Noakes to give the shepherd his job
again. You could tell him that a mistake had been made. As
it is, people are saying terribly hard things about you—that
you cannot control your own son, and are venting your
spite and vexation on the inoffensive cause of the trouble."

"Oh! That I should live to hear such things said." Mrs. Pike turned up her eyes.

Ellen went on, steadfastly ignoring the housekeeper, "Papa—think how Mama would have felt about it. She could not endure injustice. She would have said—"

"Quiet!" thundered Luke, finding his voice at last. He glared at Ellen, his face working with wrath and other, more complicated emotions. He looked so extremely angry that Ellen, quite surprised at her own lack of fear, thought: Perhaps Mama is speaking through me. And indeed the strong resemblance that she bore to her mother just then, both in expression and in attitude, did much to confuse Luke. He said hoarsely, "How dare you speak so?"

"Because it is the truth; and it is for your own sake."

"Leave my presence! Get out! Think yourself lucky I do not turn you out of doors."

Ellen left the room collectedly. I have said what I set out to, at all events, she thought; I must only hope that some part of it will sink in. If only I have not done more to push him into that woman's arms!

She ran up to Gerard's room, resolved, now she knew the cause, to break the silence into which he had retreated during the past weeks, and scratched at his door.

"Who's that?" she heard his surly voice.

"It's I, Ellen."

"What do you want?"

Despite his unwelcoming tone she opened the door and went in. He was slumped on the bed, with his head in his hands. Ignoring his scowl, she sat on a straight-backed chair and said, with a faint smile, "I need encouragement and sympathy. I have had such a set-to with Papa, and all for nothing, I fear, over that poor man Matthew Bilbo."

His head came up. "How did you come to know about Matthew Bilbo?"

"Oh, people in the town are saying how unfair Papa has been."

"So he has—confoundedly unfair! Bilbo is one of the best, most harmless fellows in the world; indeed I do believe he is a kind of saint. It was downright *wicked* of Papa to do as he did. And if he thinks that will make me more inclined to obey him, he is quite out. I shall do all in my power to go against him."

Ellen sighed. She said, "Tell me about Bilbo. He seems an odd friend for you. He is so much older, surely? How did you meet?"

"Oh," said Gerard impatiently, "Dr. Bendigo made us known to one another, one time when we were returning from Chichester and ran into the doctor on top of the Down, where he was visiting a hurt quarry hand. We met Bilbo with his sheep; the doctor, knowing of my interest in botany, said that Matthew knew a great deal about birds and fungi and orchids. Other things too, as I found out! He learned to read in jail— the chaplain taught him—he is a remarkable man, Ellie! So good and so humble, and so truly original in all his thoughts and conversation!"

The boy's face had lit up. Ellen was amazed at the transformation. If Papa could see him like this! she thought.

"Did you know that Eustace has given Bilbo work, and a cottage on Lavant Down?"

"No, has he? That is like Eustace. He is a good fellow. But"—Gerard's face fell—"that is too far away for me to call on him. I could ride Captain up to the top of Duncton Down and back in one evening. But Lavant is out of the question."

"I asked Papa if he could not see his way to have Noakes reinstate Bilbo. But he would not consider it."

"No, I daresay," muttered Gerard. "Once Papa takes up a position, nothing will shift him."

"If only you were on happier terms with him—could

you not work harder, to please him? Talk about what interests him?"

"I *do* work hard," said Gerard irritably. "But I won't pretend an interest in politics. The truth is that Papa just wants me to be *him* over again—only successful, where he failed; and I shall never be that."

"He is so lonely! And his loneliness is driving him into the company of Mrs. Pike."

"I wish him joy of her! Let him marry her! Next year I'll be at Cambridge, and then I'll never come to Petworth again… Why don't *you* talk to him more?"

"He does not care for my conversation. Indeed, just now, he was within an ace of turning me out of the house."

"I can't think why you stay here, when you need not Still, it was good of you to approach him about Bilbo," said Gerard, in a more friendly tone than he had yet used, "though I could have told you it would be useless."

⤙⤚

It took several weeks for Luke's manner toward his daughter to return to anything like civility, let alone amiability. For the most part, during that time, he ignored her. If she were so tactless as to ask him a direct question, he addressed his reply to Gerard or the housekeeper. His glance, when it accidentally rested on her, was filled with a kind of morose bewilderment, as if he really did not know how to treat her. It was plain, however, that her calm, watchful presence, and the obvious independent operation of her judgment, resent it though he might, had reduced, or slowed, his attentions to Mrs. Pike. His behavior to the latter displayed more caution and reserve. The housekeeper for her part showed her awareness of the agent to whom she owed this setback by increased sharpness, verging on downright hostility, toward Ellen. The latter bore all this with what fortitude she could

muster. Lonely and depressed, she found comfort in
Vicky's educational progress, in visits to Aunt Fanny,
and the small but definite improvement in her relations
with Gerard.

The Bishop had kept his promise and sent Ellen a
pony. This animal, shaggy and unimpressive but strong
and biddable, greatly extended her sphere of activity; she
could ride on the Downs with Gerard, and visit friends in
farms and cottages as far afield as Midhurst, Pulborough,
or Wisborough Green. Unfortunately an early and severe
winter setting in soon curtailed these excursions and also
prevented Gerard's illicit sorties to make music for the
morris dancers.

The house, during those winter months, was gloomy
indeed. Ellen sometimes looked back to her life in Paris
with a kind of incredulity. Did I really talk to Gautier,
Baudelaire, Flaubert, Turgenev? she wondered. I was
free to come and go, I lived in luxury, my work was
congenial—yet I seem to have spent most of the time in
a fret of anxiety because I could not like poor Louise.
Ah, if only I had tried harder! Let me not make that
mistake again!

After these moods of recollection and self-condemnation
she would increase her efforts to make some contact with
her father, trying to find any subject on which he was
prepared to converse, asking questions about his youth,
and the early years of his marriage to her mother. He
responded to these efforts slowly and ungraciously; but
he did thaw a little; and Mrs. Pike watched with a jealous
and antagonistic eye.

"I wonder, Miss Paget, that you disturb your pa with
subjects that can only distress him," the housekeeper
remarked acidly one day, when Ellen had been drawing
out her father on the progress of his early studies, and
comparing them with Gerard's, in the hope of persuading Luke to regard his son with a more indulgent eye.

"It would be more to the purpose if you could persuade your brother to pay more heed to your father's wishes."

A year ago, Ellen might have retorted, "Mind your own business, ma'am!" Now she diplomatically replied, "Why, ma'am, you know what sons are, neither to hold nor to bind! I understand that you have a son—pray tell me, how old is he? And what is his profession? Will he be coming to visit you? Where does he reside?"

To her surprise this random broadside appeared to have struck an extremely sensitive target. Mrs. Pike's complexion assumed a strangely blotchy hue, with patches of red and white alternating; her opaque blue eyes glazed with rage, or alarm; she snapped, "And who told you about my son, pray?"

Luke glanced up in surprise from the newspaper which he had resumed reading as soon as Ellen had left off questioning him.

"A son, ma'am? You have a son, Mrs. Pike? I was not aware of that."

"Oh—my son is overseas," the housekeeper said quickly. "Young men, you know, will go off to seek their fortune, no matter how their poor widowed mothers beg them to stop at home—"

The sharp, challenging gaze that remained fixed on Ellen while she said this seemed to dare the latter to dispute the story. She repeated, "Who spoke to you of my son, Miss Paget?"

"It was old Miss Fothergill."

"Oh, her." Mrs. Pike appeared to relax. "Poor old lady, she's so feeble-witted you can't credit a word she says. Of course, she never met my Sim—my son—but I used to speak of him—he having just gone abroad at that time and being much in my thoughts."

"What is his profession?" inquired Luke.

"The engineering line—always interested in tools or machinery he was—went away to Brazil to build bridges.

But, bless me, look at the time"—examining the watch at her belt. "I must bustle Sue about the tea, one has to be after them every minute of the day, or nothing gets done"—and she left the room.

"Singular that she never mentioned her son before," murmured Luke, half to himself. "But"—with a sigh—"if she finds the thought of him distressing, I can understand that."

He folded his paper and took himself off, oblivious of the tea which Mrs. Pike was hastening to prepare for him.

Ellen looked after her father with a curious pang of sympathy. It was the first time she had heard him speak of another person's feelings.

❧

Five days later she received a small packet of mail from France. During all this time she had heard nothing from Germaine or the Comte de la Ferté; it was true that in her hasty departure she had left no forwarding address, but her direction could have been obtained from Lady Morningquest, and she had felt hurt and troubled at the lack of news.

During her first two months in England she had found some solace in completing the translation of Germaine's short novel, and sending it to Longmans, the publishers, with instructions to them to arrange payment, should they like the book, through M. Villedeuil. They had acknowledged receipt of the manuscript, and she had heard no more. But now a bulky packet came from Lady Morningquest, who enclosed a brief note: "My dear Ellen, you showed excellent good sense in returning to England, where I trust you are obtaining comfort and satisfaction from providing your Father with companionship." Humph! thought Ellen. "The enclosed may be of interest to you," Lady Morningquest continued. "I am

also putting in some letters that were directed to you
here. I have heard curious rumors from Brussels & think
of removing Charlotte from the Pensionnat—she may
do her London season this year as well as next. Benedict
can escort her to England. You, doubtless, have your
own correspondents in the rue St. Pierre. Yr. affec.
godmother, Paulina M."

Since Ellen had heard no rumors from Brussels
she could only speculate fruitlessly as to why Lady
Morningquest should remove her daughter from Madame
Bosschère's establishment. Had the frivolity of Madame's
parties with young males in the cordoned corner given
rise to public censure? Or Monsieur Patrice written a
heretical treatise?

Smiling at her unlikely guesses, Ellen unfolded the
packet of papers, and found two letters addressed to
herself, and a number of pages cut from Paris papers: *Le
Monde, Le Siècle*—on which the name Raoul, Comte de
la Ferté, instantly caught her eye.

"Cries of an Anguished Husband," ran one heading,
and Ellen read on with horror. It seemed that the maid
of Louise had found a bundle of letters written by Raoul
to his wife, and had sold them to the press, doubtless for
a handsome sum. "My dearest Love, for God's sake give
ear to my plea," said one. "If the family succession means
nothing to you, think of *me*! Think of my comfortless
nights, my longing to be near you, to touch you, to
adore you." "Louise, Louise, you who are so sensitive, so
swift to pick up literary allusions," said another, "can you
not use your fine intelligence to envisage what my life
is like—freezing in outer darkness, suffering the Tantalus
torture of your daily presence, your continual refusals?
Turn to me again, I beg you, I beg you—soften that
flintlike heart, do not condemn me to starve in misery
for the rest of my life!"

There were many letters in the same vein. Ellen

snatched away her eyes in horror, feeling that she had committed an outrageous act in merely reading a few lines from them. It seemed a betrayal to witness these pitiful supplications. They seemed so different from the man she had known. Poor wretch, she thought, racked by sympathy, what he must suffer at having his words made public. He has such pride—has he not endured enough already?

She pushed away the clippings as though they were filthy.

One of the two letters was from the Hôtel Caudebec, and Ellen opened it hastily with trembling fingers. Surely Raoul would not have written to her? But the communication proved to be merely from Pondicheau, Raoul's agent and man of business, sending her a note of hand for the amount of salary that had been owing when she left Paris, and a bonus payment for her secretarial assistance to the Princess Tanofski. The payment was extremely generous, which did not in the least allay Ellen's bitter disappointment. Yet how could she possibly expect a letter from the Comte? Poor man, in his present state of wretchedness, was it likely that he would think of such a thing?

The other letter, in elegant, familiar handwriting, on cheap yellow paper, was from Germaine.

Couvent de Notre-Dame, Montfaucon, Ploëmel.

My dear Callisto: Here, believe it or not, you find me among the Benedictines, in the forests of Brittany. I see you smile with surprise, but the good Sisters have used me with such forbearance, consideration, and bonté that already I am half reconciled to the religious life. I came here in the first place seeking retreat—concealment—sanctuary—but the ambience has proved so congenial that—even now I have no pressing need to remain—I find in myself small wish to return to the city.

As you may have heard, the authorities are now satisfied that the miserable Louise did indeed take her own life and that of her doomed child. Raoul is exonerated, save from the blame and pity inevitably felt for a poor fool with no more sense than to marry someone who disliked him, and then persist in pestering her with his attentions long after she made her antipathy plain.

I must confess I feel a touch of guilt, now, at the thought of his sufferings—Jeanne de Tourbey sent me some Paris papers with extracts from his letters—poor boy, it is hard to have such undignified, deplorable outpourings revealed to the public eye. But let us hope that, now he is an eligible widower, he will soon find consolation.

I am to thank you, kind Callisto, for so reliably consigning my novel to the English publisher Longman. I had a very civil letter from him forwarded by Villedeuil; they will issue the book in three volumes, and they ask for another. When they pay me I shall instruct them to send you a translator's fee. But—I ask myself—shall I write any more? I confess, I find myself strangely irresolute; I have completed the work on which I was engaged, but this conventual existence does not predispose one to literature. Heigh-ho, Callisto, what will become of me? Shall I end up a dévote, telling my beads, reading my missal, thinking of the unhappiness I have caused?

And where are you, *Callisto, I wonder? Somehow I imagine you back in England; but what will those Sussex peasants make of you, now that you are almost a Parisienne? Do not allow your faculties to wither away from lack of use! I miss your grave good sense and shrewd perceptions—alas for those invigorating tête-à-têtes! The dear religieuses here are replete with wisdom, but they are a little lacking in wit.*

Well, Callisto, I wonder, shall we ever meet again? Think of me sometimes, as I of you. C.

This letter rendered Ellen decidedly melancholy. Despite the acrimony of their parting, and despite the disastrous role that Germaine had played in the la Fertés' tragedy, Ellen could not bring herself to dislike the other girl, and had also missed their lively exchanges. What would Germaine, she wondered, make of this English existence? Would it bore her to distraction? What would she think of Mrs. Pike, of Luke, Gerard, the Valdoes, Lady Blanche? Or Aunt Fanny? And how would Germaine's earthy common sense deal with the situation at the Hermitage?

She wrote to Germaine, telling little of this, but mentioning that in two years she would be in command of a modest fortune. "So, if you do return to writing, and are ever in difficulties, do not forget that you have a friend in England."

Sighing, she carried her letter to the post—what a long way Brittany seemed!—and then took a walk in the valley below the Hermitage. A hard frost for several days had rendered horse exercise out of the question, and Vicky was confined to bed with a cold. Ellen, well wrapped in her warmest pelisse, scrambled down the hillside and took the path that followed the windings of the brook, now swollen with melted snow, down to the Haslingbourne Mill, which had once, long ago, belonged to her great-great-uncle.

Returning on the other side of the valley, across a brow of hill known as the Sheepdowns, she was annoyed to see, coming toward her, the thin, awkward figure of Mr. Wheelbird the attorney.

She had met him hereabouts once or twice before, and he had explained, with a deprecating and self-conscious smile, that this was his route for returning home to late luncheon in the village of Byworth across the valley, where he resided with his widowed mother. Ellen thought it a strangely roundabout approach to Byworth, but if Mr. Wheelbird chose to take extra time from his duties at the lawyer's office, it was no affair of hers—except that she was tired of running into him and being obliged to make civil responses to his remarks.

He raised his hat eagerly with his usual air of nervous propitiation, nodding his head up and down, twitching a smile on and off his face as if uncertain of his right to maintain it there.

"Dirty weather, ma'am—Miss Paget. But you—if I may say so—appear blooming as usual—you do not let the weather d-deter you from your constitutional." Mr. Wheelbird tended to a slight stammer when he was nervous or excited. He appeared unusually so on the present occasion. To Ellen's deep dismay he turned and accompanied her along her path. "There—there is a d-decidedly slippery portion of the track farther along, Miss P-Paget; allow me to escort you past it."

"Thank you, Mr. Wheelbird, but really there is no need. I am quite used to scrambling along this valley. And a tumble would not hurt me in the least, I am protected by this thick old pelisse."

Whereas Mr. Wheelbird, she noticed, was attired with unusual splendor. His trousers and waistcoat, which both looked brand-new, were in two different contrasting checks; he had a black coat, which was so very glossy and stiff that he walked in it with difficulty as if inside a drain-pipe. His cravat was silk, and his tall hat shone as if it had just been carefully removed from the hatbox. Brilliant patent-leather shoes completed his toilet; altogether, he seemed oddly costumed for a walk along a muddy valley;

but perhaps, thought Ellen, he had just been attending on some important client.

"I could not d-dream of allowing you to take the risk," announced Mr. Wheelbird, and he took her arm in a somewhat gingerly grip. The path at this point was very narrow, across the steep hillside, no more than a sheep track, and in order to allow his companion to walk upon it, the lawyer was obliged to pick his way through the wet, soggy, frosty grass. His shoes, though highly polished, were evidently not meant for such usage, and, from his anxious glances at them, it became plain that this consideration was harassing him.

"Pray, Mr. Wheelbird," said Ellen, "do not put yourself to the trouble of accompanying me any farther. I am persuaded you must have more important duties awaiting you. I shall manage very well on my own, I promise you."

"No, ma'am, no! My c-conscience would not allow it. In f-f-fact, Miss Ellen," proclaimed Mr. Wheelbird, his stammer suddenly becoming so much more pronounced that "Ellen" came out as "Elelelelellen," "in fact, ma'am, I should wish to accompany you *everywhere*, and to manage *everything* for you. I should wish to stand between you and the world, Miss Paget! I should like to save you from m-mad bulls, ma'am—to rescue you from poverty—to d-defend you in court—"

"But I have not been accused of any crime, Mr. Wheelbird—and there are no mad bulls to be seen—" objected Ellen, nervously trying to stem this flow before it reached its obvious conclusion. She was wasting her breath, however; Mr. Wheelbird, having got himself embarked on his declaration, gathered momentum and confidence.

"Dear Miss Ellen—you must be aware that I have nourished for some c-considerable time a strong p-partiality—a most particular regard and devotion—of which you are the object, ma'am! My p-previous approach was premature—I was but a green youth (though still it was very wrong of Mr. Paget to address me as he did)"—a momentary unpleasant recollection darkening his brow—"but now matters are decidedly different, I am a man well established in my profession. Whereas *your* lot, Miss Ellen—returned home in disgrace—installed in what I cannot but be aware is a most unhappy domestic situation—"

"What should make you think *that*, Mr. Wheelbird?" Ellen spoke rather sharply. She had not been pleased by that "returned home in disgrace."

"All the town is aware that Mrs. P-Pike—that Mrs. Pike has her eye on your f-father, Miss Ellen. She is a capable woman—I manage some little property affairs for her, I know her nature—what Mrs. Pike attempts—she—she—she *achieves*! Think, ma'am, think what your position will be *then*, with such a stepmother. So, p-pray, Miss Ellen—my d-dear, dear Miss Ellen—will you not make me the happiest man in P-Petworth? Will you not give an affirmative answer to this offer of matrimony? Only say yes—and come back to tea with me and my mother. She has baked a s-seedcake," he added ingenuously.

Though she could not help feeling somewhat touched by Mr. Wheelbird's declaration, Ellen did also reflect that he seemed to take a good deal for granted. And she was distracted by a sudden piercing recollection of Benedict, with jutting jaw and scowling face on the Channel steamer, making some sarcastic allusion to "the attorney's clerk who still came calling at the Hermitage." How Benedict would laugh at this scene! Which, for some reason, put Ellen into a particularly unreceptive mood for receiving Mr. Wheelbird's proposal. Nor did she in the least wish to take tea with old Mrs. Wheelbird, who had a sweet, vinegary voice, and a lacy fluffy exterior, concealing vigilant powers of observation combined with a resentful and styptic nature.

There were really no circumstances, Ellen thought, which could persuade her to accept Mr. Wheelbird's offer. But still, it behooved her to be kind to him.

"It is exceedingly obliging of you, sir, to honor me with such a proposal," she responded, as civilly as she could. "And indeed, I am highly sensible of your regard and—and of the honor you do me." Annoyed, she realized that she was repeating herself, but found herself at a loss for a phrase that would decisively put an end to his expectations without doing too much damage to his pride. "But I am very much afraid that I am unable to reciprocate your sentiments. In fact I have no thought of matrimony at present. I wish to continue under my father's roof."

"Do not, do not be so hasty, Miss Ellen!" exclaimed Mr. Wheelbird, who seemed in agony at the thought of his prize perhaps slipping away from him. "Take some time to consider carefully. Pray, pray, think over what I have s-said! I am persuaded that if you d-do so—take a week, take a month!—and you will then, I am s-sure, arrive at a just estimate of how very *useful* I could be to you! Versed in the law—knowing, as I do, such a *great* deal of people's affairs—"

Here, to Ellen's considerable surprise, Mr. Wheelbird turned to give her an exceedingly sharp and meaningful glance—almost a wink—it was utterly different from his previous rather sheepish and propitiating expression. But the sudden movement of the head that accompanied it was his undoing, for they had now reached the slippery section of the path over which he had proposed to guide her; he lost his footing on a patch of icy mud and fell flat into the middle of it. He would have dragged Ellen with him, for he still kept hold of her arm, had she not braced herself, and hauled him up again, with all the strength that had served her so well when dealing with turbulent girls at the Pensionnat. So Mr. Wheelbird's tumble was of short duration—but during that instant, what havoc had been wrought! His hat fell off, his hair was disheveled, and he stood up plastered with semi-liquid brown mud all down one side of him, from his face to his patent-leather shoes.

"Oh, good gracious!" exclaimed Ellen. "How dreadfully unfortunate! *Poor* Mr. Wheelbird—what a horrid mishap—and in your new coat, too! Look, here is your hat." She picked it up and handed it to him, after endeavoring to brush some of the slime off it. He was quite speechless from discomposure. "Perhaps your mother will know some good way of getting that off—"

Mr. Wheelbird's confidence was not strong enough to sustain this mortifying setback. He almost snatched the hat from Ellen, and withdrew his arm from her solicitous grasp.

In a trembling voice he said, "I will wish you good day, ma'am, at this present. I d-did not—matters have not—oh, *d-damnation!*"

Turning sharply (though with considerable care) on his heel, he walked off in the direction from which Ellen had been coming. He was not going toward Byworth, but she feared that pride would not permit him to change his course until she was out of sight, so, having glanced back anxiously at him once or twice, she made haste to take her own way homeward.

She could not help smiling over the poor man's mishap, but hoped that his self-esteem had not been too badly shaken by the occurrence—although she hoped, equally, that the embarrassing conclusion of his declaration might be sufficient to prevent a renewal.

Vaguely she wondered what he had been about to say in that moment before he fell—some piece of information regarding one of his clients? But surely that would be a breach of confidence? It was a good thing that he had not spoken.

Then she put the whole incident out of her mind.

Thirteen

Mr. Wheelbird did not immediately resume his suit. It seemed probable that he wished a sufficient period of time to elapse for the memory of his humiliating accident to recede in Ellen's mind; at all events he kept strictly away from her and presumably avoided any locality where there would be the chance of an encounter, for she never ran across him.

The episode did recede from her mind, for, during this period, she was given what seemed a chance to rectify, or at least improve, her rather difficult and painful relationship with her father. He summoned her, one day, to his business room, ungraciously and abruptly, as she was hearing Vicky's recitation.

"Leave that, Ellen! I wish you to translate a French text for me!"

"Of course, Papa."

The text was a sixteenth-century bill of sale for cloth, and, by means of this, she was enabled to discover that the subject of Luke's reading was material for a history which he was compiling of the Industries and Manufactures carried on in the Parish of Petworth from 1066 to the present day, from the eels and hogs of the Domesday Survey, through the cloth trade during the reign of Henry VIII, the ironworks in Petworth Park, the glass manufactory during the time of Queen Elizabeth, and the boot and clog trade which later replaced it.

Mr. Paget did not ask Ellen's opinion of this work, nor did she offer it, but privately she doubted whether a book of such limited interest would ever be likely to find a publisher, and she felt apprehensive for her father's subsequent disappointment and chagrin. The work, however, appeared to proceed so slowly and haltingly that publication of any kind was a distant prospect. It was frequently interrupted by digressions into other projects on which he was simultaneously engaged: an essay on road making in Sussex; a comparison of the consumption of tea and gin in London during the 1740s, and deaths from the latter; a history of the Judicial System in England before, during, and after the Revolution of 1688. On all these topics he had accumulated copious notes, but he seemed hesitant, or hamstrung by doubt, when it came to the point of actually making a start on the work. Ellen soon began to pity him sincerely, for she perceived that it gave him such agonizing difficulty to frame a single written sentence—and the result, when achieved, was so tortuous and unintelligible—that it seemed quite out of the question he should ever complete a single one of his enterprises.

She marveled at this incapacity in a man who, by many accounts, had been a fluent speaker on political matters; but so it was. Nor would he accept advice from her; if she ventured to recommend a simpler form of wording in one of his statements, he would become irritable, and testily order her to mind her own business and not meddle in matters of which she knew nothing.

Nonetheless, he accepted her help in making some order out of his confused system of classification. This necessitated her spending an hour or so a day in his business room, and, almost imperceptibly, by slow degrees, as month succeeded month, growing to be on more cordial terms with him. During these weeks he paid considerably less attention to Mrs. Pike; his need for attention was, it seemed, assuaged by this new kind of companionship. Such a falling off was observed by the housekeeper with a marked lack of enthusiasm; she lost no opportunity to denigrate Ellen's help and cast aspersions on its utility.

In May a parcel arrived for Ellen from Brussels. She had not heard again from Lady Morningquest, nor from anybody else in the rue St. Pierre, and she undid the wrappings with considerable curiosity. Inside she found a handsome volume, bound in leather and gilt; on the spine: *Discours sur les Pensées Ultérieures*, par P. Bosschère. And inside, written on the flyleaf: "To my dear little interlocutress, Mademoiselle M. E. Paget, from whose conversation many of the ideas in this essay were first born!"

Enchanted, excited, deeply touched, Ellen turned the leaves, and, as phrases here and there caught her eye, memories of many discussions with the Professor flashed back into her mind. *There*, she thought, was a man of real, burning intelligence; no flash in the pan, but a thinker destined to go far, to make his mark; she could not help contrasting him with her father, much to the latter's detriment. The work looked brilliant—perhaps, as he himself said, some of the ideas had been furnished by her, but he had a right to cull his themes and observations from all around him, did he not? The use he made of her embryonic notions was something she might never have achieved herself, and she would learn and benefit immeasurably by a study of what he had brought forth.

Flushed, gratified, overflowing with pleasure, longing to share this with some other person—and also imbued, perhaps, with a faint touch of malice—she tapped on the door and entered her father's business room.

He looked up peevishly from the untidy muddle of cards and written pages that piled up on his worktable five minutes after Ellen had set it in order.

"What is this?" he demanded. "You here *now*, Ellen?

It is not your hour to assist me. I do not require your services at the present time."

"No, Papa—I am aware of that. I merely wished to show you this volume, which Professor Bosschère in Brussels has kindly sent me."

"Bosschère?"

"You recall, Papa—he is the cousin of Madame who owns the Pensionnat—he taught us divinity and literature—he has sent me this book—"

"Sent you a *book*?" Luke sounded both surprised and disapproving. "Why should *he* do such a thing? This seems a decided liberty! Why should he be sending you books, pray?"

"But he wrote it, Papa! It is *his* book. We always knew that he was at work on a history of human thought; now he has completed it. And, see, he has inscribed this copy to me!"

Mr. Paget received the volume and frowningly surveyed it. He did not seem at all impressed by the authorial inscription.

"Humph! Well, you had best leave the book with me, until I have ascertained whether it is a suitable piece of work for you to be perusing."

Ellen was somewhat dashed—for one thing, she had been eager to commence reading it herself, and knew her father to be a slow and plodding reader, especially in French, a language of which he had only very moderate mastery. But she said, "I am sure you will enjoy it, Papa—Professor Patrice was such a very intelligent man, his lessons were so inspiring—"

"Very well. Leave me now, like a good girl. And pray, another time, do not burst in and interrupt my work at this hour."

Mr. Paget did not allude to the book again that day, nor for the succeeding three days, during which time Ellen did her best to contain herself. At last, becoming too impatient to wait in silence any longer, she broached the matter at her regular hour for helping him, when she was in his study sorting out his cards.

"What do you think of Professor Bosschère's *Discours*, Papa? How are you getting on with it? Have you nearly finished? I must confess, I am very curious to read the book myself!"

"Eh? Ha? Humph! Oh, that book—a disgraceful bit of work! Full of outrageous notions—of course, one can expect no better from a Catholic—but still—dangerous, seditious rubbish, tricked up in flowery, sentimental language—despicable stuff!"

"But—good heavens, Papa—how can you possibly say such a thing? Professor Bosschère is not at all sentimental—he writes most clearly and incisively—and I cannot believe that any of his statements were dangerous or seditious—which ones can you mean? Are you sure that you have read it *all*?"

"As much as was necessary; I glanced through the chapters," said Mr. Paget shortly. "The headings were quite enough to show the kind of man he is—these foreigners are all the same, one cannot trust them. Human love—faugh! A most unsuitable book for you; it is very fortunate that you should have showed it to me first."

"Still, I should like to read it, Papa, so as to form my own judgment," said Ellen, who had a strong suspicion that her father had been foiled by the French language, and had done little more than glance at the book; she was now exceedingly sorry that she had succumbed to the impulse to show it to him.

"Well, you *can't* read it," he snapped.

"Excuse me, Papa, it is my own book, presented to me by the writer; I should like to have it back, if you please," she said, keeping her temper with a strong effort.

"That is out of the question. In fact, I have burned

it, which is the only thing to do with such stuff." He glanced toward the fireplace; following his eyes, Ellen saw, with incredulous dismay, some portions of red leather, burned almost black, in a corner of the grate.

"Burned it? You burned my book?" Sheer rage almost choked Ellen for a moment; then, in a high, shaking voice, she said, "You are a selfish, despotic, bigoted old *monster*! How *dared* you do such a thing? That book was my property—you had no right to destroy it. When Mama said you were not an easy man, she was ludicrously understating the case. You are not difficult—you are *impossible*!"

His face went a dull red. He said hoarsely, "What can you mean? When your mother said I was not an easy man—to what can you refer? How can *she* ever have discussed me with *you*?"

Ellen realized, aghast, that recklessness had led her into betraying her mother.

"It is nothing I can tell you about, Papa. I am sorry I spoke. We had best end this discussion." And she turned on her heel, and was preparing to leave the room, when he burst out into a loud, incoherent tirade.

"Insolent! Ungrateful! Unfilial! Outrageous girl! *She* shall hear of this! She-she—"

Ellen assumed that he referred to Mrs. Pike, and was only thankful that the housekeeper was not present. Her father took a step toward her, and she thought he was actually about to bar her way to the door, when, muttering again "She—she—she—" he waved his arms at her, staggered, and sank fainting into an armchair.

Mrs. Pike was almost instantly in the room. It seemed probable that she had, alerted by the raised voices, been listening outside the door; she drew breath in a long hiss of honor.

"*Now*, miss! *Look* what you have done to your poor old father!"

Darting to her employer, she felt his pulse, turned up his eyelids, then violently tugged at the bell rope.

"Is it a faint?" asked Ellen, who, sincerely alarmed, felt nevertheless a kind of disgust at the melodrama that the housekeeper was extracting from the scene. Ignoring her, Mrs. Pike turned to Sue, who had come running, scared at the urgency of the summons.

"Send John coachman for the doctor—hurry, woman! Your master has had a shocking seizure—heaven send it do not prove fatal!"

Dr. Smollett, when he came, did not take such a serious view. Mr. Paget had, he thought, suffered a slight stroke, but with care and good nursing—"Such as yours, ma'am," he remarked politely to Mrs. Pike—there should be no permanent ill effects. Mr. Paget must, however, be confined to bed for several weeks.

Ellen, who was present during this interview, studied the housekeeper with keen attention, and could not avoid the conclusion that she was a little disappointed by this favorable verdict. When she first ran into the study and saw her employer prostrate in his chair, Ellen could have sworn that there had been a momentary flash of satisfaction on her face. Was it vindictive pleasure at sight of such a shocking breach between father and daughter? But surely she would hardly take the feeling so far as to hope that Luke would die, thus leaving her out of employment?

◦❦◦

During the first few weeks of her father's illness, Ellen was excluded severely from the sickroom.

"Visit your father? When you were the cause of his affliction? I should think not, indeed! The mere sight of you might be enough to give him another turn!" said Mrs. Pike in righteous outrage.

Ellen did not press the matter. Her father's action in

burning her book had filled her with such a passion of indignation and disgust that, so long as he continued to progress favorably, which Dr. Smollett assured her was the case, she preferred to keep out of his presence. Finding the doctor intelligent and sympathetic, she had made no secret about the dispute which had brought on Luke's attack, and Smollett had agreed on the wisdom of not reviving the memory by presenting herself at her father's bedside.

"Quick-tempered kind of man your pa—ain't he?" said the doctor. "No sense in stirring up trouble." But after a few weeks he changed his opinion. "It's my belief, Miss Ellen, that he don't remember a thing about what caused his attack. In fact he has asked me several times—rather pitifully, under that gruff manner—why you never come to see him."

"Has he indeed? Mrs. Pike never told me that."

During the period of Luke's illness, Ellen had had time to master her first feelings of resentment and bitterness. Nothing would assuage her disappointment at the loss of her book, but, in the absence of her father from the domestic scene (and it was remarkable how much more agreeable the household became while he was confined to his bed), there had been leisure to reflect that this was just the kind of difficulty which her mother had asked her to bear with patience. How many such indignities and disappointments must not Mattie have suffered! While still keenly resenting the injustice of her treatment, Ellen was prepared to give her father another chance. In a way, it was exasperating that he had so conveniently forgotten the matter, and would not even be aware of her tolerance; but, on the other hand, this blank in his memory made him seem pitiable, vulnerable, at a disadvantage. Furthermore, she needed to allay the agitations of Kitty and Eugenia, who wrote by every post demanding news of poor Papa's progress. Fortunately Eugenia was confined to Valdoe Court by measles among her children, or she would certainly have visited the Hermitage before now, and been presented with Mrs. Pike's version of the affair. As it was, Ellen had merely written to inform her sisters that Papa had suffered a slight seizure, from which he was recovering satisfactorily.

"I will certainly go and see my father if he wishes it," she told the doctor.

In order to avoid a clash that might be upsetting to the invalid, she picked a moment when Mrs. Pike was out of doors, arguing with Moon the gardener, and then made her way to Luke's bedside.

He did look rather pitiful, she was bound to admit, lying propped upright against heaped pillows, his long bony face even paler than usual, the cavernous eye sockets deeper, the eyes fixed in a melancholy, absent stare, the massive hands lying idle on the coverlet.

"Papa? Dr. Smollett said you had expressed a wish to see me."

"Ah, there you are, child! Yes—I believe you have been away on a visit? I, too, have been away—I am not quite sure where," he confided. "But I am very glad to be back, and soon I shall be resuming my literary labors. In the meantime, Ellen, I shall be obliged if you will read to me for an hour or two. I find the effort is too much if I have to hold the volume myself."

"Certainly, Papa, I shall be glad to. What shall I read?"

"Oh, whatever you wish. I have no particular preference."

Ellen reflected with some irony that now would have been an excellent time to read to him from Professor Bosschère's *Discours*. Lacking that, she read him a few items from the local paper, an essay from the *Gentleman's Magazine*, which lay on his bedside table, and an article from the *Morning Post*, which was delivered daily by coach, on the likelihood of the North American

Federal Union erecting a tariff wall which would block British trade.

"It is a bad business—a bad business," muttered Luke. "Palmerston favors the Southern side—but if it should come to an armed conflict, I fancy that the Northern states, with their greater population and more extensive industry, would in the end prove victorious."

"Their cause is just, Papa. Slavery is odious."

"Do not attempt to discuss subjects which are outside of your sphere, child."

Ellen bit her tongue and remained silent. Yet after a moment he continued in a musing tone, "I cannot but be of your opinion, however. No human should be utterly at the disposition of another. John Stuart Mill expresses this admirably in an essay I have been reading; he says, 'Mankind are greater gainers by suffering each other to live as seems good to themselves than by compelling each other to live as seems good to the rest.'" And Luke heaved a long, sad sigh; on his face was a look of unappeasable regret. Ellen could not help wondering if he thought of her mother. After a moment she said in a gentle tone, "Are you weary, Papa? Shall I leave you?"

"I am a little weary—but do not leave me for a moment. How-how do Vicky's lessons proceed? Does she apply herself? Is she studious—docile?"

"She is biddable enough. She will never be my star pupil," said Ellen, smiling, "save in her talent for portraiture. She must have that from Lady Adelaide—I do not recall any artist in this family?"

Luke sighed again and shook his head. But after a moment his expression became lighter as he asked, "And Gerard? How does he go on? The boy pays me such brief visits—two hasty words and he is gone. Does he seem to be working hard?"

Ellen said truthfully that Gerard spent many hours a day with his tutor and law books.

"That is good—that is as it should be. He will write the name of Paget on the page of history."

Poor Papa, thought Ellen. How he deludes himself. Unless, indeed, Gerard becomes a famous composer of music.

"But the Doom Stone," Luke went on. "Is there no word of its discovery? I wish you will write a note to the Bishop, child, asking if it has not yet come to light."

"I am sure, Papa, that the Bishop would have informed you if it had."

"It might have escaped his memory. He is a busy man. I wish you will write, my dear."

"Very well, Papa."

Mrs. Pike suddenly appeared in the doorway. She looked extremely discomposed; the red spot burned on either cheek and there was an angry spark in her eye.

"Miss Paget! I did not give you leave to enter the sickroom."

"My daughter does not require your permission to visit her father, ma'am," said Luke magisterially. "Your consideration outruns the bounds of your duty. I sent for Ellen to read to me."

"And I can see that she has stayed too long and tired you," snapped the housekeeper. "*I* could have read to you, Mr. Paget, if you had asked me!"

"You are too occupied with your manifold duties. And," said Mr. Paget clinchingly, "your voice is too loud."

Mrs. Pike reddened with annoyance. "Well, it is time you rested now."

"I was just going," said Ellen, and moved toward the door. But her father halted her. "Perhaps, child, you would care to peruse this essay on Liberty, by Mr. Mill; I fancy you would find it of interest."

"Why, thank you, Papa! I shall like to read it."

She took the pamphlet and escaped, followed by Mrs. Pike's malevolent stare.

Mr. Newman, Gerard's tutor, was to be away for the month of August, attending a Church Convocation and visiting relatives in his native town of York. It had been arranged by Mr. Paget, some time before he had his seizure, that, during the tutor's absence, Gerard should read law with a retired judge in Chichester, staying with his sister Eugenia for the purpose. Since Luke was now progressing so favorably, it was not thought necessary to cancel the arrangement; Gerard packed up and dispatched books and clothes by the carrier, and himself rode over the Downs on his horse Captain. From his holiday air of joyful liberation, Ellen guessed that he planned many visits to his friend Matt Bilbo; she could not blame him, but she sighed a little, reflecting what trouble this would cause for Eustace and Eugenia should Luke come to hear of it, and wondering what effect it might have on Gerard himself; still, perhaps a month's unfettered association with his friend might divest the relationship of its mesmeric fascination, so that, on his return to Petworth, he might be content to let it dwindle away.

Luke missed his son; but the knowledge that the boy was in Chichester, reading with Sir Magnus Orde, was, in a way, more satisfactory to him than Gerard's actual presence, since the intercourse between father and son was generally so strained and perfunctory.

It had become an accepted practice for Ellen to spend a couple of hours a day by her father's bedside, reading him news from the paper, essays from *The Spectator*, or extracts from volumes relating to his historical research. Mrs. Pike glowered and fulminated, and was quick to object that her patient was becoming tired, but she had no power to forbid the sessions.

A cold and windy July had now given way to a chill and rainy August; Dr. Smollett allowed Mr. Paget up for an hour or so a day and said that he might sit outside if weather permitted; but so far it did not permit. Ellen, however, sometimes read to her father in the garden room, and there, occasionally, Vicky was permitted to come and play quietly (which, to her, meant drawing) while the reading sessions took place. Mrs. Pike expressed strong disapproval, but Ellen felt that if the child were not allowed to see her father even thus briefly, the pair would become utter strangers to one another.

Vicky was there one rainy afternoon when Ellen read aloud the sad case of the Unknown Female Vagrant.

"A female Pauper, of age probably approaching twenty-three or four, was discovered by the constables lying out in Pikeshoot Copse with her infant child. She appeared emaciated and very sick, and would answer no questions as to her name, age, Parish of origin, etc., etc. Having no claim on the Parish of Petworth, they at first thought to lodge her in the Jail, but the overseers of the Poorhouse at last permitted her to be admitted there and stay for the period of one night, it being hoped she would then divulge the name of her own Parish so that she might be conveyed there. But during the night, having remained resolutely silent, she died, it is thought by the Parish Medical officer, of inanition, for the weather was tolerably mild, though it is true the woman's garments, which were scanty and worn, had been wet through by recent heavy rains. Her funeral will be a charge on the Parish of Petworth, unless any person can identify her. Her infant, also ailing and emaciated, is not expected to survive her many days. A drawing of this poor Unfortunate is appended, in case any of our Readers can throw light on the mystery of her identity."

A sketch of a piteously thin, hollow-cheeked face appeared below the paragraph. Ellen was certain she had never seen the girl, but Vicky, coming to lean against her sister's knee and study the paper, said at once, "Why, that is the beggar woman who came to the back door one day while Papa was in bed. I was in the apple tree and saw her."

"You should not climb trees, Vicky," said her father.

"Are you sure, Vicky?" asked Ellen.

"Why yes, I remember her face very well, for I did a drawing of her—wait, and I will show you." Vicky riffled through her well-used notebook and found a picture in the corner of a crowded page, which showed recognizably the same girl. She held a baby in her arms, and her expression was desperate and beseeching.

"Yes, that is undoubtedly the same girl. Poor thing! I wish I had known, I would have given her some money—or perhaps helped her to find employment."

"Mrs. Pike came and talked to her and gave her something," replied Vicky. "Mrs. Pike was very angry, though, and told her to go away and never show her face again, or she would have her whipped by the constables."

"Did she indeed?" muttered Ellen.

Mr. Paget remarked, "Mrs. Pike is zealous to protect this household from mendicants and vagrants. Perhaps she sometimes exceeds her warrant, but her intention is for the best."

Ellen strongly doubted this. She wondered if the wretched beggar could be the same girl whom she had seen talking to Mrs. Pike by the track to Frog Hole Farm. Might she have been some poor relative, some connection whom the housekeeper was refusing to acknowledge? But all this was mere supposition.

Mrs. Pike, bustling in with a cup of coffee for Mr. Paget, put an end to the conversation, announcing that the patient was fatigued and must return to his chamber.

"Did you know this poor girl, Mrs. Pike?" inquired Ellen, holding up the paper.

The housekeeper answered composedly enough. "Is that the pauper who died up at the workhouse? It is a shame that such creatures should wander about the countryside, frightening honest folk at their own doors. Yes, she did come here, but I soon sent her about her business."

It was evident that she had already seen the story in the paper. But her color was somewhat higher than usual, and her hands shook slightly as she received the coffee cup from her employer.

You sent that girl away to her death, thought Ellen.

~

Two weeks later, as Ellen, having taken advantage of an unusually fine afternoon to visit a superannuated gardener who lived at Osiers Cottages, some two miles north of the town, was returning on her pony through Petworth Park, she heard herself hailed by a voice which was so familiar, and so wholly out of her present context, that for a moment she felt completely at sea. She had been riding with a loose rein, in a mood of mild and recollected melancholy, for the man from whose house she came, a retired family servant, had been very devoted to her mother, and the afternoon had been largely spent in reminiscence. Now, to be hailed so unexpectedly: "*Darling* Miss Paget! It *is* you! Only imagine the luck of encountering you here!" brought her abruptly out of her reverie.

At first the tiny, blond, exquisitely coiffed, hatted, gloved, and habited equestrienne on the big bay horse seemed a stranger; then she realized that it was Charlotte Morningquest, her external appearance sleeked and groomed into adulthood, but her bubbling, breathless loquacity unchanged since the days in the rue St. Pierre.

"How *wonderful*!" Charlotte was exclaiming. "Of course I wished to come and call on you directly, but they told me at Petworth House that your father had been dreadfully ill, and I hesitated to intrude; but, oh, I have been *bursting* to tell you about all the goings-on at Madame's Pensionnat!"

"Goings-on?" Ellen was startled. "What can you possibly mean, my dear Charlotte?" Then, turning to Charlotte's silent companion, equally splendidly mounted on a glossy black hunter, who was holding himself somewhat withdrawn from the two females, she added, with formality, "How do you do, Mr. Masham?"

"How do you do, Miss Paget?" he replied, as coldly. "Miss Charlotte, I am sure that you two ladies must have many private matters to discuss, and I am persuaded that no harm can befall you in this park, so I will leave you to your conversation," and he was about to set spurs to the black horse when Charlotte detained him, crying imperiously, "No, no, don't go, Benedict, for I shall need you to pick me some rose hips, and to open the gates, and for a dozen other things—you must not leave us! Now, *dear* Miss Paget, tell me how you go on? Was it very sad for you, returning to England? Is your papa *very* ill? Shall you ever be able to come up to London? Aunt Massingham is giving a ball for me in Berkeley Square in the autumn—could you not come to it? You must be weary of ruralizing!"

Ellen smiled and said she was not at all weary of country life, and saw little prospect of being able to come to London for Lady Massingham's ball. "But tell me about your mother. How is she? And your brother Tom? I hope that Lady Morningquest has a little recovered from her grief at your cousin's death."

"Oh, cousin Louise? She was a dismally hopeless girl," said Charlotte dismissively. "Always mooning about with her head in a book, when we were children, and then considering herself put upon and abused because she was not popular. For my part, I felt sorry for her husband— poor Raoul! And he was so handsome, too!"

Ellen kept her eyes rigidly on her pony's neck; six paces away she could feel Benedict, grimly intent on some object in the middle distance. Neither of the pair looked at the other, but they were as mutually aware as two cats stalking a garden boundary.

Charlotte went on blithely, "But that wasn't what I had to tell you. Only imagine! Madame Bosschère is in shocking disgrace, and Professor Patrice too—the scandal has all come out, and it is almost certain that Madame will be obliged to close the school. What a good thing you left when you did, dear Miss Paget, or *you* might have been involved too, and, as Mama said, it is bad enough being mixed up—"

She stopped, her cheeks suddenly turning a bright pink.

"Bad enough to be mixed up in one scandal, let alone two!" Ellen finished calmly.

"Well—yes! Not that any of it was *your* fault! Indeed," said Charlotte naively, "nobody looking at you would consider you a femme fatale, Miss Paget, and yet that is almost the role that has been thrust upon you in each of these two affairs!"

"What utter nonsense you talk, my dear Charlotte," said Ellen with a slightly heightened color, and still keeping her eyes resolutely away from Benedict. "But what is all this about Madame Bosschère and the Professor? Pray do not keep me in suspense."

"And no wonder," Charlotte went on, pursuing her own way, "no *wonder* that Madame used to become so nervous and distraught when she observed how the Professor adored you. Which it was plain he *did*—we all thought he was bound to pop the question, and were laying odds on how soon it would be—"

"Charlotte! If your mother could hear you! Besides, it is all such nonsense. The Professor liked to talk to me about intellectual matters—that is all."

"Well, so it now seems, and lucky for you, too!"

"Why, pray?"

"Why, it has come out that the Professor and Madame were *married*, all the time—had been married for ever so many years—only it was kept a secret for the sake of his fellowship, since married Fellows are not permitted. But only imagine the furore when it did come out!"

Ellen felt as if she had received a violent physical blow, somewhere between her diaphragm and her collarbone; she gasped, and turned quite white for a moment. Then she said hoarsely, "Married? They were actually *married*? He and Madame?"

"Yes! Can you conceive of such a deceit! Naturally, Madame's credit is quite sunk, and many people have been removing their daughters from the Pensionnat. As you may know, Mama heard a rumor some time since, which was why she brought me to Paris last autumn—"

"But how did the story get out?"

"Oh, it seems the Professor had written some learned book, on human thought, or an equally dry as dust subject—"

"Yes?" Now to Ellen's sensation of shock was added one of regret at the thought of her lost present.

"Well, it seems that this book won some great prize, in Belgium, National Medal for Literature, I believe it was called—so there was much public interest in him, of course, and the newspapers published articles about him—and then it all came out about the marriage, which had taken place years ago in a little village in Brabant. But what a thing! When I remember how severe Madame always used to be about *la pudeur* and *la propriété* and *les convenances*—all the time she was conducting such a deception herself. Is it not famous! How Dorothea and I did laugh!"

"Famous indeed," said Ellen rather hollowly. "But I cannot help pitying Madame. Her school, that she had taken such pains to build up! And the Professor, too—did the disclosure do him great harm?"

"Why no—I believe he has since been offered some important government position. Mama said it was unfair that, in such a case, the woman always suffers more from the scandal, while the man's credit is soon re-established—indeed, Papa, and other men, considered him rather a clever dog to have concealed his marriage for so long! He has had to give up his fellowship, of course, but then the government post will compensate for that."

"Well, I never was more astonished," said Ellen, lamely and inadequately. She felt immense relief that she had written a brief, cordial note of thanks to the Professor immediately upon receipt of his book; it would have been almost impossible to write at this juncture, withholding mention of the book's destruction at the hands of her father, and her knowledge of this extraordinary revelation.

Now uncountable memories began to come back—of conversations held with the Professor in classrooms or garden—of Madame's vigilant eye always upon him, always seeking him out; *then*, Ellen had imagined that her watchfulness was on grounds of chaperonage, or convention; *now*, she realized it had had a more personal motivation. Poor woman—what a desperate strain her life must have concealed, when she saw her husband courted by other women—as he had been, continually; his favors had been greatly sought by the teachers at the Pensionnat—while his own wife must hide any propri-etary airs or signs of jealousy.

"Remember your situation—remember your prom-ises!" Ellen remembered her beseeching him on that last evening in the rue St. Pierre. But even then she had not betrayed him—she had kept the secret.

"Poor Madame!" Ellen exclaimed involuntarily.

"How she must have suffered! And now it seems hard that she should receive a greater share of the blame."

"Oh well," Charlotte said cheerfully, "Mama thinks that, by and by, the Belgian bourgeoises will commence sending their daughters to her school again; for it is true she was an excellent teacher. But the foreign community have quite withdrawn their patronage—they do not like to feel they have been duped." The town clock distantly struck four. "Good heavens, Benedict! Cousin George Leconfield will be sitting down to dinner before I can get out of my habit and into evening dress. They keep such rustic hours at Petworth House. We must fly! Good-bye, *dearest* Miss Paget. Cousin George says that he and your papa ain't on good terms," Charlotte went on ingenuously, "so I can't very well invite you up to the house, but may *I* come and call on *you*, so that we can have a comfortable gossip? I have *such* things to tell you about Paris beaux! And Benedict will show me the way, I daresay."

"Of course you may come," said Ellen, though in fact she did not welcome the prospect of the visit, particularly if Benedict were to accompany Charlotte. He had been sedulously keeping his eyes off Ellen as much as he could; but if his gaze did chance to rest on her, it almost burned her with its cold, rejecting disdain.

"Addio, then! Till tomorrow. Come, Benedict, we must make haste." Charlotte gave her handsome mount a sharp tap and cantered away; Benedict briefly raised his hat to Ellen and followed.

Ellen made her way home at a slower pace; she was afflicted with tumultuous feelings. Chief among these at first was a considerable indignation against Professor Bosschère; he *must*, surely, have known the warmth of attachment that he might be exciting in the young teacher by his continued interest and attention; yet he had dropped not the slightest hint that there could be no future, no outcome, no chance of reciprocity for such an attachment. Or had he, perhaps, had aims of his own in view? Ellen's cheeks suddenly burned as she recalled his saying, "You *must* be free!" What had he meant? Free for what purpose?

Suddenly she found that she did not wish to think about Professor Bosschère.

And to have all this so artlessly revealed by Charlotte in front of Benedict—could anything in the world be more unfortunate? Benedict's notion of her was low enough already (not, of course, that Ellen cared a rap for his opinion); but, from Charlotte, he had now doubtless received the impression that Ellen's favors were bestowed promiscuously and uncritically upon whatever male happened to be at hand. Bother Charlotte! Why did she have to come and visit Petworth House just now? And why did Benedict have to escort her? Was Lady Morningquest intending to make up a match between them? Charlotte would not, Ellen thought, suit Benedict at all; good-natured but shallow-pated, she would soon bore him to death with her artless frivolity and prattle. Though, to be sure, it was no concern of Ellen's—let them marry if they chose! She very much hoped they would not be making a prolonged sojourn at Petworth House; it was annoying and embarrassing, too, that Papa had quarreled with Lord Leconfield about the siting of the new Infant School to be built beside the County Jail; Papa had said that was a most idiotic position for it, and there had been a consequent coolness between the two men, who avoided one another's company except for the inevitable fortnightly Petty Sessions in the Town Hall. Benedict would be confirmed in his view that the Pagets were a froward, contentious, ill-bred tribe, from whom it would be best to sever all connection…

Next morning, however, to Ellen's surprise, Benedict did present himself at the Hermitage, along with Charlotte. He looked and spoke coldly to Ellen; he paid a short formal visit on Mr. Paget, and expressed himself happy to see that his stepfather was making progress toward restored health; the chief object of his visit seemed to be that of satisfying himself as to Vicky's comfort and happiness. Ellen could not help thinking this highly officious—why should Vicky not be happy and well cared for? But then she was obliged to recall how far from happy Vicky had been under the single and despotic rule of Mrs. Pike, which, by a mixture of diplomacy, defiance, cunning, and care, Ellen had by degrees managed to alleviate in almost every particular; the child was now a changed creature indeed. And it must be admitted, too, that she seemed exceedingly fond of her grown-up half brother; she rushed to him with cries of jubilation, showed him all her drawings, and exclaimed in rapture over the gifts he had brought her. Ellen would have been a little more in charity with Benedict by the end of the call if he had not made it so abundantly clear that the purpose of his visit was not to see *her*.

"Where is Gerard?" he inquired. "Not up at Cambridge, surely?"

"No, not until next year." And Ellen explained about the visit to Chichester.

"Oh, then I shall very likely see him. I am going over to dine tonight with Aunt Blanche."

Just as Benedict was taking his leave, to Ellen's great chagrin Mr. Wheelbird was announced—news which Benedict received with curling lip. Avoiding his satirical eye, Ellen said to Sue, "Tell Mr. Wheelbird that I am engaged with Miss Charlotte and cannot see him at present."

"Oh, 'tisn't you, miss, he wishes to see, but Mrs. Pike."

"In that case Charlotte and I will remove ourselves

to my bedroom," said Ellen. "Good-bye, Mr. Masham. Please give my remembrances to Lady Blanche and the Bishop."

"Good day, Miss Paget."

"Why can the lawyer wish to see your housekeeper?" demanded Charlotte inquisitively when the two girls were ensconced in Ellen's room.

"Oh, he manages some little business affairs for her. But tell me, Charlotte, is your brother Tom quite recovered from his fall?"

"Oh Lord, yes, any time these eighteen months. But listen, Ellen—I may call you Ellen now, may I not?" What Charlotte really wanted to relate was the tale of her Paris conquests, a lengthy, breathless, and somewhat tedious recital, made painful to Ellen by sudden violent homesickness which the narrative aroused in her for the sights and sounds and society of that lovely city. To think that it was already a year since she had returned from France! How could she bear it?

"I will say, Ellen, that you do not look at all dowdy," Charlotte broke off to remark in a tone of commendation mixed with mild surprise. "That gown is still well ahead of English styles; how do you contrive it, buried away here?"

"Dear Mrs. Clarke, with whom I maintain a correspondence, sometimes sends me fashion plates, from which, with the help of a local dressmaker, I manage to keep up with the modes. Of course, I am thought something of a freak here! But it does not signify since Papa does not mix with society. And I cannot admire the bulbous English crinolines. I would rather feel elegant than worry about public opinion."

"Take care that you do not become an eccentric or a bluestocking!" Charlotte warned seriously, looking remarkably like her mother. "You cannot afford to flout public opinion *too* far. Remember poor Louise, and

Germaine. Oh, by the bye, that reminds me—Germaine
de Rhetorée has returned to Paris."

"She has? She has emerged from her convent?"

"She found that the conventual regime did not suit
her. Or she it! Also her latest romance, *Les Bichettes*, had
a great success (Mama would not let me read it), so she
has been enabled to pay off her debt to the moneylender,
and lives quite in style."

"Dear me! I had thought her entirely fixed on the
religious life."

No wonder, Ellen thought rather hollowly, that
Germaine had never troubled to write and thank her for
the offer of help in the future. She told herself sternly that
she ought to be glad of Germaine's success; could she be
so mean-minded as to envy the other girl?

"Mama says she would not be at all surprised if, in
the end, Germaine and Raoul de la Ferté were to make
a match of it."

"*What?*" This did seem to Ellen in the highest degree
improbable, remembering Germaine's strictures on the
whole tribe of men.

"No, they are meeting continually. Raoul, it appears,
suffers terrible remorse over his wife's uncompleted
historical treatise, and Germaine is advising him as to
its possible completion and publication. Oh, it is such
dreary stuff! Raoul showed some chapters to Mama. I do
not think *that* will be a success! But Mama thinks well
of the match—Germaine is of good family, after all, and
Raoul must marry again—*mercy*, look at the time! I am
continually earning scolds from cousin George. I must
go—and I have not even told you about the Vicomte
de Marigny! He is *such* a swell. But I daresay, in the end,
I shall marry Benedict Masham. Mama wishes it; he is
very dull, but Papa intends him for his First Attaché and
thinks Benedict could well be the next Ambassador, after
Papa retires; so that would be quite convenient. Getting

married is such a bore—I much prefer going to balls and having beaux! Good-bye, dear Ellen, pray try to come to town for my ball."

And Charlotte floated away, leaving Ellen to ponder on the vanity of human wishes; she had longed for visitors from the outside, for news from her lost Paris life—and look at the discomposure it brought her when it did come!

◈

Gerard and his friend Matt were talking about happiness.

"I'm so content when I'm with you, Matt," said the boy. "It feels *right*. Why, if a thing feels right, may one not have it all the time? Why should my father be so angry and set against it? Surely we ourselves must know what is best for us?"

The shepherd, without immediately answering, looked up at the sky, where gray and plum-colored clouds were massed, promising a stormy night. Last gleams from the dying sun threw an unearthly luminosity over the hillside and the quarry where Bilbo had his hut; the lumps of chalk scattered about the ground looked like jewels of congealed light, and the ash saplings and bramble growth masking the entrance to the quarry seemed carved from glittering jade.

"Do you believe in the Almighty, Gerald?" said the man at last.

"Of course I do! But not all that rigmarole they tell you in church. Why do you ask?"

"Ah! When I look about, and see how turble pretty His creation do be, and all of it so foreign to *our* notions—"

"How do you mean, Matt?"

"Look at that service tree. See that pethwine." He pointed to the brilliantly illuminated screen of ash and honeysuckle.

"Well?"

"They wasn't made for *us*. Look at they thunder pillars in the sky. What do we know of they? Our part in all that be no more than a fingernail on His hand."

"So?"

"So why should us reckon to be *happy*? In my recollects, there beant no promise in the Scripture about that. 'Happy is the man that findeth *wisdom*,' it do say in Proverbs. Not 'Wise be he that findeth happiness!'"

"But folk *are* happy—" Gerard began to protest.

"Maybe! But 'tis be rereness, not by right. 'Tis a glimpse o' heaven gate, no more. Providence dunna *lay* for man to be happy—but for to learn. Happiness do come in t'other land, not this-ere one."

"*You* seem happy enough, Matt?"

"Ah! But I had my contrairy times."

"Yes. I'm sorry. I shouldn't have said that," the boy muttered awkwardly, remembering those long years of prison.

"Now an' agen, too, I fare to grieve over a middling good friend I had, back in the lockup."

"Who was that?" inquired Gerard, curious, and not a little jealous.

"Ah. You'd not think much to him, I reckon. He were a poor, hampery, ardle-headed fellow. Drink had been his ruination. How he'll be a-faring without me I dunna like to think. But yet I'd be lief to see him, poor Sim."

"Will you not see him, sometime?"

The shepherd shook his head.

"He were down for a lamentable long stick o' time; robbed a church box, he had, when he were confused in liquor; Justices be main hard on that. He 'on't be free this side o' Puck Sunday. But, as to happiness," Matt went on musingly.

They heard a dry stick crack, and cautious slow footsteps among the bushes. Matt's head went up alertly. Gerard scrambled to his feet looking anxious.

"Who be there?" called Bilbo.

"I be seeking for shepherd Bilbo," answered a man's hoarse voice.

"Well! Here I be!"

A skinny figure came limping wearily between the bushes. Gerard thought he had never seen anybody quite so dusty, derelict, and battered-looking. The man was bleeding from cuts about the head, and had a bundle of dirty rags wrapped round one foot. He was thin as a scarecrow and trembling with fatigue and apprehension; his appearance infused the boy with a deep, troubling pang of pity, such as he had never yet felt. What could have happened to the poor wretch, to put him in such a state? And yet the face on top of this deplorable body was that of a clown—rueful, twisted, self-mocking, resigned. He gave Matt a lopsided smile.

"Matt! Man ye do be a welcome sight for a poor waygoer!"

Matt's eyes were round with amazement.

"Sim!" he breathed. "Oh, Sim! I was just a-speaking of ye. This very minute past! Man, ye've never broken out of clink?"

"Ah, but I have," said Sim. "I couldn't a-bear it no longer. Treated me so mortacious, they did, after ye went. So I clommed off, time we was put to dyke-digging on a driply day—an' I wraught clear away."

"But what got ye in such a mux? Did they send dogs after ye?"

"No, that were Sheba's folk. I went a-looking for 'er, and they lambasted me. She died, poor gal, simmingly. But they'd not give me up to the beaks; that I will say. And I knew, if I could only find ye, Matt, my hurts'd soon be mended." Slowly as a falling tree he collapsed, and lay on the thymy grass between Matt and Gerard.

Fourteen

NEXT WEEK ELLEN INFORMED HER FATHER THAT SHE intended catching the public coach to Chichester and spending the night with Eugenia. Some considerable time had elapsed since she had last visited old Miss Fothergill; also she intended to purchase new lesson books, paints, and crayons for Vicky. She would return two days later (the coach ran twice a week) unless Eustace could bring her back.

Mr. Paget was greatly discomposed by this news; he had become dependent on the daily reading sessions. "I hardly know that I can spare you" was his peevish response. Ellen waited in silence. "Well—well—if you made a promise to old Miss Fothergill, I suppose you must honor it," he added ungraciously, after a long pause. "But I see no occasion for purchasing yet *more* lesson books; cannot the child manage with those she already has? Books are costly items!"

"If you consider the expense unreasonable, Papa, I will pay for them out of my savings," Ellen said quietly. "Vicky has really outgrown the books she has been using."

"I did not say that it was *unreasonable*; do not take me up so quickly, in that way of yours. You are always far too hasty to misjudge me, Matilda," grumbled her father.

"You mean Ellen, Papa."

"Ellen, *Ellen!* It was a slip of the tongue," said Mr. Paget testily. "If I were left in peace occasionally, instead of being continually harassed with demands, and belabored with troublesome information, I would perhaps be able to reach a decision more easily on such matters."

He did look unusually perturbed and displeased; a nerve twitched at the side of his temple, and his large, well-kept but clumsy hands fumbled among the papers on his desk, creating hopeless confusion in the orderly arrangement that Ellen had just made for him.

"I am sorry, Papa; who has been bringing you troublesome information?"

It was not hard to guess; Mrs. Pike had, as usual, superintended the nuncheon which was taken to Mr. Paget each morning in his study, and she had remained with him while he ate it; this was her most favored hour for talebearing and imparting disagreeable reports about the other members of the household.

"Your brother Gerard—" Luke brought out the words with difficulty. "I find it hard to credit; but Mrs. Pike informs me that word has come to her—and from an unimpeachable source—"

Ellen waited nervously, wondering what spiteful gossip had reached the housekeeper, and from whom?

"—that your brother Gerard has once more been indulging his taste for low company; playing *music* for *money*, she was assured by her informant, with those idle wastrels who call themselves the Moorish men, or morris dancers. Can this be true, do you think?"

"They are not idle wastrels, Papa," corrected Ellen, feeling that a flanking movement might be the best tactic. "They are all honest laborers who practice the dancing in their free time. I am familiar with several of them—Ted Thatcher, whose hand I once cured, and old Mr. Randall—"

"Is it true that Gerard is consorting with these men?"

"I believe he has played music for them in the past. Whether he still does, I am unable to say. Gerard is seventeen, Papa; so long as he studies faithfully—which

I am persuaded he does—do you not think he should be allowed to choose his own diversion?"

"No, I do not!" growled Gerard's father, thumping so violently with his fist that a whole pile of books became dislodged and toppled to the floor. "Young persons must obey the precepts of their elders. They have not sufficient sense or judgment to select their own companions. And this fact is abundantly illustrated by Gerard's behavior. I am exceedingly displeased with him. It is lucky for him that he is with Eugenia at present, or I should remonstrate with him most severely. But how can I tell what kind of low associations he may be forming in Chichester? I think you had best tell him that I wish him to return home directly."

"But he has not finished his course of tutorials with Sir Magnus."

"He could manage without those. Still," said Mr. Paget, recollecting, "since Newman is still in York, he would have insufficient employment at home—no, perhaps matters are best as they are. You may tell him that I am greatly vexed with him."

"Very well, Papa," Ellen said, and escaped, sending down silent maledictions on the head of Mrs. Pike the talebearer.

That lady, when informed of Ellen's forthcoming excursion, let fall various animadversions as to the good fortune of young ladies who could afford to go jauntering about the country whenever they wished. In fact, Ellen thought, she was not ill-pleased at the news. As before, she had a number of household commissions for Ellen, and added, as an afterthought, "If you should chance to visit old Miss Fothergill, Miss Paget, remember me kindly to her. But don't forget she's half flown in her wits; you can't trust a word she says."

❧

Waiting outside the Half Moon Inn, from which the coach departed, Ellen heard herself addressed in a soft but urgent voice.

"Miss Paget! Miss Ellen—ain't it? Dear, I am *that* pleased I ran into you! I didn't like for to come up to the house!"

It took a moment for Ellen to recognize the girl who addressed her. But the lustrous black eyes in the warm-complexioned, sun-browned face were deeply familiar; as was the red smiling mouth and the tangle of black curls. Then the memory came back: "Selina Lee! Oh, but I am glad to see you!" She gripped the girl's hand. "How you have grown—how big and beautiful you have become!"

"Well, you are none so peaked and swarly yourself!" retorted Selina, smiling. "I on'y just recognized you—so city-smart as you are now! 'Tis a long cry from the skinny little elver that Doc Bendigo and I did teach to swim on Climping Strand all those years agone."

"Are your family—are the gypsies camped near here now? Are they at Eartham?"

"No, we are adown past Rogate. I caught a lift over on a carrier's cart." Selina's handsome face clouded. "I come over on behalf of Aunt Priscilla, for she's in bed with a poisoned foot an' can't touch ground—come to see about the poor thing that died, Wednesday was a fortnit, in the Petworth Union. Word just come to us about her."

"Was—did you know her?"

"Ah. 'Twas Aunt Priscilla's youngest, my cousin Sheba Smith, her that run off, three years back, with a gorgio. I saw the picture up to the Town Hall here. She'm buried now, but that were Sheba, sure enough. And they showed me a brass bangle she had; they wouldn't let me carry it away but I knew 'twas Sheba's, she'd had it from a child. Poor Aunt Priscilla will take it mortal hard; Sheba was her dowlin', her baby, and she grieved sore when the gorgio took her."

"What was his name?" asked Ellen with quickening interest.

"I forget. But he was a no-good. We heard tell the bozzers got 'un, later, and put 'un in the lockup, and Sheba was tramping the roads on her own, for she were feared to go back to Uncle Reuben—she knew he'd beat her nigh to death for taking up with a foreigner."

The coach rumbled up. "Quick, tell me—shall you be at Rogate for much longer?" said Ellen. "And what about the baby—Sheba's baby?"

"A lady took it—they wouldn't say who. Wouldn't tell a Rom!"

"I'll try to find out for you," said Ellen. "I daresay they will tell me. Where can I be in touch with you?"

"We'll be traveling south to Meon, then back to Eartham and Slindon. Look for us in Slindon come September. And I thank you kindly, sister," said Selina, adding a blessing in Romany as Ellen climbed into the coach.

As she settled herself she noticed, through the window, Mr. Wheelbird standing on the other side of the street, looking after Selina Lee with a face of strong disapprobation. Had he overheard their conversation? Well, what did it matter if he had? Mr. Wheelbird was not Ellen's governor.

❧

The visit to Miss Fothergill repeated the pattern of previous ones. The old lady was touchingly delighted to see Ellen, but found it hard to accept that she was not Matilda; since Luke, too, was tending to make this mistake more and more frequently, Ellen began to have a perplexed feeling that perhaps she was the only person not allowed into the secret of her own identity.

"Of course you are your mother, child," said Miss Fothergill, patting Ellen gently on the cheek. "Anybody can see *that*."

"But I am myself, dear Miss Fothergill. I don't wish to be anybody else—not even Mama!"

"We can't choose, child."

As before, the old lady's doll's-house apartment was specklessly clean.

"Are they treating you kindly here?" Ellen inquired.

"Oh, my dear, beautifully. Much better than that odious woman. I forget her name."

"Mrs. Pike?"

Miss Fothergill shivered. "Mrs. Pike discovered a dreadful thing about Uncle Henry's past—he had once robbed the Bank of England."

"*Dear* Miss Fothergill! I am sure the Canon never did any such thing!"

"Oh, but he did. When he was young. And Mrs. Pike found out. That was why he left her all his money."

It was just possible, Ellen thought, that Mrs. Pike had discovered some discreditable little secret, and held it over the poor old man.

"What about Mrs. Pike's son?"

A guarded, withdrawn look came over the old lady's face. "Well, dear, I never saw that man in person; and glad I am I did not, for from what she let drop about him, I believe he was the Evil One himself. But, pray, let us not discuss such distressing subjects; they make me shudder! Pass me the black canister, Mattie; it contains the ginger drops; let us have one apiece to warm us, and tell me, instead, what new embroidery stitches you have been learning."

Leaving St. Mary's Hospital after this visit, Ellen had the good fortune to encounter her brother-in-law, who had been attending a churchwardens' meeting, and he drove her out to Valdoe Court.

"I am a little concerned about Gerard," he confided on the way.

"Has he not been attending his tutorials?" Ellen asked with a sinking heart.

"No, not that. Indeed, old Orde says that he works well and has a keen brain. But, firstly, I find that he has persuaded Mr. Fielding, the Cathedral organist, to give him music lessons, and spends hours there practicing; and then in the evenings he goes out for long solitary excursions over the Downs, and comes back in such a queer, excited, wrought-up condition that Eugenia says she does not know what to make of him; she has been half inclined to write to your father, but did not like to give him additional worry when he was only convalescent."

"Oh no, no, let her not do that!" exclaimed Ellen, reflecting that, on top of Mrs. Pike's disclosure about the morris dancers, this would throw Mr. Paget into an agitation that might have disastrous consequences. "Where do you suppose Gerard goes on these excursions?" Though she imagined she knew very well.

"I am afraid," said Eustace rather uncomfortably, "that he goes to visit my shepherd Matthew Bilbo."

"Oh dear."

"I feel to blame in the matter. And yet, I do not see why I should! It was no more than human decency to give the man employment. And it is not strictly my concern if your brother persists in the association. Bilbo has not an ounce of harm in him—"

"And you are not my brother's keeper," finished Ellen. "Besides, Gerard is of an age when he should be allowed to choose his own companions—and so I have said to Papa. But you can imagine with how little effect!"

"Eugenia is not at all happy about it," said Eustace miserably.

"Well, I will see if I can reason with Gerard. By the bye, did your friend in Winchester ever discover

anything about Mrs. Pike? You said you were going to
ask him."

"Oh, ay. He did tell me, last month, that he thought
he was on the trail of something unsavory. Mrs. Pike had
had a son by a former marriage, who turned out not all
he should be. But Polwheal had not discovered his name,
or what he had done. He hopes to find out more."

At dinner, Ellen was amazed by the change in her
brother. A month's residence in Valdoe Court had
completely transformed the surly, silent youth of the
Hermitage: he laughed, he talked entertainingly about
his legal studies—the law, he said, was a series of
contradictions, linked together with lowest common
denominators—and he was fervent and inspired on the
subject of music, about which, it was plain, he had now
acquired a great deal of knowledge. After dinner he
played good-naturedly with his small nieces and nephews
(such as had recovered from measles), giving them pig-
gybacks and rides in the swing. Then he announced his
intention of taking a walk.

"May I come too?" asked Ellen.

Instantly his face clouded.

"No. I would walk too fast for you—and I compose
as I walk; I am working on a four-part setting for the
Te Deum. Another time, Ellie—I do wish to talk to
you—I have many things to tell you—but not now—"
and he was gone before she could argue, vaulting over
the garden paling and making his way through the copse,
giving her no time to protest that she would not distract
him with conversation. Besides, that would not have
been true.

Then a bold thought struck her. Gerard had said he
was going to compose as he walked, so perhaps he did
not intend to visit his friend this evening. Why should
not Ellen herself do so? She had a curiosity to meet this
man who had so bewitched her brother; and perhaps it

would be possible to warn him that the friendship was a dangerous one for Gerard.

"I am going for a ramble in the woods, Eugenia. Will you accompany me?"

"Good gracious, no, child; I have all the girls' dresses and the table linen to darn, I have not taken a walk in months! And if you had a grain of consideration you would help me, instead of roaming off."

"Well, I will help you when I return. But the evenings are still so long and light, it seems a shame not to make the most of them."

Ellen knew roughly where the shepherd's hut on Lavant Down was situated, about a mile away, along a grassy bottom, past some earthworks supposed by the locals to be fairy mounds, but which Dr. Bendigo had said were ancient British burial places.

It was a clear, still evening to be out in; the sheep, up on the hill above, were calling far and near; a breath of the sea came over the marshes from Chichester Harbor, and a large pale moon kept Ellen solemn company as she walked quietly on the dewy, sheep-nibbled turf.

The shepherd's hut stood in a disused quarry where spindleberry and young ash trees had already grown head-high, half screening it. Perhaps Bilbo won't be at home, reflected Ellen; very likely he will be upon the hillside with the sheep.

But as she approached the small wooden building she heard voices.

The door stood open, and somebody was moving inside the dusk-filled hut; beyond it, on the velvet moss of the quarry floor, she could see two people stretched at ease by a small fire. One was her brother, one a gray-haired man in a shepherd's smock.

"And what did you do then?" she heard Gerard's question.

"Ah well," said a slow, thoughtful voice. "'Twas owl

time by then, ye see, dark enough so ye'd have to blow on your hand to find it afore your face—"

Ellen passed in front of the open door and, standing at the corner of the hut, said gently, "Gerard?"

The two talkers turned in surprise and looked at her. She received an instantaneous impression of Gerard's annoyance at the interruption, and the other man's accepting interest; she met the gaze of two intensely blue eyes. At that moment she heard a man's angry, frightened voice from inside the hut—"Who the devil be that?"

Some article was knocked over or dropped inside, there came a crash and a curse; she heard a rapid limping step behind her—then came a stunningly violent blow on the back of her head.

Falling, she thought: This is the end of me. But *why*?

As she lost consciousness, the last thing of which she was distantly aware was Gerard's voice, appalled, crying, "My God, my God, man, what have you done? That's my sister!"

❧

Ellen did not recover full awareness for what seemed an infinitely long stretch of time. Now and then she realized vaguely that things were being done to her, most of them unpleasant. Light sometimes shone in her eyes, and the pain in her head became so terrible that her only recourse was to slide into blackness; she was turned and handled—"like a roll of pastry," she murmured once, achieving a brief command of speech; sometimes liquids were trickled down her throat; hot pads were applied to her feet and cold ones to her head; she was raised, she was lowered, pillows were packed behind her, coverings were laid over her and then taken off again; often, for long periods, she seemed to be hovering above her own body, physically removed from it, only detained in its vicinity by a mild interest in what was being done to it.

At one point she seemed to see the whole top of her head removed, hair and all, while intricate maneuvers were performed with beautiful ivory-handled implements, like the crochet hook and buttonhole maker in her mother's sewing basket. Two men in black coats hung over her, busy and attentive.

"But they'll never embroider as beautifully as you did, Mama," she remarked to Mattie, who was beside her. "And suppose they put my head back upside down? Then what would I do?"

"You'd sing *mi re do* while everybody else sang *do re mi*," answered Matilda. "But don't worry, that surgeon is a clever fellow. He knows what he is about. You can leave him to his task with an easy mind."

So Ellen floated away with her mother to a region of yellow lupins and blue tropic seas, breaking on black, shining beaches.

"Mama, what did Papa do to you that was so bad? Why does he feel such terrible remorse?"

"He forgot to treat me as a human being. But I was sadder on his account, because for him the sun never shone. It was like living on a north-facing hill. And now it is too late. Or so he believes."

"Can he not go back and begin again?"

"Go back and begin again? Let time run in reverse? Unknit all that was knitted up? But how can a man turn back to a child again? How can a grown tree become a seedling?"

"Why not?" Ellen asked. "Here, we are outside all that—are we not? Here time stands still—does it not?"

"Time certainly does *not* stand still, my girl!" exclaimed a voice—intolerably loud and harsh, close to her ear. "As you will presently find out, if you will only condescend to favor us with your attention!"

A not ungentle thumb opened one of her eyes, and she became reluctantly aware of light and dark, of shapes, of pungent medical smells, and of an enormous face, much too close to her own, and two eyes surveying her.

"Do I know you?" asked Ellen doubtfully.

"We haven't been formally introduced, me dear, but *I* know *you*; better than anybody else in the whole world, I daresay! Better than your own mother."

"No, never better than her." Ellen tried to shake her head, but found this was impossible; a kind of iron crown, with the spikes turned inwards, held her scalp rigidly in one spot on the pillow.

"A—a! No wriggling, if you please! You are my prisoner just at the moment, and must do as I say."

"May I have a drink?"

A cup with a spout was held to her lips; water like nectar trickled down her throat.

"Now that is famous, Miss Paget! We'll have you up, drinking tea and port wine, in no time. And none too soon, I may say! You have been playing truant for too long. Yes," mused the voice—now that Ellen was becoming accustomed to its tones, it did not seem quite so atrociously loud. "I know just what makes you function; every neat little cogwheel and spring balance; very prettily they work together, too! It was fortunate for you that I was at hand to wind you up again—the best clock mender in the business—because I learned my trade at Scutari and Balaclava, where there were more broken heads in the hospital than crocuses on the mountainside."

"Did I have a broken head?"

"You did, me dear; but I have mended it so neatly, with white of egg and plaster of Paris, that you will soon be as good as new."

"To go back and begin again?"

"If that is your wish. Now you must sleep. Mrs. Pinfold will see to that."

"Ah, I will so," said a comfortable voice, warm and

soft as the wind over those distant azure seas. "You be off with yourself, Sir Thomas, while I see to the poor pretty."

Ellen felt herself gently rearranged into an easier position; the light faded, silence enshrouded her, and she slept again.

❧

Gradually, after that conversation, she began to be aware, once more, of the passage of time. Days, nights succeeded one another; people and events slowly began to take on reality.

Mrs. Pinfold became the fat motherly nurse who fed, washed, and tended her; Sir Thomas Bastable, the brusque, white-haired surgeon who had first addressed her. After a week, members of her family were allowed at her bedside: Eugenia, wan, haggard, full of silent reproach; Eustace, nervous and friendly; Lady Blanche, solicitous but reproving; the Bishop, kindly and cheerful as always. She became conscious that she was in Eugenia's house, and later realized with amazement, when she was allowed up for a brief spell, and wheeled to a window in a cane chair, that the leaves were blowing from the trees; autumn had come, summer had ended while she was still wandering in that distant, nebulous region where her mother had seemed to talk to her.

"But what happened to me?" she asked Sir Thomas—he had been knighted for his work at Scutari, she learned from the Bishop, and happened to be staying in the Palace at the time of her mishap.

"Why, you went for a ramble, as young ladies, with their romantical notions, are prone to do on summer evenings—and a great stone fell on your head in a place called Hayes's Quarry. No doubt you were climbing up after some flower or bunch of berries."

"I remember nothing about it."

"Lucky for you your brother was not far off and ran

to the rescue. He and a shepherd fetched you down to Valdoe on a hurdle. At first all thought you were dead. But then they saw faint signs of life and somebody had the good sense to send for me. And I put you together again."

"My brother—Gerard—where is he?"

"In Petworth, my dear, keeping your father company. The poor man has many times petitioned to come and see you, but your sisters were firm. It would be too disturbing for you both, they said."

"Sisters? Is Kitty here, then?"

"No, she is at Petworth with your papa."

"Mrs. Pike won't like that," murmured Ellen, but Sir Thomas had gone, with an injunction to her to "be a good gal and mind what Nurse says."

Very soon she demanded books to read, but for a long time this solace was forbidden. "Eyes and mind must not be taxed at first," warned Sir Thomas.

However, one day when Ellen was in the cane chair, having her bed made, she chanced upon a most engrossing manual entitled *Notes on Nursing*, which Mrs. Pinfold had left on the washstand, and she read it from cover to cover before she could be stopped. "Apprehension, uncertainty...waiting, expectation, fear of surprise, do a patient more harm than any exertion...he is face-to-face with his enemy all the time, internally wrestling with him, having long imaginary conversations with him." Why, that is like Papa, thought Ellen; although in bodily health, Papa has the temperament of a sick man. The author of the manual, F. Nightingale, was very brisk about people who thought it required only a disappointment in love to turn a woman into a good nurse. This is a remarkable mind, thought Ellen. The small book stirred in her a feeling of emulation. What am I doing, lying here, being tended like a baby? She remembered that she had heard something about F. Nightingale five years ago, while still at school in Brussels.

From that moment she began to recover more quickly; she demanded to be let up for longer periods, and asked for more reading matter, for writing materials.

At last she was allowed downstairs. "It has been a shocking charge upon your household, having me here all this time," she apologized to Eugenia.

"Well—yes; it has." Eugenia was nothing if not frank "But Lady Blanche did not think it would be convenient to have you at the Palace. The Bishop has been very kind, though; he paid Mrs. Pinfold, and Sir Thomas's fees."

"I have given a deal of trouble."

"It would certainly have been better," said Eugenia, "if you had stayed indoors with me that evening and helped with the mending. What in the world were you doing in Hayes's Quarry?"

Ellen had no idea. The whole of that evening was a blank in her memory.

When she asked how soon she could return to the Hermitage: "Now, Ellen, you must not be in too much of a hurry! You need not concern yourself about the household there. They go on well enough. When Mrs. Pike left—"

"What?" cried Ellen in utter astonishment. "You say that Mrs. Pike has gone?"

"Why yes. Oh, of course, I recollect, all that occurred during the long period of your unconsciousness."

"What in the world happened?"

"Eustace had asked his friend Polwheal to see if he could not find out something about Mrs. Pike's circumstances. And this man discovered that, by a first marriage, she had a son who had been sent to jail for robbery."

"Oh yes...I believe...now a little is coming back. Eustace did say something about her having a son who was not all he should be. And Miss Fothergill said something—"

"And then, just as this information was received, something much more disturbing transpired; word came from Winchester that this son, who went by the name of Simon Enticknass, had escaped from the jail."

"Escaped? Good heavens," said Ellen faintly.

"As you may imagine, Eustace and I became very agitated. The idea that this violent criminal might come seeking his mother—in Petworth—at the Hermitage—was not to be borne! We made very strong representations to Papa—Kitty came down expressly from Maple Grove—and so Mrs. Pike was given her notice. She was exceedingly angry about it, as you may imagine."

"I can indeed," murmured Ellen, trying to picture the scene. Poor Mrs. Pike—after all her pretensions of gentility—to be confronted with such a shocking skeleton in the cupboard as a criminal son. Ellen surprised herself by saying, "In a way it seems unjust. What the son had done, after all, was not her fault."

"Unjust? Are you out of your senses?" cried Eugenia. "She had reared the son, had she not? In any case, she was given her marching orders. And she went, threatening every kind of retaliation, action for defamation of character, I don't know what else. 'I shall have the last laugh on you yet!' she was so impertinent as to say to Kitty."

"Where did she go?"

"I am sure I don't know. The main thing is that Papa is rid of her."

"I hope Kitty makes him as comfortable as Mrs. Pike used. Or there will be trouble!"

"Kitty has carried him back to Maple Grove with her; I suggested that she do so, until you are capable of taking charge at the Hermitage."

Do I have no choice? thought Ellen. But mental effort was still laborious. Her brain still felt clouded and clogged, her body weak and languid.

"I shall be able to see after it all in a week or so, I am sure. But there was a question I wished to ask—what was it?"

"Never trouble me now, child; I have so much on

my hands that I hardly know which way to turn." And Eugenia went off to organize her straitened and hard-pressed household.

Once she was permitted downstairs, to the observation post of a sofa in the drawing room, Ellen was given so many opportunities to witness the difficulties, embarrassments, and lack of adequate help in Eugenia's life, while Eustace spent every available penny on restoring his impoverished acres, that it was hard to blame Eugenia for her constant complaint that "Papa was miserably niggardly not to help them with more money, which he could very well do if he chose."

"He is worried about the possibility of civil war in America, because of his interests in the cotton industry," Ellen suggested.

"Oh, my dear Ellen! Those are not his only interests! Papa is a rich man."

Even Eustace agreed, sighing, that Mr. Paget was known to be very comfortably situated. The grass-cutting device that some Paget forebear had invented alone brought him in some ten thousand pounds a year.

"If we could have a tenth, a twentieth of that!" wailed Eugenia.

A week spent convalescing in this atmosphere was enough to imbue Ellen with a lively desire to return home; at length she prevailed on her physicians to permit this. "I am perfectly stout again," she asserted, "and must not impose on my poor sister any longer."

The Bishop doubtfully suggested that she should come to the Palace for a while; Lady Blanche found a number of reasons why this was not possible; and in the end Ellen was given her way, under a proviso that, after her return, she must spend at least a week in bed, submit in every way to the jurisdiction of Dr. Smollett, and not attempt to resume the teaching of Vicky, who had, in fact, been taken off by Mrs. Bracegirdle.

Indeed the Hermitage seemed strangely quiet when Ellen re-entered it. With Mrs. Pike gone, and her father and Vicky away, the servants had little to do, for Gerard was indifferent about meals or comfort; Ellen was welcomed with affectionate enthusiasm.

"But, oh, Miss Ellen! Your poor hair!" mourned Sue. "And you so thin and peaked—you seem like a token maid, that you do!"

Ellen had not been encouraged to look in minors while she remained at Valdoe; one had been removed from her bedroom. But since getting up she had become accustomed to her appearance. It had been necessary to shave her head for Sir Thomas's operation. Her hair, dark, fine, and silky, had never been very long, and was now taking its time about growing back; at present it was hardly more than two inches long, curling over the top of her head in a soft, unmanageable mop.

"I look like a French poodle," she said, laughing. "And all my dresses need taking in."

"Ne'er mind, Miss Ellie; we'll soon feed you up like a fighting cock."

Her brother Gerard, Ellen noticed, also seemed unusually thin and pale. It might have been expected that he would seize the occasion of his father's absence to indulge his musical propensities and neglect his studies, but the reverse seemed to be the case; he worked long hours every day with Mr. Newman, his tutor, appeared only briefly at mealtimes, and seemed unwontedly subdued, particularly in the presence of his sister, whom he treated with a kind of anxious, propitiating solicitude. Several times he asked her if she did not *indeed* remember anything about her accident, and on her assuring him that all events of that evening were lost to her, he appeared relieved, but also troubled. When he thanked him for bringing her back to Valdoe Court, and said she understood that she owed her life to his promptitude, he burst out, "Don't thank me, Ellie! There is not the least occasion in the world! The fellow you should properly thank is Matt Bilbo, the shepherd, for he played the main part in the business, and it was his idea to lay you on a hurdle."

"I don't remember any of that. But I should like to thank him. Shall I write him a letter?"

"*No!* No, don't do that," said Gerard hastily. "How ever could the postman find his hut? I believe Matt is coming to Petworth in a couple of weeks for his sister's wedding anniversary; I will tell him to come up here— shall I?"

"Yes, do; I am curious to meet the man who has had such an influence on you, Gerard!"

"Oh—that is all gone by," said Gerard. "Or at least— Matt says that, for your sake—and Papa's, not to distress him further—I must now apply myself to my books. And indeed, Ellie, I begin to think—to see—that perhaps Papa is right when he says that I ought to go into politics. Not that I want to! But there is so much wrong that needs putting right—responsible people are needed to administer the laws more justly than they are at present—"

Greatly astonished at this change of attitude, Ellen would have liked to hear more from Gerard on the subject. But she was really too weak, as yet, for long conversations, and in any case he did not seem to wish to pursue the matter.

❧

Bilbo did come to the house a couple of weeks later, and Ellen could not help being impressed by him, though there was nothing striking about his appearance: a small-ish, gray-haired man with a thin, lined face and a pair of guileless blue eyes. But he had a mild self-assurance and dignity, as he received her thanks, that made her instinctively like and respect him.

"Your brother do say as how you've forgot how your mishap all came about," he said. "Otherwise, I'd tell ye more of the matter. But, simmingly, 'tis best not to talk about it, on'y stirring up troublous memories, or laying up more sorrow. Let be how 'twill."

Ellen did not quite understand his meaning, but did not attempt to very hard; her head still ached easily if she overtaxed herself. Instead she said, "I am afraid that you have received much injustice at the hands of my father, Mr. Bilbo, for which I am truly sorry."

"Ah, never trouble your head about it, maidy," said Bilbo kindly. "'Tis all gone by now, an' forgot, like your mishap. I'm right glad to work for your brother-in-law—who'm a notable good maister an' a kindly man; as for the time in jail, 'twas your dad's duty to sentence me, if he saw fit; and I reckon 'twas the Lord's wish I should be there; I bear no grudge in the business."

"How long were you there?" Ellen asked with a shiver.

"In Petworth jail, six months; then I tried to run off, an' they shifted me to Winchester. Then, seems, I lost count; 'twere over twenty year, I reckon. Just about the length o' your lifetime, maidy," he said, smiling. "And now 'tis all gone like a dream, and I'm a free man, minding my sheep on Lavant Down."

"Winchester jail," Ellen said thoughtfully. What had she heard recently concerning Winchester jail? "Why, I know what it was," she added, half to herself, proud of catching the elusive memory. "Simon Enticknass—did you, by any chance, while you were there, come across a man by the name of Simon Enticknass?"

A curious look came over Bilbo's face—a look not hostile or withdrawn, but wary, meditative, as if he observed a hazard ahead in his pathway, and did not know how best to approach it. "Ah, I knowed him, poor fellow," he said after a moment. "Half flash, half fuddled, he were; take him the right way, not a doit of harm in him. But he were wrong led, an' mazed wi' the drink. And that 'solitary,' that done him mortial harm; turned his mind, like."

Gerard, who had been anxiously invigilating the interview, broke in at this moment "I think my sister should rest now, Matt."

"God bless ye, maidy, and see ye better soon," said Bilbo earnestly. "My sister said to thank ye again for coming to touch her Cath, time the maid was poorly wi' the ague; the liddle 'un healed up wonderful quick arter that, Sairy said."

"Thank you, Mr. Bilbo."

"An' I hope your dad get his wish to find the owd Doom Stone he be so set on! If I hear aught of it, lying out in the woodses and hillses, I'll let 'un know, surely."

He knuckled his brow to Ellen, and allowed himself to be marshalled out by Gerard, who seemed intensely anxious to bring the interview to an end.

"I liked your Mr. Bilbo," Ellen said later.

"I knew you would. He's a wonderful man!" Gerard said fervently. "He—he is *noble*, Nell! He acts by instinct as others never learn to in their whole lives."

"Yes, I can see that. What a curious coincidence that he knew Mrs. Pike's son. What did Bilbo mean by 'solitary'?"

"Oh—solitary confinement... But it is no great coincidence that they should meet," Gerard said hastily. "After all, there must have been hundreds of men in Winchester jail."

"Yes, that is just why—" But Ellen was not strong enough to pursue the matter.

❧

A few days later, Ellen, taking one of her first cautious walks, was somewhat taken aback to encounter Mrs. Pike herself. She had assumed that the housekeeper would have moved away, perhaps back to Chichester, where there would be more opportunities of employment; she could not avoid a feeling of dismay at sight of the familiar massively built white-haired figure, in opulent bonnet and fringed mantle, approaching majestically along Angel Street. However, there was no way to avoid the meeting, so she braced herself to speak and be civil.

"Good morning, Mrs. Pike. How do you do?"

"Not as well as I could wish, Miss Paget—thanks to your meddling, jealous, mean-minded sisters," replied Mrs. Pike glacially. "There's some folk who are never happy save when snatching the bread from others' mouths. And, as I remarked to your sister Mrs. Bracegirdle, you may come to rue the day when she turned me off—like a scullery maid—who had looked after him as if he was an Emperor of China—and all for a pack of idle, nasty rumor."

Ellen thought of Mrs. Pike's own talebearing. But she said merely, "I am sorry. It was a very unfortunate business."

"Mind! I wouldn't come back now! Not if Mrs. Bracegirdle was to kneel on the cobbles before me with her mouth full of diamonds!"

"Well, then, perhaps matters are best as they are."

Ellen would have liked to inquire after Mrs. Pike's son, whether he had been recaptured, or perhaps escaped to the Americas, but realized that this would not be tactful.

"Best as they are? Humph! That's as may be. You don't look so peart!"

Mrs. Pike coldly surveyed Ellen up and down, then swept on her way. Sue told Ellen later that the housekeeper was lodging with a woman in Byworth, across the valley. "Though I don't know, for sure, what keeps her here, where nobody can stand her!"

Perhaps, thought Ellen, she expects her son to come here (for Sue said there had been no news of his recapture). The thought was a somewhat uneasy one.

~✷~

Housekeeping for such a reduced household was no difficult matter, for the maids went out of their way to make matters simple for Ellen. When in doubt she had recourse to a manual of her mother's entitled *The Family Economist*, which offered practical advice on everything from cleaning decanters to preserving rhubarb. And the rector's wife kindly lent her half a dozen issues of *The Englishwoman's Domestic Magazine*, which contained many instructive articles by Isabella Beeton.

"I see no occasion to hire another housekeeper when Papa returns," Ellen said to Gerard. "We go on well enough. And Papa will be glad of the reduced expenditure."

"Not a doubt of that," he replied, shrugging.

Just now, the ménage was decidedly pressed for ready cash. Kitty, when she swept her father away, had not thought to make provision for his dependents beyond a couple of weeks; nor, it seemed, had Mr. Paget himself. Ellen wrote him, requesting a sum to pay the servants' wages, but, receiving no reply, sent a note to Mr. Wheelbird asking if, in the meantime, sums could be advanced from her father's bankers. Mr. Wheelbird came round to wait upon her and explain that this could not be done without her father's written authority.

"I am sorry about it, Miss Ellen, but such is the case. It is not in my power to assist you."

He did not seem particularly sorry; in fact she had the impression that he was quite pleased to be able to thwart her; perhaps he still remembered the undignified plight in which she had seen him last. He did, however, seem shocked at her appearance; he had gone quite pale as he came in, and she noticed that he seemed to dislike looking at her, keeping his gaze on the floor to one side of her, except when absolutely required to meet her eyes.

"Oh well, it can't be helped," said Ellen. "I will just have to write Papa again, and, in the meantime, meet the household expenses out of my own funds."

These were dwindling fast; she resolved to write again without delay.

"Ah—Miss P-Paget," said Mr. Wheelbird; his stammer, which had been in abeyance, suddenly returned. "You h-have been ill since I saw you last, and s-suffered m-misfortune—which I much regret; I d-don't suppose you have had occasion to consider the matter which I m-mentioned to you?"

"I *have* thought about it, Mr. Wheelbird," Ellen said gravely, "but I am afraid my answer is still in the negative. Indeed I doubt if I shall ever enter the matrimonial state. I shall care for Papa while—while he needs me; and then I plan to return to teaching."

A sudden intense nostalgia suffused her, for the streets, the sounds, of Paris; the silence of the Hermitage seemed to imprison her like a bell jar.

Mr. Wheelbird's pallor had changed to a dusky red; he said, with what seemed an overpowering impulse of fury and frustration, "You'll not have me, eh? I reckon as how your papa has never seen fit to inform you about his will?"

"No. Why should he?" Ellen was startled. "Naturally he does not talk to me of such things."

"Naturally! Well, it might interest you to know, Miss Paget, that he made a will leaving his fortune—apart from what is entailed upon your brother—all to Mrs. Pike. He said she was the only one as had shown disinterested kindness to him; *you* were capable of earning your own living, and your sisters had been given all they'd a right to expect. So, if you are planning to stay here in the expectation of a fortune, you had best set yourself to the task of persuading him to change his testamentary dispositions—if it ain't already too late!"

"What *can* you mean?" she asked, quite shocked by the sudden unconcealed malice in his tone. "Papa is not likely to die—he is not ill?"

"No; but what if he ain't in his right wits? A man can't change his will if he is of unsound mind!"

With which parting broadside, Mr. Wheelbird walked out and slammed the door.

Ellen began mechanically rearranging the contents of her father's desk—she had conducted the interview in his business room. She recalled that on her first arrival home, the papers had seemed in even greater disorder than usual; was the disorder such as might have been left by a deranged man, or merely that contingent upon a hasty departure?

Having set matters straight and paid the bills, Ellen wrote some letters of her own. There had been a note from Aunt Fanny: "Dearest child, I have been so Anxious about you & long to see you, but think I had best not at present, for I have a little head cold which you, in your Reduc'd state, might easily take, and then I wd never forgive myself! But I have a surprise which I shl take Pleasure in showing you, & shl beg your company as soon as we are both on the Mend." Ellen wrote a loving note in reply, wishing her great-aunt a speedy recovery, and gave it to the garden boy to deliver. Then she answered kindly, solicitous inquiries from Lady Morningquest and Mrs. Clarke in Paris. Still no word from Germaine! But no doubt, thought Ellen with a sore heart, she is so busy and successful that she has scant time for correspondence.

There was a one-line note from Benedict. "Deeply regret to hear of your misfortune. If I can be of any assistance, pray command me. B.M."

The note was from Matlock Chase, Derbyshire; had

Benedict gone to his family seat to introduce Charlotte Morningquest to his brother? Ellen did not immediately answer it; she put it thoughtfully on one side.

◈

Some weeks passed, during which Ellen slowly regained her strength. She remained pale and thin, but each day she could walk a little farther and take more interest in what was happening outside Petworth. She read in the paper that peace was almost concluded in Peking, that the French Empress had been visiting London incognito as Miss Montigo, shopping, and staying with the Duke of Hamilton; that meanwhile her husband, the Emperor, had actually assembled a real French Parliament with a right to talk and vote; the era of imperial despotism was coming to an end, it seemed. The intellect of France was at last to be set free. How happy they will all be— Germaine, Madame Sand, Gautier, Gavarni; perhaps Victor Hugo will now be allowed home from exile, thought Ellen. How I wish I could be there to see!

She expressed something of this to Gerard one night at supper, and he remarked, "Well, why don't you go over to Paris for a holiday? You could stay with Aunt Morningquest—it would do you good. You still look as pale as a leek!"

Ellen was greatly tempted, but: "For one thing, I have hardly any money. And for another, I am anxious about Papa. I wish he would answer those letters I wrote him! And why do we not hear from Kitty?"

"Oh, Kitty never has time for anything but her own concerns," growled Gerard. "Listen, Ellen—I believe we are on the track of the Doom Stone at last!"

"The Doom Stone?"

Ellen had almost forgotten her father's obsession, which she had never taken very seriously. Now, it seemed, Gerard had caught the infection too.

"One of the stonemasons working in Chichester Cathedral is a friend of—a friend of Matt Bilbo. And he sent me word that they have found a corner of a carving protruding from the wall in a kind of undercroft below the nave, which they excavated while attempting to shore up the central piers of the tower. Exposing it further is a difficult and delicate business—in fact the architect is against attempting to do so—but only think if it *were* the stone! How delighted Father would be!"

"Are you going to write him about it?"

"Oh no. That might be to excite false hopes."

Ellen felt touched that Gerard should display such consideration.

Next day she had a letter from Luke. She had not recognized the superscription when it arrived, for it was enclosed in another cover, written in a round, uneducated hand.

"Dear Miss Paget: I make Bold to write on behalf of your Papa & to send you this Paper. Miss what is being done is not Right & you shd know it. I ask you to Come and fetch your Pa away. Well you shd do This. It is not Christian what your Sister is doing. Please not to mention that I writ this or I shd be Turned off without a Character. Yrs respeckfully, Martha Alsop."

Aghast, Ellen unfolded the dirty scrap of paper that was enclosed in Martha's letter.

"Dear Ellen, pray come take me home from here. I do not like it here. Pray Mattie come take me home. If not I'll have to run for it. Luke Paget."

"Good God!" said Gerard when Ellen showed him the two letters. "What *can* have happened to him?"

"I shall have to go there and see. I plan to start tomorrow morning."

"I'll come too. You are hardly fit to travel alone—and the weather is vile; I read that in London the ice is ten inches thick on the Serpentine."

"No, Gerard, I think you had best remain here. If we both arrive at Maple Grove, Kitty will be suspicious, and the fact that this Martha wrote might come out; but if I arrive and say I have come to take Papa home it will seem natural enough. And if he should run off—as he suggests—someone should be here to receive him."

Also, she thought, we hardly have money for two railway fares.

"That's true," Gerard said thoughtfully. "The deuce! What can be going on?"

Ellen thought of the will, leaving Luke's fortune to Mrs. Pike. Had Kitty discovered about that?

Next day—again bitterly cold and frosty—she traveled up to London. She would dearly have liked to spend some time there and visit a few bookstores, but thought it best to go straight on, in order to arrive at Kitty's home by daylight. She sent a telegram from a London telegraph office (so that it would not be possible for Kitty to put her off), and then caught a train from St. Pancras station. Her spirits became lower and lower as it carried her through the flat, dismal Midlands, set in the iron grip of frost.

Fifteen

THERE WAS NO ONE TO MEET ELLEN WHEN THE SMALL local train arrived at Coldmarsh, which was the nearest station to the village of Burley. This did not much surprise Ellen. She hired a fly, reflecting ruefully that she had now almost exhausted her small supply of cash; she would need to borrow from Kitty for the fare home.

A sudden fear assailed her: suppose Kitty and her husband were away, had decided to take Papa with them to some health resort? But the doubt was quashed almost as soon as it had arisen; after all, Martha Alsop had written from Burley; *somebody* must be there. She asked the driver of the fly if he knew whether the Bracegirdles were at home, but his reply came in so thick a Derbyshire accent that she could not understand him.

Dusk was falling when she reached Maple Grove. It was a large, new, ugly house, on the outskirts of a straggling semi-industrial village which contained a cloth mill, a small foundry, and a printing works; the prospect from the house was of factory chimneys and roofs set against a rough, shapeless hillside. None of the maples suggested by the name were to be seen, but a number of young coniferous trees had been planted around the house, intended presumably to exclude the dismal view; at present they were only ten feet high, and the house, made of liver-colored stone, stood awkwardly in the midst of them like an oversized, self-conscious child. Its garden, now caught in the grip of winter, was laid out with rigid formality, the beds railed off by iron hoops. Poor Kitty, thought Ellen, so fond of comfort and elegance; how can she endure to live here?

Having paid the jarvey with the last of her money, she rang the bell. The door was answered by a plain strong-faced woman in apron and cap; an instant flash of comprehension crossed her face when she heard Ellen's name, but all she said was "Please to step this way, miss, and I'll see if Missis is at home."

Ellen was ushered into a gloomy little closet of a room while the maid went up a broad flight of stairs to the floor above. Ellen glanced about her curiously. All the furnishings—carpet, curtains, tables, chairs—were new, solid, of good quality, and hideous; Kitty must have absorbed her husband's taste completely, for none of them were things she would ever have chosen when she was single.

Now Kitty herself came down the stairs, rustling importantly in a heavy flounced pink satin evening dress with a long frilled and beribboned train; she wore elbow-length white gloves and her hair was elaborately dressed and frizzed in front. Her cheeks were flushed with annoyance.

"*Ellen!* We received your telegram only an hour since! What in the world brings you here? There was no occasion for you to come! We did not send for you. And your arrival is not at all convenient; Samuel and I are on the point of going out to dine with Sir Marcus Bagnall at Draycott Hall."

"Well, never mind!" said Ellen. "I daresay your housekeeper can find me a bit of bread and cheese? I have come to take Papa home; but if you are just going out, we can talk about it tomorrow."

"Take Papa home? There can be no question of that! Sam cannot think what caused you to come here—it is most vexatious!"

"Well, I suppose," said Ellen temperately, "that you

can at least give me a bed for the night? I am rather tired! And perhaps I can talk to Papa and see how he feels about it?"

"Talk to—well, I don't know about—it is not at all—oh, good gracious, as if I had not enough to plague me—" Then, seeming to observe her younger sister's appearance for the first time: "Tired? Yes, I should think you are! It was most imprudent of you to make such a journey, in your present state of health. How came you to do such a thing?"

"Oh, I am really much better—indeed, quite recovered. And now all at home is running smoothly since Mrs. Pike departed—"

"Mrs. Pike!" Kitty almost spat out the name. "That woman! But we can't go into all that now... Alsop, make up a bed for my sister in the Pink Room. Light a fire and take her some supper there. You look like a wrung-out clout, Ellen, you had best go to bed directly." Kitty had fallen back automatically into the half good-natured, half bullying manner of the past.

"Well, I would be glad to; and thank you," said Ellen. "But may I not first see Papa? Does he accompany you to dinner with Sir Marcus?"

"Good God, no! Certainly not. No, you cannot see him tonight—he has already retired."

Sam Bracegirdle came stumping down the stairs at this moment, settling a black evening jacket more comfortably on his thickset frame.

"Now then, what's all this caper?" Without the least pretense at any kind of welcome, he eyed Ellen disapprovingly, and added, "Infirmary ward's the place for you, my girl, by the look of you—not gadding about the countryside! Well, there's no time for argufication now; come on, Kitty, the carriage is waiting. We'll talk to you in the morning, miss; meantime, as Kitty says, best gan off to bed."

And he hustled Kitty away down the stairs, grabbed a fur wrap from a maid, and, bundling it round his wife, thrust her out of the front door.

Ellen was left to wait in a large drawing room filled with opulent stuffed and fringed upholstery while her bedroom was prepared; then the maid, Alsop, reappeared, said, "Will you please to step this way, miss?" and led her up to the next story.

In the bedroom, with door closed: "It was you who wrote me?" said Ellen.

"Yes, miss—but for anything's sake, don't let that out! I'd have my notice in an hour! And then there'd be no one to take the poor old gentleman's part!"

"But what is happening? What are they doing to him? Can I not see him—where is he?"

"His room's on this floor, miss—the door across the landing from yours—but you can't go in. Master's man keeps the key."

"You mean that my father is *locked in*?"

"Ay, indeed, miss, he is, and niver allowed out. And the food he gets not enough to feed a bare golly!"

"But *why*? I can hardly believe it!"

"Something about a will, miss; that's all I know."

Ellen felt a cold chill of foreknowledge; in a flash she saw what must have occurred. Kitty had somehow learned about the legacy to Mrs. Pike; perhaps Mrs. Pike herself, in her rage, had made the disclosure; or Mr. Wheelbird had told Kitty, as he had later told Ellen. And of course, if Kitty had begun to storm and demand of her father that the will be changed, matters would swiftly have reached a crisis; Luke's obstinacy would have met head on with his daughter's and deadlock would soon have been reached.

But to lock him up! To deprive him of food! Could Kitty really have become such a monster?

Martha Alsop retired, after leaving a tray with soup

and tea and a wing of cold chicken. Ellen, who had been
hungry and exhausted on arrival, swallowed the soup
but found that she could not touch the chicken. The
thought of her father locked up, powerless, underfed,
so close at hand, was too appalling; she thought food
would choke her.

It was many hours before she managed to get to sleep,
and then her slumber was a light, broken one, disturbed
by dreadful dreams.

Long before daylight she was up and dressed, having
woken at the first sound of movement in the house.

Opening her door the slightest crack, she kept a
careful watch on the one which Alsop had said was her
father's. At last, after about forty minutes of watching,
a small, thickset man, evidently a servant, came up the
stairs, carrying a jug of water and a pail.

He took a key from his pocket, opened the door, and
went inside. Presently he reappeared with the pail and
a bundle of dirty linen, and went downstairs, this time
leaving the door shut but not locked. It seemed likely
that he would soon be back; but meanwhile, seizing her
chance, Ellen tiptoed quickly across the hallway, tapped
on the door, and, without waiting for a summons,
opened it and went in, closing it softly behind her.

The room was much more sparsely furnished than
hers. It looked as if it had originally been intended
for a children's room or nursery; the single bed, chair,
and small table were plain; there were bars across the
window, but they were not new. The room was very
cold, although the window was shut, and the air was
close and smelt bad.

Her father lay in the narrow bed, propped against a
couple of pillows. Ellen was inexpressibly shocked at
the change that had taken place in him since she had
seen him last. He seemed to have aged twenty years.
His hair was limp and scanty, his cheeks hollow, his

back and shoulders hunched and drooping. From a tall, big-boned, elderly man, he had deteriorated into a thin, stooping, lantern-jawed ancient. He was unshaven, with a three-day stubble of beard, and the nightshirt he wore was spattered with food. His look was vacant and wild-eyed; when it fixed on Ellen he at first seemed to stare at her without recognition; then a flicker of intelligence came into his eyes; glancing warily from side to side, he worked his jaw once or twice before beckoning to her and whispering urgently, "Mattie? Have you come to take me away?"

"Papa! Oh, dear, *dear* Papa!"

Ellen was wrung to the depths of feeling by his pitiful, tremulous look. He could not articulate very clearly, for he did not have his false teeth in his mouth—nor were they anywhere to be seen; nor were his clothes. There was no cupboard in the room.

Ellen knelt by the bed and took his bony hands.

"Dearest Papa. I am so *sorry* to see you like this!"

"It is Blanche—she thinks it best to keep me here," he confided in his broken, toothless utterance. "But I do *very* much wish to come home, Mattie. I am glad you are here at last. Why did you not come sooner? Have you my clothes with you? Blanche took them away. But I can walk—my leg is much better—only it is so cold in here—" He would have scrambled from the bed had she not restrained him.

"Hush! Wait, Papa! I do not have your clothes with me now, but I will come back with them soon—I promise."

"You won't leave me here?" His hands clung to hers.

Blinking to keep tears of outrage and pity from her eyes, Ellen said, "No, I won't leave you."

Now she noticed more strongly the horrible smell in the room—a rubbery, cankerous odor, of decayed food or flesh. He is ill, they are killing him, she thought; how can they *do* this?

Luke said falteringly, "I believe this place—where they keep me—is in my house."

"No, it is Kitty's house, Papa."

He shook his head. "It is *my* house—my dream room. Perhaps it is my own fault—I should have furnished it long ago. I knew this room was always here—inside my head, you know—but I did nothing about it. For years! But you will get me out of it, Mattie, will you not?"

"Yes, yes, of course I will. But I am not Mattie, Papa, I am Ellen."

"Ellen?" Slowly his gaze focused on her. His face, if possible, seemed to become even more drawn, grief-racked, agonized. He cried out loudly, "No—no—you are not Mattie! Mattie is dead!"

"Hush, Papa! That was long ago. She has been happy in heaven for—"

"No, no. *Listen!* You don't know. You don't know what I did. She was in so much pain—I couldn't endure her pain. I stood outside her bedroom door, I heard her crying for me, Luke, Luke, oh, Luke, won't you come to me. Help me!"

"That is all over now, Papa," said Ellen, though her hands were clenched in anguish on her father's.

"No, but I would not go in! I was unable to, I could not bear to go in! I stayed away from her room. A week before she died, I told Bendigo I was obliged to go to Bath on business. I couldn't endure even being in the same house with her pain! I went to Bath! I stayed at Pratt's Hotel!"

"Oh, Father!"

"And I did not come home until the nurse wrote to me that she had died. After five days more of terrible pain. *This* is my punishment," he said, looking at the bare room. "I deserve it but—you *will* take me away, Mattie, will you not?"

A brisk step came up the stair, and the manservant

entered, carrying a bowl of gruel. He checked sharply at
sight of Ellen, and his face turned plum color.

"Oo the deuce said *you* could come in here? That ain't
allowed! Clear out, afore I call the master!"

"I *beg* your pardon!" Summoning all the authority of
the rue St. Pierre and the Hôtel Caudebec, Ellen drew
herself up and gave him a freezing glare. "I am Miss
Paget. I have come to see my father. Who—pray—
are you?"

He advanced and put the bowl of gruel on the bedside
table. "I'm Consett, Mr. Bracegirdle's man, that's who
I am, and no one's allowed in this room without Mr.
Bracegirdle tells me first. Sorry, miss, but orders is orders.
The door's to be kep' locked at all times."

Ellen did not choose to discuss her father's state with
this underling. She said frostily, "Then you should have
left it locked just now."

"Didn't think there was anyone about to nip in like
you done," grumbled Consett, who was a very unpre-
possessing individual with a round greasy face, thinning
black hair, and quick-moving shifty brown eyes.

Mr. Paget's attention had been deflected from his
daughter by the gruel, which he was gulping down with
clumsy haste, dropping more splashes on his garment.
Wrung by pity, Ellen said loudly, "I will come back later,
Papa! Enjoy your breakfast." Then she left the room.

Consett followed her to the door, where he said in
a low voice, "The old gentleman's not safe to be left,
miss. That's why the door has to be locked. Master'll tell
you all about it." Then he shut the door smartly and she
heard the key turn inside.

Ellen returned to her own room. The hour was
still early—half past seven. She drew the curtains and
looked out. A hard frost lay in the garden; the factory
chimneys belched black smoke; the prospect was unutterably dreary.

Shivering, she dragged a blanket from her bed and wrapped it round her shoulders; then sat down to wait for the sound of the breakfast gong.

∽

At breakfast, which was served on a massive mahogany table, with porridge, ham, kidneys, muffins, herring roes, toast, oatcakes, and urns of coffee and tea, the Bracegirdles, who had evidently enjoyed their dinner party, showed more cordiality to Ellen than they had on the previous evening.

"Did you sleep well? You still look shockingly tired. It was folly, to travel here until we summoned you. You had best go back to bed after breakfast. Besides, I have a very busy day," said Kitty, "with the Dorcas Society, the Sunday School teachers, and the Women's Christian Aid. And the Poor Basket. And Mr. Bracegirdle, of course, has to go to the mill. No, you had best spend the day in bed. Then, this evening, perhaps you may see Papa."

"I have already seen him," said Ellen.

A freezing silence filled the room. Ellen went on, "How *can* you, Kitty—who call yourself a Christian woman—have the conscience to keep *anybody*—let alone your father—in such a state? What can you have been doing to him? He looks like some wretched old tramp! He is cold—dirty—hungry. And it is barely four months since he was a strong, active, intelligent man."

"Upon my word!" said Mr. Bracegirdle indignantly. "Didst ever hear sooch ingratitude? Here we've looked after him all the time you've been laid oop—and *that's* all the thanks we get!"

"Really, Ellen!" exclaimed Kitty, with extremely heightened color. "I'd thank you to reflect a little longer, before coming here and condemning us out of hand! Wait till you hear both sides of the matter, pray. Papa has been behaving like a lunatic—like an utter, raving madman! For his own sake, it was necessary to restrain him. You need not think we *enjoyed* having him here. It was no such thing, I assure you!"

"Then you will allow him to come home with me today," said Ellen. She recalled her total lack of funds—but, after all, Luke must have money at his disposal—there must be some cash of his somewhere about the house?

"Leave with you today? Are you mad?"

"That is quite out of the question."

"Why?" said Ellen. "I shall write, then, to Eugenia. If she and Eustace knew what you were doing here—"

"You little fool! It was Eugenia's idea in the first place! She suggested that I bring him here and—and reason with him. *She* could not do so—Eustace is too soft—"

"Soft-headed," said Sam Bracegirdle. He rose, mopping his mouth with the damask table napkin. "I'll leave you to make the matter plain to the lass," he said to his wife, and, to Ellen, "Joost get this into thy head, miss. Your pa's not leaving this house until he and I have come to an agreement over something Kitty wants him to do."

"Change his will, do you mean?" said Ellen.

The same icy silence followed her words.

"If you know about the will," began Kitty. Her husband interrupted her.

"Your dad's clean daft, girl—that's the long and the short of it. He's not sensible. He's not responsible. And, until he is, he stays here. Who knows what other idiocy he might fall into? He stays here until he agrees to alter that lunatic testament. And if he won't do that—then we'll be obliged to get medical men to have it set aside, because he's of unsound mind. Do ye see? Leaving all his brass to that harpy—the idea!"

"I don't like Mrs. Pike any better than you do," said Ellen, "but Papa was not mad when he made that will, and you know it. Whether you have *sent* him mad, since, with your cruelty, is another matter—"

"What?" shrieked Kitty. "Us sent him mad? I like that! Mind your tongue, miss! Anyone would think you wanted that woman—that mother of a jailbird—to get Mama's money!"

"I can't say I want that. Though I would not be prepared to go to such lengths to prevent it. But has it not struck you that you are going the best way to drive poor Papa out of his wits? He is terrified—wretched—it makes me sick to see him. How can he ever change his will now?"

"Roobbish!" said Sam Bracegirdle vigorously. "You don't know what you're talking about, miss! Ony road, you're ailing—fevered—yourself, in no case to joodge. Your pa's aging, that's all. It's four months since ye saw him last, and that's a long time at his age. It can be sudden—when old ones goes downhill. Now: you go and rest, like a sensible lass. Later in the week ye can talk to our doctor, Barney Oldthorpe, as clever a man as ye could wish to meet; and he'll be able to put your mind at rest. We've not been oonkind to the old gentleman—it's joost that he's a thick-skulled, obstinate, self-willed old devil, and ye can't reason with him."

He had begun this statement in a very reasonable tone, but worked himself into a passion by the end. Ellen felt danger in the air. She said quickly, "I'll be glad to talk to your doctor. Perhaps he can write to Smollett at Petworth. I do think, Mr. Bracegirdle, that if Papa were at home—in his own place—allowed to lead a normal life—he would be much more likely to see the force of your arguments. After all, Mrs. Pike has left his employment now—several months have passed—very likely he has almost forgotten her."

"Nay, but if he went home, likely he'd remember her again and invite her back," objected Sam. Ellen thought of Mrs. Pike, still in the vicinity of Petworth, and feared there might be some truth in his argument. He pulled the watch from his fob and exclaimed, "By gum, I'm half an hour late! Talk to Ellen, Kitty—reason with her—you can make her see sense, I daresay."

And he left the house at speed.

❧

After another hour spent in fruitless argument, Ellen was glad to retire to her room while Kitty busied herself with her various charitable occupations. The door to Luke Paget's room remained shut and locked; nobody went up or came down. Listening outside it once or twice, Ellen heard her father mutter to himself fretfully; she heard the name "Mattie" several times repeated, and sometimes a kind of whimpering. She was greatly tempted to talk to him through the door, but decided that this would only be unkindness, since she had no means of access.

She thought with horror of the story he had told her. It had the ring of total truth. Ellen clenched her hands again, thinking of those five days during which Mattie had writhed in pain, calling for her husband, while he had stayed in Bath, safely out of earshot. Why should one trouble oneself to rescue such a man? And yet she must.

"When does Papa get his meals?" she asked Kitty at luncheon. Kitty gave her an angry, silencing look—there were a couple of local ladies from the Christian Aid Society at the table.

"Consett takes him his meals twice a day; the doctor told us he should be on a light diet. Old people can easily become overheated and poisoned by too much rich food, he says. And my father is in a very delicate state of health," Kitty explained to her guests, who nodded sympathetically and murmured that elderly people could be a great care and a problem and that Mrs. Bracegirdle was showing exemplary filial piety in tending her difficult old parent. Ellen longed to speak up and disabuse them. Two basins of gruel a day! she thought, looking at the fricassee of veal and chicken patties with which the ladies were being regaled—but she was aware that her own position in the house was highly precarious, and she had best mind her tongue, or she might find herself turned out summarily, and lose any chance of helping her father.

That evening she was allowed to pay a short, formal visit to her father's room, but Kitty and Bracegirdle accompanied her, and Luke was evidently so alarmed by their presence that he fell into a violent tremor and hardly looked at his youngest daughter.

"Well, Mester Paget, hast thought any more as to what we were talking aboot?" said Bracegirdle. He evidently intended to speak in a calm and measured manner, but his voice rang so loudly in the scantily furnished room that it made Luke start; his great anxious eyes fixed on the other man, and after a moment he shook his head and muttered: "Not—subject—coercion—free—dispose—as I choose!"

"Don't be foolish, Papa!" said Kitty sharply. "You know that your testamentary dispositions are utterly unreasonable."

An obstinate, vacant, cunning look came over Luke's face. "Mattie will take my part," he mouthed at Kitty. "*She* knows what you are—vile demon! Get you back to the pit!"

"There! You see!" said Kitty furiously, and she pulled Ellen from the room. "He raves. He is not rational. Sam says we must have him declared of unsound mind."

Ellen saw many practical objections to this, but she had decided not to expend valuable strength on arguing with the Bracegirdles. She really did not feel very strong, and was turning over a wild plan in her mind, for which all her resources would be needed.

"When does the doctor come next?" she asked, after a considerable pause.

"On Saturday." Kitty sounded relieved that her sister had given up expostulating and seemed to have begun accepting the situation.

Ellen resolved to possess herself in patience, and accordingly spent a couple of days resting, thinking, and observing the habits of the household. Kitty was out a great deal of the time on her various charitable activities; Sam left the house at eight every morning and did not return until five. The key of Luke's room was entrusted to the disagreeable Consett, who kept it at all times on his person.

❧

On Wednesday evening, when Alsop brought her washing water before dinner, Ellen asked, "Martha, could you send a telegram for me?"

"Not tonight, miss. But tomorrow I could, when I go to the grocer's."

"The thing is, Martha, I have no money to pay for it; but would you take this brooch instead?"

It was a little pearl one her mother had given her when she was ten.

"Bless you, miss, I 'on't take your brooch! I can find the money—I get good wages—and you can pay me back some time or other."

"I shall need to meet somebody in the village; is there a decent inn?"

"The Crown's noon so bad; that's where the business folk mostly stays."

Having dispatched her message, Ellen was free to remember that it might never reach its recipient—who might, in any case, be unable or unwilling to help her; any number of things might go wrong with her plan, and she had best occupy herself by thinking of some alternative course. None presented itself, save an appeal to the better feelings of the doctor (who was probably too well paid by the Bracegirdles to indulge in the luxury of better feelings), and Ellen was in a wholly despondent and pessimistic frame of mind when, on Thursday afternoon, she walked down to the Crown Inn.

Kitty was away at a charity bazaar in Tunstall. Ellen had already ventured out, two or three times, into the gardens of Maple Grove and the outskirts of the village; her departure from the house excited no remark.

The Crown was a large, respectable-looking hostelry with an arched entrance for carriages and a number of people coming and going; evidently it was used as a place of call for manufacturers, and Ellen was able to slip into the coffee room without anyone asking her business or particularly observing her. Once there, she looked anxiously around her. A tall, elegantly dressed form removed itself from the seat nearest the fire and came toward her.

"My dear Ellen! May I ask what all this is about? I am come, as you see, in answer to your summons, but—" Then he looked more closely at her and exclaimed, "Good God, Ellie! What is the matter with you? You look like a ghost!"

"Oh, Benedict! I am so thankful that you have come! It is all so dreadful! But"—she glanced about—"we can't talk here."

"No, I have reserved a private parlor. And you look as if you would be the better for some coffee. Come this way."

Comfortably established by a brisk fire in an upstairs room, Ellen poured out her story. She was careful to keep her language and tone as moderate, calm, and objective as possible; she did not want Benedict to think that she was indulging in hysterical exaggeration, fancy, or melodrama; and she was infinitely relieved to see, as she proceeded, that his expression grew more and more appalled.

"Benedict, if Papa is left there much longer, I think he will die! Or he will go truly mad, and then they will consign him to Bedlam. And he is not mad; I am positive of that. Poor old man! He is wholly confused and wandering—and no wonder, after such treatment. But I am certain that, once restored to his own home, he will regain his usual sense."

"I always did think Kitty hard as nails," muttered Benedict. His brows knit, he rubbed his forehead, then asked, "Who has the key to your father's room?"

"Sam's man Consett. He keeps it in his pocket. And he is devoted to my brother-in-law."

"No man's devotion extends beyond a certain point," said Benedict drily. "Try him with fifty pounds, Ellie; if that fails, raise it to a hundred."

"A *hundred*?"

"You wish to rescue your father—well? Now let's think. He will need clothes. I can bring a suit of my brother's from Matlock—he is a big fellow, they will do well enough. You say Bracegirdle is out all day—what about Kitty?"

"She too is out a great deal. But when—when could you come?"

Ellen's voice trembled. She could hardly believe, even now, that Benedict was really going to help. Angry at her own weakness, she shook the tears from her eyes.

"Tomorrow at this time. How would that be?"

"That would be capital. I heard Kitty say that on Friday afternoon she was to attend a meeting of the Overseas Mission Society at Cheadle. She—she occupies herself a great deal with charity."

"*Charity!*" Benedict muttered something which Ellen thought it best not to hear. "Wait here a moment, Ellie; indulge yourself in another cup of coffee while I go on an errand."

He was absent for ten minutes, while Ellen sat in a state of such relief and exhaustion that it felt like vertigo; to have found someone prepared to share her burden was an alleviation she had hardly dared expect. It was almost a surprise to see Benedict come back through the door.

"There!" He slapped down an envelope full of dirty bank notes on the table. "I have discovered there are some advantages to being an earl's brother; your credit is excellent within a twenty-five-mile radius of his seat! Try this on your Cerberus and I am fairly certain it will succeed."

"If not?"

"If not, then we shall be obliged to call in the law; but I am sure you, and your father too, would wish to avoid that if possible."

Ellen's spirits sank at the suggestion. She said falteringly, "Benedict, the next problem that has been occupying me is, where can we take him? For he is too frail to undertake the whole journey to Sussex, and—"

"Nothing simpler. We take him to Matlock Chase. Easingwold wouldn't have the least objection, but he is not there at present; he stays at Melton for the hunting. Aunt Essie is there; she's a kind old soul with her head in the clouds, nothing surprises her. And it is only two hours' drive from here; that won't harm your father."

"Oh, Benedict! I h-hardly kn-know what to s-say—"

"Come, now, Ellie!" he said kindly. "This is no time to break down. You have to go back and recruit your strength for tomorrow; show an innocent face to that atrocious pair, and set to work on the manservant. But not too soon!"

She stood up obediently, and he wrapped her mantle closely round her. "That's the dandy. Now—one last point—is there a side entrance to the house?"

"Yes: to the left, past the shrubbery."

"Can one take a carriage along?"

"Yes, it is where coals are delivered."

"Excellent; I will be there at this time tomorrow. Till then—keep your heart up!"

He clasped her hands briefly and was gone.

Sixteen

EVEN WHEN THEY WERE IN THE COACH, ELLEN COULD hardly believe that they were safe. She kept looking anxiously out of the window until Benedict, laughing, said, "Don't worry, Ellie! After all, if Bracegirdle did come home unexpectedly early, and start in pursuit, he would assume that you had taken the road south to Lichfield; or, more probably, gone into Stoke to catch a train."

"Yes, that is true," agreed Ellen, relieved.

"It commences to snow," Benedict said, glancing out at the hillier country through which they were now passing. "What a piece of good fortune that it did not start any earlier! A heavy fall was the one thing that might have prevented our plan."

Luke, all this time, had been sitting with a dazed, vacant expression on his face, which, though she would hardly admit it to herself, deeply troubled his daughter. He had submitted quietly, without utterance, to being dressed, wrapped up warmly, and escorted downstairs to the carriage. But even since the day she arrived at Maple Grove he seemed to have deteriorated. What—she now had leisure to think—what if the Bracegirdles and their doctor had been right about his mental state? What if by now he were too far gone to recover—too disturbed, too confused?

"Don't distress yourself," said Benedict quietly, guessing at her anxieties. "This must all seem to him like a wild dream. It may take days—weeks—before he is himself again."

By the time they had reached Matlock Chase the snowstorm had grown to a blizzard; the horses could only just battle against it.

"This weather will be a stopper on my brother's hunting," said Benedict, carefully, with the help of a couple of footmen, assisting Luke to climb out of the carriage. "I suspect, Ellie, that you may have to resign yourself to several days'—if not weeks'—incarceration here. I only hope Matlock may not prove as much of a prison as Maple Grove!"

"It is a little larger!" Matlock was an immense house, thrown up by Vanbrugh for the third earl. Just the same, the thought of not being able to leave—of being uninvited guests for so long—was very disagreeable. Ellen went on doubtfully, unhappily, "Benedict, I am sorry for this. Indeed I had not expected—I do not wish to be a burden on you—or disarrange your plans—or—or those of Charlotte Morningquest."

"Charlotte Morningquest?" He sounded astonished. "How does she come into the business?"

"I thought you might have invited her to stay here?"

"Over my dead body!" said Benedict. "There are limits beyond which I will not endure to be bored."

They walked into a huge hall, decorated with gray-and-white parti-colored marble statues in niches, and a great many weapons. An elderly servant with a benevolent face came forward to welcome them.

"Now this is Hathersage, who will be taking care of your father, and I assure you if Hathersage looks after anybody they are guaranteed recovery from anything up to bubonic plague; he has seen me through whooping cough, scarlatina, and a broken thigh, and I was a difficult patient, was I not, Hathersage?"

"Tolerable difficult, Master Benedict," said Hathersage, smiling. "Don't you fret, now, miss, well soon have the old gentleman on the mend. Just you come this way, sir, and the young lady can come up and sit with you, soon's you're between the sheets."

"Meantime, *you* come with *me*," said Benedict. "There is somebody else who has been on tenterhooks ever since I told her this morning that you would be arriving."

In fact they did not have to go anywhere; Vicky appeared, hurling herself down a vast staircase, crying, "Ellen, Ellen! I am so happy to see you! Is not this a splendid palace?"

"Vicky! I was just about to ask Benedict if it might be possible to visit you at school!"

"I did that last week," said Benedict. "Your sister Kitty was so obliging as to inform me of the action she had seen fit to take; not out of consideration! She felt it proper to tell me so that I might contribute toward the school fees. Being one who likes to be sure that I am getting value for my money, I went to inspect the place, found Vicky miserably unhappy and learning nothing, so took her away and brought her here, where she can tyrannize it over Easingwold's brats—who are much younger, of course—and share the attentions of their Miss Flyte."

"Oh, Benedict! And are you enjoying yourself here, Vicky?"

"Tolerably," replied Vicky with her usual caution. "But I shall prefer it when we can go home to the Hermitage. I am *very* glad to see you, Ellen. Oh, but your poor hair! What happened to it? And you are so thin! Have you been *very* sick? Did you nearly die?"

"No, no; and I am quite better now, and my hair will soon grow again and I shall be as fat as a pig. Have you drawn many pictures here?"

"Hundreds! And we have been skating in the park— Benedict taught me. I will show you—if only it will stop snowing."

But it did not stop snowing for three days and nights. Most of that time Ellen spent at her father's bedside, talking to him, listening to him, feeding him, coaxing him slowly back to lucidity and reason. He took a chill from the journey, and, for a time, she feared that her impulsive action might prove his death. At times she was in despair. But, little by little, recognition returned to his eyes and intelligibility to his utterance. The Earl of Radnor's personal dentist attended on him to measure and construct a new set of false teeth, and this addition greatly improved both his appearance and his diction, once he got into the way of wearing them, which did, however, take a little time.

Ellen herself suffered something of a relapse after the mental, physical, and emotional strain of the days at Maple Grove; she felt desperately tired for several days following the arrival at Matlock Chase.

She could not avoid a good deal of speculation as to the Bracegirdle's' reactions when they discovered that Mr. Paget and his daughter were missing. None of the servants save Consett had witnessed the departure, for it had been managed at a time when they were belowstairs having their dinner; and Consett, wholly won over by the hundred pounds, had said he intended to break the lock, so that it would not be thought he had any hand in the escape. Kitty and her husband might well think that the fugitives had perished somewhere in the blizzard. How would they act then?

As soon as it was feasible to do so, Ellen sent a reassuring telegram to Gerard, and followed it with a detailed letter. After a week she received a note from him in reply:

"Have had no end of kick-up from Kitty and Samuel, who seemed to think I should know where you and Papa had got to: telegrams every hour for a day or so. I replied that I had no notion where you were. Now they have quieted down. I daresay Kitty may be ashamed of making the matter public. Very sorry to hear P. was in such poor health, hope he is on the way to mending now. Tell him another portion of slab uncovered in Chi. Cath. undercroft; mason fairly certain it is the Doom Stone. Hope to see you soon. G."

"I have had a letter from Gerard, Papa," said Ellen. "He tells me that the masons working in Chichester Cathedral really believe they have found the Doom Stone, in a small crypt-like chamber under the nave."

"The Doom Stone?" Luke spoke slowly and ponder-ingly. "Ah yes—I remember. They found a Paradise Stone—did they not? And there should be two. There should always be two. Black and white. Up and down. Good and evil. Man and wife."

"In and out," said Ellen, smiling, pleased to play this game with him and exercise his rusty wits. "Brother and sister. Here and there. You and I."

"Ah. But you, Ellen, are two—are you not? You are brother and sister both. For you had a twin—little Luke, who died."

"Why—so I did," said Ellen, utterly astonished at this unexpected evidence of memory and recognition. "My poor little brother. That is why the people in Petworth say that I am a healer."

"A healer. Yes, of course. They used to come to the door—did they not? And somebody—some person—did not care for them to do so. She said we would be having our poultry stolen."

"That was Mrs. Pike," said Ellen softly.

"Pike? I do not recollect the name. But Mattie—Mattie *always* lets the people come."

"Does she, Papa?"

"Invariably! Ask her yourself! She was here but a moment ago. She brought me"—he looked about—"she brought me those flowers." He pointed to a little glass full of snowdrops that Ellen had brought from the con-servatory. "She is nearly always with me now."

"I am glad of that, Papa," Ellen said steadily.

"Poor Mattie. I did her great wrong." Luke's hollow eyes moved round and rested on his daughter. "I used her as I might an armchair—a desk. As if—as if she were there only for my convenience. I seldom talked with her, or asked her opinion. And yet she was a person—a spirit! One human being should not use another so."

"Never mind, Papa. You would not have done it if you had considered more. You know better now—it seems we never stop growing. And Mattie would not hold it against you."

"No, she has forgiven me. She tells me so," said Luke contentedly. "She tells me so every day."

❧

At last the snow stopped, and Benedict announced that it was time Ellen had an airing.

Ever since Mr. Paget's rescue, a certain cautious confidence had replaced the cold formality which had for so long characterized the relations between Ellen and Benedict. It is hardly possible to participate in such an enterprise without, to some degree and almost involuntarily, relaxing one's defenses against the partner who has assisted in the adventure. Ellen's gratitude to Benedict for his promptitude in action, efficiency, and subsequent tactful solicitude made her feel it incumbent upon her to infuse into her expressions of proper obligation a degree of warmth and friendship which he seemed quite disposed to reciprocate. In fact the pair were getting on very comfortably.

Each day Benedict made kind inquiries as to Mr. Paget's progress and, when the patient became equal to company, was prepared to help entertain him in any way that might be acceptable. Much conversation was still fatiguing to Luke, but Benedict played spillikins with him, and read aloud Shakespeare's plays, from which

Luke seemed to derive considerable pleasure, especially *Timon* and *King Lear*. He then asked for the poetry of Cowper, explaining somewhat wistfully that this poet was "Mattie's favorite." Fortunately Lady Dovedale, Benedict's aunt Essie, a kindly vague soul, proved to be greatly addicted to Cowper and to possess his complete works; she was prepared to read them aloud ad infinitum.

"Very good," said Benedict. "Hathersage is in the next room; your father is in excellent hands; you have not been out of doors since you arrived here, and your cheeks are the color of whey. I am going to teach you to skate; put on your pelisse."

A dozen gardeners had been set to work, sweeping the snow off the frozen lake.

"The ice looks dreadfully hard," said Ellen dubiously, eyeing the dark-gray surface, on which Vicky and Radnor's two little daughters, aged six and four, were already tumbling about with Miss Flyte, screaming with laughter and falling flat more often than they stood upright.

"Don't think about that. These are my great-aunt Georgiana's skates—I think they will fit you very well. Now take my hand—trust me—just think that you are a bird, skimming along."

Never had Ellen felt herself so helpless. Her feet slipped away from her in what felt like an infinite number of opposing directions simultaneously; her weight never seemed to be where it would help, but always pulling her disastrously out of balance.

"I feel like a sack—a lump!" she gasped. "It is *hopeless*, Benedict—quite hopeless! I shall never, never learn."

"No, no, it will come. That's the way—push forward, not back. It is more like dancing than walking."

Unsteadily, they glided off down the lake, toward distant dark woods and a snowy hillside.

"The last time I danced with you," said Benedict, "was at Kitty's wedding. Do you remember?"

Did she not! Vividly the occasion returned to Ellen. After dancing with her four times, he had taken her down into the Valley Walk, and told her that she looked like a wild hyacinth. They had walked to and fro, to and fro…

"Very good!" said Benedict. "Now you are quite getting the feel of it. I knew that you would be a quick learner—such a clever girl as you are!" He spoke teasingly, as usual, but there was affection in his tone.

They were a long way from the others now, going faster and faster. The air that rushed past was like breath of diamonds.

…And then next day…

"And then next day," he went on, "you caught me kissing Dolly Randall in the dairy—oh, how angry you were! You told my mother about it—telltale tit!—and she gave me a great scold, and dismissed poor Dolly all for a silly piece of boy's nonsense."

"Oh, and you cannot believe how bitterly sorry I was the very next day for that spiteful act of priggishness! I would have cut my tongue out not to have done it. But I was dreadfully unhappy just then: homesick, missing Mama so painfully, about to be sent back to Brussels—but still I should not have tattled on you and Dolly in that odious way."

"And all the time," said Benedict, "it was *you* that I wanted to kiss."

He did so now, very lightly, on her parted lips, but even so it was enough to upset Ellen's precarious equilibrium, and the two of them crashed down together in a flailing tangle of arms and legs and skates.

"I *told* you," said Ellen, as they lay prone, but with her head gathered comfortably onto his shoulder, "I told you that it was hopeless! I shall never be a skater. The least thing oversets me."

"No matter," said Benedict, without making any

attempt to get up. "We do very well as we are. Now I can scold you as much as I please and you cannot escape. Why did you give me such a shocking setdown that time when I invited you to Petworth Fair?"

"Because you had already asked Kitty and Dorothea Morningquest, and only seemed to invite me as an afterthought!"

"I was scared to death of you, Amazon that you are."

"Why were you so teasing and unkind whenever we met? You would snap my head off at the least provocation!"

"What about you, pray? Good heaven, those freezing, withering looks you used to give me—like the east wind in person."

"It was because I was so miserable. I longed to make peace—but never had the opportunity. I loved you so much—and it seemed so hopeless."

"And do you think I did not? I began to fall into despair. I have got to forget that fiend of a girl, I told myself—go off—gamble-travel—enjoy the world. But I *couldn't* forget you."

"*Despair?* It was like living in the Arctic!"

"Benedict and Ellen!" scolded Vicky, skating staggeringly toward them, with a gardener's boy in anxious pursuit. "What are you *doing*, lying there on the ice and snow? You must get up at once! You will catch cold!"

"No, we will not catch cold," said Benedict, rising with caution onto one knee. "In fact we are so warm, Vicky, that we shall probably never catch cold again." Climbing to his feet, he picked up his small half sister and tossed her into a pile of snow as she squealed with delighted laughter. Then, turning to assist Ellen, he exclaimed, "Good God, though, we shall probably run into no end of trouble when we marry! Do you suppose that we come within the forbidden degrees—am I permitted to marry my Mother's Husband's Daughter? Well, I intend to, whether permitted or not."

"You may not marry your Stepmother," said Ellen, after some consideration, "or your Mother's Brother's Wife—"

"That would be Aunt Essie. I have not the least intention of marrying her. It's you I wish to marry."

"But, Benedict—"

"What? Oh, are you going to allude to that Frenchman? I never for a single moment believed that story, even then, and I don't now!"

"In that case, why did it make you so angry?"

"Because, you monstrous girl, you would go to such lengths to hurt me. When all I wanted was to protect you. Didn't I travel to Brussels, just to break the news to you about your cat—?"

"Oh, what a wretch I was! But I will make up for it now."

∽

The bitter weather continued for another three weeks, and during that time it was thought ineligible for Ellen and her father to attempt the journey back to Sussex. Lord and Lady Radnor appeared at Matlock Chase for a night, gave Ellen friendly, absentminded welcome as their prospective sister-in-law, then hastened away to another of their houses in Dorset, which, though humbug country for hunting, was at least now free from snow.

"Hunting is all they think about," said Benedict. "I used to wish that Easingwold would break his neck at a rasper so that I could be Earl, but now I am quite of a different opinion. Think of having to sit in the House of Lords and listen to all those old windbags!"

"Oh, fie, Benedict," Aunt Essie said mildly.

"You are not interested in a political career, my dear boy?" Luke, now allowed downstairs in the evening, regarded Benedict wistfully. "But what nobler aim can there be than to represent your fellow man in our glorious legislative assembly?"

"I can represent him just as well in an embassy!"

"It is time you went upstairs to bed, Papa," said Ellen gently. "See, here is Hathersage to help you."

❧

During the fourth week, the snow began to melt; roads and railways were said to be clear; and, after more telegrams, Benedict, Ellen, and Luke set off by train for Sussex. Vicky was to remain with her small half nieces at Matlock for another month, until the household at the Hermitage was running smoothly.

The journey passed without difficulty. Benedict had with him his man, Bakewell, an expert at procuring cabs, reserving compartments, buying tickets, and providing foot warmers and sandwiches. Ellen recalled her trip with Lady Morningquest from Brussels to Paris, and sighed, thinking of poor Louise and Raoul. But she could not be really despondent, leaning against the warmth and comfort of Benedict's shoulder, observing with satisfaction how her father demonstrated more and more signs of reawakening intelligence. He read the newspaper in the train and commented on the shocking damage sustained by the Crystal Palace at Sydenham daring the late gales; upon the lucky officer who had bought a book for £50 during the French sack of Peking, for which the Emperor of China was now offering him £16,000; on the extraordinary notion of having a Female Artists' Exhibition—where in the world could they possibly find enough Female Artists?—and on the necessity for the French Emperor removing French troops from Rome. Then he fell asleep and only woke when they were obliged to change trains at Pulborough for the last lap of the journey.

Gerard was waiting to meet them with the family coach at Petworth station. He hugged Ellen, affectionately saluted his father, and shook Benedict's hand up and down a great many times. "I say, Benedict, what a tramp you have been! You make me feel a wretch for not having accompanied Ellen—but I daresay you made a far better hand at the rescue than I should have done."

"It was just fortunate that I happened to be close at hand," said Benedict. "Even if I had not been, I imagine your sister would have managed it on her own. She is a dauntless creature. But come, here we are standing in the rain and wind—let us get your father under his own roof."

The drive was soon over; Sue and Agnes welcomed them joyfully at the Hermitage, and Benedict stayed to supper before going on to Petworth House (it had been arranged that he should stay there with his cousin George so as not to put an undue strain upon the slender resources of the Paget household. Ellen reflected that her father and Lord Leconfield must now make up their minds to forget that silly dispute over the Infant School).

"I must say, it is very agreeable to be at home again," said Luke, looking fondly round his own dining room, after drinking a small postprandial glass of port. "But I think I will go upstairs now; Mattie will be waiting for me."

"I will help you, Papa," said Gerard, springing to his feet.

❧

During the next couple of days there were many business matters to arrange. Money had to be withdrawn from the bank to meet the servants' outstanding wages and other household expenses. Ellen went in and out of the house a great many times. At one point, crossing the town square, she came face to face with Mr. Wheelbird.

"Ah, Mr. Wheelbird. What a lucky meeting! I was on the point of writing you a note. Would you be so kind as to come up and call on Papa, tomorrow afternoon?"

Now she noticed that the young lawyer had gone as white as a cheesecloth.

"M-m-m-miss Ellen? Are you—are you perfectly all right?"

"Why yes. Why should I not be? In fact I have never been better," she said with a radiant smile.

"B-but we understood that you—and your father—had p-p-p-passed away in the blizzard! I had n-numerous telegrams from your sister Mrs. Bracegirdle—"

"Oh, well, yes, my sister may have been under that impression at first. But it was a false one." Ellen reminded herself that she really must write to Kitty—but this did not seem to have a high priority among the hundred and one things that needed to be done.

"So, Mr. Wheelbird, will you please come round tomorrow? Papa has decided to change his testamentary dispositions—as I believe you very properly suggested he should consider doing, on the last occasion when you and I met. In fact he has already destroyed his will, and has made various notes for a new one, which he wishes you to put into legal order for him."

If Mr. Wheelbird could have turned any paler, he would have done so; he stared at Ellen with his Adam's apple working convulsively. In a hoarse voice he said, "A new will. Tomorrow afternoon. Y-yes, Miss Paget—" then turned and walked hastily away.

Ellen looked after him in vague bewilderment for a moment. Why should he be so startled? Mr. Paget was proposing to divide his property among Gerard, Eugenia, and herself. Kitty was to be struck out of the inheritance entirely, as a reprisal for her heartless usage of her father. Ellen felt that this was not entirely just, since Eugenia had also played a part in the business, had certainly condoned and encouraged the abduction and coercion; still, she probably would not have gone to such lengths as Kitty had done. However, Ellen did not feel called upon to attempt any intervention—which would, besides, be quite useless. Mr. Paget had quite made up his mind. Absently, she thought, Mr. Wheelbird ought to be pleased that Papa is changing his testamentary dispositions, I remember his giving me some warning about them—that day when he proposed to me. Gracious! What a long time ago that seems! And she was laughing to herself over the memory when, to her surprise, she heard her name being called in strangely familiar tones from the opposite side of the square.

"Callisto! *Mon dieu, que tu es maigre!*"

Thunderstruck, Ellen turned and saw Germaine de Rhetorée waving at her from the doorway of the Half Moon Inn.

The two girls ran to each other and embraced in the middle of the square.

"Germaine! But what in the world are you doing here, in Petworth—how long have you been here?"

"Since last night. I came because I was concerned about you—I thought I would come over and see for myself. And when I arrive—what do I find? That you have been on some mad quest, some quixotic errand, to rescue your papa from the harpy of a sister!"

"Who told you this?"

"Benedict Masham—I saw him riding by, not ten minutes since."

"I would never have succeeded without his help," Ellen said.

"Oh-ho! So there has been a rapprochement! Do I scent a romance?"

"How can I tell what you scent, you bloodhound?" said Ellen, smiling broadly with pleasure at this meeting with a friend she had thought never to see again. "But yes, it is true that Benedict and I are to be married."

"*Hélas!* Poor Raoul! And so he has come all this way for nothing?"

"What? Good God, you do not mean to tell me that *Raoul* is here also?"

"Why, you do not think that I would travel to this barbarous island without an escort? I suggested to Raoul that he should come with me as my cavalier, he was happy to do so. He had long been meditating an approach to you, but lacked the courage to write and propose it. And now he is too late!"

Full of wonder at this utterly unexpected development, Ellen asked herself whether, if Raoul had written to her during those melancholy months last winter when all seemed so hopeless—if he had proposed then—would she have accepted him, just to escape, just to return to her beloved Paris?

"Where is Raoul now?" she asked, looking around.

"Oh, he is paying a call on Monsieur le Baron Leconfield, whose aunt is Raoul's grandmother's niece by marriage—or something of the kind; Raoul will always put family proprieties first. I was about to come and call on you—for he, full of diffidence, suggested that you and I should first have our reunion alone, so that I could plead his cause. *En effet*, there he comes now with the Honorable Benedict—I wonder they do not have their swords at each other's throat!"

In fact there did, Ellen thought, seem to be some constraint about the two young men who strolled toward them in the cold February sun. Benedict's former look of chill reserve had settled once more over his countenance, and Raoul appeared simply worried and apprehensive. He looked years older than when Ellen had seen him first: a sober, thoughtful man, the white stripe on his hair still in evidence. But when he set eyes on Ellen, his expression changed to pure affectionate compassion, as he exclaimed, "Oh, my friend! What you have been through! You look as frail as a snowflake. How you must have suffered!"

He kissed her hands, holding them tight and looking intently into her eyes.

"It is no use, Raoul," said Germaine, brisk and cheer-ful. "You are too late, *mon pauvre ami*! Ellen and Benedict are to be married."

Ellen's eyes met those of Benedict; he raised his brows, giving her a slight, wry, questioning smile. She shook her head at him, smiling also.

"Then," said Raoul with exquisite French gal-lantry, "you are the luckiest man in England, Monsieur Masham, and I congratulate you with all my heart—*hélas*, poor laggard that I am! What shall I do now?"

"Well, you cannot marry *me*," said Germaine, firm but friendly. "One mistake of that nature is quite enough! But I will be your friend, your copain, and give you excellent advice, until you find the right person." She took Raoul's arm in a comradely manner. "Come along now, you must escort me to the bank, where I wish to change some money. You may return and call on Ellen later; just now I can see that she has business to transact."

The business was with Benedict, who said simply, "Are you sure that you know your own mind, my love? Are you certain that you are not going to be pining after that French fellow?"

"Oh, Benedict, no! I am dearly attached to Raoul—but as a brother, not a lover. I have told you this already—"

"Poor fellow," said Benedict, looking benevolently after his defeated rival.

※

Gerard had ridden Captain over to Lavant Down. He was planning to spend the night with Eustace and Eugenia, to give them the full tale of the rescue from Kitty. Eustace would be appalled, no doubt; what Eugenia's reaction would be, Gerard could not imagine.

But his first business was with Matt Bilbo.

"Matt—you *cannot* be keeping Sim here any longer! It

is too dangerous. I have heard that the police are looking for him in this part of the country. His mother still lives near Petworth—and it is known that you were his friend in prison—they are almost certain to come to your place sooner or later. Where is he now?"

"He be a-working down thurr in Chiddester." Matt's face was troubled. "Working for the church, he say, be a way to pay off the money he took from the poor box. 'Twas on'y five shilling. He be paying it back, penny by penny..."

"But he escaped from jail. And you will be in terrible trouble, Matt, if he is caught with you. When his foot was hurt, I can see you could not ask him to go, but now he is better—"

"Ah, poor Simmie! He've dyed his hair wi' walnut," Matt pointed out hopefully. "And none do know him hereabouts."

"Except his mother."

"He wouldna go anigh her. She used him mortal hard when he wed—said she'd have namore to do with him, he'd get nor crust nor crib from her, never again till snow do fall in hell."

"Is there nowhere else he could go?" Gerard felt it strange and hard that he should be arguing on the side of heartless, cruel common sense, against the calls of loyalty and love.

Matt raised eyes so guileless and full of light that he was even more abashed.

"Sim be such a poor skiddery fellow, Gerald; who'd look out for 'un if *I* cast 'un off? And he be main set on digging out that Doom Stone, for you an' your dad; he be turble grieved, still, at what he done—"

"But it was a mistake! And it's all over now, and she took no harm—"

"Ah, I know, but Sim do be dogged-set to make amends; an' by his way o' thinking, if he grub out the owd Doom Stone, that'll be a jonnick way to do it. You'd not stand betwixt a man and his upsidement, Mus' Gerald?"

Matt had never called him Mus' before; the touch of formality cut Gerard to the quick; the shepherd seemed by it to be putting a distance between them.

"No, I'd not do that, of course! But when—if—it is found—if I can find the money for him to go overseas—?"

"Well!" said Matt, with his candid, happy smile. "When 'tis found, then let be how 'twill!"

❧

Back at the Hermitage, Sue the housemaid was in fits of laughter.

"Oh, Miss Ellen, what *do* you think? My cousin Nancy just told me. Mr. Wheelbird and Mrs. Pike got married at Egdean Church last Saturday as ever was! And she a good twelve year older, if a day! And a head taller! Did you ever hear such a thing?"

"What? No! Mr. Wheelbird and Mrs. Pike? I can hardly believe it!"

Then Ellen recollected his horror—his pallor and dropped jaw—at the news that Luke Paget was still living and in his right mind; in a flash the whole picture presented itself to her.

"I mind how, whenever he came to the house, he used to make up to her a bit," Sue said comfortably. "After her money, he was, I'll be bound; well, they do say she's a tidy bit put by, what she 'herited from the old Canon in Chiddester."

And might have had even more, thought Ellen. But still, very likely Mr. Wheelbird had not done so badly for himself; at all events, he must make the best of his bargain.

"Is there any more news of Mrs. Pike's son who escaped, Sue?" she asked.

"None, miss, not a word. Vanished clean away, he did; off to Ameriky, most likely."

❦

But that night there came news of Sim Enticknass.

At half past eleven, after Benedict had returned, reluctantly, to Petworth House, Sue appeared in the parlor with a troubled face to say, "There's a young girl at the back door asking for ye, Miss Ellen. She says it be urgent. Will you see her?"

"Of course," Ellen said, thinking that perhaps somebody was sick; but at the back door she found Selina Lee, her shawl and skirt soaking wet from a new gale that had blown up.

"Selina! Are you in trouble? Come in! What can I do for you?"

"I'm in no trouble, Miss Ellen, but I'm feared for your brother, an' thought ye should know."

"For Gerard? Why? He's over at Valdoe with my sister."

"No, Ellen, he's over to Chiddester, after the Doom Stone,'"said Selina. "And Sim's there too, and he've been drinking. When he's sober he's sensible enough, but a drop makes him reckless-foolish."

"I don't understand! Who is Sim?"

"Why, Sim Enticknass, that was wed to my cousin Sheba."

"You mean—Mrs. Pike's son?"

"Ay—he that was in Winchester clink. He've been hiding with shepherd Bilbo on Lavant Down."

"Oh!" breathed Ellen. Suddenly a great many things fell into place. "That was why that poor girl came to see Mrs. Pike—"

"Who wouldn't help her. His ma cast him off. Well," said Selina, "he were always a poor, no-account member. Shepherd Bilbo were good to him an' doctored his hurt foot. *We* knew he was there, we Romany, as we knows most things, but we wouldn't go after him furder. Leave him find his own way, Uncle Reuben said. Poor Sheba's dead, and we've got the babby."

"Sheba's baby—I was going to inquire—"

"Your aunt Fanny took it." Selina smiled briefly. "She took an' nourished it till it was thriving; then sent us word. There baint much gets past your aunt Fanny!"

I will go and see her tomorrow, Ellen resolved. "But about Gerard?"

"Why, the Doom Stone. Everyone knows your brother be main set to dig it out, for to pleasure your pa."

"Yes," Ellen said, thinking how strange it was that the obsessional quest for this, to her, unimportant piece of carving should thus have been transmitted from father to son.

"And Sim, who was a stonemason afore the drink undone him, he've been working in Chiddester Church. An' he told as how they were going to cover up the stone again tomorrow—the foreman said as 'tweren't safe to shift it. So they are all there now, Sim and Bilbo and your brother; they reckoned to go in quiet-like after the regular workmen was gone for the day."

"But in that case—good God, the men at work there must know—if *they* could not shift it—it is the most crazily dangerous escapade! How can Gerard be so foolish as to become involved in it?"

But, with a hollow heart, she could imagine how, because he had not accompanied her to rescue their father, he might be bent on proving himself in another way, on bringing home this trophy.

"Shepherd Bilbo went to try an' dissuade 'em," said Selina. "But Sim had drunk hisself obstinate and would hearken to none. He said he knew a secret way in, that one o' the men had showed him. An' if he got your dad's reward, that'd set him on the way to Ameriky an' rid shepherd Bilbo of his charge. So will you come, Ellen? Maybe you can make one or other of 'em listen to reason."

"Give me five minutes," said Ellen. "Sit by the fire, Selina; drink some milk."

She flew upstairs, dressed in a warm old riding habit, cloak and hood, wrote a brief note to her father, and returned.

Sue, shocked and distressed, had already been to the barn and saddled Ellen's pony. "I doubt riding's the quickest way, Miss Ellen; and I do see you *got* to go; though it rives my heart, it do, that ye have to go out at such an hour, on such an errand. Wait, just, till I see Mus' Gerald, won't I give him a sorting!"

Selina had a hardy, shaggy gypsy pony and the two girls rode fast out of the town, along the two-mile stretch of road that led to the rampart of the Downs.

"How did you ever discover all this, Selina?" Ellen panted as they walked their horses through the winding village of Duncton.

"Us Rom gets to hear most things. My uncle Reuben were in Chiddester doing a bit o' business wi' the landlord o' the Dolphin and Anchor; an' he see Sim in the tap, all lit wi' drink an' hopefulness; so followed and saw 'em go down the undercroft."

"Perhaps no harm will come of it," said Ellen, trying to put herself into a hopeful frame of mind. But she thumped her pony to hurry him as they approached the daunting climb onto Duncton Down.

The night began to pale, just a little, as they reached the summit. But the wind blew as hard as ever, and the rain stung their eyes. When they surmounted the second ridge, which was known as the Top of Benges, the sky had become perceptibly lighter in its eastern quarter, on their left; at the edge of the flat land ahead they could faintly distinguish a thin silver stencil which was the line of the sea.

"Now you can just about see the owd church spire," said Selina, pointing half right. "Stand out thirty mile off, that do."

A wild and ragged dawn was beginning to break as their ponies, glad of the favoring slope, cantered at a fair pace down over Open Winkins, past Molecombe and Waterbeech. We may be able to have breakfast with Eustace and Eugenia later, thought Ellen; how relieved Eugenia will be to hear that Papa is going to change his will. But I shall never be able to feel the same way to her as I did.

They had lost sight of the spire as they rode through the beech copses on the seaward slope of the Downs; but now, from the flat farmland, they could see it ahead like a fingerpost, standing against the brightening sky.

And then, as they approached Burnt Mill, a terrifying, a portentous thing happened. Ellen, eagerly looking ahead at the steeple over her pony's ears, saw the whole structure vanish from view, downward—like a sword pushed into a scabbard. One moment the slender point was there—next moment it was gone, and only the stump of tower remained in view.

∽

By the time they reached West Street a huge crowd had gathered in the precincts of the Cathedral. It was still very early in the morning, but evidently the news had spread fast; the sound of the collapse must have been enough to shock many people out of sleep. They were lined up, silent, twenty deep, along the iron railings around the grass plat.

"We'll niver get through," said Selina, but Ellen had seen the Bishop near the west door; he was directing emergency operations with ladders and ropes. Giving her pony's reins to a boy, Ellen thrust her way to the front of the crowd and managed to attract the Bishop's attention.

"*Ellen Paget?* Heavens, child, what are you doing here at such a time?"

"Oh, sir—I am terribly afraid—my brother was down in the undercroft with two other men!"

The Bishop looked aghast and disbelieving.

"Child, how *can* he have been? I myself made sure that the Cathedral was locked at a quarter past one last night, when all the workmen came out. The spire had been giving great anxiety—they were working on it—"

"A friend of my brother's knew a secret way in!"

The Bishop made a gesture of despair, then turned and shouted to the men who were gingerly attacking a colossal pile of crumbled masonry. A great gash had been torn through the center of the church when the spire telescoped down into the nave—the surprising thing was how little damage had been done to the transept or the ends of the nave.

"Watch out, lads, there may be men under there. Take the utmost care!"

Sick with suspense, shivering with cold, Ellen watched as the men lifted stone after stone from the mountain of rubble.

Hours passed like minutes.

"Child, why don't you go to the Palace?" the Bishop said. "Blanche will give you something to eat—"

"Oh no. I couldn't go. I must stay—"

A shout from the men working.

"He've broke through!"

The Bishop hurried away.

It seemed hours longer before a slow procession emerged—twelve men carrying three improvised stretchers made from builders' planks. The bodies on them were shrouded with dust sheets.

The Bishop came back, very slowly, to Ellen.

"My poor child. What can I say, but that he is in God's keeping?"

"Dead?" Ellen could hardly articulate. The Bishop bowed his head.

"One of the other men—the gray-haired one—had thrown himself over your brother to protect him. But it was a vain attempt—"

"Was he—were they very much injured?"

"No. Slater thinks they were suffocated, poor fellows, by tons of dust and grit. What possessed them to do such a thing? Ah well, no use to ask. Do you wish to see your brother, my child?"

"No—no. Not now. Not yet… And—and the Doom Stone?" Ellen asked in a shaking voice.

"Crushed to powder—as was its fellow, which had been left in the nave. My child—your poor father! I will come and visit him later—"

"Thank you—thank you, sir. I—I must go home, to be with him." Hardly aware of what she did, Ellen left the Bishop and made her way back to where Selina still waited beside the horses.

❧

"Papa: I have some dreadful news for you. It is about Gerard."

Thank God that Benedict was with her; close beside her, holding her hand.

Mr. Paget heard the short tale in silence, with a puzzled frown on his face. Then he looked down at his interlocked fingers, and opened them, as if letting go something that he had held for too long.

"Dead? Gerard dead? And Bilbo too? And the other man? The innocent…punished with the guilty?"

"Bilbo tried to save Gerard—"

"Bilbo…" Luke seemed to have gone a long way back in memory. "Why do I remember that name? There was something…about a hare?"

He lay against his pillows as if his large frame had

lost the strength to remain upright. After a few minutes, during which neither Benedict nor Ellen spoke, he said slowly, "Now they are together."

"Gerard and his friend?" ventured Ellen.

But Luke's gaze had gone past her. He went on, thoughtfully, to himself, "Both my sons. And their mother. She said... No one will ever be so close again. But I think...I think that I too..."

Sighing a little, he turned his head away from the pair at the bedside. His hands relaxed. Two or three minutes passed.

Then Ellen said in a frightened whisper, "Benedict? He isn't breathing?"

Benedict said gently, "His heart is broken."

Clasping her arm, he led her out of the room.

Note to Reader

Readers who think they recognize Madame Beck's Pensionnat in Brussels are not mistaken; in 1854, Madame Beck sold the goodwill of the establishment to her cousin, Madame Bosschère.

On the twenty-first of February, 1861, the spire of Chichester Cathedral did fall straight down into the center of the church. Nobody was hurt. At a cost of £60,000, the tower and spire were later rebuilt under the direction of Sir Gilbert Scott. Previously, Sir Christopher Wren had tried to protect the spire with an ingenious pendulum and had advised shortening the nave and erecting a classical facade, which had, however, not been done. Perhaps that was just as well.

The SMILE *of the* STRANGER

The arrival within sight of St.-Malo was an occasion for joy. They stopped for the night in the small fishing village of St.-Servan, where, for a wonder, the inn they chose proved clean and comfortable. And on that evening her father dictated his last paragraph to Juliana, concluded his final peroration, and announced with a sigh, "There! It is finished. And I fear a weary work it has been for you, my pet! You have been an angel—a rock—a monument of forbearance and industry. How many pages of manuscript?"

"Six hundred and two, Papa," she said faintly.

"Hand me a sheet of paper, my love, and I will make it six hundred and three by adding the title page."

With a weak and shaky hand he dipped his pen into the standish, and wrote in staggering letters: *A Vindication of King Charles I*, by Charles Elphinstone. Then, underneath, he added, "This work is dedicated to my Dear and Dutiful Daughter Juliana, without whose untiring and faithful help its completion would never have been achieved."

"Oh, Papa!" Reading over his shoulder, Juliana could hardly see the words; her eyes were blinded by tears.

But then he somewhat impaired her pleasure by depositing the unwieldy bundle of manuscript in her arms, and observing, "Now, as soon as you have made a fair copy, Juliana—a task that should prove easy and speedy once we are at your grandfather's, for there will be no household duties to distract you from the labor—the book may be sent off to my publisher, Mr. John Murray. How long do you suppose the copying may take you, my love? Could you write as many as ten pages an hour?"

"I—I should rather doubt that, Papa," faltered Juliana—even her stout spirit was a little daunted at the prospect ahead, for the book was more than twice the length of any of his previous works. "For the first hour it is very well, but—but presently one's hand begins to tire! However, you may be sure that I shall do it as speedily as may be. You cannot be any more eager than I am to see it on its way to the publisher's. Only think! Instead of having to ask the British Envoy to undertake its dispatch, you may be able to travel up to London and leave it with Mr. Murray yourself."

"So I may," agreed her father, coughing.

At this moment they were startled by a tremendous noise of shouting, the clashing of sabers, and musket shots in the street outside their bedroom window.

"Mercy! What is it? What can be happening?" exclaimed Juliana in dismay, running to the window to look out.

"Have a care, my child. Do not let yourself be the target for a bullet. If there is a disturbance, it is best to stay out of sight."

But Juliana, reckless of his warning, struggled with the stiff casement, pushed it open, and hung over the sill.

"It is a mob," she soon reported.

"As usual," commented her father, who was lying on his bed. "Pray, dearest—"

"Men in red caps shouting, 'Down with the foreign spy!'"

"You do not think it is us they are after?" he said uneasily. "Are they coming this way?"

"No—no—they have got hold of somebody, but I cannot see who it is. Yes, they are bringing him this way. They are all dancing and yelling—it is like savages, indeed!" Juliana said, shivering. "They are shouting, 'To be the Tree, to the Liberty Tree! Hang him up!'"

"Poor devil!" said her father with a shudder. "But there is nothing *we* can do."

"Oh!" exclaimed Juliana in a tone of horror next minute. "It is the man who was so kind to you in the diligence, when you were sick! Oh, poor fellow, how terrible! How can they be such monsters?"

"Which man?"

"Why, our fellow traveler in the coach from Rennes— the Dane or German, or whatever he was, who gave you the cordial and was so kind and helpful when I was in despair because you seemed so ill I feared you were dying. Oh, how *can* they? I believe they do mean to hang him!"

"Well, that is very terrible," said her father, "but I fear there is nothing in the world we can do to hinder them."

Juliana thought otherwise.

"Well, I am going to try," she asserted, and without wasting a moment she ran from the room, despite her father's anguished shout of "*Juliana!* For God's sake! Come back! You can do no good, and will only place yourself in terrible danger!"

Running into the street, Juliana saw that the mob had dragged the unfortunate victim of their disapproval some distance along, to a small *place*, where grew a plane tree which, for the time being, had been garlanded with knots of dirty red ribbon and christened the Liberty Tree. Toward this the wretched man was being dragged by his red-capped assailants.

"Spy! Agent of foreign tyrants! Hang him up!"

The man, who had struggled until he was exhausted, was looking half stunned, and as much dazed as alarmed by the sudden fate that had overtaken him. He was a tall, thickset individual, plainly but handsomely dressed in a suit of very fine gray cloth, with large square cuffs and large flaps to his pockets, and a very high white stock which had come untied in the struggle. His hat had been knocked off—so had his wig—revealing untidy brown hair, kept short in a Corinthian cut. A noose had been slung round his neck, and the manifest intention of the crowd was to haul him up and hang him from a branch of the tree, when Juliana ran across the cobbled *place*.

"Citizens!" she panted. "You should not be doing this!"

Luckily her French, due to a childhood in Geneva, was perfect, but it seemed to have little effect on the crowd.

"Mind your own business!" grunted one of the three men principally in charge of the operation, but another explained, "Yes, we should, Citizeness! The man is a spy."

"He is not a spy—he is a doctor! And a very good doctor! He gave some medicine to my father that cured him of a terribly severe spasm. And my father is an important professor of Revolutionary History. Think if he had died, what the world would have lost. But this man saved him! Think what you are doing, Citizens! France cannot afford to lose a good doctor! Think of all the poor sick, suffering people!"

Juliana had raised her voice to its fullest extent in this impassioned appeal, and her words penetrated to the outer fringe of the crowd, which had come along mainly out of curiosity. She heard some encouraging cries of agreement.

"Ah, that is true! We can't afford to waste a doctor. There are plenty of sick people in this town!" "Let him cure my Henri, who has had the suppuration on his leg for so long." "My daughter's quinsy!" "My father's backache!" "Do not hang the doctor!" they all began to roar.

"Are you a doctor?" demanded a man who carried an enormous smith's hammer.

The victim's eyes met those of Juliana for a moment, and a curious spasm passed across his countenance; then he said firmly, "Certainly I am a doctor! If you have any sick people who need healing, I shall be happy to look after them. Just find me a room that will do as a surgery, and provide me with the materials I shall ask for."

This suggestion proved so popular with the crowd that in five minutes the man was accommodated with a small parlor of the same inn where Juliana and her father were lodged. A large queue of persons instantly lined up, demanding attention, but before he would even listen to their symptoms, the gray-suited man demanded supplies of various medicaments, such as rhubarb, borage, wine, brandy, oil, egg white, orris root, antimony, cat's urine, wood ash, and oak leaves. Some of these were not available, but others were supplied as circumstances permitted. He also asked for the services of "the young lady in brown" as a nurse and helper.

"You have gone halfway to saving my life, mademoiselle," he muttered as the crowd chattered and jostled in the passageway outside the door. "Now do me the kindness to finish your task and help save the other half."

"How do you mean, monsieur?"

"Help me devise some remedies for these ignorant peasants!"

"But—are you not, then——?"

"Hush! I am no more a doctor than that piebald horse across the street. But with your intelligent assistance and

a little credulity from our friends outside, I hope that we
may brush through."

The next hour was one of the most terrifying and yet
exhilarating that Juliana had ever lived through.

"What are your symptoms, Citizen?" she would inquire
as each grimy, limping, hopeful figure came through the
door. "Sore throat—difficulty in swallowing—pains in
the knee—bad memory—trouble in passing water—"

Then she would hold a solemn discussion with the
gray-coated man—he told her in a low voice and what
she had now identified as a Dutch accent that his name
was Frederick Welcker.

"Sore throat—hmm, hmm—white of egg with rosemary beaten into it—take that now, and suck the juice of
three lemons at four-hourly intervals. Pound up a kilo of
horseradish with olive oil, and apply half internally, half
externally. A little cognac will not come amiss. Next?

"Toothache? Chew a dozen cloves, madame, and
drink a liter of cognac.

"A bad toe? Wash it with vinegar, mademoiselle, and
wrap a hank of cobwebs round it."

Combining scraps of such treatments as she could
remember having received herself in her rare illnesses
with some of old Signora Fontini's nostrums, remedies
she had culled from *The Vindication of King Charles I*, and
various ingenious but not always practicable suggestions
provided by Herr Welcker, Juliana was able to supply
each patient with something that at least, for the time
being, sent him away hopeful and satisfied.

"Now what happens?" she asked breathlessly as the
last sufferer (a boy with severely broken chilblains)
hobbled away smelling of the goose grease that had been
applied to his afflicted members.

"Now, mademoiselle, I have a moment's breathing
space. And, with the French mob, that is often sufficient.
They are fickle and changeable; in a couple of hours

they will have forgotten me and discovered some other victim," replied Herr Welcker, washing off the goose grease in a finger bowl and fastidiously settling his white wristbands and stock.

"But what if the sick people are not all cured by tomorrow? They will come back and accuse us of being impostors," pointed out Juliana, who was beginning to suffer from reaction, and to feel that her actions had been overimpulsive and probably very foolish indeed. What had she got herself into? Her despondency was increased when her father burst hastily into the room, exclaiming, "Juliana! There you are! I have been half over the village, searching for you—I was at my wits' end with terror! Never—never do such a thing again! Rash—hasty—shatterbrained—"

"I am sorry, Papa! I am truly sorry!" Juliana was very near to tears, but Herr Welcker intervened promptly.

"I regret, sir, but I must beg to disagree with you! Your daughter's cool and well-thought intercession indubitably saved my life—for which I cannot help but be heartily grateful—and was, furthermore, the most consummate piece of quick thinking and shrewd acting that it has been my good fortune to witness! Thanks to her, I am now in a fair way to get back to England, instead of hanging from a withered bough on that dismal scrawny growth they are pleased to call the Liberty Tree."

"England?" said Juliana in surprise. "I thought you were a Hollander, sir?"

"So I am, but England is my country of residence."

Charles Elphinstone brightened a little at these words.

"If you are bound for England, sir—as we are, likewise—perhaps you can give me information as to what ships are sailing from St.-Malo?"

Herr Welcker looked at him with a wry grin.

"Ships from St.-Malo? You are hoping for a ship? I fear, sir, your hopes are due to be dashed. No ships are sailing at present. Those wretched devils of Frogs have closed the port."

"Then—" gasped Juliana's father. "My god! We are trapped! Fixed in France! Heaven help us, what can we do?"

He tottered to a chair and sank on it, looking haggardly at the other two occupants of the small room. But Herr Welcker, strangely enough, did not seem too dispirited.

"Well, I'll tell you!" he said. "Damme if I haven't got a soft spot for you two, after the young lady stood up for me with such spunk. Pluck to the backbone you are, my dear. I'll take you both with me—though," he added puzzlingly, "it will mean throwing out some of the Gobelins, half a dozen of the Limoges, and most of the wallpaper too, I shouldn't wonder. Devilish bulky stuff!"

"Sir? I don't understand you."

"Walls have ears," said Herr Welcker. "Let us all take a stroll out of the town. And if you have any luggage that can be carried in a handbag, fetch it along. The rest will have to remain here."

"What?" gasped Mr. Elphinstone. "Leave my *books*? My Horace—my Livy—my Montefiume's *Apologia*— Dieudonné's *History of the Persian Empire* in fourteen volumes? Leave them behind?"

Herr Welcker shrugged.

"Stay with them if you please," he said. "Otherwise it's bring what you can carry. I daresay the innkeeper will look after your things faithfully enough if you leave a few francs in a paper on top—you can come back for the books when the war's over! Who wants a lot of plaguey books? The Frogs don't, for sure. Unlettered, to a man… Well, are you coming, or not?"

Anguished, Mr. Elphinstone hesitated, then sighed and said, "Well, Juliana, my dear, if you will carry my own *Vindication*, I daresay I could make shift to bring along a few of my most treasured volumes. We shall just have to leave our clothes behind. I collect, sir, that you have at your disposal an air balloon?"

"You collect rightly," said Herr Welcker.

About the Author

The daughter of Pulitzer Prize–winning poet Conrad Aiken, the late Joan Aiken started writing from the age of five. During her lifetime she published over one hundred books for children and adults. She received an MBE from the Queen for her services to Children's Literature and is well known for her Jane Austen continuations.

The Weeping Ash
The Paget Family Saga
by Joan Aiken

— ❦ —

New bride Fanny Paget experiences shame and torment in her loveless arranged marriage, finding solace only in her budding friendship with estate gardener Andrew Talgarth. He never seems too busy to listen and sympathize.

But Fanny is trapped, until her husband's cousins arrive from India and a series of explosive events unfold that change the lives of all involved. Andrew is there through it all, strong and steadfast, awaiting Fanny's greatest self-discovery—no matter how long it takes.

— ❦ —

What readers are saying:

"Romance and high adventure flow at a rapid pace!"

"Cracking entertainment, with lots of romance and thrills."

"A fast, satisfying read."

"Vivid and vibrant!"

For more Joan Aiken, visit:
www.sourcebooks.com

The Five-Minute Marriage
by Joan Aiken

—— ❧ ——

First comes marriage

Desperate to help her ailing mother, Philadelphia "Delphie" Carteret agrees to partake in a sham wedding ceremony to her cousin Gareth. This fulfills Gareth's obligation to marry before his sick uncle passes, and in exchange, Delphie's mother will be guaranteed an annuity for life. The plan is perfect.

Then comes love

But perfect plans usually go awry. Not only was the marriage ceremony valid, but Gareth's dying uncle makes a miraculous recovery. An imposter is threatening Delphie's identity and her life, and the whole family is on the brink of scandal. As Gareth and Delphie try to mastermind a way out of this mess, they begin to discover that what's between them may be surprisingly real...

Then things start to get really complicated

—— ❧ ——

Praise for Joan Aiken:

"Delightful and humorous."
—*Historical Novels Review* for *Eliza's Daughter*

"Ingenious...a country dance in high style, twirled to the tune of a proven virtuoso." —*Kirkus Reviews*

For more Joan Aiken, visit:
www.sourcebooks.com

What the Duke Doesn't Know

The Duke's Sons
by Jane Ashford

A proper English wife, or the freedom of the sea?

Lord James Gresham is the fifth son of the Duke of Langford, a captain in the Royal Navy, and at a loss for what to do next. He's made his fortune; perhaps now he should find a proper wife and set up his nursery. But the sea calls to him, while his search for a wife leaves him uninspired. And then, a dark beauty with a heart for revenge is swept into his life.

He can't have both, but he won't give up either

Half-English, half-Polynesian Kawena Benson is out to avenge her father and reclaim a cache of stolen jewels. She informs James at gunpoint that he is her chief suspect. There's nothing for James to do but protest his innocence and help Kawena search for the jewels, even though it turns his world upside down.

Praise for *Heir to the Duke*:

"Engaging characters, plenty of passion, and a devastating secret in this heartwarming read." —*RT Book Reviews*, 4 Stars

"Fabulous romance with wonderful characters... I couldn't put this book down."
—*Night Owl Reviews*, Reviewer Top Pick

For more Jane Ashford, visit:

www.sourcebooks.com

Discovery of Desire

London Explorers
by Susanne Lord

--- ❧ ---

The one man who's not looking for a wife

Seth Mayhew is the ideal explorer: fearless, profitable, and unmarried. There is nothing and no one he can't find—until his sister disappears en route to India. His search for her takes him to Bombay, where Seth meets the most unlikely of allies—a vulnerable woman who's about to marry the wrong man.

Discovers a woman who changes his dreams forever

Teeming with the bounty of marriageable men employed by the East India Company, Bombay holds hope of security for Wilhelmina Adams. But when the man she's traveled halfway around the world to marry doesn't suit, Mina finds instead that she's falling in love with a man who offers passion, adventure, intimacy—anything but security…

--- ❧ ---

Praise for *In Search of Scandal*:

"Smart and sexy." —*Booklist*

"Beautifully written, deeply romantic, and utterly magnificent." —*New York Times* bestselling author Courtney Milan

"Delightful… Passionate characters and personal adventures come alive." —*Booklist*

"An emotional adventure, with moments ranging from sweet to sexy, funny to heart-wrenching." —*Night Owl Reviews*, Reviewer Top Pick

For more Susanne Lord, visit:

www.sourcebooks.com

The Untouchable Earl

Fallen Ladies

by Amy Sandas

❧

Lily Chadwick has spent her life playing by society's rules. But when an unscrupulous moneylender snatches her off the street and puts her up for auction at a pleasure house, she finds herself in the possession of a man who makes her breathless with terror and impossible yearning…

Though the reclusive Earl of Harte claimed Lily with the highest bid, he hides a painful secret—one that has kept him from ever knowing the pleasure of a lover's touch. Even the barest brush of skin brings him physical pain, and he's spent his life keeping the world at arms' length. But there's something about Lily that maddens him, bewitches him, compels him…and drives him toward the one woman brave and kind enough to heal his troubled heart.

❧

Praise for *Luck Is No Lady*:

"Smart and sexy." —*Booklist*

"Lively plot, engaging characters, and heated love scenes make this a page-turner." —*RT Book Reviews*, 4 Stars

For more Amy Sandas, visit:

www.sourcebooks.com

How to Impress a Marquess

Wicked Little Secrets
by Susanna Ives

―――――――― ⊱⊰ ――――――――

Take one marquess—Proper, put-upon, dependable, but concealing a sensitive artist's soul.

Add one bohemian lady—Creative, boisterous, unruly, but secretly yearning for a steadfast love, home, and family.

Stir in a sensational serialized story that has society ravenous for each installment.

Combine with ambitious guests at an ill-fated house party hosted by a treacherous dowager possessing a poison tongue.

Shake until a stuffy marquess and rebellious lady make a shocking discovery!

Take a sip. You'll laugh, you'll swoon, you'll never want this moving Victorian love story to end.

―――――――― ⊱⊰ ――――――――

"I have never, ever laughed so hard or swooned
so much while reading a historical romance."
—*Long and Short Reviews* for *Wicked Little Secrets*

"Will touch readers' hearts. Ives delivers
on every level." —*RT Book Reviews* Top
Pick for *Wicked, My Love*, 4.5 Stars

For more Susanna Ives, visit:

www.sourcebooks.com